THE JUDGE'S BRIEF

John Gastineau

Route 4 Press

Library of Congress Control Number: 2017907705
CreateSpace Independent Publishing Platform
North Charleston, South Carolina

In memory of my father, a well-read man with whom I shared books and much more.

EXPECTATION

The boy is eighteen, shrill and insistent. He wants to know who and when and how, and he wants his answers now. To him, it is simple. We are friends. I was there. I should tell. I have been a fool to think we were past the point of pure obligation, his or mine. In his company, I must always reassess. I knew his father. I should not be surprised.

And who better to ask than me, a specialist in conclusions? His mother hardly knew his father, nor does she have the perspective that I have. The boy's grandmother, his father's mother, by necessity, lives in a "facility" now. She greets visitors—the boy and I included—with a slow, cocked smile, a nod of momentary recognition, and a savage twisting of her rings before she turns away, back to her window, blank and staring. His father, his uncle, his grandfathers, his other grandmother—the rest of the boy's family—all dead, and I am not long. The knot in my gut has unraveled, the doctors say. The boy may suspect.

And even if he does not, he insists nonetheless, as he has always done in one way or another. When he was little and would lisp in my ear as I carried him on my back across his family's fields, he would point a stubby finger across my shoulder to a tractor crawling along the horizon. "Da?" he would pipe, precise and ruthless to one still raw with memory. Then I could quietly say no and let it go at that.

Later, the questions began to appear again in the letters I encouraged him to write to me during the school year. Perhaps some memory of our walks and my hesitancy caused him to plant them half exposed, like stones that snag a plow, among his thoughts on the drudgery of multiplication tables and his triumphs at soccer. "Did my dad hate math?" "What sports did my dad play?" It is a lawyer's distinction, but I answered each directly, if not completely, then since I knew, even if the boy did not, the larger questions to which they led.

Now he believes he must march to sand and blood. Old men with motives no more revealed or understood than the boy's childish questions have told him they need him to avenge the lives lost and the souls pierced when the Towers burned and shattered.

He is energetic. He is altruistic. He is prey. The old men see him and his naive generation as instruments in the fulfillment of pride and the settling of scores. I know about old men and the way they treat young men, as he will see, but at his age, I cannot stop him.

And with his resolve, his curiosity has evolved into something direct, obsessive, blunt. I fear that he will become bitter that he must ask at all: "Who was my father? How did he die? Why?" And I fear even more his reaction when he finds that I have no better answer to the last question than anyone else. Still, he is owed, and accounting, if not reckoning, is the least we require of justice.

This much I do know: For a time around noon on only a few days early in June, Holoce County is encased in crystal. It is held fixed like a scene in an antique globe on an end table in an aunt's parlor. The soil's promise impels the land, stretching thin the air and nudging the sky deep into blue. Poised against that rim is an armada of white clouds that dapple the land in shadows below. There, inlaid among blocks of yellow wheat, green threads of young crops seam thick stripes of black soil. Sunshine defines these facets; a low, steady breeze turns them to the light.

All this, you take in by looking straight ahead. The shimmering heat that blurs the vision later in the season has not yet arrived. But clarity's price at these moments is stillness. Birds forsake the sky. Their songs may ring off the landscape, like a moist finger pulled across a wine glass rim, but mar its surface with flight? They do not. Only men are conspicuous, carving and buffing soil yet another time. Their growling machines rattle the birds from their perches and bat them aggravated back into the sky.

Once in a while though, when they're young and maybe again when they're old, some realize the bargain that is offered. They will turn off their tractors, stand perhaps, and gaze. And in silence comes purchase. A few understand the yearning and feel no guilt when they must turn the key again. Fewer still feel no regret when the note comes due and they find they could never afford it in the first place.

It is not merely an old man's sentiment that causes me to begin this way. I have spent damn near fifty years in a profession that rewards observation, evidence, and logic. I have seen the farmers in my walks, I have stopped myself, and I would have the boy understand at least that much to balance the other.

The question then is how to proceed. I must be truthful this time and objective. Third person would be best, but I know myself well enough to make no promises and, at any rate, it is not enough. The testimony of the witnesses and the gossip of the town were, by necessity, neither entirely accurate or complete.

Still, my neighbors' ways do help. In Holoce County, we are given to prefacing our small daily judgments with "I 'spect." "I 'spect he's gone to town." "I 'spect she's pregnant." Whether we expect or suspect is not always clear, even to someone like me who's lived here nearly all his life. Sometimes it seems both so that neither the "I reckon" or the "I guess" we occasionally use in its place is adequate. "I speculate" is accurate but affected. "I imagine" comes closest to the mark. Therefore, I imagine:

On one of those painfully clear days in June, in the year before you were born, a redwing blackbird bobbed on a cattail that topped a deep drainage ditch that cut one boundary of your grandfather's farm. The bird had turned its attention from insects to a tractor lumbering toward it in the distance. Through the wire fence separating the ditch from the field, the bird could see the machine weave. The blades of a cultivator the tractor pulled diligently carved dollar signs across the parallel tracks of the packed-clay lane. The engine complained against the drag, and the bird's head jerk-turned with each belch and groaning surge. As the nose of the tractor snagged and stretched fence wire, a locust post bent, snapped, and exploded in splinters. Instinct conquered curiosity. The bird leaped from its perch in blurred flurry of scarlet and black.

A front wheel dropped over the edge of the ditch and the equipment keeled with a gentleness that belied the whump when it hit the ground. Driven by the force of wheels that still turned, the tractor ground to the bottom of the ditch and jackknifed back into the cultivator. A blue, billed cap tumbled out of the wreckage and into the mud at the bottom of the ditch. Given everything else that happened afterward, perhaps it is some small comfort to know that by that time, in the opinion of the coroner, your uncle was dead.

RELIANCE

1

We are no longer on the way to anywhere. You must have a mind to come to Lindley, and tourists from Chicago sometimes do. They reach us about the time their stomachs growl or their gas tanks dry up and after they have disdained shiny, self-service stations and brusque, repetitive, plastic restaurants. Thinking themselves the adventuresome sort, they are looking for something different, a bit more bothersome perhaps but all the more memorable for it. Smug, they veer off the interstate, wishing God's speed or something like it to those they leave behind.

They are disappointed at first. The herbicide plant sprawls just past the exit. Gray and smudged, thoroughly industrial with its flame towers burning off waste, it is too much like what they have left. But the two-lane state road is straight and smooth and soon they glide through the patchwork of fields. Neat homesteads, outposts in more than just the geographic sense, serve as anchors in billows of gently rolling land. A bank barn, some smaller sheds, and a granary usually stand behind the home. Most homes are white, although here and there one sees blue and yellow to suggest modernity or distinction. The older homes are tall and cubic; the newer ones rectangular and flat. The differences in color and design are probably negligible from a moving car. Only the occasional foul cloud of manure odor that makes the children giggle and squeal might cause one to wonder just how people live out here. But the trip is hardly that long, and just as the thought might occur, there is the new high school, spare and simple as a child's building blocks, and the signs. "Del-O-Mar Motel Free TV Low Rates" says one about seven miles out. "Taylor Insurance Agency: Your Friend in Need" reads another a couple of miles closer. "Kathy's Kountry Kitchen" stands a mile beyond town. And then, at last, on a green rectangle in silver letters, "Welcome to Lindley: Our home, Your haven Pop. 3,478."

The outskirts are obviously newer: a cluster of tri-levels behind spindly trees, a supermarket knotted with traffic, a dealership glutted with new pickups, the Del-O-Mar advertising its low rates here with a pink metal door on each of its rooms, a drive-in theater, a gas station, a McDonald's. Or was it a Burger King? No matter. Tourists from Chicago do not come to Lindley to eat or rest at one of those.

The outer edge gives give way to another, more tightly packed neighborhood. Here, the homes are smaller, one-story, and some bear chipped paint or a jagged hole in a garage window. The tiny front lawns are well groomed and the landscaping is what your last realtor might have called mature.

A sign that says "Downtown" points left into a long street bordered by tall maples that slouch their shade like an old, bored honor guard. Behind them, the large homes echo their rural counterparts, but these are introduced by porches with thick columns and occasionally gingerbread. Many still project their owners' quirky but highly acceptable pride with unmarked siding and green or brown trim. Just as many report their owners' efforts to make do. They are coated in gray deck paint, and four or five narrow black mailboxes have been tacked to the wall by the front door.

The trees step back to welcome the tourist to the town's core. At the center on a rise sits the square limestone courthouse. It is ringed by more maples, the oldest and elite of the guard, and a spacious green lawn. Setting the building in a park, however, does little to leaven its ponderous authority. The charcoal slate dome that rises from the center of the square has been, after all, the tallest manmade landmark visible for miles.

Across the streets, on all four sides, are the businesses: a pharmacy, a dimestore, clothing stores that divvy up the trade by age and sex, a hardware and appliance store, a jeweler, a market, a photographer, and a couple of restaurants. A bank stands on one corner, a church on another. Both proclaim in large letters that they are the first of their kind in Lindley, and both seem to be the only buildings around the square that do not mask their lower exteriors behind plate glass or shiny ceramic siding. Sooty rough brick creeps up from behind the glossy finishes to second and third stories. Signs painted on a few of the tall narrow windows up there announce the office of a lawyer or an accountant or a frilly curtain here and there suggests an apartment, but for the most part, the panes are black, dirty, and empty. The light goes in but no longer comes out, not as it once did after the turn of the century when Lindley bustled into maturity.

A long stretch beside the car is enough for the tourists to take this in, and once settled down for lunch at the Kountry Kitchen, they might turn their attention to the people. Noticing a man in a leisure suit or a woman who still favors a bouffant, the tourist might conclude that styles arrive late and die hard here. This is 1984, after all. Noting the common names in the paper, he might surmise that we don't waste much time thinking about ethnic heritage, that we are so far past immigration that it never occurs to us to hyphenate our allegiance, if we bother to think of it at all. And after hearing the people talk of coming downtown–to work, to shop, to eat, to play, to get married, to pay taxes–he might realize that Lindley's heart is neither up or down. The tourist, after all, has passed inversely through Lindley's layers of progress, and the core really seems to hold none of the special distinction the residents grant it, especially not for someone from a place of such size and diversity that it must call its many hearts by flavorful nicknames such as the Loop, the Gold Coast, or the Miracle Mile.

Still, there are the persistent ones who refuse to let their detours be wasted by insight. Once in a while, a particularly observant traveler will point to the calendar behind the cashier, the one that lists one Catholic and thirteen Protestant churches, and ask "Why is there a Star of David on your courthouse clock?" Or the plaque on the courthouse lawn–the one that tells how Lindley was founded by four men who stopped under one of those very maples to sleep off a drunk–will intrigue her husband when he discovers he cannot buy beer with his meal on Sundays. But the answer they get is the same as the reason we say *downtown*: a puzzled stare, a dismissive shrug, and "I guess it just suits us."

Tourists from Chicago should know better. Any number of them have left, even fled, places like Lindley and any number secretly long to return. The tension that nudged them off the interstate in the first place sends them racing back out there when their business here is done. Allen Pierman was beginning to understand that about the time Randy Grable died, but Allen was no tourist.

Beware what I say about him. I have promised to be truthful, but time alters perception, and if I am to be honest, I must say that I loved him as both a person and an idea. Now, he is Allen, dutiful son of Carter, my late friend and former law partner, and Elizabeth, Carter's wife. Then, some would say, he was Pierman, even young Pierman, a project and a projection, as was Joe Calkins, I suppose, to a lesser degree.

Allen I knew in nearly all his aspects. First, as a child, skinny, sandy-haired, and tanned, prone to appearing in our offices without appointment in smudged clothes: T-shirt, jeans, and sneakers. He would burst in, then catch himself and stop, for he was curious, always curious, peeking into offices and fiddling with typewriters, but quiet and respectful and careful not to interrupt Carter when he met with clients. Elizabeth would have spoken to him about that, I'm sure, and for her, he kept an excellent memory.

In his teens, when I would come to the Piermans' home for dinner after my wife died, he was tall and lean, frequently flushed from track or cross country. He was more willful than fast, and the coach prized him for the seconds and thirds in the long distances that he delivered with consistency. At these meals, he was capable of both warm, adult conversation for me, the guest, and sidelong glances and cold fury for Carter, the father. Carter had a quick mind and a sharp tongue. The boy inherited both, and each expected more understanding from the other than either seemed capable of giving.

Manhood moderated all that came before. Sometime after college and before law school, probably during that stretch in the Peace Corps Carter despised as time wasted, he acquired glasses and a placid expression apparently born of confidence and maybe a drop or two of the old man's arrogance. Sometime during law school, he threw off his father's plans for him, crossed to the other side, and took up criminal defense. Sometime after law school, he acquired the pale, waxy complexion of one who works long hours indoors and the gauntness of one who jogs. Here and there, though, one caught a glimpse of the devil. He drove a red Triumph convertible, and Carter said he kept the motorcycle. His hair remained long well after others began to cut theirs. And behind the wire rims, the eyes remained bright and always watchful.

At the time with which we are concerned, Pierman was the Holoce County Prosecuting Attorney. He had held the position for less than two months, by appointment since his father died, although Pierman would have been the last to say he inherited the job. He preferred to say he was dragooned.

The prosecutor's position was then part-time work. Carter also maintained a civil practice consisting mostly of personal injury, real estate, and probate matters that did not conflict with his criminal cases. His son claimed that I purposely declined to put his father's civil cases on the calendar, that my intent was to prevent him from cleaning up the most pressing of his father's affairs and rushing back to his job as a deputy public defender in Chicago. He claimed that my professed reasons for not scheduling his father's cases–a desire to keep the docket open so that criminal matters would not be impeded when a prosecutor was finally found and the certainty that few, if any, of Carter's civil matters needed immediate attention–were merely ruses. Young Pierman was also quick to point out that without consulting him I had called on old school ties with his boss to obtain permission for him to take an extended leave.

But I need not ask myself again whether my choice, that choice at least, was right. There had always been a certain diffidence, sometimes running to damned stubbornness, about Pierman that would make the manager of any large organization wary. Indeed, my chum, the Public Defender, said that given a recent episode, in which Pierman had managed against his superior's instructions to get all charges dismissed against a drunk driver who had killed a certain alderman's granddaughter, it was just as well that he take some time away. It was either that or lose his job. As for old ties, Pierman conveniently forgot that they had helped him obtain his job in the first place, and because it was contrary to every one of his father's hopes and wishes, they had been employed just as furtively.

Besides, what choice was there? Mayne was a drunk, then and now; the police were not likely to trust him and I certainly did not. Hardesty wouldn't take it if it were offered; he was too old and too comfortable. D'Agostino, that kid from East Chicago whom Hardesty brought in, wanted it so badly he came to see me the day Carter died and that was just too fresh. We deserved better, and there was no reason I could think of why we shouldn't have it. Pierman was smart, he was seasoned, and whether he wanted to believe it or not, he was local. He had the most sense of what we're about, even if he did not like it.

I don't remember being as specific as three months when I called the county chairman to remind him of my past contributions to the party and to recommend that Pierman's name be forwarded to the governor. Pierman seemed to think that is what I said, though, and then it seemed helpful to allow him the mistake.

When he was a senior in high school and feeling particularly spiteful, Allen said to his father that it must be a dreary prospect to be prosecutor in a jurisdiction where crime ran *merely* to the petty, no more really than vandalism, theft, and drunks. The remark produced on Carter the expression he saved for the hubristic witness he was about to gut on cross. He adopted the dead-eye gaze and mildly amused smile of a reptile; you half expected him to extend his tongue to sample the air. In his son, the reaction evoked first the thrill of finding yet one more pressure point, then self-loathing, for he found that, even though he was closer to man than boy, his father could still make him afraid.

We were at the table. Elizabeth instinctively placed her hand on Carter's arm.

"The *first* crimes were against property," Carter said finally. "Eve defrauded Adam, they conspired and stole the apple, then they perjured themselves before God." He spoke to Elizabeth with his amused look. Talk that mocked religion made her uncomfortable, he knew, but to his mind she was holding him back. For his son and me, Carter trotted out the hard victor's smirk he wore after every trial, win or lose. "Not until the *next* generation was there a crime against the person," he said, "and even *that* was about possession and control."

On the morning of Grable's fire, as the school superintendent explained his plight, Pierman's thoughts alternated between that lecture and the limits of his tenure. The ironies were not lost on him, his taste for the ironic having been whetted at his father's table.

Maybe if the boy had not made Elles scream, the superintendent was saying. Maybe if he had not made her cry.

Surely Pierman remembered Miss DeMott, the superintendent said. Indeed, he did. She had been the school librarian for as long as Pierman could remember. She was sour, short-tempered, and of that school of her profession who believed her primary role was to collect and hoard, not facilitate and share. Pierman did not doubt that the boy had made her scream and cry. He had trashed what she loved most.

The background of the case was well known, even to someone like Pierman who made it a point of honor not to read the local paper. Brother Austin Barton, pastor of the Little Flock New Faith Tabernacle and a UPS delivery driver, had discovered his son, Matthew, a 16-year-old junior, reading *The Grapes of Wrath*. It was for a book report, Matthew said; he had found a copy in the high school library. Brother Barton was appalled. He would be the first to tell you that he was not widely read himself. There was no need. Scrupulously each day he read his Bible and each month the newsletter of his denomination. Only recently, the newsletter had published a list of books that "rend the moral fabric," and *The Grapes of Wrath* was one of them. As were five other books, which, upon further investigation, Brother Barton was also appalled to find on the shelves of the high school library. Not only were such books available from the library, but the school was teaching evolution in biology and the children were studying "values," which, as Brother Barton was quick to point out, was not about values at all since what was valuable depended on the situation.

Brother Barton's eyes had been opened, he told the Little Flock. It was too much, he said. He was not about to stand for it, and neither should they. Talk to your school board, he told them; demand that *those* books be removed from the library and that *those* courses of study be stricken from the curriculum.

We are a churchy place, and as a man who had found his cause, Brother Barton exhorted not just the Little Flock, but also his colleagues among the other denominations. The next Sunday, most brayed at their congregations and pounded the pulpits. They demanded to know: What kind of country is it that allowed such books in our schools but would not allow children exposed to their influence to pray?

Attendance, and with it, collections, increased, just as Brother Barton promised, and each week that followed, most yielded to the temptation of just one more sermon on the subject. Only the old Jesuit who led the Catholic parish spoke out against censorship. A man of his education and training could not be ignorant of his own faith's long history of imprimatur, but he declined for the time being to share that insight with his parishioners. The Presbyterian and Methodist ministers would not join the coalition, but they addressed the issue in general terms. In the one worrisome sermon each chose to give on the matter–after long consultation between them by telephone–they said they preferred to incline their focus heavenward and urged their members to draw a sharp line between the sacred and the secular.

Brother Barton's son came down hard on the side of the secular. The day after Brother Barton and his allies confronted the school board for the first time, signs bearing the handwritten message "Fuck the Censors" were found taped to hallway walls at the high school. These provoked little more than snickers among a student body primarily concerned with the sectional basketball tournament and the Prom. A grateful administration held its breath rather than ferret out the vandal and raise issues that could interfere with the resolution of the book problem. The day after Brother Barton confronted the school board a second time and demanded the impeachment of any board member who voted to retain the books Matthew simplified the investigation. He appeared at school wearing a jacket across the back of which he had written "Fuck the Censors." When the principal asked him if he had written the signs, he said yes. When the principal ordered the boy to remove and hand over the jacket, he merely sat down on the floor. When he would not be reasoned with, the principal and the janitor carried him cross-legged out to the curb, where they left him while the principal went back in to call his parents. Since he returned without the jacket, he was allowed to enter the school the next day. One teacher said she thought he walked kind of stiff and funny, and another mentioned a mark on his face that might have been a bruise, but, really, he was a grim, runty kid who tended to be aloof, and nobody bothered to ask him how he was.

Elles DeMott cried the next day. When she came to work, she found the entire fiction section of the library strewn across the floor. Most of the volumes had been slashed, torn, or doused with some kind of odorous fluid she did not care to know the source of. The windows of the audiovisual room were broken, and the equipment it contained had been smashed. Only six volumes remained on the shelves, each a brand-new copy of the books Brother Barton wanted banned. Just to be sure no one missed the point, "Fuck the Censors" was written across the glass of a display case with the blue marker Elles used to sign hall passes for her student aides. Matthew Barton provided authorities, specifically Sheriff Joe Calkins, with a statement. He said he had hidden in a closet in a vacant classroom, emerged at night, and carried out the vandalism. He said he was "defiantly proud."

If you could get far away enough to see it, Pierman decided long ago, the criminal law had many pleasures. It addressed both sides of human nature, the way it is and the way we would like it to be. There were constitutional issues to be addressed in even the simplest case, and every case came with real human beings, not the "legal persons" of corporations or governmental bodies. But after all this time, the law had developed a fairly complete picture of the range of human behavior and a fairly complete set of rules and procedures to direct it. Thus, most of the prosecutor's work was routine. The boy's statement resolved the question of culpability, and there appeared to be no problem with the procedure. In his methodical way, Calkins had carefully obtained the signatures of the boy and his parents attesting to the facts that Calkins had advised them of their rights and they had understood them. For Pierman, the only remaining issue was what he should advise the Court to do about it.

Dr. Fulton, the school superintendent, had no desire to see the boy jailed—that would be counter-productive politically—but he did think something just short of stocks and rotten fruit would be appropriate.

"The Board and our insurer expect full restitution," he said. "And some money for counseling for Elles."

"You have some reason to think this boy has money?" Pierman asked.

He was careful to keep the smirk off his face and out of his tone. He had declined Fulton's summons to come to the administration's offices, insisting instead that if Fulton wished to see him it would have to be in the prosecutor's office, an aerie of cheap, knotty-pine paneling and worn, government-surplus furniture atop the northeast turret of the Courthouse.

"The father's got a salary and a house. It'd serve him right for stirring up all this vitriol about our books."

"An entirely unnecessary distraction from the bond issue you're trying to sell to your constituents to finance another addition to the high school," Pierman said. "A swimming pool, this time?"

The superintendent was short, round, and fussy. No one could remember ever seeing him anywhere without a tie. He wore round, wire-framed glasses that fogged when he was excited and left marks on his pudgy cheeks when he dragged them off to wipe them down. He had run the high school for decades, first as principal then as superintendent. He knew most of his current board of trustees from the time they were students and exerted a great deal of residual influence over them as a result. He had known Pierman "when," too, and now gave him the long, silent appraisal he deployed on chronic troublemakers.

"We insist on community service," he said, when he thought the look had taken its toll. "A lot of it. Better still if we could call the newspaper for a photograph of this boy cleaning up the library."

"A man in your position would have to make sure lessons were learned, Mr. Fulton," Pierman said. "Notwithstanding the facts that the boy is a juvenile and the records of his case are therefore confidential."

"In the good old days," Fulton said, "most students who stood on the other side of my desk wound up there because they skipped school or got in a fight." He limply raised his hands and let them fall back to his lap. "As I recall, your mouth was a problem."

"Yes," Pierman said amiably. "It always surprised me how much words, even those that were true, could make my ass sting." He swung a cupped hand through the air. "A testament, no doubt, to your excellent eye-hand coordination and years of practice."

The juvenile cases he had handled as a public defender had only reinforced the opinion Pierman reached while bent over Fulton's desk years before: School administrators usually were little more than narrow-minded bureaucrats, more concerned with indoctrinating than teaching. He knew he should tie off this conversational thread, but he could not resist. His time here was short and he did not expect to be back when he left.

"Nelson, I have the impression that part of this conversation is still about my mouth," he said. "I guess those ass-paddlings didn't teach me much."

The color rose in Fulton's face and his glasses began to fog.

"I would prefer that you not use that language in front of me." Pierman had to think what he referred to. "And I have earned the right to be addressed as 'doctor.'"

Fulton took a deep breath and let his gaze drop to the desk. He smiled to himself, pulled out the lapels of his suit coat, shifted in his seat, and placed the lapels back across his midriff. Pierman gave him the skirmish.

"What I do should not make a difference to your decision making," Pierman said, "After all these years, you should know better than most that we don't parade convicted juveniles. Their proceedings are closed and their records are sealed."

Fulton sputtered. "As if that would make a difference in a gossipy place like this."

Pierman's telephone rang. His secretary quickly announced it was the sheriff calling and dropped off the line before he could scold her for interrupting his meeting.

"Allen," Calkins said, "we have to go."

He sounded calm; it was the gap in context that made the call seem urgent.

"Go. Go where? I'm in a meeting. Who's we?"

"You and me. Now."

"Where?"

Calkins spoke very quietly. "Allen, we have to go now. Meet me at my car," he said and hung up.

Pierman sat nonplused. Fulton acted as though there had been no interruption. "So what will you do?"

Pierman focused on him a moment. "I'll talk to the boy and his parents."

"But."

"Doctor, for better or worse, I'm the prosecutor. The decision is mine. It's called discretion."

"But I need to know now. We're deciding this matter very soon."

Pierman savored his sputtering. "Yes, you are," he said, smiling. He rose and pulled his jacket off the back of his chair. "Doc, I'll be in touch."

2

Allen would be of a number of minds and even more emotions that day, but at the end of it, he vowed to stop assuming. Whatever he thought he knew of us and this place would be called into question. Death does that, of course, particularly one like that.

There was first Calkins, from whom Pierman expected explanation but received none, at least not in the beginning.

For the Courthouse steps, Pierman saw standing with one foot in the open door of his unmarked, beige squad car and his arms limply draped across the roof and the top of the door. The car door obscured much of him. He was not tall, and at the age of 31, he was already broad and thick. His face was growing round and his dark hair was thinning to tonsure. He preferred the utility of a brown, polyester jumpsuit to the well-pressed, two-tone brown shirts and slacks he required of his deputies. Calkins was capable of subtlety but at that point of his life usually disdained it.

At the bottom of the steps, Pierman caught the low, incomprehensible garble of radio traffic, like burps and whines of jungle creatures, coming from the car. The creatures seemed agitated.

Calkins bounced a radio microphone by its cord like a yo-yo. That and Calkins' clenched expression made Pierman quicken his step, but when he arrived at the car, Calkins went slack. He swung himself leisurely into the car, he carefully checked his mirror before backing out, and he slowly headed west out of town. Only when the car was well beyond the town limits did Pierman notice the speedometer touch eighty.

For a time, Pierman was willing to be patient. They had, after all, known each other a long time. They were bound to; Lindley is a small town and they were the same age. But Calkins and Pierman had been more than mere acquaintances. From first grade through high school, they had eaten at each other's table and slept in each other's bed. For twelve years, they had played, talked, and fought with, for, and against each other.

To a large extent, it was an attraction of opposites: town boy in the country and country boy in town; one given to enthusiasms and impulse, the other plodding and methodical. Perhaps as a result, one would periodically take time away from the other to see if it was still worth the effort. At one point in their senior year, both came to understand that their lives would diverge. In the way that drives women mad, neither man felt the need to speak of it, and neither felt much regret when the other made little effort to stay in touch. Now, neither could honestly say, if the question would ever have occurred to him, whether they were still friends, but they treated each other as such because it seemed right and the alternative laughable. Even if they tried, they could not remember the heel-sniffing days of first acquaintance.

"Are you going to tell me who died?" Pierman said.

"How do you know anybody did?" Calkins turned his head sharply. "I didn't say anything about that."

Pierman explained with some effort at patience that he could not think of any other reason why Calkins would pull him out of a meeting for a drive in the country. "Beyond that," Pierman said, "Don't question me like I'm suspected. As I remember, I was at the other end of the phone when you called." It came out sharper than he intended, and he looked away.

The county was swept clean of life. There were tractors here and there, and black, moist, newly turned soil glistening in the sunlight. In other fields, balers were poised to lap the tails of pale, green windrows, and even with the air conditioning, Pierman caught the sweet, weedy scent of cut clover. But in each scene, people were missing, and the implements untended. Only at the horizon could Pierman see activity; a blue light winking at the top of a vehicle.

"So," Pierman said, "let's try again. Are you going to tell me where we're going or not?"

A funnel of black smoke rose from a field off to the north. It held Calkins' attention for a moment.

He said, "You going to give Fulton what he wants? Let him out? Some community service and restitution?"

Pierman remembered the game now. They played it as boys. The one who answered the other's question first lost. Pierman said nothing.

"He walked by my office," Calkins said. "He didn't come to see me, so he must've come to see you."

"Maybe he was just paying his taxes." Pierman looked away again.

"Then he's late, and that doesn't sound like him."

As a defense attorney, Pierman knew the cop's position without asking. "Your preference would be to lock up the boy and not let him out."

"He broke the law."

"And the rules are the rules."

Calkins drove another mile or so.

"Ever met a rule you wouldn't bend?"

"Like the one you're bending? Let's call it breaking. You've now reached ninety-five."

When Calkins did not respond, Pierman said: "I use rules every day. I'm a lawyer."

Calkins laughed. "So they're tools, like a wrench or hammer. You don't apply a rule. You use it."

"If you want to put it that way, whether I apply a rule depends on the facts. The right tool for the right job."

"Well, is there a rule that always applies? That you won't try to alter? How do you feel about 'Thou shalt not kill'?"

Pierman blew out some air. "I'll tell you what I told Fulton. I'm going to talk to the boy before I decide."

"But you'll probably go ahead anyway, won't you. Probably."

"Probably," Pierman said. "Yes, probably. What's the difference? We're talking about at most mischief and trespass and that's if he were an adult. Morrison's not likely to jail him for that, not on a first offense. He'll order restitution. Besides, he's a juvenile; even if there's a record it's sealed. So I repeat, Joe. What is the difference?"

Calkins nodded once, confirming something for himself. The speedometer reached ninety-five.

"Shouldn't you be using lights or sirens or something?" Pierman said.

Calkins smirked and swept a hand across the windshield. "You see anybody else on this road?" The blue light was gone.

"We're going to be the last ones to this party," Calkins said. He sucked in his breath, the front end of a sigh or a shudder. "But then I don't reckon I'd want to be the first one either."

Pierman caught the name as Calkins turned in. The mailbox across the road from the farmstead said *Grable*. A state trooper, insect-eyed in silvered sunglasses, had pulled his car across the driveway. He held up his hands for Calkins to stop, but Calkins declined. He drove into the lawn and around without even a wave.

The gravel drive led past a white, two-story, box-frame farmhouse and a detached garage into a fenced lot that contained a large white barn in one corner and a smaller white pole shed in another. The column of smoke they had seen previously towered ahead of them rising from the end of a dirt lane in a third corner of the lot. Calkins pointed the car there without hesitating.

From the portable console beside him on the seat, Calkins took a pair of sunglasses and a brown, billed cap with the sheriff's yellow, five-point star sewn on the front. He put them on and wiped his hand across his mouth.

"'Course, you're right. We've got a body," Calkins said. "Don't know who for sure. It's cooked. Burned." He looked at Pierman. "Don't imagine you've run into that."

Pierman shook his head.

"No," Calkins said, "no, I didn't think so." He touched his left breast pocket, fingering first the badge then the pens he found there. "Been a while for me." He pulled the cap low over his sunglasses. "Well," he said quietly, as much to himself as to Pierman, "just breath through your mouth."

"Joe, this is a homicide?"

"Don't know. It could be an accident." Calkins shrugged. "Anyway, homicide's a legal word. That's one reason you're here. You'll have to tell me."

Then there was the site, which offered any number of unfinished, mostly conflicting stories and one, unalterable fact.

We are practical and considerate, and we wish to be helpful. The lane made a ninety degree turn to the left, then two hundred yards further a ninety degree turn to the right. From the second turn on, cars and pickups were parked bumper to bumper on either side of the lane. Many were askew, pulled up short, but the drivers had been careful to leave the lane clear without pulling too far into the fields and mashing the crops. As they passed between the rows, Pierman noted the pickups came in all sizes, colors, and styles, but the cars tended to be large, boxy, and neutral in color. They were the women's vehicles, he knew, purchased in the knowledge that they would be driven to fields one day and church the next and made to serve years beyond the last payment.

Men, women, and children—maybe thirty or so—were gathered where the first of the vehicles had come to a stop. They stood before a ladder truck that had been parked along the ditch that ran the width of the fields, arms crossed or hands in their pockets, talking in small knots. Occasionally, someone would crane her head and peer around those in front, then draw back and look around to see whether anyone saw. The men were in T-shirts, jeans or overalls, and a kaleidoscope of billed caps. The women wore sundresses or shorts and tops. Quiet expectation, like moments before the prayer at a church picnic, was in the air.

They clustered at the wide end of a pie slice of burned wheat field. A breeze out of the southwest had urged the fire through the field, and the blackened area radiated out from the crowd across acres. In the middle of the burned area, men on a pumper played water up and down the torso of a single, gnarled old tree. A tractor plowed a fire break between the wheat field and a bean field to the north while another pumper followed dousing embers. Stragglers were returning to the fold. Men and older boys trotted singly back toward the crowd. Women and girls walked behind, pairing and tripling as their paths converged and they drew closer to the crowd. Most everyone dragged blankets and sacks, their faces flushed and grimed.

"Smells like somebody's smoking dope," Pierman said as they got out of the car. Calkins was already out, ready to move through the crowd. He turned and cocked an eyebrow at Pierman. "I would've said burnt toast."

The crowd was skittish. Calkins' touch on an arm or a shoulder was enough to make them start and part. The expressions of those he moved aside alternated between expectant and apprehensive when they saw who it was. To Pierman, the scrutiny was nearly stifling. He could only nod stiffly to the few he recognized.

A deputy stood guard before the ladder truck. Darrell Ardmore had wanted to be "in law enforcement," as he called it, since he was eight. Now he was a young twenty-one. He carried patches of acne high on his checks, and he still wore his mouse-brown hair in a flat-top. He faced the crowd with crossed arms and a grim set to his mouth, but his eyes darted constantly across the faces before him, and he had sweated through his uniform. When Calkins emerged from the crowd, he jumped to attention.

"Yeah?" Calkins asked, holding up a hand at the array in front of him. Pickups had been parked at the front and back of the ladder truck, and fire hose ran waist high from their bumpers to the ladder truck.

"It's a goddamn homemade . . ." The deputy caught himself when Calkins frowned and lowered his voice. "It's a police line, Joe. I didn't have no tape." The deputy shrugged and his eyes slid sideways. "It was the best I could do. Gawkers. Too many of them."

Calkins pursed his lips. "Where?" Darrell tipped his head toward the other side of the truck, and Calkins started around.

"It's kind of a mess," Darrell called after him. Calkins turned and waited for an explanation. Darrell moved closer so that he would not be overheard. "It was burning. They hosed it. I let them. I couldn't just let it burn."

"You look?"

Darrell lowered his eyes and nodded.

"You go down?"

Darrell nodded again.

"Dead?"

"Long dead."

"Who?"

Darrell slowly shook his head. "Can't tell." He pointed beyond the front pickup truck to the tracks the implement had made in the lane. "It come out of that field. Somebody who was working it, I reckon. This is Grable's place. It'd have to be Randy or the old man, wouldn't it?"

"You haven't seen either of them?"

Darrell shook his head again. "I've been looking."

Pierman had held back at the front of the ladder truck. Calkins noticed and waved him over. "Watch where you step," Calkins said, pointing to muddy ground.

Each of them took a position at the top of the ditch. None seemed to want to stand too close to the others.

At first, Pierman allowed himself to see only a tangled, charred heap. He decided it was best for the time being to think that it looked like the carcass of some dinosaur. That he could accept.

Curiosity soon made him examine the sight methodically. The ground around it was burned black in an ellipse, an inverse spotlight. The tractor lay on its side in the middle. No doubt, it had been a bright color–green or red or orange–they always were. Now, it was merely black, gray, and white. The tires had burned away, leaving only huge rims. The blades of the cultivator curled up, toward him and away, so that it was easy to imagine rows of teeth.

Calkins pointed to something near the tractor. It looked like another cultivator blade bent almost perpendicular by the torque of the accident, but the end was rounded, a knob.

"An arm?" Darrell was saying. "Some limb, at any rate."

The breeze died and dropped a cloud on Pierman. It smelled like warmed-over steak. His empty stomach burned from the inside out.

"Sweet Jesus," he croaked. Calkins didn't turn. "Give him a hand," he said.

Darrell parked Pierman on the running board of the ladder truck. "You going to puke, do it somewheres it won't interfere with the area in question," he said and returned to the edge of the ditch to talk and point with Calkins.

The tractor's bellow pulled Pierman out of the fog. When he walked around the truck, he found the crowd turned away to watch its approach from the burned end of the field. The driver pulled the rig up to the crowd, shut down the engine, and let himself drop stiffly to the ground. When the crowd saw who it was, the murmur of conversation ceased. We may not believe in ghosts, but sometimes they come to mind to explain what we do not expect.

Paul Grable was in his fifties then, and after a lifetime of physical labor, he was compact, flat-bellied, and unlikely to go to seed anytime soon. Hatless and wearing a short-sleeved white shirt and a striped tie, he should have looked out of place, but he moved with the rolling, paced gait of the other farmers and like many of them the whiteness of his bald spot crowned a tanned face.

The crowd parted at the sight of him. One man who was quicker than the rest removed his hat. A woman genuflected. Grable stopped in their midst to consider them curiously, then turned and walked directly to Pierman.

"Tell me what's going on here," he said.

"You are?" Pierman said.

"This is my place. Who're you?"

Pierman was about to ask him to wait at the barrier when Calkins came around the truck. For a long moment, each considered the other.

"Paul," Calkins said finally. "Why don't you come under that hose for a second."

Calkins held the hose up for the older man, then positioned himself in front of him. "Where you been, Paul?" he asked casually, as if Grable was merely late for a meeting.

"In town. Had business. What is this?"

"Paul, where's Randy?" The question gave nothing away. It occurred to Pierman that whether the old man was going to be a suspect depended on his answer.

Grable turned north, the direction that the tractor had come from, and pointed. "He should be . . ." Grable stopped. His eyes scanned the bean field then the tracks the cultivator left on the lane. His expression did not change, but his Adam's apple jumped. After a long moment, Calkins put a hand on Grable's shoulder and told him about the tractor and the body in the ditch. "We don't know who it is or how it happened yet, Paul."

Grable shook off Calkins' hand and marched to the lip of the ditch, where he stood looking down into it. Darrell hovered nearby, ready to grab him should he attempt to interfere with the crime scene. Calkins waved him off.

Grable returned to Calkins, flicking something off his cheek with his little finger. "I 'spect it's him," he said, looking Calkins in the eye.

"I expect so, too, Paul," Calkins said," but we'll have to find out." He turned to Darrell. "Get rid of those people."

As Darrell started around the truck, Grable sighed. "I'll help," he said. Calkins started to protest, but Grable shook his head. "My place," he said.

Each little conversational knot fell back as Grable approached, then drew closer when he planted himself in its center. Pierman could hear murmured thanks for their help and a request to let the police do their job. When he had finished, they would glance at each other sideways, one or two would touch him on the arm or shoulder, then they would leave without another word.

"How do you like that?" Calkins said to Pierman.

The last group leaned against a telephone company van. To Pierman's eye, Grable stood off from this group as he talked. He also seemed to be talking to one person, a slender, bearded man about Pierman's age. As Grable returned, the bearded man waved. Pierman had the impression it was for him, but when he turned to ask who it was, Calkins was heading for his squad car and Darrell had resumed his post at the lip of the ditch. Grable showed no sign of following either one of them. He sat on the bumper of the ladder truck, his head bowed and his hands between his knees. Pierman saw his lips moving.

To the south, four vehicles battled their way through the flow of outbound traffic. Two state police cruisers, their red lights flashing, led the way. They were followed by a state police van and a black hearse. The first three jacked to a stop near the ladder truck. The hearse carefully halted some distance off.

A tall, sharp-featured man emerged from the first cruiser. He wore a blue sport coat and tan slacks. He covered the distance between the car and the truck in three strides, eyed Pierman for a moment, then spotted Calkins. "You selling tickets to this thing," he called. "Jesus, I like to never got up that goddamn lane." He started to say more, but Calkins silenced him a stern look and a jerk of his head toward Grable.

A second man appeared from around the ladder truck. He wore a three-piece suit, but even across the rough ground, he glided like a priest, with folded hands. Cross was a convenience. He was a funeral director and the county coroner. He had signed Carter's death certificate, embalmed him, and buried him in one efficient, unbroken chain of service. He would have to send this one off to an autopsy, but the rest would probably be the same, and nobody had to tell him how to conduct himself. Cross nodded to the officers standing along the ditch, looked for Grable, and walked directly to him.

"Paul? Paul." Cross had to shake Grable a little. "I'm sorry. It will be over soon. Paul? Bear with us a while." He waited until Grable gave him a responsive look before turning to Pierman. "Allen, you're looking a little green. I've got salts in the wagon."

Embarrassed, Pierman declined, excused himself, and approached Calkins, who introduced him to Detective Lt. Purcell of the State Police.

"Carter's boy?" Purcell's eyes widened. "Nifty. Me and your old man, we didn't get along too good."

Up close, Pierman could see that Purcell was of his father's generation or one step removed. He turned back to Calkins. "We holding court out here today, or you just worried you'll screw this up?

Anybody been down there yet?" he asked without any recognizable break in his thoughts.

Calkins said no curtly.

"Well, let's get at it." Purcell beckoned to the van. A young, clean-cut man in navy blue overalls snapped to then trotted forward with a camera. "Lots of pictures," Purcell ordered. "You hear me? Loads of 'em. The prosecutor here's going to need 'em. Makes a jury sit up and take notice."

Several thoughts passed through Pierman's mind with a speed that could not be measured. In the end, he did not like cops. This guy was one reason. His time in Holoce County was not long. He did not have to get along with this man.

"Lieutenant, I don't think it's been established yet that a crime's been committed," he said, tracing a circle in the soil with his toe before looking at Purcell. "Until it is, why don't you shuck that tough guy routine and keep your fucking voice down. You know. For that fellow over there."

Purcell's eyes widened again before he turned to the coroner. "You bring a bag," he asked in a stage whisper, "or you want to use one of ours?"

Calkins caught Pierman as he started forward, and Cross stepped in front of him. "If I could suggest," the coroner said as calmly as if he were addressing a church board meeting, "perhaps Allen could take Paul back to the house for us. I don't think we need legal services right now and Paul does not need to watch this."

Calkins spun Pierman around and gave him a discreet shove. "We'll need him," Calkins said when they were out of earshot.

"Or not. The guy's an asshole."

Pierman jerked his arm away from Calkins, who had been channeling his disappointment in Pierman's behavior into the grip he had on it. Calkins took Pierman's arm again and turned him. "Sometimes," he said, "I get tired of pulling your ass out of jams." He took his keys from his pocket and jingled them in Pierman's face to get his attention, as Cross escorted Grable toward the squad car. "Get him settled," Calkins said. "See if anybody can stay with him. Tell him we'll want to talk to him later."

As Pierman turned the car, he saw Purcell standing at the top of the ditch. He was bent at the waist unfurling a huge black plastic bag. Silhouetted against the afternoon sunlight, he was a matador beckoning the bull.

If Grable expected Pierman to apologize for the episode, he showed no sign of it. Throughout the slow ride back to his house, he stared straight ahead, dry-eyed but oblivious. They had pulled up to the house and parked before Grable snapped to. "Just let me out," he said. "I can make it from here."

"If it's all the same to you, Mr. Grable, I'll walk you in."

A narrow porch doubled as a covered walkway to the garage. They used the back door under the porch, entering directly into the kitchen. It was a pale pink, except for frilly white curtains on the window above the sink and deep purple tiles above the counters. Black spots showed around the stove rings and fingerprints smudged the refrigerator around the handle, but the counters were clear. One clean frying pan, two plates, two cups, and some silverware had been left in the drainer in the sink.

Grable sat down beside a small Formica table with chrome legs and began to unlace his boots. "The bathroom's there," he said, motioning toward a door across a dining room that also looked too tidy.

Pierman closed the door, turned on the tap, and waited for the coldest water to rise from the deepest part of the well. He splashed it on his face with cupped hands. It did not help. If Grable's boy was dead, he was sorry, but mostly for his own sake. It tended to complicate his notion of leaving. Beyond that, he could not think of anything to say.

Pierman found Grable in a recliner in one corner of the living room off the kitchen when he emerged. The furniture was plain, unmatched and arranged for comfort and convenience, with low tables for glasses and feet pulled close to chairs and the couch. Pierman decided the pieces had been purchased one at a time as money allowed. A desk in another corner was chaotic with paper and three magazines lay open and askew on the couch.

Grable let Pierman's eyes stroll the room. "I haven't kept it as nice as my wife since she died," he said finally. The words were merely factual and asked no sympathy. Pierman cast his only line.

"Can I get you something? A drink?"

"We keep no liquor in this house," Grable said, but today it lacked zeal. He waved Pierman toward the couch. As he sat down, Pierman saw that the magazines had not been tossed but left carefully open to ads for shiny new farm implements. The low angle of the photos and the bright light in which they were shot made the tractors look huge, powerful, and bulbous, like trains hurtling past.

"He was coming back, you know. Randy." Grable pointed to the ads. "I was doing a little shopping, a little daydreaming. We would've needed another tractor." His upper lip ballooned before he let the air leak out. "It would've been expensive. The boy would've wanted a radio, but I guess that would've been an investment, too."

Pierman nudged the magazines away. "You know, Mr. Grable, we don't really know yet."

"Mr. Pierman, I think we do."

It took all of Grable's attention for several moments to straighten the terry wash cloth that covered the recliner's arm.

"Dr. Fulton tells me you're clearing the path for us on this book deal," Grable said. Pierman scowled. "Oh, don't worry," Grable said, "he said you were skittish about it."

"It can wait," Pierman said.

"It's the same thing in a lot of ways," Grable said aloud but mostly to himself. "The books, the equipment. Investments."

Pierman blinked, incredulous, before he remembered: We are a place bent on instruction. Our answers are hard won and certain, and we will not be deterred from sharing them, in school, in church, around the table, on the street. Mention that you met the friend of a friend on a trip and someone in Lindley will tell you that just went to show what a small world it is. We are never short of life lessons, each of which had a logic. No one seemed capable of acknowledging that there might be no meaning in a course of events, and variables such as money, cunning, and chance were mentioned with ridicule if anyone spoke of them at all. Those things you learned to appreciate later, Pierman thought, on your own.

In his reverie, Pierman did not hear Grable ask him whether he had kids, and Grable had to ask it again. When Pierman shook his head, Grable said, "Well, they're a gamble." He toyed with the cloth on the arm of his chair. "You give them all you can. Time, money, as much as you can afford." He frowned again and cocked his head. "But you can never tell. My children . . . It's the only gambling I ever allowed in this house. I guess it paid off." His voice caught. "Trouble is, it just never stops."

Pierman listened to the songs of birds outside. "Mr. Grable," he said finally, "we ought to call somebody."

The older man sank further into his chair, his chest almost concave. "Yes, Kay," he whispered. "My daughter," he said louder and roused himself from his chair. "Do you know her? She's about your age."

"Maybe she was a few years behind me," Pierman said.

Grable went into the kitchen. Pierman could not hear what was said, only Grable's tone of voice, which was abrupt and severe, like a bark, then softened.

"She's coming," Grable said when he returned. From somewhere he had found a blue bandanna, which he held balled in his hand, palm up, exposed and vulnerable in the way of old ladies. Looking at it, Pierman decided he had to go and said so.

"You've been real kind," Grable said. "I wish she was closer. It's what I was talking about before. You give them all you can to make them independent, and you hope what you'll reap is a place in their lives."

Grable took Pierman by the arm as they moved toward the back door.

"I was sure with Randy," he said. "But Kay? With her, I can only guess."

At the door, Pierman extended his hand, but Grable ignored it at first. "You ever read any of those books?" he asked.

"The ones in the library? Most of them, at one time or another."

Grable's hand was calloused and meaty. He squeezed hard and held on for a moment.

"At our school?"

"Some, I'm sure."

"Well," Grable said, releasing Pierman's hand. "You seem to have turned out fine."

The compliment did not jibe with Pierman's sense of accomplishment, but Grable closed the door before he could respond.

3

Five more state police cruisers towed dust clouds like drag chutes as they crawled back the lane. Pierman followed. He could barely see.

"Reinforcements, Lieutenant?" he said to Purcell, who trotted to meet him as he got out of Calkins' car.

"You don't think we got a homicide, Al? Here."

Purcell pushed two plastic bags into Pierman's hands. In each, under a red identification tag, was a lump of metal.

"Bullets?" Pierman said to Calkins who had joined them.

"One fell out of the body when we took it off the rig." Calkins said quietly. "We looked a little closer after that. The other was on the ground."

"Where was he hit?"

"Who knows?" Purcell was indignant. "I mean, Jesus, the obvious holes are burned away. Autopsy may tell us, but I doubt it." He pointed to the contents of the bag. "And them. They are a fucking mess. How're we supposed to identify those?"

Calkins explained to Pierman that the fire had destroyed any rifling marks. "You might be able to determine caliber, if none of the weight's melted off. That's not likely, and you probably can't tie it to any particular weapon anyway."

Purcell took the bags back from Pierman. He turned and scanned the fields, rubbing the slugs through the plastic between his thumb and forefinger. "So, Al," he said. "Where d'you think they came from?"

"That's twice, Lieutenant. You can call me Allen."

"Allen. Sure. Where'd these items come from? Which direction? What would you tell your jury about how this murder was perpetrated?"

"Perpetrated," Pierman said. He turned to Calkins. "This a test?"

Calkins was scrutinizing Purcell's back. "Probably." He turned his gaze on Pierman and pursed his lips. "Or it settles an argument. Maybe both."

A dozen troopers stood around their cars with their arms folded, kicking clods and watching them sidelong from under campaign hats. To a man, they were tall and built like swimmers, with broad shoulders and hips so narrow Pierman wondered how they kept their gun belts up. They looked confident and neat, with pleats sewn into their navy-blue shirts so that they aligned with the pleats in their lighter blue trousers. In contrast, separate and to one side, stood Darrell. His shirttail was out and his pants were stained. He looked hot and winded.

"Aren't we wasting time here?" Pierman said.

Purcell wheeled around. "My point. My point, exactly."

Calkins' eyes remained fixed on Pierman. He refused to indicate what was at stake or whose side he was on. It was, in Pierman's experience, typical cop: You're for me or against me, but don't let me stop you from deciding.

"Pistol or rifle, Lieutenant?" Pierman finally looked away from Calkins. "Judging by the size of those slugs, what'd they come from?"

"Rifle, probably." Calkins nodded agreement.

"The shooter didn't want to get too close."

"Or," Purcell said, rocking on his heels, "it was handy. Lot of rifles in Holoce County."

"No glass in the tractor cab?"

Purcell sputtered, perplexed. Calkins almost smiled.

"It's not that easy, Allen," he said, "and we're not that dumb. The tractor had no cab. There aren't any spiders in glass to show where the shots came from. It's a roll bar with an awning. Open on all four sides.

Trying to imagine, even surrounded by police, Pierman felt a chill, as though he were naked. He wondered if either the victim or the shooter had felt that way. Behind him, across the ditch, corn stood four feet high and ran the length of the ditch and the lane. Pierman did not think the skinny stalks and narrow leaves would provide much in the way of cover until one went in so deep that he couldn't fire out of it.

He walked to the lip of the ditch. The technician was down there taking samples off the tractor.

"Any footprints?" Pierman asked. The technician was curt. "I'm standing in a foot of water here." Pierman gave him his father's hard grin. "And the answer is you're going to look, you just haven't done it yet." Pierman held the technician's glare for a moment before turning around.

Before him, the wheat field lay divided along a diagonal line, charred black on the north side, golden on the south. Soybeans separated the wheat from a woods, which apparently marked the boundary of Grable's farm.

The beans had been planted in rows that ran east-west, the longest dimension of the field, for efficiency's sake. Turning equipment more than you had to wasted time and money.

From the darker color of the turned soil, Pierman could tell the tractor had worked the bean field in a looping pattern. To accommodate the cultivator's broad turning radius, the driver would have started at the middle of the field's width, run the length of the rows, turned north toward the woods, harrowed the northern border of the field, then turned south to run the rows that adjoined the rows he started with on the south. He would have continued to loop until the field was finished.

But he had not completed the field. Half the width of a football field stood between the last of the southernmost harrowed rows and the wheat field, and within that width, Pierman could see a gap of a dozen or so yards between the points where the harrowed rows ended and where the tracks the cultivator made on the packed-clay lane began.

"Grable would've raised the cultivator to come out of the field and onto the lane," Pierman said, "but then he dropped the cultivator so it made tracks on the lane. Why is that?"

Purcell shrugged. "Probably the point where he got it. People don't always get thrown by a shot. Sometimes they drop. If that's what happened to him, he may have dropped and hit the lever that dropped the equipment."

Looking at the point where the tracks began, Pierman said, "Shots come out of the wheat field?"

"What makes you think so?" Calkins asked, but his eyes looked beyond Pierman's shoulder to meet Purcell's.

Pierman walked into the charred part of the wheat field. "The angle. Whoever was shooting had time to put at least two shots into the victim. If he didn't hit him, you'd never have found the bullets. The body stopped them."

Pierman paused to look at Calkins, who nodded. Pierman turned so that his back was not to Purcell.

"That means he probably would not have shot directly from the victim's side because that's a smaller target and he'd have to be a very good shot and very quick."

"So what'd he do, Al?" Purcell turned to Pierman. "Face him down like a gunslinger."

"Maybe. I don't know." Pierman pointed. "The tracks weave in a lazy pattern, not like someone jerked the wheel in fear or to avoid being shot, but like the driver had already been hurt or killed."

"Maybe he was shot from behind," Calkins said but without enthusiasm. Purcell waited with raised eyebrows, obviously relishing that theory more than the other.

"If Grable started on this side and worked the field east to west and north to south, he'd be facing south toward the wheat when he was on this side," Pierman said. "Besides, wouldn't shooting him in the back be the harder shot? He walked to rim of the ditch and looked at the tractor. "Wouldn't that seat back make the target smaller? Which gets us back to the accuracy and speed of the shooter."

Pierman's eyes again swept the fields around him. "How he got in here without being seen is what I don't understand. Surely, he didn't just drive up the lane."

"Well, he might, Allen, if he and the victim knew each other. That might explain the lazy tracks," Calkins said evenly. But Purcell cocked his head at Darrell. "Of course, no thanks to Deputy Dawg," he said, "it was gawker city out here. If there ever were any other tracks, we'll never know."

Calkins looked at Purcell coldly. "Unless we look." To Pierman, Calkins said, "The other possibility is that the Halsey Highway runs on the other side of that woods. Someone could have parked there and hiked in."

"Parked," Purcell said. "In plain view. On a well-traveled road. And walked clear around a bean field—without being seen—to nest in the wheat. That's not what I'd call efficient, and pursuing it at this stage is not what I'd call efficient. Boys, let's get a dog and a chopper in here and stop fucking around."

Pierman now saw not only the shape of the argument but what started and drove it. It was about who was going to run the investigation. The banality of it depleted him.

"Lieutenant," he said, sighing, "you'd have the shooter fire from behind the victim but not come through the woods, which would put him at the victim's back." He turned to Calkins. "You'd place the shooter in the wheat field—or in front of the victim—but you think he would've swung across a field and a half of short crops without being seen."

Pierman turned his back to them, one hand hooked in his belt, the other held like a blade. "If I *had* to tell a jury about this, Lieutenant, I'd say that at noon in broad, goddamned daylight, somebody came into this field, took aim at a moving human target, and put not one but two slugs into it. Then, he may have set fire to a tractor to destroy evidence or to cover his escape. If I were talking to a jury," Pierman tapped his head with the blade of his hand, "I'd said that's pretty damned brash. If I were talking to a judge, I'd say it's deliberate and almost certainly premeditated." He turned back to Purcell and Calkins. "Offhand, either of you know anybody that skillful or cold-blooded?"

Purcell accepted the question as rhetorical and merely returned Pierman's gaze. Calkins eyes glazed, then he shook his head as if clearing it. "No," he muttered, "probably not." He had to clear his throat after he said it.

Pierman massaged his forehead. He was tempted to ask Calkins where he would've known such a person, but he decided it was a question for another time.

"The deal, as I understand it, is the county has jurisdiction and the state assists unless the county yields." Pierman looked up. "That right?" Both Calkins and Purcell nodded warily. "Then, Lieutenant, you want me to talk to a jury, give me something to say. Line those men up at the south side of that wheat field and march them through both fields, the ditch, and the woods, if necessary. Tell them to put their eyes on the ground and not come back until they find something that tells us how this happened."

Pierman looked over the knot of men and back to Calkins, who showed a trace of a smile. He met Calkins' eye.

"Darrell can go with them."

Calkins and Purcell retired to their cars to make notes. They later helped each other measure the cuts made by cultivator and distances from the tractor to various points in the field. They sought no more advice from Pierman, who stood with his arms folded and his heel hooked on the bumper of Calkins' car while he watched the progress of the march through the fields. Another deputy arrived shortly before five. After eyeing Pierman for a moment, Calkins sent him off to walk the fields with the others.

When the searchers returned, the troopers' crisp uniforms were wrinkled and stained black and green below the knees. They had found nothing. There were no trails or depressions in the wheat that still stood, the ground was too dry and trampled to find anything where the wheat had burned, and there were no footprints or markings in either the soil or the bean rows or the ditch.

"If there was ever any to begin with," the technician said. He looked at Pierman when he said it.

"Did you check the bean field for evidence of someone trying to cover their tracks?" Calkins asked the technician.

"Sir," the technician now spoke to Purcell. "The soil was turned this morning. If the guy was obliterating his prints as he walked, we'd never find it. The ground's already broken."

"Nothing in the woods?" Calkins said.

The troopers were silent. Some looked away; most looked to the technician.

"Sir," he said again to Purcell, "there was no point to going in the woods if we hadn't found anything before we got there."

"Fine," Purcell said.

Darrell had straggled in behind the rest of the group. He had not joined them at the water cooler in the back of the state police van. Instead, he put his back to the door of Calkins' car and lowered himself to the ground in a crouch. Now, his legs were splayed out in front of him as he wiped his face with a handkerchief.

"There were depressions in the grass along the fence row," he said dully. "The one between the woods and the beans."

"There was one place. It might've been a depression or it might not," the technician said quickly. "The growth was bent but not broken. Might've been an animal."

"They were near a post where there was a scrape on the fence wire," Darrell persisted in the same flat tone.

"The fence was old, sagging, and rusty," the technician said. "He's assuming that because there was slight variation in color it was scraped."

"Fine," Purcell said, looking at his watch. "Saddle up, boys. The sheriff here's running this show. Give me a call, Joe, you realize you're out of your league. I'm not the one who has to get re-elected, you know."

"I want your reports tomorrow," Calkins said to the backs of the state officers as they moved away. Purcell waved over his shoulder.

Darrell said, "I found a guy in a car on the other side of that woods a couple nights ago."

Purcell and the troopers stopped.

"Who?" Calkins said.

"Old Billy McQueen."

"Bet he was dead drunk," said one of the troopers who spent more time in the county than the others.

"Where's the report?" Calkins asked evenly.

Darrell said nothing. Purcell and the troopers began moving off again. Pierman saw Purcell and a trooper smirk at each other out of the corner of his eye. Calkins considered Darrell for a long moment before he instructed him to go back to town. He could do his report on Bill McQueen before he went off duty, Calkins said. He could take Mr. Pierman with him, if Mr. Pierman was ready. Darrell shrugged and headed for his car.

Darrell declined Pierman's offer to drive the police car back to town. "County property. Insurance," Darrell said, by way of explanation. Pierman doubted that it would make any difference if he pointed out that he, too, was a county employee.

"We used to play cowboys and Indians in fields like that one back there," Pierman said when they were on the highway. "Bang, bang, you're dead. Hard to imagine it's become real."

"Yeah, well," Darrell said. His eyes were fixed; they did not roam in the way cops' do when they drive.

"Did you know the victim?" Pierman asked.

"I knew Randy Grable some, if that's who you mean. I don't know he's the victim."

"Say he is the victim, why do you suppose anybody'd want to kill him?"

"I reckon that's another thing I don't know."

Farmers were back cultivating their fields or baling their hay. To make up the time spent at Grable's place, they would work late into the night. In one field, a woman leaned against a car watching a tractor approach while two small children ran around her legs. A picnic basket sat on the roof of the car.

"Why'd you think there was a scrape on the fence?" Pierman said.

Darrell turned to see what the joke was going to be. Pierman raised his eyebrows.

"It was one strand, knee-high, at a post," Darrell said. "You climb a fence near a post or they sag," he said, in case Pierman, a suit, had never climbed a wire fence. "And there weren't any other 'variations in color' on that fence I could see."

Darrell was raised to respect authority. "But," he said and shrugged in deference to it or his exhaustion.

It should have been simple. Pierman had Darrell drop him off at the Courthouse so he could make sure his office was locked. The building, however, had been shut down for the day. When he let himself in the back door, the lights were out, and he could not find a switch. He made his way along a wall to the elevator, but when he pressed the button, it did not light and he could not hear the car clanking in the shaft as it normally did.

Pierman was ready to let the office go, when he heard the slow steps on the stairs. A circle of light, a flashlight beam, bobbed on the wall of the first landing. Before he could think, Pierman pressed himself against the elevator door. As soon as he did, he felt foolish; he knew he had been spooked by the events of the day. All the same, he did not relax. The light sliced the black hall.

"Who's there?"

It sounded like "who's ear?" The words were methodical, slightly slurred, absent of the fear that had made Pierman swallow back his heart.

"Me, Willie," Pierman said finally and identified himself.

If the janitor had been young once, I could not remember it. What everyone did know was that he had always been slow in speech and thought. The story was that sometime before anyone presently working in the building could remember the county commissioners had given him the job of cleaning its toilets in lieu of welfare. In the years since, without being asked or denied, he had taken on the rest of the building's chores.

He always wore a short-sleeved, white shirt and bolo tie with a silver and turquoise clasp. Given his job, it was an outfit no one required him to wear. The getup made him look like a poor copy of the other Courthouse employees, particularly since the shirt was frequently smudged, but he wore it every day nonetheless.

Pierman and his friends ragged Willie unmercifully when they were boys roaming town after school, until Carter caught him and I sentenced him to helping Willie with the toilets for a month. Since his return, Pierman tried to give the old man time and respect as repentance.

Willie shuffled down the last flight of stairs and put the flashlight beam directly in Pierman's eyes.

"Hello," he said. They could have been meeting on the Courthouse square at noon. "Ever'body's gone home."

"Put the light down, please, Willie," Pierman said. It took a few seconds for the command to register. "What're you doing here?"

Willie explained that he always came back to shut off the lights and elevator. "Sometimes people ain't done at four-thirty. I'm supposed to save money."

Pierman asked him for the time. He tucked the light under his arm and drew hand over hand a large pocket watch attached to a leather thong out of his shirt pocket. After an annoyingly long pause, Pierman heard the watch click open.

"Past six."

"Well, I hope you get overtime."

"No." Willie didn't seem to think it unfair at all.

Pierman asked him to turn on some lights, so that he could go up to his office and lock it. As with all things, Willie took time to consider it.

"Switches are on the fourth floor," he said finally. Elevator's, too."

To Pierman, that sounded like the closest Willie would get to no.

"I'll borrow your light then," he said. "It'll just take a minute."

Pierman grabbed the light before Willie could react and sprinted up the stairs. He didn't like leaving the old man in the dark, but he figured he'd be back before the Willie realized it.

Pierman loved his mother, but he refused to live with her. She said it made no sense for him to live in the cramped efficiency, but when he had offered her rent, she had refused. She had Carter's pension and his investments and her family's trust, she said; he was the one who might not have a job to go back to. That was enough to convince him to keep the place two blocks from the Courthouse, but he stopped by to see her every evening, usually for dinner.

The yellow house on Taylor Street was a two-story affair with a white, rounded colonnade on the front instead of the porch that most of the other houses on the street had. It had always been too large for the three of them. In settling Carter's estate, Pierman was learning the sources of his family's assets, and he suspected now that his parents had bought the place with his mother's money. The old man must've loved her to have accepted that.

Tonight, as he approached from the Courthouse, the house was not only too large, but too still. From outside, he saw no lights. The door was open, but inside he smelled no cooking and heard no sound from the kitchen. The storm door's slam was the last sharp rap sealing in the silence, and Pierman had had too many abrupt shifts in volume that day.

He called her and heard nothing. A car crunched gravel in the alley behind the house. He called again and moved quickly checking rooms.

"In here."

It was faint, from her bedroom at the back of the house. He found Elizabeth rocking in a chair next to the four-poster bed. The evening sun strained enough light through the sheer curtains to make the shadows thick. She had moved the rocker into one of them.

"You all right?" he asked.

"I . . . I was indulging. Having a little cry." She laughed through a snuffle. "I told myself it was for Mr. Grable, but it was really for me."

"You heard then."

"The phone's rang all day. They always think I should know something. Because of you men, your father and you."

Pierman sat on the bed, his back to the window. She squinted for a moment, trying to read his face.

"I was out there," he said. "Had to babysit Grable." He cocked his head in a dismissive gesture. "Keep the cops in line."

"I wondered if it wasn't something like that. I'm sorry."

She put her head back, closed her eyes, and rocked slowly. She was a tall woman with a long face and short hair she had let go silver. She favored elegant light-colored blouses and dark slacks that said but did not boast that she had money. She had been gawky and shy when she was young, but sometime during her middle years, her manner evolved into loose-limbed reserve. It was not uncommon for men of her age to attempt ultimately awkward conversations with her in lines at the grocery or the post office.

As she rocked, the wrinkles and puckers of her face deepened for long seconds as she approached the light, then softened as her face melted vague back into the shadow. It was like an image dragged with difficulty from a dream the night before. Pierman reached out and stopped the chair.

"Lonely?" he asked, probing delicately for the source of her mood.

"Yes, that."

"And?"

"And afraid, mostly."

"Of?"

"Of being alone, I suppose."

She opened her eyes, but they looked over Pierman's shoulder.

"I've been thinking of your father today. God help me, but this was the kind of day he lived for." She shook her head ruefully. "He was kind of a bumpkin, you know."

Carter's son started to object, but she raised a hand to silence him. The light caught the big diamond, and a ray, like a tiny spent star, shot off into the dark.

"I loved him for it," she said. "You can be assured of that. Why else would I come here with him if I didn't? This was *his* home."

She started rocking again. The hand hung over the arm of the chair, the ring blinking like a lazy strobe. Pierman watched it.

"But I was always afraid," she said. "Especially at first. It was different here. There were no concerts, no plays. Well, those at the high school but they're so dreadful. There weren't many places to eat. People didn't go anywhere. It was after the war then. I was afraid."

The ring disappeared into the gloom. Pierman heard the rustle of tissue before it reappeared.

"I was afraid," Elizabeth said again. "You have to live so close here. People fight. Actually hit each other. The young ones at least, even the girls. Last one standing wins, and the adults seem to think that's natural."

She was quiet for a time, rocking, the ring winking.

"I was afraid people wouldn't like me," she said. "Afraid I wouldn't like them. Afraid I wouldn't understand them and hurt your father's career." The chair stopped; the ring glowed. "I didn't, you know." She was leaning forward, looking at him when he raised his eyes.

"But I could *not* understand how these people could do the same dreary things day after day, year after year, and not be crushed by it. Family and work, more family, more work. The only relief seemed to be their churches, and those, too, were an imposition all their own."

How often do we hear our parents' secrets? They are either not good enough or far too compelling to be yielded up easily. Sometimes we do not even know they exist without the subtle markers: the aversion of eyes at some innocent, chance remark, the way they hold their breath when they meet someone who knew them when.

It was not that Pierman was not curious. Growing up in a place where people went out of their way to be friendly, he had wondered why his mother held herself apart and he worried that people thought she was stuck up. Under other circumstances, Pierman might have drawn her out, asked questions, gently sought examples. But tonight his head was far too cluttered. He could think of only the most routine and inane ways to cope with her.

"Mother," he said too quietly for tact. "Wouldn't you like a drink or something?"

"Do not patronize me." But she sensed his helplessness and softened. "It feels good to talk right now. I'd just like to talk."

Her son shrugged and nodded, and the ring flickered again.

"It's not like I could talk to people around here about it. They'd have marked me for life. They would've said I thought I was too good for them. That wouldn't have helped me or your father. Although I suspect people have thought that about me anyway."

Again, she was quiet for a time.

"And then, after the first few years—they were so . . . uncomfortable—it ceased to matter much." Her voiced warmed with the zest of confession and memory. "I was so busy. Your father was setting up the practice with Donald then. I had to be secretary and bookkeeper.

I was bad at it—they were always scolding me—but I learned. We bought this house, and it had to be fixed up. I was not young. We had you right away. There just wasn't time for all that reflection. Things seemed to be working out for themselves, and once in a while, we had fun. I guess I decided maybe that's how they lived, too."

The light was fading, and the shadows were growing thicker. Elizabeth did not notice. She let her chair cut its path silently, then giggled.

"Carter knew. He was always giving me gentle, little lessons. I'd come home from a card party muttering about their cattiness, and he'd just laugh and say, 'Now, Beth, people have to talk about something.' Or I'd make some snide remark about a notice in our silly little newspaper, and he'd cluck his tongue at me. 'Beth, it's an accomplishment. Let people enjoy it.'" Her good humor left as quickly as it came. "I think I must've hurt him when I said things like that."

The heat was gone from the diamond. In the last light, Pierman could see only cold blue as she brought her hand to her face.

"And now this thing with the Grables," she said. "It shouldn't upset me so. We hardly knew them. But everyone was saying it was murder and I began to think again I still didn't understand. It seemed like I'd answered all but the last little bit of the question and it was the part that mattered most. And now I'm old and I'm not up to it and I'm afraid all over again."

Her shoulders were shaking when Pierman reached out to grasp them.

"We don't know anything yet," he said. "Somebody's dead. That's it, that's all we know. We don't who or why or anything else. And it's got nothing to do with you, Mom. Just let that go."

He had missed the point, but perhaps she had expected more than he could give. She missed Carter and had wanted then, more than anything else, another buffer, and he would not offer it. Even if he could. And hadn't it always been so? Hadn't she encouraged his independence, she and Carter, in his way? She shook his hands away and stood up. "Let's eat out tonight."

Elizabeth affected gaiety under the harsh light and the noise and the chatter of the café. She talked of a dozen events in town, none related to her or to him and gave no hint of loneliness or fear. But later, as they walked home, she asked him if, this once, he would mind staying overnight. In case of prowlers, she admitted finally. That much he could do, but it apparently was not enough. Later, after he had slipped into the bed he grew up in, he could hear through the wall the mumble of her voice talking on the phone. He did not know whom she talked to and he did not later ask. At the time, Elizabeth and I often spoke.

4

We expect our sheriffs to live their work. The sheriff is, after all, not just the county's chief police officer; he is also the head turnkey, and there are no frills in the budget for personnel. The men who occupy the office are obliged to live at the jail.

At first glance, it doesn't seem like a bad deal. The county provides an apartment rent free for the sheriff and his family on the first floor. The building sits off the square, and from the front especially, with two elms in a yard and a picture window behind a swing on a wide front porch, it could be any other residence.

It was, however, common knowledge that Calkins' wife hated it. Approaching the place early on the morning after Grable's fire, Pierman could understand why. The grimy, cherry-red bricks, the barred windows on the second and third stories, and the pair of dusty patrol cars at the side were more than enough to defy first impressions. Pierman had heard enough at the dinner table growing up to know that Mrs. Calkins was not the first sheriff's wife to ask herself who had whom caged here.

Calkins was barefoot, tucking in a crisp shirt, when he answered the door. He registered no reaction to Pierman's appearance; people of all types showed up on his step at all times.

"I didn't think lawyers got up much before ten," he said by way of greeting.

"I wanted to catch you before you got too busy today."

Calkins turned and led the way through the apartment, sweeping toys out of the way with his foot as he went. From somewhere above and beyond, Pierman heard muffled whooping and metal striking metal.

"The natives are restless this morning," he said.

"Always at this time of day." Calkins had long ago ground all but the slightest trace of disgust from his remarks on the subject. "They sleep all day and roam all night. They are nocturnal animals."

In a hall leading from the apartment to a darkened area at the back of the building, they stopped outside the kitchen door, a solid steel slab with a large key lock and hinges the size of sausages. A shirtless boy of four or five years of age, his eyes barely open, sat on a metal stool at a steel table mechanically chewing cereal. A short woman with a mushroom-cap hairstyle stood at a counter in a pink bathrobe buttering a foot-high stack of toast. She registered Pierman's presence with a suspicious scowl and returned to her task. Catching his wife's expression, Calkins did not introduce her. He offered Pierman coffee and waved him toward a door at the end of the hall. Pierman heard Calkins mutter something hushed and clipped to the woman as he walked ahead.

The office was cramped and uninviting, another unpainted concrete block cell if you took away the furniture. A chipped, metal desk that Pierman suspected was Army surplus took up most of the room. Squeezed behind and around it were a card file, a silent radio console on a table of the same mud green color as the desk, and a smudged Olivetti on a listing stand. An aquarium containing three goldfish and a snail had been placed on a low table under a window. Pierman had difficulty believing they belonged to Calkins; perhaps Calkins used them as a means of coaxing his son into his office.

The window high on the wall above Pierman's head reflected green leaves onto the glass of a gun cabinet on the wall above the radio, but not so much that Pierman couldn't see the weapons inside. Three rifles and two brutish shotguns, pump models with short barrels. Pierman wondered when Holoce County police last had use of riot guns.

In one corner of the cabinet, contained in their own frame were Calkins' discharge certificate from the Army, a photograph of a younger Calkins stripped to the waist wearing only dog tags and a shy grin, and two newspaper clippings about awards he had received from local service clubs. Pierman was leaning across the desk reading them when Calkins arrived.

"Here." Calkins pushed a white mug into Pierman's hands to get him off the desk.

"So you're a hero?" Pierman said, lifting his chin toward the clippings.

"Hardly." Calkins settled into the chair behind the desk. He sipped from his own mug and winked across its rim. "Unless I'm up for re-election."

"What happened after you had me driven off last night?"

Calkins leaned back in his chair, assessing Pierman's mood. "I went to an autopsy," he said. "It was a damned pretty sight."

"I take it you'd like me to feel sorry for you."

Calkins stared at Pierman, his chin set and his lips pulled tight in what might have been a grin. He was comfortable with the sulkiness. It was one of the things he knew about Pierman. But when Pierman did not blink or look away, Calkins shrugged and put the mug down, all traces of amusement gone.

Calkins had stopped to talk with Paul Grable on the way back to town, he said. He still could not identify the body at that time, but no one had seen Paul's boy for hours so it was at least worth asking about him. The old man had last seen his son at breakfast. The boy—"Hell, he wasn't a boy; he was twenty-one years old"—had gone to the field while his father had remained at the kitchen table settling accounts. As president of the school board, Paul Grable had later met with Fulton to discuss how to approach Pierman on the library vandalism. Fulton confirmed that he and Grable had met.

"You spoke with Fulton?" Pierman asked.

"Sure. You think I'm going to take old man Grable at his word?"

Pierman raised a hand in submission. "I've gotten soft. Something about this place makes me think I should take what people say at face value."

"Grow up."

Grable was on his way home when he saw the smoke, Calkins said. He had hopped on a tractor when it was clear that the fire was on his land. He said he did not think anything about Randy until he saw the way people treated him at the scene. Grable couldn't think of anyone that would want to kill his boy. He personally wondered if it didn't have something to do with the damned book business. Maybe they were aiming for him.

"Well?" Pierman said.

"Over books? Come on."

"Over power, politics, control of the minds of our children. Tell me in our lifetimes we haven't seen violence in service to political ends."

Calkins nearly smiled again. Sometimes Pierman would argue just to listen to his voice. Sometimes he liked to ride a farfetched idea just to see if he could do it. Sometimes you had to shut him up or knock him off.

"A minute ago, you wanted me to be nice to everyone." Pierman said nothing. "You think anybody around here gives that much of a shit? Wars are about politics. I was in Viet Nam. I killed for politics. Murder is personal." But when Pierman merely continued to stare, Calkins shrugged. "It's a theory, I reckon."

The autopsy verified that the body was Randy Grable's, Calkins said, hoping to move on. They did it by dentals, Calkins said, but only just barely. There were thermal fractures. "The kid's bones looked like used firecrackers," he said. But the pathologist had found a rounded hole in the skull and a nick in the rib cage, so his educated guess was shots to the head and chest. Who knew which one killed him?

"Mighty accurate," Pierman said. "And the when?"

"The when." Calkins was wary.

"Is there any doubt that the shots killed him? Or could it have been the fire?"

Calkins was growing tired of Pierman's attitude. "Are you asking because it makes a difference or 'cause it busts my ass?

"One way would be evidence of premeditation while the other may not. It could make a difference in the way it's charged, first or second degree."

"Any difference'd be damned little," Calkins said. "If you're asking if I asked that question, the answer is yes. The coroner is ruling it a homicide resulting from gunshot wounds to the head and chest."

The state police technician confirmed evidence of an "accelerant" around the tractor, Calkins continued quickly, but those things are filled with gas and oil so what do you expect? Calkins hadn't heard yet whether the burn patterns would tell them anything about whether the fire was accidental or deliberate. "I'm betting deliberate." He shrugged. "Which ought to eliminate any difference in the way it's charged."

Pierman seemed to have heard enough. He stood, looking out the window. Calkins noticed a set of index cards on the corner of the desk. He picked them up, tapped them into a neat stack, and thumbed through them.

"Three more for the hopper." He read off the names and flipped through them again. "One from here, one from Illinois—never heard of the place—and from the Capitol." He tapped the cards into a stack again and tossed them back on the desk. "The usual stuff. All young, 20 or less. All minor shit, one public intox, one bad check, one DWI. We don't do a lot of premeditated murder around here." Calkins leaned forward in his chair.

"I've only done one of these, Allen. A manslaughter in a domestic. Nothing like this. Take another ride with me."

Looking out the window, Pierman thought about how in all the years they had known each other they never apologized. Pierman thought about how he was at least curious. Pierman thought about how as prosecutor he had to be careful about participating in too much of the investigation. If he wasn't careful, he could wind up a witness and that would mean he would have to get another lawyer to try it. But then he didn't think he'd be around by the time this one came to trial.

Through the window, Pierman watched a skinny figure loping up the sidewalk. The man's plaid pants were an inch too short, his white shirt looked yellowed, and his tie was askew.

"If we're going," Pierman said, "now's the time. The press is at the door."

The buzzer produced indignant shouts and catcalls from the residents upstairs. They were just bedding down for the day. Calkins put a portable radio in the holster on his belt and snapped it on. A burst of static and a nasal voice reciting codes accompanied them out the back door. It was official. The day had begun.

5

Lindley's neighborhoods, like its business district, bear no distinctive names. It is purely a matter of necessity; in a town this size, there is none. The streets have names, of course, but mailmen are about the only ones who know them. A cordial but blank stare is the typical reaction to a visitor reciting a street name and number from a crumpled piece of paper. More often than not, the visitor will have to name the person he seeks to get accurate directions.

The rule's proof is its exception, Sparky's Knob. The visitor giving that as his destination will be met by no trace of blankness and paler shades of cordiality. We all know where it is, but not many will admit to knowing anyone there.

The Knob lays along a low ridge on the other side of the old graveyard. There are few hills here and what there are wouldn't have amounted to much more than bumps to the Pennsylvanians, New Yorkers and Kentuckians who settled here. They would've appreciated what rises there were, though, and perhaps that explains the name.

Sparky himself is lost to contemporary memory. They used to say he was actually a dog, a snappish, low-slung, loose-jointed hound, the Abraham from whose loins all the packs of the neighborhood traced their common ancestry and disposition. The story had it that the people who set up housekeeping on the Knob took their inspiration from Sparky: They lived too close to the ground. Children fell like rain from bitter men and exhausted women. In the winter, they cooped in tiny, brown or gray asbestos-sided houses that reeked of bacon, diapers, and booze. Summers, they roamed in rowdy, tumbling packs, punctuating the days with the percussion of warped screen doors yielding to their advances. The children and the dogs came and went, the story's punch line had it, but the numbers stayed the same.

The tale has its elements of truth, I suppose, but I could never stomach it. God damn tellers of tales. I grew up there.

As a boy, Allen, of course, had heard the story, but it made little sense to him. We talked. The Knob kids at school did not seem so different or bad, he said. Some were slower maybe, he said, and I suggested it might be more be boredom more than simplemindedness. They got mad quicker and look out when they did, he said, and I wondered aloud whether it was because they carried extra measures of anger and frustration. And they stood up for you, he said. One kid, a boy to whom Allen gave his apple each day and a man his father later sent to prison, had broken a classmate's nose when the kid mocked Allen for wasting generosity on "trash". I did not have the words then to tell Allen how the Knob boy felt.

By the end of the conversation, we agreed the Knob kids laughed when they were happy and cried when they were hurt. It just took them longer to reach either point, and Allen, when he was very young, marveled at them.

The Knob now did not look as Pierman remembered it. Two or three trails of rubbish still smeared the side of the ridge down to the wider

road below. Three or four house trailers were parked where houses once stood, but the homes that remained were still mottled and
small with the occasional fender or kitchen appliance wallowing in
the back yard. The difference was that the neighborhood seemed
lifeless. He saw no children or dogs, as if their seed had finally dis-
sipated like milkweed on wind.

"Billy McQueen's a drunk," Calkins was saying, "and has been
long as I've known him. Drove off his wife. Lives with his old ma here
'cause he can't keep a job."

"You're talking about the guy Darrell found passed out on the
other side of the woods."

"You don't remember Billy?" Calkins asked.

"Should I?"

Calkins looked at Pierman as though he thought Pierman was
pulling his leg, then shrugged. "Maybe not," Calkins said and paused,
choosing his words. "You ought to know Billy used to work for Grable
as a hand."

"A hired man? Really."

Calkins nodded. "I 'spect it was charity as much as anything."
Calkins paused again. "But, you see, Paul fired him when he found
out his boy was coming back to work the farm, and I don't think
Billy's worked since."

Pierman took his turn to consider. "And that would make it
personal."

"It would," Calkins said.

Dilapidation wins no favor from daylight, and the house cowered
from it. Tree roots from ragged-top stumps split the sidewalk and
made the men step long. They walked past the shell of a pickup
truck, cancerous with rust. The wooden steps swayed under their feet
and made them skip up onto the front porch.

A tiny, sour woman watched them through the screen. She reminded Pierman of one of the crabapple dolls girls would bring to school after a weekend at camp: a small round head, deeply crinkled and set on a stick, gray hair the texture of corn silk pulled back in a bun, cloves for eyes, and faded material wrapped loosely as a housedress. The dolls might've looked shriveled but never frail.

"Wha' you want?" Her voice was the bleat of a cat.

"Billy," Calkins said, ducking his head in greeting.

She jerked her head back into the house, unfazed by the curt response. "Sleeping." Pierman had the impression she had been through exchanges of this sort before.

"Sleeping? Or passed out?" Calkins said.

She glared at him to show she was not intimidated, then stepped back and held the door. It opened directly into a stark living room. A threadbare sofa, two equally worn armchairs and a coal stove clustered on a bare wooden floor around an oval braided rug. Cheap paneling that bowed at the seams in a place or two made it dark.

"There," the old woman said, cutting off Pierman's study of the room. She pronounced it "thar."

A bare lightbulb grazed Pierman's head when they entered. Calkins stepped to the window and snapped up the shade. "Jesus Christ," he muttered under his breath.

The room was rank with boozy sweat in the heat. A T-shirt hung from the back of a wooden folding chair. More clothes spilled from a cardboard wardrobe onto the floor in a dirty, matted pile. Between that and the iron bedstead was a half-empty whiskey bottle and from under a dingy sheet came a low, drooly snore.

"Billy," Calkins barked and punched the heap on the bed. "Damn you, Billy, wake up."

Reflexively, Pierman turned to see how the old woman would take this treatment of her son, but she was not there. When he stepped out the door, he saw her in the kitchen across from the living room. She was standing on a crate talking on wall phone.

"Billy." Calkins stripped away the sheet. A man curled fetally, in Dickies work pants and socks. "Get your ass up, Billy." Calkins poked him in the kidney. "Come on."

With poking, the snoring broke into hacks, like the backfire of a car. The man slowly pushed himself up and rubbed his eyes on the knuckles of his hands.

"Late f' work," he muttered with a slur and grabbed for the shirt more quickly than Pierman would have thought possible. Calkins caught his hand.

"Billy, we're going to talk."

The man inhaled deeply, blew it out loudly and belched. "Joe?" he said, then started when he realized Calkins was not alone.

"This is Mr. Pierman, the prosecutor," Calkins said.

The blood drained from the man's face. Only the red nets across his nose and cheeks remained. He sat up, eyes darting back and forth between the two of them. "I didn't do nothing," he whined.

Calkins pulled him to his feet. Upright, the man was only a little taller than his mother, and just as skinny. His chest was sunken, his arm muscles were slack, and his hair was matted by sweat.

"See the line," Calkins said, pointing to where two floorboard met. "Do it." Billy knew the procedure; he walked shakily but straight enough. Calkins spun him around and pulled his arms out straight on the sides. "Well?" he said impatiently. Billy reeled a little when he closed his eyes but he touched his nose with each forefinger. "Competent?" Calkins asked Pierman over his shoulder.

In his mind, Pierman went down the checklist he followed as a public defender when he looked for cop screwups. "Mirandize him," he said.

Calkins gave the man his rights off the top of his head and asked him if he understood them. The man nodded. "We need to hear yes or no from you, Mr. McQueen," Pierman said. He put his back to the wall next to the window so that he could watch Billy's face and crossed his arms.

When McQueen answered yes, Calkins ordered him to sit down. The man kept his eyes on Calkins and backed around him, like a dog about to be whipped. "Didn't do nothing," he said again. When he stumbled back onto the bed, Calkins pulled the wooden chair up close.

"Return with me, Billy, to yesteryear," Calkins said. "Or in your case, last week."

The older man only looked puzzled.

"Think back a couple, three days ago." Calkins put his head down and the tips of his fingers together between his knees. "My deputy found you out on Halsey Highway. You remember?"

"Well. Well, sort of."

"What's that mean? Sort of."

"Well, I know I was brought in, Joe, but I don't remember being brought in."

Calkins let out some breath between his teeth.

"You'd been drinking."

"Yessir."

"A lot."

The man shrugged. "You know."

"Yeah, Billy, I do. You drink a lot. What were you doing on the Halsey Highway when Darrell picked you up?"

"Well, sleeping, I imagine."

"How'd you get there?"

"My car, I guess."

"Is there a reason you're acting smart with me, Billy?"

"No, Joe, no. That's what your deputy said he found me in. I couldn't find my keys."

The man's eyes had wandered off to the whiskey bottle and locked on it. He started squeezing his fingers. Calkins had been watching his face and followed his eyes across the floor. Pierman saw the slightest of smiles appear.

"Where'd you go that night, Billy?"

"What?"

"That night. Where'd you do your drinking? You stay home or go somewhere?"

"Allie's," he said. "Allie's, like always." Allie's was a roadhouse on the outskirts, a place furnished in Formica and metal. Pierman had been there once long ago; it was like drinking alone in a stranger's dark kitchen. Lindley didn't have cocktail lounges.

"Anywhere else?" Calkins asked.

"Joe, why you asking me this all?"

Calkins leaned forward and clapped him on the side of the head. It brought Pierman off the wall, but Calkins held him in place with a stare. To the older man, Calkins remained calm and reasonable.

"So I'll ask again, Billy. Anywhere else?"

"I don't remember." He raised his hands, expecting another slap.

"Anybody see you there? At Allie's?"

"Lots of people, I reckon." It came out a whisper. Billy sat completely still except for his hands. They knitted the air in his lap.

"You ashamed, Billy?"

Billy shrugged again. "I drink too much," he whispered.

"Billy, look at me," Calkins said. "Now look at me." The man did but just for a second. "When was the last time you saw Paul Grable?"

"Paul," Billy said, a toddler's goofy, nearly toothless, grin appearing in the middle of a face full of stubble. "He's a fine feller."

"So you like Paul?"

Billy nodded amiably.

"When'd you see him last then?"

Billy stared blankly at the floor. His eyes strayed to the bottle and he rubbed his face as if to wipe the sight away. Billy started when Calkins leaned forward.

"When he fired me," Billy squealed, as though he was suppressing a sob. "When he let me go."

"You haven't seen him since?"

Billy shook his head.

"You haven't been to his house, his place?"

Billy shook his head again.

"How about his boy? When'd you see Randy last?"

"Boy, Joe, I don't when I seen him last."

Calkins raised his gaze to Pierman, who shrugged. Neither of them thought the man was capable of squeezing off two accurate rounds.

"At Allie's," Calkins said. He put a hand gently on the older man's knee. "I need to know who you talked to, who you were with."

"Well," Billy said. "Nate, I reckon. He was there."

"Nate was there? What happened to Nate?"

"Maybe," Billy said, his expression now haunted. "Maybe you better talk to him yourself." He cocked his chin toward the window. "He's out there."

𝒵

Pierman assumed the man stepping down from a telephone company van was the person the old lady had called. For reasons he could not then explain, Pierman recited details in his head: Medium height, built hard and compact, black hair, bearded. The man wore a gray, short-sleeved work shirt, company emblem above the pocket on the left, jeans, and black cowboy boots, of all things. At his waist, he carried pliers in a leather holster. A baby blue telephone handset hung from his belt on an O-ring.

The man considered the sheriff's car then the house and marched. He did not bother with the steps. He sprang onto the porch, entered without knocking, and let the screen door slam with a whack. He gave the living room a long, inquiring scan before calling the old woman by her name. Only when she appeared in the kitchen door and he saw a smile crinkle her face did he swagger into the bedroom.

"Boys," he said. "The Lone Ranger and Tonto, Batman and Robin, Poncho and Cisco. Back in the saddle, I see. But I got to tell you it's hard to know which is which."

"Nate," Calkins said. Without taking his eyes off the man, Calkins casually placed his hands at his waist, letting the right one rest on the handle of his gun. Pierman was surprised, until he looked at the man's face.

A few of the regulars in the Chicago criminal courts had been disfigured, victims of shanks and reflexes slowed by dope or booze. But people of unnatural appearance were rare in Lindley, where they kept or were kept to themselves. One razor straight scar, perhaps an eighth of an inch wide, ran from near the top of the man's forehead down across a puckered left eyelid, his left cheek, and a corner of his mouth into a black beard. He gave Pierman what might have been a smile. It was difficult to tell. Only one end of his lower lip opposite the scar moved. It came down square, turning the expression into a grimace, like he was biting a fart.

"You want ID, Pierman?" he said.

"No, Nate. I recognize you."

"Knew you would." He raised his hand, forefinger extended and thumb up, like a pistol, aimed it at Pierman, and let the hammer fall. "But I made you look."

"Like yesterday. You waved at me in the field."

The two men looked at each other, remembering, yesterday and before that.

"Like then," McQueen said. He turned to Calkins. "You guys going to tell me or I have to ask?"

"Just some questions for your dad," Calkins said.

Nate suddenly stepped forward. Calkins backed off. Pierman heard a hollow pop from Calkins' holster as he unsnapped the strap holding his gun.

"Whoa," Nate said, advancing still but more slowly, holding his hands up empty. "We got a little family matter here."

During the interruption the older man had made a dive for bottle. He was holding it high and sucking it hard. The son snatched it away viciously, and his father scrambled crablike against a wall. To Pierman's disgust, the son poured the last inch onto the bed in front his father's stricken eyes and dropped the bottle onto the sheet at his feet.

"So," Nate said pleasantly to Calkins and Pierman, "You were asking about?"

"Your dad says you and him went drinking at Allie's a week or so ago," Calkins said.

"We're both a long way from twenty-one."

Pierman had folded his arms and leaned back against the wall. "If you don't like your old man's problem so much, how come you're going out drinking with him?"

McQueen considered Pierman for a long moment. "Well, Allen, I guess it's your business, considering the circumstances, but if I want to spend any time at all with him, it usually requires a tavern."

Calkins rushed in. "Where'd you go afterward?"

"Afterward we were supposed to get a bite at Skelly's. The drunk old fart never showed. I looked for him but I didn't find him until your boy called me from the jail."

Nate picked up a sock from the end of the bed, tossed it onto the floor, and sat down. It crossed Pierman's mind that he was assuming the suspect's position, sitting under the gaze of Pierman and Calkins, who stood. McQueen gave Pierman the smile. He knew it.

"You boys're working fast, I see." McQueen leaned back on his arms and crossed his legs. "'Course, working fast is one thing. Working sloppy's another. My old man's too shaky to shoot straight. And look at him. He still hasn't figured out what this is all about."

Billy sat quivering, with his knees pulled up and his forehead resting on them. Calkins had said nothing for some time. A long look from Pierman drew no response from him.

"You think this is about Grable?" Pierman said.

"Isn't it? Both the sheriff and the prosecutor standing in my grandma's house the day after a murder?"

"How do you know it was a murder? We haven't said anything about that?"

"Come on. How long you been back? Small town. Big mouths."

McQueen watched a pointed toe jiggle up and down.

"How about you?" Pierman said. "What were you doing when the boy was killed?"

McQueen held up a finger. "Whoa now. Cheap trick. I don't know who was killed or when they were killed."

"What were you doing when the fire occurred, then?" Pierman said.

"Checking lines. Passing time."

"Where?"

"Five miles away. Check the assignment sheets."

"We will. How'd you wind up at Grable's?"

"Same as everybody else. Saw the smoke. Followed the traffic."

"Why didn't Paul Grable want to talk to you that morning? I saw him standing off from you. You scare him?"

The light in the man's good eye dimmed for a moment.

"You know," he said. "I am a true believer in law enforcement. And I'd like to cooperate in any way I can, but I think if you boys're done you can get the fuck out of here."

Calkins shrugged and started to go, but Pierman held his ground.

"If you're a believer, you'll let us look around."

McQueen looked at him and slowly brought up the grimace that passed for his smile. "Not my house."

"Billy," Pierman said, his eyes on Nate, "you mind if we look around?"

Billy shook his head. On his haunches, he rocked and rocked.

❦

The old woman was not as cooperative. She rooted herself in front of her bedroom door. Pierman introduced himself, stated his purpose, and promised to disturb as little as possible, but she did not move until her grandson appeared and motioned her away toward the kitchen.

Her bedroom was off the living room next to her son's, but walking into it was like walking into another house. While Billy had fouled his nest, she had embroidered hers. A simple, single pine bed was carefully made and covered with a green afghan. The curtains were just nylon sheers, but she had added tatted blossoms, like dandelion balls, to the borders. Two more pillows, one orange and the other beige, were laid plump and inviting in a torn armchair by the window.

There were also books, rows of them on shelves made of planks and bricks behind the chair. Most were fiction or history, and most were classics. Some bore the stamp of the town's library, apparently on permanent loan. The bindings were faded, but there was no dust on them or the shelves. The rest of the room was similarly tidy. Mother and son obviously lived by different rules. It was as if they left the sterile living room as neutral ground on which to meet.

Pierman looked under the bed and in the closet. Cops probably had a way of searching a room thoroughly, but Pierman didn't know it, and now that he'd had his way, he admitted to himself he didn't really know what he was looking for. A gun, a rifle, he supposed.

He was standing before the dresser, considering whether it was necessary to open the drawers, when he saw that the doily on top had a large lump under it. The scrapbook had a wooden cover, blotchy with stain and the name *nathanial* carved in crooked letters along the bottom by a young, unskilled hand.

Calkins apparently had given up quickly on Nate's room; Pierman could hear him outside clattering in the garage. When Pierman peeked, Nate and the old woman were sitting at the kitchen table, eating lunch and talking in quiet, earnest voices. He assumed Billy was in no shape to sneak up on him.

A birth certificate with tiny footprints was pasted on the first page beside yellowed newspaper announcements. Nate's mother had been named Barbara. A pressed rose—the note said it was from Billy to Barbara on the day Nate was born—was taped on the next page. The rest seemed to be just about everything in Nate's life that could be put on paper. A baptismal certificate, a crayoned valentine to the old lady, report cards with her signature replacing Barbara's in the middle of the second grade, swimming lesson certificates, a notice commending the boy for winning a *Time* magazine current events contest. Scout badges, curled and loose from the old glue, fell into the cracks. The pages grew whiter. Nate's name was underlined in clippings about football games and the National Honor Society. The high school diploma was laminated before it was attached.

The last few pages bulged. Pierman thumbed quickly by letters admitting McQueen to one of the smaller state universities and awarding him two different scholarships. The Purple Heart was behind the letters, dark against the white page and alone. The next page carried a photo of a young Nate and two other boys, maybe young men. Their hair was short, nearly shaved, and they were barechested, wearing only dog tags. Some numbers and the letters LURP were handwritten at the bottom of the photo. It was not unlike the one Pierman had seen in Calkins' office, except that each of these young men had a rifle propped on his hip.

"You go?" Nate asked from the door. Pierman started, but he knew exactly what McQueen asked. The question of whether a man had been to Viet Nam defined their generation, and Pierman had never been comfortable in the face of it. Even then, what seemed like many years later, when you rarely heard it anymore, the ones who asked the question were the ones who had already answered it to their satisfaction, one way or another; and Pierman always sensed a moment of tension in them, a second of readying for welcome or revulsion, as they waited for the answer.

"No," Pierman said, turning to McQueen. "I had a high number," he added and immediately disliked the sound of it.

"Well, boy, you were lucky. This"—McQueen lazily traced his forefinger along the scar down the left side of his face and into his beard—"this here's my door prize. You march?"

"What?"

"Against it, against the war?"

"No."

"You didn't go. You didn't march. Did you fucking pay attention?"

Pierman looked for a sign of anger or resentment, but instead McQueen favored him with the twisted grin.

"Hey, listen, I'm not the VFW." McQueen held up his hand at arm's length to push the notion aside. "If you marched? I wouldn't hold it against you. It blew. Royally."

"I imagine most people'd like to forget it."

"Exactly." McQueen sniggered. "Just like you and me, man. Right? Just like me and you. Course, for some, it's kind of a trick. Forgetting it."

Pierman knew he was being baited. One part of him wanted to end the conversation, but another could not resist the temptation.

"Why'd you come back then?"

"Home, man. It was home. After a round of shit like that, where else you going to go? You go home." McQueen shook his head in wonder at Pierman's ignorance.

"And you never thought of going back to college? Like on veterans benefits?"

McQueen found that idea amusing.

"Like I didn't know more than I did before? Well, I did. Considerably more. For instance, I knew killing. Oh, and telephones," he added as though wanting to be fair to the experience. "I earned a master's in killing and communications. The Army taught me both. The first, I have to say, has been a complete and utter waste of time, but now the second"—he held the blue line phone away from his leg and waggled it at Pierman—"the second, that made me a fully productive member of society."

McQueen leaned against the door frame. "They been busy," he said.

"Pardon?" Pierman said.

"The phones, man. The phones."

"What're you talking about?"

"That murder. Grable's kid. You and me. Remember? We were out there?"

"I still don't understand."

"People're talking. They're shook. They're locking their doors and buying guns."

"How would you know that?"

"You're a very suspicious guy, aren't you. I suppose you have to be in your business." McQueen dropped his hand to his belt and the blue line phone and patted it.

"You listen in?" Pierman asked.

McQueen's lips pulled back from his teeth. "Did I say that?"

"That would be against the law," Pierman said, but he knew it was weak.

"Yeah, well, you got to pass the time, and you got to check the lines. Better get it wrapped up quick."

Pierman shook his head. "Nate, are you getting off on this?"

The mischief went out of McQueen' good eye, and Pierman pressed the advantage.

"So, Nate, why was your father parked on the road that runs along the back of Grable's place a couple of nights before Randy Grable was killed?"

The confidence had returned to McQueen' gaze. "I wouldn't have a clue. And neither, apparently, do you. Time to go."

They met Calkins on the sidewalk.

"Guns," Calkins said without being asked. His shirt was sweated through.

Pierman stopped and looked at McQueen. "Oh," he said.

"Your buddy here'll tell you there are a .22 and a 12 gauge in a gun rack in the garage," Nate said. "Both mine. They're chained to the rack and each has a trigger lock so that crazy fucker inside won't kill himself or my grandma. I'm the only one with the key. If you want to take them, fine, but you'll find that neither has been fired in some time.

Calkins shrugged. "He's right. I checked."

"I don't suppose you'll apologize," McQueen said, walking them to the car.

"Any empty slots in the rack?" Pierman said to Calkins.

McQueen grinned in his horrible way, walking backward toward his van, but only for a second. "Don't come back," he said. "No sir. Not without good fucking reason. Better yet, a warrant."

He beeped the van's horn, like the ice cream man, as he drove away.

6

They drove a couple of miles in silence. Pierman wanted to ask Calkins what it was about McQueen that frightened him. Instead, he said, "Let's see, my last question to you was, 'Were there any empty slots in the gun rack?'"

"A month with your arm in a sling," Calkins said. "And you don't remember?"

The sigh escaped Pierman before he could catch it. Remember seemed to be all he had done since the old man died. Still, this memory was an exception, one he held face turned, at arm's length, in the way of all humiliations. At the time, the episode had struck him as emblematic, symptomatic at any rate, of some important principle. Age and circumstance now made it appear merely strange and all the more fascinating for the change.

Always, it came back through the senses first. The stink of sour socks. The brittle crack of shattering plastic. Moist, stinging heat rising and welling in his eyes while bruising cold tile chilled his chest and groin. And yes, more than anything else, the burn and snap of muscle tearing across the curve of his shoulder like frayed rubber bands. Plink. Plink. Plink.

The sunglasses, mirrored lenses in thick black plastic frames, had started it. They had been Pierman's idea. The cross-country coach was a short, blond, bristle-haired man, with a terrier's snappish disposition. At every meet, rain or shine, he wore the glasses. At the last meet of the season, his team showed up wearing them as tribute and joke. When the gaunt boys huddled around him before the meet, trying to keep straight faces, the coach looked up from one knee at each of them, his own reflection filling each of their eyes. At first, he said nothing. He then rose to stand face to face with Pierman. "Maybe you ought to win," he said.

Pierman had no recollection of the race itself except for the last two hundred yards: the startled face of the leader when he glanced back, the sense of heightened alertness that Pierman had since come to recognize as the onset of ruthlessness, and cool autumn grass come to meet him. "He's all right," someone said, and a pink sky dissolved the darkness. His mother had held his hand tightly as his teammates had grabbed him under the arms and walked him around. He had cramps and the congratulatory pounding nearly drove him to his knees, but neither diminished the glow of accomplishment.

Even as a boy, Pierman distrusted good feelings. They did not last, and in the locker room, his disappeared. The cross-country team shared the room with the football team, and neither cared for the other. The runners pegged football players as Neanderthals, and the football players expressed doubts about the runners' virility and sexual preferences. At the appearance of the runners in their sunglasses, the hoots and whistles rose and echoed off the concrete block walls like morning in the bird house at a zoo.

Calkins was a football player. "Very studly," Pierman remembered him saying. He smiled wearily until he found a hand on his shoulder. Nate McQueen was a year older than Pierman. He had a reputation as a vicious lineman and an outstanding student. Other than by that reputation, Pierman did not know McQueen then.

"Let's see who we got behind these," McQueen said. He was stripped to his football pants and cleats. His hand tightened on

Pierman while the other moved swiftly toward the glasses. Pierman twisted out of the grip, but McQueen had a finger hooked under the shaft and the glasses fell to the floor. McQueen put his cleats on them and pivoted. He did it so casually that Pierman at first could not believe that it was intentional. He stared at the shards and the twisted frames.

"You son of a bitch."

McQueen shoved him. The lockers boomed when Pierman hit them. He pulled himself erect, chin to chin with McQueen.

"I didn't hear what you said, Hollywood," McQueen said.

"Yeah, you did," Pierman said, his voice cracking.

"Help me out. Say it again," McQueen said in a low voice.

Pierman felt the crowd of half-naked boys watching and waiting for his answer. The door flew open. The cross-country coach stopped and looked around.

"Problem? Or you guys planning to dance?"

"No problem, coach," McQueen said, without taking his eyes off Pierman.

"You, Allen?"

"None."

"Then, hustle up." The coach clapped his hands and turned to go back outside. "All of you. Let's go."

Pierman had not been uneasy in a locker room since his first year of gym, but the feeling crept over him again. The usual chatter had dropped off. The other boys were spending too much time dressing and packing their gym bags, watching without looking, waiting. Coming out of the shower, Calkins winked at Pierman and patted him on the rump. McQueen took interest in the way Pierman rolled down his socks and peeled off his trunks.

They entered the shower at the same time. Two of Pierman's teammates rinsed quickly and slipped a bit on the wet floor in their rush to leave. When Pierman turned his back, icy water hit him. He was blinded by the spray when he wheeled.

"Lay off, McQueen." It sounded whiny in Pierman's ear's, but it was the best he could come up with.

McQueen readjusted the temperature and stepped in.

"Say, Pierman," he said. "Is it true that you cross-country guys always suck cocks?"

He luxuriously soaped the subject of the question with both hands, and Pierman almost laughed. It was the old joke, lawyer's trick, and English teacher's example. *Always* confounded the purpose of a simple, if obscene, question: *yes* was an admission; *no* could mean sometimes. Either way, at their age and at that time, it was incriminating, but Pierman was mature enough to recognize that it was also silly. That McQueen, a guy who was supposed to be smart, would try a taunt like that was reassuring.

"I don't know, Nate," Pierman said. "Is it true that football players always have shit for brains?"

They rolled across the greasy floor in a tangle of flailing limbs, throwing punches that didn't land. Then Pierman felt himself lifted to his feet by an arm twisted behind his back, and McQueen jammed him against the wall.

"Maybe you didn't mean that," McQueen said into Pierman's ear.

Pierman heard feet scuffling across the floor as the pain lifted him to his toes. Gathered in a semicircle at the shower room, the other boys watched and shushed each other so that the coaches would not hear.

"What, about you being stupid? Fuck you," Pierman said. And fuck them, he thought.

McQueen pushed Pierman's hand higher up his spine.

"Take it back, faggot."

Pierman tried kicking back through McQueen's legs but slipped. McQueen deftly nailed him back up on the wall and raised the hand another fraction.

"I said take it back."

Pierman tried again. He swung his free arm wildly, first at McQueen's groin and then his face. McQueen pulled it down and leaned heavily against him.

"This turning you on, queer boy."

The repugnance of the suggestion made Pierman rear back. He tried twisting down and away, but McQueen was too quick and too strong. The first tissue tore. Plink. Pierman moaned.

"Maybe that'll do," McQueen said. "First you take it back and then you beg me to stop."

"Fuck you," Pierman whispered, and McQueen raised his arm higher. Plink.

Pierman swallowed back the nausea. He fixed his eyes on Calkins, who stood at the back of the semi-circle, but Calkins would not look back.

"Hey McQueen," Pierman whispered. He felt McQueen's weight shift as he leaned in closer. "From what I'm feeling, I don't think I'm the one with the hard-on here."

"I said say it," McQueen shouted and banged Pierman's head against the wall. "Say it." Plink. Plink. "Say it. Say it."

Pierman's cheek dragged the cool tile wall as his legs buckled. The gray tiles unraveled in rainbows before his eyes. "Say it." Raspy and hoarse, it came to Pierman from a long way off.

It seemed strange that McQueen would suddenly pat him on the butt and let go. When his ashen hand, numb and useless, hit the floor beside him, Pierman realized the pat had been it falling and ricocheting off his backside like a stone off a cliff. When he raised his face from the floor, McQueen was dancing and howling in the air above him like a crazed marionette. Behind him, fully dressed and soaked to the skin, Calkins held McQueen around the throat and through the legs by his balls.

"What the hell?" The cross-country coach and the football coach pushed through the scattering crowd.

"You hurt?" Pierman flinched when the cross-country coach propped him against the wall. "What happened?"

"Accident. Slipped." Pierman would not look at the coach.

"What was Calkins doing in here?"

"Friend. Came to help."

"Look at me. You expect me to believe that?"

Pierman held the coach's stare. "Yeah."

Calkins and McQueen stood outside the shower, listening and looking everywhere but at their coach, a little brick of a man.

"What'd you do?" he growled at McQueen.

"Nothing."

"Joe, what happened?"

Calkins looked to Pierman. Just perceptibly, Pierman moved his head to the side.

"He fell, coach." Calkins shrugged. "That's all."

The football coach jabbed a finger at Calkins. "Don't you fucking shrug at me. What were you doing to McQueen?"

"Just horsing around."

The coach moved to within inches of Calkins's face. "Going into showers with your clothes on is stupid. You stupid, Calkins?"

"No, sir."

"Is he stupid, McQueen?"

McQueen hesitated, looking at Pierman with a puzzled expression. "No."

The cross-country coach put Pierman's good arm around his neck and hoisted him gently.

"Will you tell me, Allen?"

"No."

The football coach prowled the room, bellowing, calling his players "jerkoffs," "demonstrators," "fucking hippies." He'd investigate and he'd find out, and goddamn it, he would suspend. He would, by God, not have goddamned dissension. The cross-country coach, still dragging Pierman, stepped him in front of him.

"Forget it, Terry. We'll never find out anything. I'm taking him to the doctor."

Terry. That was the guy's name. Not a very manly for a football coach, Pierman thought at the time. Terry—his eyes bulging, his face red, the veins on his thick neck close to bursting—looked like he wanted to hit someone. Pierman was pretty sure it was him.

⌒

"Did I thank you for that?" Pierman asked Calkins as he eased the patrol car to the curb behind the Courthouse.

"So you do remember."

Pierman shrugged. "We got along all right after that."

They were never going to be friends, but Pierman and McQueen were civil to each other in a curious way. Their first meeting after the episode occurred in a crowded study hall. With plenty of people around to hear him, McQueen reminded Pierman that he'd called McQueen a son of a bitch, said he didn't like people talking about his mother, and asked Pierman if he took it back. Pierman, who had earned a measure of respect for his stoicism under pain and the persistent questioning of school officials, said he did not. "I didn't think so," McQueen said, and shook his head as though any other answer would have been a disappointment.

A couple of days later they happened to meet in a school parking lot. No one else was around, and Pierman froze, but McQueen just nodded and went on his way.

The pattern repeated itself from then on. If someone was around, McQueen would ask Pierman if he took it back, and Pierman would say no. There were no more threats, but no apologies either. Pierman didn't know what to make it, but much of the world's ways were strange to him that year, and once McQueen graduated, he no longer had a reason to think about it. Climbing out of the patrol car, he supposed that the episode contributed to McQueen's behavior toward him, even if it offered no real explanation for it.

"I don't have anything against Nate," he said, leaning back into the open door of the patrol car.

Calkins shrugged. "I wonder if you ought to."

Carter maintained his private practice at the top of treacherously steep and dark stairs in rooms behind two of the tall windows above a store on the square. When Pierman and his father filled it, the prosecutor's job was not full time. As Carter's son had observed, there was not that much crime in Holoce County, and the county commissioners were not inclined to pay for a full-time prosecutor even if there had been. The probate, real estate, and personal-injury cases rarely conflicted with his criminal work and they made him good money, but he was the first to tell you he didn't care for them much.

It is a myth—a tale we tell ourselves to explain and assure—that we did not lock our doors then. We did, at least when we were to be away from home for a long while and certainly the offices. At that time, privacy far outweighed fear as the concern, but surely that is no lesser reason to throw the bolt. It is understandable then that Pierman was not a little surprised and more than a little annoyed when he reached the landing outside the door to his father's private office and found it unlocked.

In his consternation, Pierman failed to see the woman sitting in the chair behind the door. Without saying anything, she watched him as he placed his hand on the light switch and look up puzzled at the lights, which had been left on. She saw him peer and then turn his ear first toward the door to the rather cluttered office behind the reception area, then toward a room adjacent to the office and reception area that appeared to be both library and conference room. She remained silent as he scowled at the empty secretarial desk in the reception area and then examined and knocked aside with a disdainful forefinger each envelope in the mail stacked on the desk. Her concentration and the directness of her gaze makes it safe to say that she held silence not because she was shy or meek.

As Pierman started toward the cluttered office, she rose and said, "Could you see me now?"

A slight flinch, as though he had a catch in his neck, was the only sign that Pierman was startled. "That depends," he said, turning. "I don't recall any appointments."

"I don't have one."

"You are?"

She had dark brown hair that fell beyond her shoulders and settled in glossy folds around an oval face like a cowl. Married women of his acquaintance, particularly those with children, tended to cut their hair. Glancing at her left hand and finding no ring, Pierman decided she was probably single. The face itself was not as beautiful as the hair suggested, but her eyes, which were the same color as her hair, were level and direct. They held the observer's away from the rest of her features long enough to make them unimportant. She was familiar to him.

"You are Miss Grable," Pierman said, answering his own question.

"Kay. Yes." She stopped and considered. "You were in the house. You saw pictures."

She was inquisitive and intelligent, too, Pierman decided. He introduced himself formally and expressed his condolences.

"If it's about your brother, you should talk to the sheriff," he said.

"It is, but not that. My father sent me."

She waited, suggesting she would prefer a more private setting. Pierman motioned her toward the office. She wore a blue blouse and black slacks. As he followed her, admiring her figure, it occurred to Pierman that seeing an attractive woman alone in his office was something out of Raymond Chandler. More realistically, he knew it was likely to cause talk. He pushed the notion aside quickly, dismissing it as another sign that he had been in town long enough. But he was not alone in his thought.

"Your secretary said I should come back later," Kay Grable said. "She said she had to go to lunch and she couldn't wait any longer. I don't think she liked us meeting unchaperoned."

With her back to him, Pierman could not tell if she was joking. "She tends to be protective," he said.

When he died, Carter left open casebooks, documents, and brown expandable files on nearly every surface but the seat of his own, high-backed, stuffed chair and the client chair on the other side of his formidable, mahogany desk. Pierman had not gotten far enough into his father's cases to make much of a dent in the clutter. Pierman waved her toward the client's chair, but she stood for a moment looking around.

"I'm not sure whom she wanted to protect," she said, sitting finally and looking up at him wryly. "I got the impression it wasn't you."

"Edith was my father's secretary," Pierman said. "When I was little, she'd give me gumdrops if I said please. There came a time when I would not."

She nodded slightly and smiled. She said, "Edith also seems to think there'll come a time soon when you'll close this office and she'll be out of a job." Any traces of amusement and approval were gone.

"If she told you that much, you must've been here for some time," Pierman said. "I'm sorry you had to wait."

Pierman drew a yellow pad out of a drawer and took his seat. When he looked up, she was considering him again, sizing him up.

"Are you?"

"Am I what? Closing the office? Why would that concern you?"

"My father wants you to handle the legal work on Randy's death. He wasn't very old so he didn't have much in the way of property. But he had no will and Dad seems to think that will complicate matters."

Pierman put his pen down. "Surely, your family already has an attorney. It wasn't my father. Despite this mess, I've been through his records."

"Dad says he wants you." She shrugged.

"Why?"

"He didn't say. I suspect gratitude. For being kind yesterday. If there's something else, he didn't say and I didn't ask. He just insisted on you."

The mere fact that she would mention the possibility of something else made Pierman wonder. Was the old man using his son's death to somehow influence Pierman on the vandalized library? Grable had not seemed like the type to be cynical or devious. Or was there something about his son the old man was trying to keep quiet by drawing Pierman into a confidential attorney-client relationship? Kay held her purse firmly on her knee, but not so tightly that she looked nervous. McQueen was right; he was a suspicious bastard.

"Why send you?" he said. "Why not come himself?"

"He didn't want to run into people. All the sympathy, the questions. And it wouldn't look right. So soon after my brother's death." For once, she avoided his eyes. "Maybe planning takes his mind off it. Or maybe he just wants to get everything out of the way as quickly as he can."

The critics have said that the whole mess could have been avoided if Pierman had listened more closely that day. That is the purest speculation, of course. They forget he was witnessing the same impulse—the obsessive fits of cleaning, sorting, and giving away—in his mother after his father died.

He said, "But you don't really care for it much. Or for being the messenger."

Her tone told him how she felt was none of his concern, and as for her role, the logic was simple. "I don't live here anymore. People aren't as likely to recognize me." She pursed her lips. "It's one of the few times he's liked that situation."

"I see."

"I doubt it."

The high-backed chair listed to the left, sprung in the direction Carter leaned when he talked on the phone. It squeaked when

Pierman swung to the right and arose. He went to the tall window overlooking the square and looked down.

"I expect I understand more than you think." Perched on the sill, he explained the death of his father and his intention to leave. "The fact that I don't want any more work is one, purely selfish, reason for not taking your brother's estate."

"And the others?"

"Conflict of interest primarily. I can't, as prosecutor, mix the civil and criminal sides of your brother's death. Whether I like it or not, I'm involved in the investigation."

She wrinkled her brow. "Will you leave before that's over?"

He had no answer for that. "Pick whatever reason you want to give your father," he said.

"I can live with either one," she said, revealing again the look of amused approval. "But I think I'll stick to conflict of interest. Dad'll understand that one."

She rose and extended her hand.

As Pierman took it, he remembered what his job was.

"No one from the sheriff's office has spoken with you?

"No."

"State police?"

"No."

As a litigator, he had learned long ago that sometimes it's a matter of how you phrase the question. If he had asked her if she knew who killed her brother, the answer would have been same but quicker. Instead, he asked, "Do you know why someone would want to kill your brother?"

It made her hesitate, the deliberation glazing her expression.

"No," she said emphatically and withdrew her hand.

"Why do you have to think about it?"

"It is an important question," she said returning his gaze now without effort.

"Will you think some more about it and let me know?"

"Of course," she said and turned to go.

"I'm sorry about your brother," Pierman said.

Her shoulders sagged slightly. She was unused to hearing it yet.

"Yes," she said. "Of course."

At that point in time, Pierman, I'm sure, was not nearly as sorry about the death of your uncle as he was to see your mother go.

7

On the third day, we bury our dead, and Randy Grable was no different. His funeral was scheduled at eleven that morning, but over breakfast, Elizabeth announced that Pierman would have to go. She did not know the Grables well, hardly at all, she said. Still, it was a loss, tragic. Someone from the family should go, she said. To pay respect, she said. It was only decent. She, though, had had her fill of funerals lately.

The prospect hardly appealed to her son either; his own memories were as fresh and raw as hers. He had the impression that this sudden call to duty was at least partially the price she demanded for his intractable response to her depression the other night. Still, her attitude was encouraging; there was a touch of the old, suppressed haughtiness he hadn't seen since he returned home. The family banner would be his to bear this time, he decided.

Pierman did not stumble under the weight of it until he climbed the steps to the Cross Mortuary. Edith could not or would not trouble herself to learn the idiosyncrasies of his handwriting and had spent most of the morning asking him how he wanted documents typed. Coping with the whole infuriating process had caused him to lose track of time. He resisted the urge to sprint the four blocks to the funeral home by telling himself he was already late and five minutes either way would not make any difference, but he walked fast nonetheless and the sun was high and hot. He arrived damp and rumpled.

The parking lot was full. The hearse, the same one that had hauled the body out of a burned-over wheat field, stood waiting alongside a large Victorian building that had once been one of the town's more stately mansions. Everyone was inside, of course. Pierman knew the preacher would register his appearance with a glance or some other nearly imperceptible gesture that would still be enough in those tense, suspenseful quarters to make several heads turn and look. He doubted there would be reproach in their stares; more likely, he would be a welcome distraction. The sermon about the hope that salves the loss had been delivered too often in too many dreary and unbelievable ways to offer much relief from the powdery face before them. Those who would turn yearned, with an eagerness they would never be so shameless to admit, for any reason to look away.

Decked out in his best black suit and a deep blue silk tie, Cross nonetheless stood like repentant Adam, hands folded across his crotch, in the hallway just outside the room. He smiled a tight-lipped welcome and beckoned Pierman with one upturned hand toward the door. For the moment, though, Pierman was arrested by the scent of flowers. It cloyed at him again, as it had during the two exhausting days he had been required to hover beside his father's body in the same room. By the time he had learned to ignore it, it wasn't necessary. The brilliant, symmetrical arrangements had been heaped on a long, low mound, and were soon carried off by the breeze, the scent first, then, singly and in clouds, the blossoms' petals.

Pierman chose to stand with Cross just outside looking in at the room. It was full to the point that people stood at the back and along the sides. From his position, Pierman was hidden from the preacher and his glances, but he could still see the casket. He had been stupid to expect a gray face. How could he have forgotten? The casket was closed, of course, and Pierman shuddered remembering, too well now, the black knob thrust up like a sentinel's command from the wreckage. He tried not to think what Cross must have done to close the lid. He wondered instead how many of his other perceptions about the day would be distorted by his feelings about his father's funeral.

"He that believeth in Me shall not die," the preacher was saying in his earnest singsong, "but shall have everlasting life."

Should be playing to a hostile crowd with that line, Pierman thought. This one was too final; the sealed casket left no doubt of that. One could not fix on a face to envision the possibility of resurrection, only on oneself and each other. At times like this, were either ever enough?

But Pierman was wrong again. Those gathered hung on each word. There were no coughs, no sniffles, no squeaks from shifting chairs, no remembrances murmured with tight smiles, as there had been at the old man's funeral. There was no sound at all but the low, urgent voice of the preacher. All heads were upright and turned to receive his words.

Except one. A sandy-haired man in a lime suit still looked to see who had admitted bird song and traffic noise into the proceedings. He sat alone in the back row, and in spite of his severe expression, he nodded. Pierman scanned the crowd, trying to connect him. A group of young men, also in light-colored suits, sat in a row near the front. Young Grable's friends from college, Pierman guessed. The man could've been one of them, a little older maybe—perhaps he got lost and arrived late, too—but Pierman decided he was too aloof. He had tipped back the wooden folding chair he sat in, and he crossed his legs wide, while the boys at near the front were hunched, shoulder pressed against shoulder without shame. The man's eyes had followed Pierman's into the crowd, but when they met again, he discreetly pulled back his coattail. On his belt, pulled around to one side was the silver badge of the state police. Christ, even here, Pierman thought, and glared at Cross, who shrugged. In neither of his roles was it his place to deny people admittance to these functions.

Pierman scanned the mourners again with a new awareness. He spotted Darrell, Calkins' deputy, standing to one side, looking down at his hands, his eyebrows raised, his whole attention fixed on running a blade of his pocket knife under his fingernails. Calkins sat in a middle row, at one end so that he could slip out easily. Both wore plain clothes, which made Pierman wonder if they were traveling on business or pleasure. Well, not pleasure, of course.

Kay Grable sat in the front row. He saw her when the preacher called for prayer and all heads dipped but hers. She wore a black, sleeveless dress. She sat perfectly still, one bare arm enclosing the shoulders of her father. Pierman, too, knew that position; he had welcomed the needles that ran across his arm as his mother quivered and bit her lips. The sensation had kept him from his own thinking and biting. We do not wail.

When the prayer ended, people filed out as quickly as propriety would allow, their faces set. Few looked at each other or Pierman, who remained near the door as they passed by. Only Dr. Fulton started to open his mouth to say something, but Pierman emphatically shook his head. He would not do business now.

Cross left to guide the college boys, who shuffled in a restless pack at the front of the room between coffin and family. There had been none of that awkwardness for Carter. Two rows of men strode forward to flank the casket then. The inner row of younger friends did the work for the outer row of the old man's contemporaries, who were no longer in any shape to grapple a maple casket. We, the men in each row, were separated by age and infirmity, and if none understood the answer suspended between us, at least all were familiar with the question.

The boys at Randy Grable's funeral were not, and it showed in their dismay. Cross finally whispered a few, gentle words to the calmest of them, and he, in turn, spoke to the rest. Amid stolen glances, they moved forward. Each extended his hand and mumbled something to the family before assuming his station at the box. Only one, a slight boy with outrageously bleached, yellow-blond hair and a jeweled stud in one ear, hung back, holding his position off to one side. He gazed at the casket. He started to step forward, thought better of it, and left. Paul Grable, Pierman noted, watched the boy's every move.

Pierman decided he had carried the family banner about as far as he cared to go; he did not think it necessary to haul it to the cemetery. He expected Cross to usher the family out at that point and told himself that now would be a good time to express his sympathy privately and leave. But when he at last entered the room, Cross was gone. Instead, from a corner on the side of the room Pierman could not see, Nate McQueen stepped over to the family. He moved with assurance and dignity. He gently touched Kay's arm. She whispered something to her father, but he curtly shook his head and she went alone to kneel before the casket. When she returned, McQueen placed himself slightly behind and between Kay and her father and escorted them up through the empty folding chairs. Kay caught Pierman's astonished, furious stare, but he was quick to drop it and leave.

"Need a ride?"

Calkins stood with one foot in the door of the unmarked car, just as he had behind the Courthouse on the day of the murder. The car was parked at the head of the procession, the only one without a small, purple flag fluttering on the fender.

Pierman looked around, his hands on his hips, thinking. "Apparently," he said.

Under Cross's watchful eye, the boys loaded the casket into the rear of the hearse. As he dispatched the boys to their own cars, Cross looked to the driver of a big Chrysler that was parked behind the hearse with its engine running. Following Cross's expression,

Pierman could see McQueen at the wheel. Paul Grable sat beside him, and Kay was in the back. McQueen gave Cross an index-finger salute. Cross nodded to Calkins, and both men swung in behind the wheels of their vehicles.

"So," Calkins said as he slowly pulled away, "see anything out of the ordinary in there?"

"Other than the abnormally high ratio of cops to citizenry? No. Not a thing."

Calkins looked at Pierman.

"Is that a shot?"

"Was it necessary to stake out that young man's funeral? Did the family really need that?"

"Yeah. Yeah, maybe they did if they want the guy caught who did it? Or maybe they need a little protection if, as you pointed out the other day, somebody's stalking old Grable about those goddamn books."

Calkins rolled his head and checked his rearview mirror.

"You telling me cops in Chicago don't do that? Don't go to the victim's funeral to see who turns up?"

"Yes," Pierman said. "Yes, I'm sure they do, but probably too damned often for all the good it does."

"Spoken like the damned defense lawyer you are," Calkins said.

They stared at each other. Calkins broke it first to look back at the road, but Pierman knew cops. Calkins had withdrawn a measure of the trust Pierman had earned.

Pierman looked out the side window. The procession was passing through downtown. An old man walking a spiky-haired dog mongrel removed his billed cap and cranked himself upright. A woman in running shorts and curlers stopped and turned off her lawn mower to peer into the car behind the hearse. A child craned his head and pointed until his mother slapped down his hand.

"You've got someone guarding them at the farm," Pierman said.

Calkins looked back at him with narrowed eyes. "I didn't hear a question mark at the end of that sentence."

"Well?"

"No. I offered. They—Paul, the daughter—felt otherwise. Paul said no."

At an intersection, a shiny car with oversized chrome rims sat at a stop sign perpendicular to the procession. Its mufflers grumbled and popped and its rear end humped as the driver gunned the engine. Calkins removed his sun glasses so that the driver could have the full benefit of his glare. He aimed thumb and forefinger out the window. When Calkins' thumb fell, the rear end of the car dropped like a rock and the procession passed in silence.

"We don't seem to be getting anywhere," Calkins said without prompting. "It's been three days. We know the boy was shot and that he died as a result of those shots. We're pretty sure the shooting was deliberate. But we don't know why."

"Background?" Pierman asked.

"Next to nothing. So-so student in high school. Didn't do sports, which disappointed his dad. Liked band. Went to college, studied ag. That made the old man happy. He didn't have a steady girl. In fact, he didn't date much in high school or after. He drank now and then, but no drugs and he didn't get into trouble. Nice kid, although he kind of kept to himself and not a lot of people seemed to have hung out with him."

"Isn't that what they always say about people accused of murder?"

"What?"

"'He was a loner, but a really nice guy. I can't believe he did it.'"

"We're talking the victim here, not the shooter."

"Maybe it's the opposite side of the same coin," Pierman said. "When it's deliberate, somebody shoots and somebody gets shot for the same reason."

Calkins studied Pierman. "I reckon that's why I brought you to the party, to keep my thinking straight. If there's a reason, I'm goddamned if I know what it is."

A gimpy, bowlegged, old man in muddy, green work clothes pushed open the iron gates to the cemetery and pivoted around out of the way on one arthritic leg like a door on a hinge. He removed his engineer's cap and waved them through. The cap snapped in his hand with each sweep, the only sign he respected anything but soil, grass and trees. Pierman would not let go.

"Randy Grable gay?"

"Gay," Calkins repeated as though he did not know the word.

"Homosexual."

"Queer?"

"Be as derogatory as you like, you know what I mean."

Calkins' reluctance to address the question did not surprise Pierman. It was something they had joked and teased each other about as boys, but neither he or Calkins would have been able to remember anyone in Lindley who lived openly as gay when they were growing up, and he doubted that anything had changed since then.

"So," Calkins said, "I tell you the guy liked band, didn't date much, you decide he's gay, and you think I'm a bigot?"

"No. I was wondering what Randy was to that shaken kid with the bleached hair back at Cross's place. And I was always pretty sure you were a bigot."

Calkins started to scowl, then realized Pierman was putting him on. He pursed his lips and shrugged. He maneuvered the big car down a narrow gravel lane at a creep.

"And what's Nate McQueen to Kay Grable?" Pierman asked.

"You noticed that, too. He works for Cross. Part-time, side job. But they used to date."

"They don't now?"

"Don't know. Did in high school. He went to Viet Nam. She dumped him."

"You make it sound like a crime," Pierman said. "They would've been teenagers."

Calkins looked at Pierman to see if he was kidding him again. When he saw the intently curious expression on Pierman's face, he realized he might have exposed a part of himself he had not intended to. "Dumping him while he was there, " Calkins said, shrugging again. "Shitty thing to do."

They had too little and too much in common right then. They took the last hundred yards in silence, hearing only the murmuring within.

⚘

As the topic for their last, great argument, Elizabeth and Carter chose trees and the logistics of death. Only in the practical sense was the dispute resolved and then only partially. The intense, individual feelings, the stew that makes family fights crucial and petty in equal parts, still swirled, and time had served only to magnify the former for the combatants and the latter for the observer.

"I want you in on this," Carter said to his son one evening when Pierman was home. His trips home were few enough, the old man grumbled; they would have to take care of it now, while they could, even though everything hadn't been worked out yet.

"You'll need to know these things someday," Elizabeth said to her son as the three of them arranged themselves in the living room.

They had been discussing final arrangements. They did not want to leave them to a time when a grieving survivor would have to make hard decisions. "Mostly, it's her," Carter said. "She figures I'll go before she does. She's probably right." He spoke indifferently, as though he was not interested in making such decisions, just in making sure his son was informed of them, but Pierman saw him check Elizabeth's reaction as he said it. She winced, and a flicker of a smile crossed the old man's lips.

They'd settled the wills and the funerals, right down to music and pallbearers. It was on the issue of cemeteries that they disagreed. Lindley had two. One sat on a knoll out of the way on the edge of town. It was old, established long before the town incorporated. Lindley had grown away from it and had been so busy doing so that nobody had bothered to name it. The other cemetery was newer. It sat along a main road into town; you couldn't miss it. It was called Maple Lawn.

"And that is the problem, Allen," Elizabeth said. "The trees."

Despite its name, Maple Lawn had only a few spindly saplings—mostly oaks at that—planted well away from the graves. The lawn was thick and green, broken by straight rows of low, rectangular stones, the style and size of which were specified and limited by the deeds. The old graveyard—nobody called it anything but that—was filled with trees, old ones, thick, knobby and loaded with leaves. It was cool there year-round. Sunshine had to fight its way in, Carter joked, and then it needed the wind to move the branches to get the job done.

Elizabeth did not care to be buried there. The plots were small and roots continually upended the stones. "Just think," she said and shuddered. "What must they doing to the caskets?" And the caretakers did not like the place, or so she had been informed by a bridge partner whose husband had been buried there. The stones were packed in and set every which way. They had to hand rake the place in the fall. And they never really saw much need to mow, what with the stones and the shade. Only moss grew in the shadows and that—she, too, had been willing to joke at first—that never got very high.

The worms'd get you sooner or later, Carter replied. He had his practical country boy persona turned up high now that things were getting serious. So what if the roots forged the way? He like the way the place looked: well used, maybe, but kind of peaceful and content. A lot of his friends were buried there, family, too, for that matter. And what would he care how the placed looked like after he was gone?

And what about her? Elizabeth demanded. What of her if he passed first? She would have to see to its—that night she could not say *die*, she could not say *grave*—its care, its appearance. And were his friends paupers? There where the county buried them, or didn't he know that?

It was just like him to be thinking only of himself, she said. And it was just like her, the old man said, to be thinking of appearances, to be carrying her airs right to the damned grave.

To Pierman, red-faced and exasperated in the cross-fire, it was just like both of them. In the long run, a generation or two at the most, who would care who went where or what it looked like.

They argued it twice more before he left. Pierman was excused from these sessions, but it was not as though he was left out. Their voices carried to any room he chose as sanctuary. Neither could find any new reasons to persuade the other.

In the end, it remained just like both of them. Elizabeth let Carter buy two plots in the old graveyard and they buried him there. A few days later, when his son opened his will, he found a deed for one plot in Maple Lawn and an eight-month-old codicil leaving the plot to Elizabeth. Hers, if she wanted it, the old man said in a note addressed to him, but he hadn't bothered to tell her about it. So much for keeping his son informed. Pierman could not decide whether the bequest was a posthumous jab, one that he would be forced to deliver or, as the note suggested, merely the old man's idea of letting his wife have her way if she wanted to take it. In the end, he decided that it was a little of both and that his father probably was no more capable of sorting out his motives than his son was. He had not yet figured out how to tell his mother.

And perhaps his mother had a point, Pierman thought as he and Calkins climbed out of the car. Let it, and the old cemetery could be morose. In summer, under the trees, it was clammy and dark. In the winter, slate sky congealed into gray, cold knobs of gravestones in snow. Naked trees, by then withered talons, were merely the sieve. It might look inviting in the fall when the leaves flamed and the air was rough enough to abrade your face, but that, too, was dying. Call it nature's eulogy, if you wish, a mask for the incredible.

All in all, though, it still seemed right to bury the old man here. The darker side of people always held his attention, and he had accumulated his allotment of history. But not Randy Grable. Someone so young should be buried in Maple Lawn, a new, sleek place, Pierman thought, but that was before he looked under the green-and-white, striped tent that would define the truly bereaved.

The tent floated above a hole in the last open corner of a rectangle bordered by a low cement wall. In the middle of the rectangle, a red marble obelisk bearing the name "Grable" arose. Around that were a dozen, stubby stones of similar color, specific names and dates chiseled in each. The father would follow the son from now on. Pierman doubted they had ever argued about where they would stop.

The crowd stood along the cars, whispering and straightening their clothes. At least three dozen cars and pickup trucks snaked along the gravel road back toward the entrance. The coffee shop crowd, the loafers who gathered each morning to assess the world, would appreciate the number, good-sized for one so young.

The college boys slid the coffin from the rear of the ambulance, paused to adjust the weight among them, and tacked toward the tent. The weight was probably more than they expected, and they were not practiced in the slow, rolling gait that would keep them on a straight course. One tripped on the low fence. The crowd sucked away the cool air. When he recovered, they sighed it back, hot and relieved, and began to move forward. The loafers, Pierman knew, would appreciate that, too.

McQueen had left the wheel of the limo to lead the Grables forward. He ushered them to their chairs before the casket and melted back into the crowd, as did Pierman when he saw it. The father turned and motioned with his head for the pallbearers to join them under the tent. Pierman noted that blond kid was nowhere to be seen. With some chagrin, he noted, too, that his surveillance was exactly what he had criticized Calkins for earlier.

The father sat erect now, staring ahead if not seeing. Kay gazed at the ground. She had worn down finally, Pierman thought. She had wept in the limo.

The final words were brief. Dust to dust, ashes to ashes, the real point of it all. But Pierman did not take that too literally either. He had seen the vault wagon parked off to the side with the thick concrete box swaying slightly on a chain. They'd all be long gone before nature worked her way through that.

People shyly approached the family with a few last words of their own when it was over. Pierman knew he should get on with his duty, but he could not. He wanted to blame it on McQueen, who stood by protectively inspecting each person who approached, but that really was not the reason. The truth was he had no more comfort to offer than he had had before in Paul Grable's living room.

Pierman, frankly, thought too much about death for someone his age. I suppose I was at least partially at fault for it, but it stunts buds and withers blooms, and maybe that is one good reason why I've waited this long to tell you the tale.

℞

Calkins waited at the car.

"You go on," Pierman said. "I'll walk."

"It's a hike."

"I need the exercise."

Pierman wandered over to his father's grave. He had not been back since the funeral, but his mother apparently had. A pot of geraniums was centered on the green rectangle of fresh sod. He wondered how she felt knowing that a month or two of shade, leaves, and tree sap would mottle the grave gray and brown like its neighbors. He knew she would not care for the bird droppings that splattered across the new lettering on the stone. He squatted beside the stone, looking for a twig.

"Thank you for coming," Kay Grable said.

She had done it to him again, sought him out when he least expected it and found him rooting.

"My father says to tell you there're no hard feelings," she said. "About your not taking our case." Her voice was high, not quite angry but sharp. "He thought maybe that's why you didn't say anything back there."

Pierman looked back toward the Grable grave. Her father was out of sight, probably in the limo. McQueen leaned against it, watching Kay and him. He gave Pierman one of his mocking salutes.

Her father might be generous in reasoning out Pierman's behavior, but she was not. She stood over him with her arms crossed and her eyes glistening behind a black veil. Outside of movies, Pierman had never seen a woman wear a veil to a funeral. Then he thought she was the only person he had not weaseled in some way since his return.

"Your friend there," Pierman said. "I don't care for him much."

"Nate? He's not . . ." She caught the tumbling words. "I don't think you could call him. . . . He's an old boyfriend."

She looked for understanding in Pierman's face, but he was impassive. "What's he now?" Pierman said, turning back to work on the stone.

She sighed. "I don't know. He was nice to me once. He's being nice now." She stopped to consider again. "My father and I aren't in any shape be choosy." Her voice rose. "And what business is it of yours anyway?"

"It's not," Pierman admitted meekly.

"You missed a spot."

He had enough things to think about now, and she was tied to the most difficult of them. And how would it look? Her brother in the grave, and his father not far beyond. "I hear you've found something to distract you from the burdens of your office," he could hear me say as a dryly, amused prelude to another lecture on the manner by which he should conduct himself.

"I'm sorry," Pierman said, rising and brushing the knee of his trousers to avoid her eye. "And I'm sorry about your brother."

"Thank you."

Her tone remained brittle, perfectly tuned for ending the en-counter and huffing off. Instead, she suddenly reached behind her head and removed the pin that held the veil.

"I hate this goddamned thing," she said. Her purse swung wildly as she tried to jam the wad into it. "Dad said it's what women wear. I wouldn't win for arguing."

Pierman steadied the bag for her. Five minutes they'd stood over his father's grave, and she had not mentioned it. And now this. She apparently thought better of it.

"Now, I'm sorry," she said. "That didn't sound right, did it." She shrugged. "Life goes on. That's all."

Life goes on. When everyone else had left the graveyard, even his mother, Pierman stood alone before his father's casket, just as he had for two days, bug-eyed and salty, waiting. The scent of flow-ers irked him. Behind him, he could hear the bow-legged old man and his assistant clanging their shovels in their impatience to put the tarp-covered mound behind the coffin back in the ground. And in a few moments, it came. He cried, with four, maybe five sudden, shud-dering sobs. And just as quickly, he stopped. He stood for another moment, quivering as though the torrent still washed in him. Then, he stilled. He wiped his nose and left, asking his father's forgiveness. It had been the best he could do.

"What," he said to Kay Grable, hoarse and still a little dazed, "What are your plans?"

"I'm staying." She sighed. "Here. For the summer. It's one of the advantages of teaching. Free summers." She brushed the long, loose hair from her face. "I was going to finish my master's, but that's out now. Dad's taking this worse than he lets on." She dropped her eyes. "Any hints? On survival?" She lifted her eyes and smiled wanly. "As one prodigal to another."

It was what he had sought and feared. For two months, Pierman had taken pride in his stamina and resolution. At the office, at home, the only thing on his mind had been to get the job done and get out.

There was no place to go and no one to go with, he had told himself, so he may as well get on with it. And the somberness and melancholy had been useful, like drugs that took his mind off a hunger even though he knew they did nothing to relieve it.

And did she know some better way? Really? Or was she looking for something else? A direct line to her brother's case, perhaps, although he couldn't imagine why. A way to get away from McQueen, who sauntered toward them now. Pierman couldn't say, but then this was Lindley, whose poverty of resources often forced one means to serve many ends.

"Maybe dinner sometime?" he said. "I advise better over food."

It grated, a singles bar line in a cemetery. He would've laughed but for her directness.

"Yes. When?" she said, then reconsidered. "We probably should wait a week or so. For propriety's sake."

"Kay," McQueen said, touching her elbow and giving Pierman his hard, cockeyed grin. "Your dad's waiting."

Pierman did not know what came over him. "I'll see you in week or so," he called after them. It echoed in the trees and wiped the grin from McQueen' face. He stared, first back at Pierman then at Kay. Pierman did not know whether that or the knowing half-smile Kay returned him over her shoulder gave him the greater, inexcusable pleasure.

8

In summer, people here talk with an eye on the sky. Their gaze flits constantly from your face up and back, for those who plant wait, for either sun or rain. Even the shopkeepers and businessmen, who plant only gardens in a corner of their yards but depend on the farmers for daily bread, join the chorus of silent, persistent appeals that rise and weave like swallows from March through November. At any given time, they'll agree it's too wet or too dry to plow, plant, hoe, bale, combine, pick, or plow again. Only at the end, when everything is in, does it seem both, regardless of how much, were enough.

The Halsey Highway is not really a highway. Certainly, it is paved and flat, but it is really no more than a narrow, country road that runs among the farms between Lindley and Astor. Calkins drove the Halsey at high speed on a sunny day one week after Randy Grable's death. It had been an age since Pierman had been on it.

"Kids still hide their booze in the culverts along this stretch?" he asked.

"More likely grass, pills, and angel dust now." Calkins said glumly. "Technique's the same."

Pierman remembered lifting a bottle of vodka from the old man's stock on a Saturday night, heading for the Halsey with a girl whose name he could not recall, and putting away half of it. After he took her home, he went back, tied a string around the bottle and secured it to a branch in the third pipe past the stop sign. In the moonlight, the frayed ends of other cords skittered like water bugs on the surface of the stream. The old man asked him the next morning how he got mud on his shoes.

"How they keep the stuff dry?" Pierman wondered aloud.

"Baggies, cans, shorter strings," Calkins said. "If they bother at all."

They stopped at a woods. As they got out, Calkins said, "Know where we are?"

Pierman stood by the car listening to the deep-throated cacophony booming through the woods. "I'm guessing the back side of Grable's place. From the tractors."

"No fooling you, is there."

"We starting over?"

Calkins skipped over the shallow ditch that ran between the fence row and the edge of the road and began walking, his eyes sweeping the ground.

"Looking," he said, "just looking."

"It's been a week. It's rained."

"You never know. We got nothing else."

Standing on the side of the road, like a figure on a Bavarian clock, Pierman rotated 180 degrees. He could almost take in the entire section, and it made him think of Mrs. Lacey, sixth grade history, and the Northwest Ordinance. The ordinance decreed that roads should be laid out in square miles to impose order on the restlessness of a young people. Holoce County had complied. Now, two or three homesteads stood on either side of the road in each mile, blocks on a parquet floor of green, brown, and gold.

"How could anyone park along here and not be seen?" Pierman asked when he had silently run out the string of his own improbable answers.

"We've been here fifteen minutes," Calkins called back from down the road. "You seen anybody?"

Pierman hurried along the road to catch up. "There're houses along here. People live along this road. They didn't see anything?"

Calkins kept his eyes on the ground, his hands in his pockets, bending away weeds with his foot in an arcing stride that made him look like a tap dancer in slow motion.

"Purcell and his people say not," Calkins said. "People work in town. People work in the fields. They don't work on the roads."

"It was around noon," Pierman said. "Farmers eat. That--"

"That what?" Calkins flared.

"Joe, you're the one keeps dragging me out here. Okay. Forget it."

Pierman clumsily stepped across the ditch, trying to avoid snagging his trouser cuff on the weeds. He began sweeping the weeds with his feet like Calkins, but he moved in the opposite direction.

Calkins stopped and turned. "You were going to say?"

"I was wondering about the guy who called in the fire. Didn't he live along here somewhere? Didn't he see anything?"

"No," Calkins said. Pierman decided not to ask whether he or Purcell had actually asked the question.

At late morning, the sun was high, simmering out the humidity left in the land from the previous week's rain. When Pierman got past the edge of the woods, he loosened his collar and wiped his brow with his forefinger. He put his foot through the wire fence and leaned on a rotted, wobbly post. Calkins joined him. A quarter mile to the south, down the slope of a corn field so gentle it took a while to realize, machines crawled across their gaze. Small clouds of dust, glowing in the sun, rolled after four tractors running parallel as they harrowed the bean field. They drove out of sight behind the woods. Beyond them, a larger machine, a combine, moved back and forth on a shorter path. A truck traveled at its side and a tractor pulled a baler and a wagon along the same course behind them.

"They'll make short work of what's left of that wheat field," Calkins said. He pointed at the combine as the truck pulled away. "They're dumping the combine on the fly and baling straw behind it," he explained as though Pierman had never seen it.

But he had. Calkins' father farmed, and when they were thirteen, he hired them as hay hands. Seeing a lone figure stumble with the rolling motion of the wagon the baler pulled brought it back to Pierman: the suffocating heat of the hay mow, the black phlegm from the dust, the sting on his forearms as sweat poured into furrows gouged into his skin by the stubble, the pain of making a fist after six, seven, or eight straight hours of hooking his fingers on toothpick-thin baling wire. Why did it take so much more effort to remember the serene, boastful exhaustion that took him in the hot bath each night?

"Remember that work?" Pierman said.

"Sure," Calkins said quietly, staring straight ahead. "It was shit."

"But you miss it sometimes?"

The chains that grabbed corn stalks into a picker snatched the pants leg of Calkins' father on a misty November day the year they had graduated from high school. The chains chewed off a leg and spit it out while Calkins watched. He tied off the stump and ran two people off the road getting his father help. After that, Calkins did most of the farming, but the accident cost both men their heart for it and a year or two later, a poor crop cost them the land. Or so Pierman had heard. He was long gone by then.

"Miss it," Calkins said. "Shit." He blew out some air. "'Cept this week, maybe. A lot of pressure."

The four tractors had turned and come back into view.

"Look at 'em," Calkins said. "Like ducks in a shooting gallery."

※

They waited at the driveway for a tarp-covered truck to crawl out. An empty one they had followed to the farm sped back to the fields. A tractor and wagon had just pulled up to a long, green hiker that stuck out like a tongue from a mouth on the second story of the barn. The wagon was stacked high and neat with bales of glistening straw.

The driver of the tractor, a beefy, red-faced man in bib overalls, flagged them down. When Calkins got out to talk to him, he went to his tractor, retrieved a greasy, rumpled grocery sack from the tool box in the fender, and handed it to Calkins. Calkins looked inside the sack and listened a little more to what the man had to say. He went back to the wagon to talk to the shirtless, stringy, teenage boy in a red baseball cap, who leaned against the bales. As the boy talked to Calkins, he removed his cap and pointed with it off in the distance. Two heads wearing the same sort of caps watched the conversation from an open window in the loft.

When the conversation ended, the beefy man wrapped a cord around the hiker's flywheel and yanked all in one motion. Calkins flinched when the engine kicked in, then waited, perversely Pierman thought. For a while, bemused, Calkins watched the boy teeter on the wagon's edge as the hiker lapped up toward the mow each bale the boy dropped onto it.

"You have to put yourself through that?" Pierman said as Calkins got back into the car.

"Look in there," Calkins said and tossed the sack into Pierman's lap.

It held a narrow, slatted, metal box. It was dented and mangled. Calkins explained that it was the magazine from a rifle.

The boy had found the magazine a couple of days ago while mowing fence rows for his father, the beefy man. The rotary mower the boy pulled behind a tractor had chewed up the magazine and spit it out. The boy didn't see it until the mower threw it out onto the road.

The site was a couple of miles from Grable's place. Father and son would come in so that Calkins could get a set of comparison prints. Calkins' mood had brightened considerably, but it didn't last long.

"Where's the rest of it?" Pierman asked. "The rest of the rifle?"

"Good question."

"What took them so long to turn it in?"

"They didn't know what they had."

"What do they have?"

"Why do you act like you're stupid?" Calkins said. "Maybe it's part of the murder weapon. These things aren't coffee cups. As a rule, people don't just toss them out their windows."

"Maybe it dropped out while some hunter was climbing a fence."

"Nobody hunts Taylor's place. No woods, no weeds, and it's posted."

"So," Pierman said, "the operative theory would be that whoever shot Randy Grable decided to get rid of the weapon one piece at a time."

"Well, yeah," Calkins said suspiciously.

"And do we search every fence row in the county to find the rest of it?"

Calkins had no answer.

"And," Pierman said, "you understand what it means if we do start finding pieces in the fence rows of Holoce County?"

"No," Calkins said.

"More than likely, the son of a bitch's still here."

As they drove toward the back of the Grable farm, they passed a half-dozen boys armed with hoes and wearing only short pants and high-tops trudging through a bean field. Each stopped here and there to chop out a weed in his row. In the same field, two tractors drew harrows down the rows, the implement's vicious blades blurred like pinwheels. Calkins stopped for a moment where the lane bent to the left to let the behemoths pirouette with slow grace back into the field. On the other side of the lane, the implements behind two more tractors rent the black stubble left by the fire. A third pulling a wide planter tucked new seeds into the moist soil.

"What do they expect to get out of the ground this late? Pierman asked.

"Beans," Calkins said. "If they're lucky."

The "ducks" Calkins and Pierman had watched earlier continued their race across the field to the north and the east. The noise that was merely loud a half mile away was now deafening. The roar dipped and coughed only when oil surged through the hydraulics to hoist the implements out of the ground at the end of each pass. The air was confused with the rich scent of moist earth and the bitter odors of fertilizer and petroleum.

Heat shimmered off a row of cars and pickups parked along the edge of the burned-over field. At the front of the row were two stake trucks from which the side racks had been removed. On the far one, an older man and a boy sat on short stacks of seed and fertilizer. Around the nearer truck, a dozen or more bantering women arranged covered dishes on red-checked cloths they had spread on the bed. Four or five preschoolers scampered in the shade underneath.

"Come to help or eat?" Kay Grable called as they approached. She was the only one of the women who smiled. The others looked at them suspiciously and then at each other before they went back to unloading their coolers and shooing flies.

Pierman did not notice. She appeared to wear no makeup, and she was plainly dressed in white T-shirt, tight jeans, and a blue bandana over her long hair. But on a clear, sunny morning, she shined a little brighter than the other women. For a moment, he was dumbfounded. Large, round, tortoise-shell sunglasses obscured her eyes, but the set of her mouth gave Pierman the impression she was amused, perhaps at the fact that he was tongue-tied or maybe at the thought of him driving a tractor in a suit.

"I don't think anybody here'd like it if I ate without helping," Pierman said finally, taking his eyes off her. "And I'm the last guy you want driving one of those things." He lifted his chin toward the tractors. "Why aren't you out there?"

"Ah. Well." She bit her lips. "I'm just womenfolk." She waved a hand dismissively toward the first truck. "Or so he says." The man sitting on the seed sacks on the first truck turned out to be her father. Paul Grable looked down on Calkins, who stood before him talking.

Kay touched Pierman at the elbow to move him away from the other women. "Are are you here to investigate then?"

He caught the scents of shampoo and sunshine on her skin, and at that moment, he could not honestly say. "Joe is investigating. I appear to be advising."

"'Appear to be.'" She repeated it not quite sarcastically, as though she had contained the impulse. "That's very lawyerly. And what has the sheriff found and what have you advised him about it?"

Before he could answer, Pierman saw Paul Grable vault down from the truck bed and step toward Calkins, who put a flat hand on his chest to keep him at bay.

As Pierman and Kay approached, Pierman heard Grable say to Calkins in a low, hoarse voice, "You don't have shit, and you ask me that?" Grable pressed against Calkins' hand trying to get closer. "How dare you?" Kay caught his hand as it came up and threw an arm around his shoulders to hold him back. Pierman stepped in between.

"You know what he asked me?" Grable said, looking from Kay to Pierman. "You know what he asked? He asked me if my boy was a pervert."

"You mean," Pierman said, "Joe asked you if your son was gay."

Grable shook off his daughter's hold on him and turned to Pierman. "Of course, goddamnit."

"Did he?" Pierman said, looking at Calkins then back to Grable. "So what's the answer?"

"You, too?" Grable's bit his lips closed in a hard line.

"Me, first, actually, Mr. Grable," Pierman said. "Was your son homosexual?"

"No, goddamnit, he was not."

"He wasn't," Pierman said. "Did you and he ever talk about it? I mean, sex."

"No."

"Then, how do you know?"

"'Cause I know. I goddamned raised him, didn't I. There's your answer. Now get out."

Calkins stood grim and resigned. A tear trickled down Kay's cheek. Pierman looked from her to her father. Grable glared back. Kay would not look back at Pierman. Pierman nodded to Calkins, and they headed back to the car.

She caught his arm and turned him before he got there.

"Why was that necessary?" she asked in a hiss. Her sunglasses were off, and her eyes flashed.

"Somebody stood before your brother at high noon and shot him twice." He talked over her shoulder, looking at the sky. He did not really want to say these things. "That's deliberate. That's personal. I have to assume he really pissed somebody off. Or maybe your dad really pissed somebody off, and they just made a mistake." When he returned his eyes to her face, she was wide-eyed, stricken by the news. "Either way, the more we know about your brother and your father, the more we know about whom they might've pissed off."

Kay had turned from him. She pressed the flats of the fingers of one hand against her mouth. Paul Grable had followed them.

"I told you to get out," he said, putting an arm around his daughter's waist.

She turned out of his embrace. "Call me?" she asked of Pierman.

Pierman looked from her to her father. "Yes," he said.

9

In the week that followed, the same people who took time away from their own fields to work in Paul Grable's answered Calkins' call to walk ditches along Holoce County roads. They and many more. Convicted drunks worked off community service time. Boy Scouts earned badges. One or two became Eagles, bent at the waist in service to the dead.

Calkins organized them into teams and assigned the teams one-mile stretches radiating out from Grable's place. He told each team to walk their ditch twice and if they found anything leave it in place until he or a deputy, Darryl usually, got there. Purcell predicted there would be chain of custody problems with anything that was found if cops didn't do it, but he did not volunteer his troops. Pierman told Purcell in front of Calkins he ought to let lawyers practice law, then warned Calkins in private he damned well better document each find by time and location and the name, address, and phone number of the finder for they would certainly have to testify.

Three times that week, Calkins silently appeared like the Passover angel at Pierman's office door. Ginny, the prosecutor's secretary, a very young woman of only modest intelligence and skill, told Pierman Calkins was creepin' her out. Each time, he laid a piece of metal in a red-tagged plastic bag on Pierman's desk. Each time, Calkins looked a little grimmer, and Pierman went a little colder.

"Where?" Pierman asked the third time as Calkins stood before him refusing to meet his eye.

Calkins told him. Pierman look at a framed county map his father had used as wall dressing. Pierman had marked the location of each of the other three pieces with a dot of yellow highlighter on the glass covering the map. If he connected the dots, there would be no straight line or any logical shape.

"Who?"

"This time? Your buddy. Nate McQueen."

Pierman thought about that.

"What was he doing there?" he asked.

Calkins shrugged. "Same as everyone else. He took a day off work."

"I don't want him around. He's too close to the situation."

"The situation? Or the woman?"

Pierman only stared. Calkins shrugged again.

"Prints?" Pierman asked.

Calkins pursed his lips and shook his head. "No prints. No smudges. Clean," he said.

"Like the others," Pierman said.

"Just like the others," Calkins agreed.

"Same gun?" Pierman asked, guessing the answer.

"Same make and model. Can't say same gun."

Purcell's techs had identified the type of gun after the second part, a mechanism for ejecting shells, was found. It was from a hunting rifle, a caliber used for deer and the type of gun that might be found in the rack in the back window of any number of pickup trucks in Holoce and any one of its contiguous counties.

Pierman look back at the map. "Seems unlikely parts from the same make and model of a gun would just happen to be sprinkled around fence posts all over the county if it weren't the same gun."

"Unlikely," Calkins agreed.

"Where's the rest of it?"

"Rest of it? Well, hell, Allen, there's a river here, a lake or two, and I couldn't begin to tell you the number of farm ponds."

"You're saying you've run out of roads?"

"Yes, sir, I have. We've walked every goddamned road in Holoce County twice, and we've run out of roads. You called it. The gun and the son of a bitch who shot it are probably still here, but they aren't along the roads."

The prosecutor's office was on the top floor of the Courthouse and enjoyed a view of nearly half the square. Pierman turned his chair toward the window and watched the reporter for the local newspaper loping toward the Courthouse from his office down one of the alleys off the square. The plaid spider, as Pierman had come to think of him, had taken to visiting Pierman every day since Randy Grable died, just to make sure Calkins was not holding back on him. The ditch walks had made quite a story; the spider expected follow-up. Pierman looked back at Calkins, who was looking over his shoulder at the spider.

"I'd keep that to myself," Pierman said. He took off his glasses and rubbed his eyes. "Son of a bitch," he said.

On another day that week, we—Pierman and I—stood at the door of the courtroom watching a young man in an azure suit chopping his hand like a blade beneath the chin of an even younger man.

"Your colleague, Mr. D'Agostino, is, no doubt, telling his client that if he doesn't like his advice he can find another attorney," I said.

The younger man wore jeans, a ragged denim jacket open to mid-chest, and cowboy boots. He greasy blond hair, cut close on the sides of his head but long to the shoulders in the back. He also appeared to be wearing mascara, eyebrow pencil, and rouge.

"Look at that damned suit," I said.

"Look at that damned makeup," Pierman said. "Mr. D'Agostino is now ten minutes late for the pre-trial conference."

"He's standing 10 feet away with his client, and you would default him? This is hardly Chicago."

"Maybe it is," Pierman said. "This is probably the first time he's met his client, and he gives this public performance for everyone of them to train them so they won't question him again."

"Ah, you have been around." I peeled the cellophane off a white tipped cigar, shook my head, and settled into one of the pews in the spectator's gallery. I pulled a wooden match from my vest pocket and pointed it out toward the hall. "He's going to come in here and ask for a jury trial."

I scraped the match along the underside of the pew and lit the cigar. Pierman remained by the door, watching.

"From the way it looks, I'd say he's going to come in here and ask to withdraw his appearance," Pierman said.

D'Agostino had put down his briefcase. He held out a handkerchief he had taken from his back pocket. His client pouted, arms crossed, shoulders sagged, looking away as if he hadn't heard.

"Lover's spat." I said. "That's all. He'll patch it up and demand a jury trial. Probably a change of judge, too." For a moment, I was quiet, letting the aggravation build. "It's just a hearing to young D'Agostino, and it's just before old me so it doesn't make any difference. But you can damn well bet he'll be in here wearing funeral black when the jury hits the box. I should hold him in contempt just for wearing a suit like that in my courtroom."

Pierman had heard it all before. His father and I frequently discussed decorum when we were partners. Carter gave little thought to his appearance, but Pierman could remember him saying, "Donnie's the closest thing to elegant we got in this county," using the nickname he knew irritated me.

On this day, I sat before him in a charcoal three-piece suit that was, in fact, tailor made and crisply pressed. The wavy white hair was combed back from a high forehead, and the shoes had a high gloss, although I doubt Pierman imagined me applying the polish myself as I had. "Donnie's as sleek as a greyhound," Carter had said once to his son, " but he's got the heart of a jackal. That's why I like him."

Carter did not talk behind my back. He had said the same to me.

10

When he was a boy, lying in bed after a bad day, Pierman would tell himself the moral was not to get carried away, not to let his expectations rise so high. He would vow to be a pessimist always, to buffer himself against highs that fell without warning, to make all surprises pleasant. As an adult, he came to understand days were oblivious to morals and always was more than anyone could manage, but the flux an ideal of moderation masked could not be relieved.

As he turned into the driveway that evening, then, he understood quite clearly why his shirt stuck to his chest even though he had the air conditioning running full blast. He hadn't approached a woman that way in years. The corners of his mouth lifted slightly. In a way, it was a relief.

Kay stood on the porch alone. She wore a salmon dress with thin straps, and in the glow of the evening sun, she looked incongruous and uncomfortable in the plain frame. She was at the car door before he could turn off the engine.

"You're early," she said.

"As are you apparently."

Once in, she seemed more natural. The dress drew out the color of her cheeks. The sun had lightened her long hair to the color of tea, and under it, her shoulders looked warm, toasted deep brown. Pierman noticed there were no lighter stripes bordering the straps.

"You'll burn up the air conditioner," she said, "letting the car run like this."

"Where would you learn something like that?"

"It's what Dad says."

"He's not home?"

"Yes. Why?"

"You were waiting outside. Perhaps I should go in, say hello."

He reached for the ignition, but she stopped him.

"Not after last week. And I don't have to be in by midnight. Or any other time, for that matter."

Her scent wafted across the seat to him when she tossed her head. The impatient gesture exposed a shoulder from under her hair and an uneven row of freckles along its brow. Pierman wondered what it would be like to walk his fingers across them like stepping stones.

They had agreed out of town was best. They had no need really to discuss it; they both just knew. There was nothing to do in Lindley. The city had far more and better restaurants. It was nobody's business. They did not want people to talk. For appearances and ethical reasons, they had to be discreet. Given the number of people in Lindley who thought the same things on a Saturday night, the odds of running into someone you knew sometimes was only marginally smaller than staying in town.

It was a forty-five minute trip. Someplace different, nice, he had thought. Ballantine's, he had remembered. Through green fields and a hazy, screened sunset, they connected the dots of blinkers, the summer-drowsy hamlets of no more than a couple dozen houses, a convenience store, and a grain elevator.

She talked about the weather. They needed rain again. She talked about an old friend she had met in the grocery and hardly recognized. Three children and a divorce already. She talked about the flowers she had added around the garden.

"Which you planted in your bathing suit," he said. "A bikini, I'd guess."

Her gaze was appraising. "It's blue," she said and wrinkled her nose. "Dad would've died."

She hummed with a tune on the radio. Sooner or later, he thought.

"How's he doing?" he asked.

"All right."

"Just all right?"

"Fine."

"And you?"

"Are we on business or pleasure tonight?"

"I won't be turning in a receipt to the county if that's what you're concerned about."

She smiled without laughing.

"And will you be treating me like some fragile, crystal bird the rest of the evening?"

"Not intentionally."

He heard the nylon whisk as she turned toward him and crossed her legs.

"He's making me crazy," she said.

"And guilty?"

"Bikinis. Guilt. Aren't you perceptive."

"I've been through it, too."

"Not quite the same, is it." Her flint struck him again as it had at the house.

"I stand corrected."

She bit her lip and looked away across the luxuriating land.

"Bumping into each other a lot?" he prompted and she nodded.

"He can't accept it yet. The legal stuff, the thank yous, the sorting. He's handling all that pretty well, but the others. . . ."

Pierman took his eyes off the road to look at her. She watched, dry-eyed, for him.

"Randy had replanted the end of a field," she said. "It came up thick. Dad took a hoe and went out to thin it today. When I went out to call him for lunch, he was standing between two ragged rows with his eyes full and a hundred little chopped stalks at his feet." She sighed deeply. "He said, 'That's what it felt like, dammit.' But he wouldn't let me touch him."

Pierman remembered how she had waited for him on the porch.

"So you wanted to hug him and strangle him."

She sucked in her breath and shivered.

"I'm sorry," he said. "That was thoughtless."

She pushed back her hair and dismissed it with a wave of her hand.

"That was about the order of it," she said.

She shut off the air conditioner and rolled down a back window. Clammy air, scented with freshly cut clover filled the car. Wisps of hair danced around her face. When she pulled the rest of it away from her neck, it floated out the window.

"I wish now those people had never come out to help," she said. "Or that he'd never hired that boy, Rodney." A smile stumbled out. "He keeps sneaking little looks at me."

"Obviously, a young man of good taste."

"We have too much empty time," she said.

"Could your father do it all by himself?"

"I could help."

"Would he let you?"

She pursed her lips.

"No. He wouldn't think it was right." Her voice rose. "Of course, Mama worked right alongside him for years, until Randy came along. And did the housework. And raised us."

"He doesn't understand he's raised a feminist then." Pierman gave her a sly glance to jolly her, but she bristled.

"And if he did?"

"Fine by me."

She waited for the punch line, but none came. They drove through well-packaged suburbs. She watched the houses slide by.

"I don't think he knows quite what to do with me," she said.

"A daughter's curse?"

"A single one's maybe. He was different with Randy."

"Man to man."

"Something like that, I guess. I'm afraid that sooner or later he'll try to find some way for me to take Randy's place."

"Big job."

"Even if I could. Or would."

Gritty exhaust began to enter the car. She rolled up the back window and turned the air back on.

"The only way I can see," she said, toying again with her hair, "is to find someone and settle down in Lindley. It's what he's always wanted anyway."

"Rodney," Pierman said. "It should be Rodney. You'd solve everyone's problem that way."

"Bastard."

But she caressed his arm and laughed for the first time.

Since he would not lie, like some he knew who grew up in small towns, Pierman always had to answer not one but two questions when strangers were serious about knowing where he was grew up. "Where are you from?" and then "Where's that?" He had thus used the city as a reference point for as long as he could remember, but he hadn't been there in years and time and progress confounded him that night. He knew where to leave the bypass, but the wide inner loop that connected the city's spokes was new to him and matching the names on the green signs overhead to the scenes in his mind was impossible with relentless weekend traffic passing him on both sides. When he finally decided to just to get off, it was no better. Clean, sleek buildings congratulated themselves in their size and each other in their walls of copper- and gold-mirrored glass. The aged, grimy landmarks he knew were hidden or gone.

"We'll be late if you don't turn here," Kay said, mildly.

That gave Pierman his bearings. Ahead was the Circle, the city's literal hub, a roundabout surrounded by concave office buildings and stores, and in the middle, the war memorial, the city's symbol.

Pierman knew it well; the old man considered it a treat to walk his young son around the spire whenever they were in town. He would point out the heroic features of downed horses and screaming men in the battle scenes carved at the base of the memorial and try to explain why ship prows, which jutted out from all four corners a third of the way up, had such a prominent place on a monument in a landlocked state. Afterward, his father would take Pierman's hand and lead him to a phone booth-sized elevator, which took them to the observation windows in the spiked knob at the top. From there, at that time, you could look out over the entire city. To Pierman now, the monument looked like no more than a tall, bristling thistle rooted tenaciously in a crack of the city's newfound urbanity.

"Field trips," Kay said, before Pierman could ask how she knew. "Teacher conventions."

An older black man in a white shirt with epaulets met them when they pulled up to the door. He studiously avoided looking at Kay's legs as he opened and held her door, but he winked at Pierman as he took the keys and squealed the tires down the alley.

"No dates?" Pierman asked as he waited for the sound of metal crunching.

"Not here." She looked expectantly through the faceless lobby.

At the bottom of the stairs, the hostess frowned and looked at her watch when Pierman gave her his name.

"It's *Doctor* Pierman," he said, and tapped his name on her clipboard. "I was in delivery. It was twins."

"Of course, sir. Forgive me."

The woman led them through murmuring twilight rooms to a place in a corner.

"You're terrible," Kay said, when she was gone.

"She would've been insulted if I'd tried to slip her a five just to get our table back."

Soft lamps in the shape of bent tulips hung along the walls over each table and made the cracked oil portraits and still lifes and the mahogany paneling behind them gleam. The menus listed the entrees in French, and gilt trimmed the rims of the china. He followed her eyes around the room, noticing two or three male heads, still turned, if not quite looking, her way. Around them, people were dressed in the colors of earth, wood, and stone. The men didn't wear lime or burgundy jackets or shiny white shoes, and the women didn't wear pants suits. Patrons here did not aspire to look like so many pieces of plastic fruit, Pierman thought.

"And how do you know a place like this?" Kay asked.

"Don't you like it?"

"I do. Very much."

A middle-aged waitress, bleached, rouged, and powdery outside her stark black and white maid's uniform, appeared, took their drink orders, and bustled away.

"My parents used to bring me here," Pierman said. "Dad would come over for court or some other business. Mom would shop or take me to the art museum. We'd meet here for dinner, then go see my grandparents, her folks."

"They live here?"

"They did. They're dead now."

"Where did they live?"

"On Meridian."

"In one of those estates?"

"You could call it that. It was near the governor's mansion."

"Well." She stretched it, and he colored.

"Whatcher pleasure tonight, folks?" the waitress asked when she delivered the drinks.

"Let me," Kay said, "It's my subject." She read off the menu in fluent French.

"You mean the veal, honey?" The waitress asked without looking up from her pad.

Pierman was amused, but Kay did not allow herself the humor of it until their eyes met. Then she changed the subject by asking how his parents met.

"Mutual friends," he said. "A party after the war. They were both in their thirties. He needed a wife; she needed a husband. Time was running out."

"That's harsh."

He had meant it to be wry. She leaned on her elbows, her face in the circle of light cast by the lamp above her head, attentive and waiting.

"Maybe I've never quite understood what they saw in each other. Sometimes it was like she was just a trophy, a way of proving to himself he could've made it here if he wanted to."

"And what was he to her?"

"I don't know."

But her stillness demanded more. He remembered his mother's conversation the night Kay's brother died.

"Maybe the call of the recently civilized wild. A boisterous country boy who struck some sort of new chord in a sheltered city girl. My grandparents didn't care for him much and the feeling was mutual, but they'd compromised by the time I came along."

"By coming here for supper."

"Among other ways." Pierman looked up at one of the oils. "My mother would comment on the paintings, the composition, use of light, that sort of thing. He'd razz her about it, and the fact that I always wanted a hot dog here amused him to no end."

He turned in his chair so that his back was against the wall and put his chin in his hand.

"But he liked it, even more I think when the old folks were gone. He'd get expansive. Big tips, calling the maitre'd—they had one then—by name. They'd run into my mother's friends here, and he'd do the whole squire-comes-to-town bit just to show them he wasn't living off her inheritance or dragging her down."

"This'll be the last time you'll see these," the waitress announced as she gathered up the gilt plates and served the food on plain white china. "Enjoy."

Kay had pulled her hands into her lap to let the woman serve. She stared at them for some time.

"Did I say something to upset you?" Pierman asked.

"No," she said, "it's not that."

They ate in silence for a time. Two tables away, a handsome, older couple, raised champagne flutes. She watched them for a moment.

"We came over once in a while," she said. "I saw Cinerama at the Indiana. There was a tobacco place or something next door. It must've sold something smutty. Dad would always park on the other side so we wouldn't walk past it. I remember Debbie Reynolds in *How the West Was Won*."

Unlike her father, she did not balk at drinks or the wine Pierman had ordered. As she sipped it now, the reflection deepened her blush.

"We'd go to the 500, too," she said. "Dad liked that. All I remember is the terrible noise and coming home bloated on brownies and pop. You must've gone."

"Not till I was in college," Pierman said. "My mother thought such things"—he leaned forward and whispered—"unseemly."

"Of course." She reached over and squeezed his hand. "Let me guess." She withdrew her hand and tapped her temple. "A Hoosier boy who waited until college to go to the Race would probably swill beer in the Snakepit, shout for boob flash in the infield, and never see any of the cars."

She paused for his reaction, but got only a cocked eyebrow. She pressed on.

"You probably went to some small, private liberal arts place where the buildings're all colonial or Greek and ivy grows up the walls. I don't think you would've needed a scholarship; you probably even had your own car. Grades would've been no problem, but they were nothing spectacular because you had other fish to fry. You joined a fraternity, flirted with debauchery on Saturday, and worried about it on Sunday. How'm I doing?"

"Aside from gross generalization? You're failing to take into account my father. No car and I went to a state university. I also worked in the summer."

"Oh, but that built character. I'm right otherwise? Midwestern prep?"

The playful way she mocked his cynicism forced him to smile. "It was long before alligator shirts," he said.

"But not before starched Gant shirts and penny loafers with your jeans."

She sat primly with her hands in her lap, but she met his smile with a sly twist of her own.

"Now taking into account your dad, you went to law school, which made him happy, and went off to Chicago, which didn't."

Pierman willed himself not to look away. "His chest was known to swell occasionally when he mentioned it to friends," he said.

"But he might've been happier if you'd come back. Your mom, too, if for no other reason than to please your dad."

"Who've you been talking to?"

"No one," she laughed. "I've been there and you just fit the type."

"Maybe we should discuss your type."

The waitress returned, noisily gathered up the plates, and took the dessert order. Throughout, Kay watched Pierman glower with an innocent expression.

"You don't have to," she said, when they were alone again. "My type tried the wide world and didn't like it." She paused to give him a chance to cross the line she was drawing. When he did not, she went on.

"I went to a state school, too. I needed a scholarship. They threatened to take it away from me when I got arrested for marching against the War." She waved dismissively. "Yes, I had hair to my ass, wore beads and peasant blouses without a bra, and smoked dope."

"I would've liked to have seen that," Pierman said.

"I'll bet you would," she said. "I had already dumped my boyfriend. I told myself and him it was because I could not be involved with someone who was serving in Viet Nam, but I think we both knew it was a relationship that'd never go anywhere."

She paused to see whether he would respond. "You know Nate McQueen, I believe," she said when he did not. Pierman looked away and shrugged.

"Dad found the money to send me to France. I learned the language cold, but the plumbing was bad and the people were rude. It was like having a compass without a map."

"So you found a little town not unlike Lindley and settled down."

"It's near the city," she said. "I teach. I'm tenured." Her smile remained, but sharp, raised eyebrows dared him again.

"Even though your father could've gotten you a job at the high school," he said, crossing the line this time.

"Or I could've married good old Nate McQueen."

The waitress put the match to the baked Alaskas and gingerly set them down. Pierman watched the handsome couple leave, hand in hand, through the nearly empty room. He wondered what they understood of each other.

"Blow 'em out when they look good, honey," he heard the waitress say. He followed the instruction without noticing, but when he still felt the thin heat on his face and the odor of burned sugar grew stronger, he looked up. Kay's eyes were fixed on the flame, and a tear flickered blue in its light.

"Excuse me," she said, leaving him to put out the flame.

She was gone an embarrassingly long time. Pierman had just received the check when she returned. New lipstick called attention to the disappearance of her eye makeup.

"That waitress is such a bitch," she said with a choked laugh. She raised her glass, but no words came.

"We've slain the fatted calf and feasted," he said. "And we have only her to say it was meet."

"Or meat," she said, willing the grin.

The glasses rang, but then she snatched up her purse by its strap and left. Pierman had to throw down the bills between the creamy puddles to catch up.

She headed north toward the Circle. When she had stiffened at his touch, he gave her space. The streets were crowded on a warm, summer night, but she did not notice. She brought traffic on the roundabout to a blaring halt when she crossed to the monument without looking. She circled it twice, at full speed. She stopped finally and stared at one of the fountains at the monument's base.

"Once he got lost in the corn," she said. "He was four; I was thirteen. It was harvest. Mama was driving for Daddy, and I was supposed to watch him. But he was sort of a big, dumb puppy who piddled on the floor and chewed up shoes so I patted him and let him wander off while I mooned about boys and being cold."

She crossed her arms and shivered.

"He could've gotten out. All he had to do was follow the rows—they were Daddy's pride, the straightest rows—but the machinery scared him. Somewhere, it was out there, coming closer, and he couldn't see it. I heard him crying and crashing through the stalks. The leaves were dry and cut my face, but I ran to get him anyway because all I could think about was how mad Daddy was going to be about the damage and how mad I was with him. When I finally found him, he was sitting in the middle of a nest of broken stalks just blubbering. It almost broke my heart, but I was still mad, so I slapped him."

There were no tears and she would not turn from the fountain, but she let Pierman draw her under his arm.

"I cannot think of him as an adult," she said.

"He barely was."

"I was born too much older than him. Nine years. I was long gone when he was growing up. I didn't know him very well."

She went still under Pierman's arm, then turned out of it to face him.

"Would you go somewhere with me?"

Pierman hesitated.

"Maybe it'll answer one of your questions," she said. "And mine, now that you raised it."

♫

She headed north again on Meridian, the broad artery that bisected the Circle.

"A year, maybe a year and a half, ago, he called me," Kay said, taking Pierman's arm. "Said he wanted to stay at my place for the weekend. Said he wouldn't bother me. He was going into the City to hang out with some people."

As they moved farther from the Circle, the number of people on the sidewalk began to thin.

"I was kind of surprised," Kay said. "Since I'd left, outside of family gatherings, he'd never really spent any time with me, and he sure hadn't stayed at my place before." She shrugged. "Still, he was family. I said okay."

"Of course, what he wanted was an alibi," she said. "When he dropped his gym bag on my floor the first time, he said he wondered if it'd be okay if he told Mama and Daddy he had visited me that weekend. That's, of course, if they asked."

"The first time?" Pierman asked mildly.

She pulled him to a stop and studied his face, but she did not take her arm from his. "I keep forgetting you listen well," she said after a moment, "and that you're pretty much a cop."

"Which ear would you like me to turn off," he said,"the personal or the professional?"

She blinked. "Shit," she said, "I don't know." She tugged his arm and walked on.

A plaza begins beyond the federal courthouse and runs a few blocks north. It is a block wide and criss-crossed with sidewalks that meet at fountains and statues. The only substantial structures on the plaza are the national offices of the American Legion, which are long, low, and gray like a huge concrete block tipped on its side, and a three-story granite memorial to war veterans that looks like a cubic fireplug. At the time, there was little to draw most people to the plaza at night. Street lamps illuminated it, but only at its margins. In the shadows, Pierman could see here and there lone white men with beards and grubby clothes and small groups of young black men and boys. He kept himself between Kay and the plaza and listened with two minds, one for her and the other for steps behind and to his right.

"The first time," she said, emphasizing it, "he came home about one. In the morning. He smelled like smoke and he looked a little glazed. I asked him where he'd been, what he'd been doing, but all I got were grunts and guilty looks. I figured maybe he'd smoked a little dope and hung out with his friends and so what? I'd done it, he was an adult, it was none of my business."

"After that," she said, "he'd show up maybe once every month or so, and it was sort of the same thing, except he stayed out later and later. It went on for several months until one time, he didn't show up until noon the next day. He was in bad shape. Glassy, barely conscious. I'm not even sure how he got home. I let him sleep it off, then I told him I didn't want him worrying me, not knowing where he was, whether he was fucked up in an accident, scaring me like that."

Traffic was heavy on Meridian. Occasionally, a car would honk at them, or a group of kids would catcall them. Kay was oblivious.

"He said, fine. Mama was dead, he didn't need another, and I wasn't the boss of him anyway. 'Wasn't the boss of him.' Jeez, just like we were children again. Besides, he said, he wouldn't be back. He didn't need this anymore."

"What'd he mean by *this*?" Pierman asked. "He didn't need an alibi? Or he didn't need a place to stay?"

"I don't know."

Kay had stopped at the end of the plaza. Across the street was the city library. The building looked like the federal court building at the other end of the plaza, four or five stories high and gray, sooty stone, nearly as wide as the plaza. Its front columns, tall windows, and doors were flooded with lights, drawing them out from the night and leaving deep shadows at its back.

Kay had removed her arm from Pierman's. She clutched her purse strap with both hands and stared at the building.

"He left his underwear on the floor one time when he got back to my place. It was . . . stained."

"Stained," Pierman said carefully.

"Yes." Her voice caught. She breathed deeply a couple of times. "In the back."

Pierman saw figures crossing the street and moving around the side of the library toward the back.

"There was a story in the newspaper about this place once," Kay said. "People," she said. "Men," she clarified and tipped her chin up, "they meet there."

"And you want to find out what your brother was doing."

"You asked the goddamned question."

"You never did? Even when he was coming back to your place with stained underwear?"

"No," she said and shuddered. "I never did."

Pierman breathed deeply.

"Let's let the cops ask the question," he said.

She shook her head.

"Then let's go back and get the car. We can come back here, you can wait in the car, and I'll go ask."

She shook her head again.

Pierman looked at her for a long time.

"You carry a picture of him?"

Without taking her eyes from Pierman's face, she reached into her purse and pulled out a photo. She didn't have it in her wallet, he noted. She had it ready all along.

They were of various ages from teenagers to old men, and they appeared to be of various backgrounds. Some wore tight T-shirts and short shorts, others wore jeans and work or cowboy boots, others a jacket and tie. A few were tricked out in leather and chains, but they did not look entirely comfortable assuming the testosterone swagger of the rough trade Pierman had encountered coming out of the holding cells under the Chicago courts. Standing at one corner of the building, trying to size up the situation, Pierman exhaled in relief.

We don't much care to be reminded that we, too, are animals. When it comes to sex and violence—those traits that most remind us that we are not so high on the evolutionary scale after all—we cloak them in ritual and shadow. Here, some promenaded back and forth along a drive that ran the width of the building. They peered into the deep shadows of the loading docks and private entry ways or stopped occasionally to chat with others met on the stroll. Periodically, someone would emerge from the shadows. There would be conversation and sometimes gifts: a bottle in a paper sack, a baggie palmed in a handshake, or occasionally, money. Pairs periodically moved off to the dimly illuminated parking lot that adjoined the drive. Sometimes the car they got into left the lot; sometimes it did not.

Kay stood wide-eyed and confounded. Pierman nudged her and they moved forward along the stroll.

"Excuse me," he said to the first person they met, a small, gray-haired, respectable-looking man with a linen sport coat and dress slacks. Expressions of uncertainty then fear passed across his face as his eyes moved from Pierman to Kay, and he scurried on without saying more. The next man—this one in his twenties wearing a polo shirt and jeans—would not even make eye contact.

"You're gonna have to come over here, honey, you want *anybody* to talk to you," a voice called out from the shadows.

"Fucking tourists," a second, gruffer voice said.

"Careful, sweetie. Maybe cops," a third voice said.

"Shit, no," the second voice said, "Can't be. They were, we'd be busted by now."

Pierman turned toward the voices. "I'm looking for someone."

"As are we all. As *are* we all," said the first voice, "But, honey, I'm telling you, *nobody* is going to talk to you out there. We're shy around strangers here, least the straight kind. Come here now, and let's talk."

"Yeah, but leave the bitch out on the drive," the second voice called.

"No, no, let's see her," a third voice said. "He said he was looking for someone. Maybe he's looking for a three-way."

"Or maybe she's a he, shaved her apple. Hard to tell from here." the second voice said. "I fucking hate that."

When Pierman looked around, the drive was empty. The voices had created enough of a scene to drive the shy away. He took two steps and held up Randy's photograph toward the shadows. "I'm looking for information about this man."

A bald man with a walrus moustache emerged from the shadows with the blinking, innocent, trusting air of a child coming into the light. He was white, aged forties, and wore plaid Bermuda shorts and a frayed T-shirt that said it was the property of a high school athletic department. Two men half his age appeared on either side of him. One was black, tall, and obviously muscular under a tight, dark T-shirt and tight, pressed blue jeans. He had short-cropped hair, and a very carefully trimmed moustache. The third man was white, pear shaped, and dressed in short shorts and a tank top.

"You expecting the Village People, honey?" the black man said, amused by the uncertain expression on Pierman's face. His voice was the first Pierman had heard, and Pierman, despite what he considered to be an open mind, was surprised.

"Cop?" the pear-shaped man said. His had been the second, angry voice, and again Pierman was surprised. He had expected the man to sound like Richard Simmons.

"Nope," Pierman said quickly to cover his reactions. "Just a public defender from Chicago."

"Prove it," the pear-shaped man said. Pierman produced his wallet and from it his bar card and office identification card.

"Excellent, Allen," the older man said reading both carefully. "I like it with educated men in the professions. And one on the right side of courtroom at that."

"Phillip, shut up," the black man said. He pulled himself up and closer to Pierman. "What's your interest?" he said very seriously.

"This guy," Pierman said, holding up the picture for each of them to see. "This guy was killed a few days ago. Shot."

"His sister," Pierman turned to Kay, who had come forward when it appeared it was safe. "She wants to know why."

The pear-shaped man had moved closer to Pierman, too. "So why come here?"

Pierman put a hand on the man's chest. On instinct, he looked at the black man, who gave him one stiff nod of approval, and Pierman pushed him back.

"We know he was living some kind of secret life," Pierman said. "The cops need to know more about him to find out who killed him. His sister needs to know who he was to put her mind at ease." Pierman shrugged. "This looks like a place where people come to lead secret lives."

"Shit, that *is* true," the black man said. "Sister," he said to Kay, "you troubled, what you going to do if the answer isn't what you want to hear?"

Kay put her hand on the black man's large forearm. "Would you help us, please?"

"Let's see the picture," the black man said. He looked at it for some time, then handed it to the other two. "Looks like a bumper."

"Which is?" Pierman said.

"Somebody who ain't sure," the pear-shaped man said. His tone suggested he thought Pierman was stupid because he was not familiar with the term. "Somebody that don't know if he's queer. They just want to bump up against it and see."

"Or a bumpkin," said the older man. "Some hayseed that comes into town from the hinterlands to get his ashes hauled. Either way, both're kind of fun."

Kay looked directly at the black man. "He could fit either category."

The black man looked at her again, then down the stroll, to which a crowd had returned while they were talking. "Give me the picture," he said. "I keep telling you, nobody's going to talk to you."

He disappeared into the shadows for a time, moving from one knot of two or three to another. He came out onto the stroll where he stopped three or four men and showed them the photograph.

"That guy the president or something around here?" Pierman said to the other two men while they waited.

"A black guy?" the pear-shaped man said. "Yeah, and we're the fucking cabinet."

"Not the president exactly," the older man said, giggling. "More like the queen."

Twice during the conversation, Kay flicked away tears, but she said nothing.

"He's been here," the black man said when he returned. "But not for a while. Some people remember he came on weekends maybe four, five times, about a year ago, then he stopped showing up. Like maybe he decided he wasn't gay. Or like maybe he found somebody." The black man looked at Kay with a gentle expression. "It happens."

The black man turned to Pierman. "You don't know where you got this," he said sternly. "I don't want to see no cops around here, and I sure as hell am not going to testify."

"Have I asked you or anybody else your name?" Pierman said.

"No," the black man said, thinking about it. "But haul ass anyway. You're making people nervous, and we don't come here to be nervous. We come here to be unnervous."

The street lights drew orange, stroboscopic veils across her face on the way out of the city. She was still, in taut profile. If she blinked, it was in the shadows. She let him take her hand in the suburbs, covering his with the other for a moment before withdrawing them both. In the country, she turned her face away from him. Only the occasional cold headlight illuminated her. Her face would appear momentarily like an apparition on the side window, then dissolve into stars. The only thing she said during the trip, when they were nearly to Lindley, she whispered like a prayer. "God, he must've been lonely. And sad."

At her house, she folded her arms and laid her head back on the seat.

"He didn't like school," she said. "When Mama died, I came home for a couple of weeks and left. I'd get home as often as I could, but I didn't have to live there. He and Dad worked it out, and when it came time for college, he didn't want to go. He just wanted to stay here and work with Dad. You suppose he was afraid he'd find out what he already knew about who he was?"

"I have no idea," Pierman said gently.

"Well, Daddy made him go anyway. Said it'd give him a chance to change his mind about farming and make him better at it if he didn't. I guess Daddy got more'n he bargained for."

Thinking back to Grable's reaction when Calkins first asked about whether his son was gay, Pierman said, "Maybe he already knew."

A single light glowed in the kitchen window. She looked up at the second story for a moment.

"Randy asked me what to do, about going away" she said, "but what could I tell him?"

"That maybe you understood both sides of it."

She gave Pierman a long, inquiring look.

"Sorry," he said. "It's none of my business."

"He didn't listen to me anyway," she said. "He didn't follow the rows." She sighed. "If he found someone–anyone–who made him happy, I'm grateful."

Kay walked to the door with her head down, her hands behind her back, placing her feet, one in front of the other, carefully like a child on a low wall. At the door, she made no effort to find a key. It was unlocked.

"Maybe I should check," Pierman said, but she shook her head. "Then, in the future, use this." He touched the keyhole, avoiding her gaze. She looked back at the car, toward the city from which they had come, then at him.

"Personal or professional advice?"

"Does it have to be one or the other?'

The bolt snapped as he walked away holding in his mind a kiss that had chosen no sides.

11

The solstice fell on that Sunday. Pierman called Calkins when he awoke to tell him about what he had discovered about Randy Grable. Pierman could hear the voice of Calkins' wife in the background. She did not sound happy, and Calkins acted preoccupied. Pierman was relieved he did not have to go into detail about how he had learned what he knew; he merely suggested that it was background that needed to be pursued. Otherwise, for Pierman, Sunday was a lazy warm day of dreamy memory and vague plans. Monday turned out to be the longest day of the year.

Pierman decided the weekend surveillance report Darrell laid on his desk first thing that morning should not have been unexpected, either in the fact that it had been done or its contents. "Subject helped father work on truck Saturday. . . . Father practiced sermon while subject changed oil. . . . Subject at church all day Sunday listening to reruns. . . . Home both nights." Only Darrell could have withstood that tedium, and all he had to show for it were eyes that, in Carter's words, looked like two peeholes in a snowbank.

Pierman leaned back in the big chair and tossed the report onto the desk.

"All by yourself?" he asked.

"Mostly," Darrell said. He stood ramrod straight on the other side of Pierman's desk, looking over the top of Pierman's head. "Little help from the town boys."

"No need."

"So you said." Pierman caught the edge of contempt in Darrell's voice, but Darrell quickly blunted it. "You never know."

"Where's Joe?"

"Commissioners. We need a new car. Got to take care of business."

"Meaning it's been three weeks, we don't have much to show for it, and he's got a department to run."

"That's pretty much what that would mean. Yes, sir."

"Have I done something to offend you, Deputy?"

"No," Darrell's eyes slid away to the book shelves on the side of Pierman's office. "You, you ain't done a single thing."

Pierman was impressed. He would not have guessed that Darrell was subtle enough for innuendo.

"That's good," he said, "'cause I'm not the one who maybe took you off the Grable matter." When Darrell glanced at him, he knew he had scored. "That is, of course, if you were on it to begin with. And I certainly didn't tell you to spend your weekend babysitting Matthew Barton, particularly when his old man seems to be doing such a good job of it."

Pierman batted a paper clip between his hands on the desk pad, giving Darrell a chance to respond. He only stared straight ahead.

"On the other hand, I would understand the frustration of an ambitious young cop if he wasn't involved in investigating the biggest crime to hit this burg for decades or if that investigation had run out of steam."

"How would you understand that, exactly, Mr. Pierman?" Darrell said, lowering his gaze to meet Pierman's. "You're a defense attorney."

"Ah," Pierman said. He twisted the clip into an "S" then into a pretzel, smiling now that he understood. "You think they turned the fox loose in the henhouse," he said, looking up. "Is that the problem?"

Darrell's eyes rolled from one side of the room to the other.

"So, we're talking an absence of trust between police and prosecutor," Pierman said. "Well, deputy, I'm not sure that's a ditch I'll be able to jump any time soon."

"It might be," Darrell said, "if you handle this kid right."

"Meaning string him up."

The clip clanged off the side of the empty metal wastebasket.

"Deputy," Pierman said. "Out of curiosity, how much of this concern about my orientation is actually yours and how much of it is the result of whatever you've heard Sheriff Calkins say?"

Darrell said, "I'll go bring the kid and his dad in."

Matthew Barton entered with his father's hand on his shoulder. Support? Pierman wondered or something less: No shackles, please, officer; he'll come quietly.

The elder Barton no longer looked like the photograph of him with his family that ran in the church's newspaper ad each week. The round, boyish face of the ad was longer and lined, and the blond, wavy hair was duller. His wife, a small woman with a sharp chin, a hairdo that swirled high like cotton candy, and eyes obscured by the absence of makeup, always stood behind him in the photo. They always smiled. Reverend Barton frowned today.

The boy's attitude was harder to make out. He was short-haired and freshly shaved, so much so that one of the pimples he'd raked off his chin still oozed. He had his mother's build and his father's wardrobe, a white shirt and plaid polyester pants. Unlike his father, he wore no tie. Instead, three buttons on his shirt were open to reveal a scant dollop of manhood. His expression was blank until his father nudged him toward a chair. He scowled then, but sat down and stared at something on the front of the desk.

"Rights?" Pierman asked Darrell.

"Sure. Outside, in the hall."

"Just once more. For the record." He passed Darrell a form he had drawn from his desk. He clicked on a tape recorder that sat on one corner of his desk. Holding the form out and away from him like a hymnal, Darrell announced the time, date, and persons present, then chanted the rights to son and father.

The boy's gaze fixed on Pierman. Defiance and contempt stood ready behind a mask of fearlessness. In Chicago, Pierman had seen old people cross the street to avoid looks like that from the young, and Pierman, for an instant, felt old himself. He began to doubt that much was going to come of this.

"Do you understand, Matthew?" he asked when Darrell finished.

As though someone pulled a string on his chin, the boy's eyes closed and the corners of his mouth came down. His head tilted forward just short of a nod.

"Look at me and answer aloud, yes or no," Pierman ordered. It won an approving look from the father.

"Sure," the boy hissed, giving Pierman no more than a glance, contempt broken through. Pierman saw the father's hand clench.

"Do you understand, Mr. Barton?"

"Yes, sir."

"And neither of you wishes an attorney?"

"We believe in God and the laws of this nation," the elder Barton said in the measured, fully enunciated tones Pierman suspected he favored in the pulpit. "They will," the elder Barton said, "guide and protect us."

"If that were entirely the case, Mr. Barton, there wouldn't be any need for people in my line of work or yours."

The father looked perplexed and Darrell scowled. Only the boy smiled.

"Matthew, do you want an attorney?"

"I already said we don't," the father answered. "This boy is prepared to accept his punishment."

"Matthew, yes or no?"

The boy enjoyed another moment's satisfaction from the backhand to his father, but given his chance, he opted out.

"No," he said, "no, thank you."

A small break, Pierman thought.

"Matthew," he said. "Do you know why you're here?"

The boy shrugged. His father popped him on the arm with an open hand.

"Let's try again, Matthew," Pierman said to the boy while he scowled at the father.

"The books, I imagine."

"The books," Pierman said. "What're we going to do about the books? And what're we going to do about you?"

The boy had managed to sink fully into a slouch, his legs outstretched and crossed, his hands folded on his stomach, and his head fallen to one side. He stared at the front of Pierman's desk. He shrugged again.

It launched Darrell off the wall he leaned against. He bent over the boy's shoulder in close to his ear. "What were you doing three weeks ago today, the first?"

Matthew turned his head slowly to face Darrell. "What's that got to do with books?" The same question ran through Pierman's mind, but he could not inquire without making Darrell look bad so he bided his time.

"What's that got to do with the answer to my question?" Darrell said.

The boy's lips parted in amusement.

"You see something funny about this?" Darrell demanded.

"I was just wondering," the boy said, too much aware of his own precociousness, "is this going to be like a good cop-bad cop routine? Are you going to yell at me then let him be my friend?"

Darrell followed the boy's limp finger to Pierman. Are you? Pierman asked with upraised brows.

"Mr. Pierman is not a cop," Darrell said.

"Oh," the boy said.

Oh, Pierman thought.

"That's TV stuff," Darrell said, stepping back from Matthew. "Anyway, why should we have to do something like that? It's a straight-forward question."

The boy's chin rested on his chest, his eyes on his outstretched legs.

"'M I boring you?" Darrell asked. "I hurt your feelings?"

"I don't understand why you're asking," Matthew whined.

"You don't have to understand why!" The color had risen out of Rev. Barton's collar. He lashed his son in his best hellfire voice. "You tell him, boy!"

The father gave the other two adults a satisfied look of dispatch. Pierman saw the boy him side-eye a dagger at his old man.

"So, Matthew?" Darrell prompted.

"I don't know. Hanging around, I guess."

"Doing what?"

"Nothing special."

"Where?"

"Nowhere?"

The color had reached the elder Barton's cheeks. His head pivoted between Pierman and Darrell. He had been on the other end of conversations like this before.

Watching him, Pierman thought, God was lucky. There'd been nobody but Him to hear the apple bite. "Let's get back to the books," Pierman said.

"Let's let him answer my question first," Darrell said. "Is there some reason why you don't want to tell me what you were doing that day, Matthew?"

"It was a long time ago." Darrell's seriousness and the way he put the question seemed at last to be getting through. The boy straightened, trying, before he shook his head and gave up. "It's hard to remember."

"What's so hard about two, three weeks?"

"He would've have been with me," the father said through clenched teeth. "On the truck?"

Pierman caught another slit-eyed glance from the boy.

"That so, Matthew?" Darrell asked.

"Oh, probably." He put the chair back on two legs and rolled his eyes around the room. "There's not been just a whole lot of variety in my days lately."

If the boy had not been looking the other way, the blow might have broken his nose. As it was, his father's big, back-handed fist caught him just below the eye. Darrell was quick. He caught the boy's chair before it tipped, grabbed the father's hand on the rebound, and blocked his advance from the other side.

"You shit," the boy said, holding his face. "You fucking bastard."

"I've had enough of your devilment." The father struggled up against Darrell, who pushed him back into his chair and held him there by his shoulders.

"Get him out of here," Pierman ordered.

In one motion, Darrell pulled the father out of the chair, spun him, and pushed him out of the door.

♌

The boy rocked on his haunches, his hands covering his eyes. Pierman sat quietly, watching and trying to collect his thoughts. The tape ran out, the recorder snapped off, and the boy looked up. A welt the size of a silver dollar swelled on his cheek. His eye teared, but only from the blow. He'd live, Pierman decided.

"Get what you wanted?" Pierman asked, when he'd broken the boy's gaze with his own.

"He didn't have any right to do that."

"Certainly. It was entirely unprovoked."

The boy leaned his head into his short shirt sleeve to wipe his eye. Pierman reached behind him, took a box of tissue off his credenza, and tossed it across the desk.

"You don't know what it's been like," the boy said.

"Try me," Pierman said. The boy's surprised expression settled into suspicion. "The recorder's off," Pierman said.

"He works me all day. And he preaches to me. He makes me stay home and pray. I can't go out alone."

"Short leash," Pierman agreed.

"More than that. It's like a fucking test for him, like if he can wring the sin out of me, he'll get a promotion or something."

Pierman wondered how many other kids Barton's age could use the word *sin* without smirking. He leaned back in his chair and put his feet up on his desk.

"Our lessons for today will be Job and the Parable of the Good Shepherd," he said.

"Jesus." The boy threw up his hand. "You, too. That's just fucking great."

"That's twice you've used the all-purpose word. I'll bet you didn't get that out of the Bible." The boy fumed. "Relax, Matthew. It was a joke."

"That's all he lets me read." The boy was single-mindedly working himself into a fit of shrill, adolescent outrage. "He made me burn my books. Burn them! Made me! I can't get to the library."

"I wouldn't say you're the best risk in that regard."

The boy crossed and recrossed his legs. He folded his hands and pushed his thumbs together until they were white.

"You want to hear a fucking joke?" he said. "You want to know why people in my church don't screw standing up? Cause they're afraid someone'll think they're dancing." He had thrown the anger into a wider, deeper channel. "I have heard every sermon fifteen times," he said evenly, "and not one of them—not one—makes any sense to me. People at school know things I don't. I am missing things." His voice clenched. "He's trying to cut me off."

Pierman said nothing.

"I'm waiting," the boy said with a touch of the old defiance.

"For what?"

"The lecture. Honor thy father. The limits of civil disobedience."

Pierman smiled. "If you know the titles, you've heard 'em."

Disappointed, the boy probed the welt carefully with his fingers.

"What if I told people you guys did this? You and that pimply-faced cop."

"At your age, I'd be careful about judging a person by his skin condition." Pierman pointed to the box of tissue. "Wipe your eye."

"Well?"

Pierman entertained no thoughts that the boy had been involved in Randy Grable's murder, as apparently Darrell did, but he admitted to himself that Matthew was a devious little shit. He swung his legs off the desk and leaned forward.

"I grew up with that sort of thing," Pierman said. "Marches, protests, sit-ins. It never cut much ice around here. We like people to be nice around here, compliant, and that sort of stuff just made people tense or pissed them off. It's not the kind of material I'd use if I were trying to be a hero."

The boy stared, then dropped his eyes quickly. Pierman punched the eject button on the recorder and turned the cassette.

"I'm going to bring your father back in now," Pierman said. "Let's you and me agree you're done trying to kid a kidder."

He left the boy sitting in his office and the father in the reception area. He took Darrell into the hall.

"This subject, we're wrapping it up now," Pierman said.

Darrell stood with one knee crooked, his hands in his back pockets, appraising Pierman.

"You wanted your shot at closing the Grable case. You hijacked the interview. I thought I'd do you a favor, stroke your ego. I let you do it. Now I'm telling you, I'm wrapping it up and we're going to get on with the reason for this meeting."

"I'm entitled to an answer to my question," Darrell said. "There's enough ties between that boy and the Grables to ask."

Pierman almost laughed.

"Course, that's bullshit, Darrell. But just so you won't think it's the sleazebag defense attorney in me talking, I'll get you an answer. It probably won't be one you'll like, but regardless, we're done."

Pierman realized as soon as they returned to his office that he had managed to unite Darrell and the father against him. Darrell put no restraining hand on the elder Barton, and he joined the older man in glowering at the man's son.

"Reverend Barton," Pierman began.

"It's Brother Barton," the man said, cutting Pierman off. "No one of us is above the others."

"Mr. Barton, you're here because the law requires a parent's presence during the interrogation of a minor. I–"

"You will not tell me how to discipline my own boy. You have no right."

Pierman blinked at the man's conviction.

"In this office and in this matter, I do and will," Pierman said, matching him.

"He that spareth the rod hateth his son," Certitude buoyed the preacher's voice. "Thou shalt beat him with a rod and deliver his soul from hell."

"Hit him again and you will deliver yourself to jail." Pierman took a moment to restrain himself. "There are laws, Mr. Barton, against assault and interference with an investigation, and I will proceed with them all if you hit him again."

The man's hostility was fully focused on Pierman now, away from the boy, and for the time being, Pierman aimed to keep it that way.

"You said you believed in those laws. Consider it a rendering unto Caesar if you want."

Barton was silenced, but he'd had too much experience with the unwashed. He met and held Pierman's gaze, giving up wrath for unconquerable forbearance. Pierman stabbed the button on the recorder and turned his infuriated attention on the boy, erasing his knowing smirk.

"Matthew, whom do you hate?"

Darrell, who had scowled at Pierman throughout the exchange with the father, was as startled as the boy.

"I don't understand," Matthew said.

"Come on. We agreed there'd be no more of that. Whom do you hate?"

"The boy glanced at his father. An irrelevant answer. Even the father wasn't surprised.

"No one," the boy said.

"No one?" Pierman said. "How about the librarian at school?"

"Wasn't her fault."

"Ah, she was just doing her job? How about the principal? The superintendent?"

"What could they do?"

"You're very understanding." Pierman said. "I guess that leaves the school board. They were the ones who banned those books, weren't they."

The boy hesitated, considering.

"No," he said finally.

"No? You tried to get back at them once."

"Well, yeah."

"They've brought these charges," Pierman persisted. "You wouldn't be here, you wouldn't be in trouble at home, if it weren't for them."

"Well . . ."

"That make you angry?"

"I guess."

"Enough to hurt someone?"

Darrell had overcome his surprise. Pierman's sudden enthusiasm rekindled his own.

"Your dad tells me you hunt," he said. "Out there, while we were waiting, that's what he told me."

The boy's mouth opened, but he didn't know whom to answer and said nothing.

"Your dad says you sneak out to do it now," Darrell said. "That right?"

The boy caught his father's self-congratulatory expression with another sidelong look. He bit his lips.

"You never bring anything home, though," Darrell said. "Aren't you any good?"

"No," the boy said.

"Your dad says he locked up your gun after you trashed the school. What do you use?"

"What?"

"To hunt now," Darrell said. "What do you use?"

"Another gun."

"Where'd you get it?" You steal it?"

"No," the boy said, with an insulted expression.

"Then where'd you get it?"

"A friend. I borrow his."

"A thirty-thirty."

"A twenty-two."

The answer sidetracked Darrell. Pierman jumped in, but he was more kindly now, not a little afraid of where this was leading.

"Why do you do it, Matthew? Why do you sneak out?"

"I need to get away sometimes. To think. Relax." The boy addressed himself fully to Pierman. "People don't understand that. You've always got to have a reason for doing nothing here. "He—" the boy gestured at his father—"he told the neighbors to keep an eye on me, to spy on me."

Reminded of his own jogging, Pierman nodded and lost the advantage.

"Sure," Darrell said. "Nobody wants to come close enough to find out what you're doing. A gun scares them off. That right?"

"That's right!" The boy wanted to spit in Darrell's face. The words served instead.

"Matthew!" the father warned, rising.

"Sit down," Pierman said.

After a moment, Darrell said, "So maybe you went hunting three weeks ago."

The boy had covered his face. His hands moved with his head as he slowly shook it.

"I told you," the father said. "He would've been with me."

Pierman thought he heard a note of panic in it. So did Darrell. He turned on the father, sympathies abandoned. "All the time? Every minute? You didn't stop at the church? Have another errand to run, a delivery?"

From behind his hands, muffled, the boy said, "I did it."

Pierman had been watching the boy. He was faster.

"Did what, Matthew?"

"Killed that Grable guy." The boy put his hands in his lap and squared his shoulders. "That's what this is about, isn't it."

Pierman answered without meaning to. He looked at Darrell, who smiled.

"The father put his hand on the boy's head. "Oh, Jesus, Jesus, grant us–" The boy slapped it away.

"You knew what they were getting at all along," he said to his father. "Didn't you. Didn't you? But you were afraid to say. Just leave me in the dark as usual. No facing up to failure."

The fist coiled, but Darrell caught it and held it against the man's chest.

The recorder snapped off. Pierman jumped. "Shut up, kid," he said.

Again, he separated father and son, and again he and Darrell went into the hall.

"Don't pull this shit," Darrell said before the office door closed.

"That kid should have a lawyer."

"He's waived his right to everybody but you."

Pierman looked into the next office, trying to think it through.

"This could be the only way to close it," Darrell said. "We lucked out. "If it'll make you feel better," Darrell said, still pitching, "we'll check the story. Completely."

"This make you happy?"

"Not yet." Darrell shrugged. "Maybe later." He thought about it some more. "Maybe not then."

It was a day for sighs and shrugs. "Let's do it before he changes his mind," Pierman said finally.

"That's supposed to be my line," Darrell said.

The boy claimed he had snuck out on a day when his father had left him alone on the delivery truck while he went to pray over a gravely ill member of his father's congregation. The father did that occasionally, he confirmed, but he did not want his employer to know about that or the fact that the boy was driving the truck without a commercial operator's license.

"Faith healer," the boy said. "Like it did any fucking good. Brother Hampley died."

The boy's scorn was wasted. The father sat behind the boy, staring at his hands, which he held clasped between his legs. There was no sound, but his lips had not stopped moving since Darrell brought him back in.

"I drove the truck out, jacked it up like I had a flat, and sneaked through the woods," the boy was saying.

Despite the recorder, or in spite of it, Darrell took notes. "Time," he demanded, without looking up from a long, narrow pad he had drawn from his back pocket.

The boy's eyes darted across the front of the desk.

"I don't know," he said. "Eleven, I guess."

"Where'd you park?"

"On the Halsey."

"Where?"

"Along a fence."

"Where in relation to the woods?"

"Woods," the boy repeated.

"Yeah," Darrell said. "At the woods, east of it, west of it, where?"

"West," the boy said, after he thought about it.

It caught Pierman's attention. "Aren't you sure?"

"It was west," the boy said, addressing himself now only to Darrell.

"Then what?" Darrell said.

"I made for the wheat."

"Through the corn?" Pierman asked.

The boy paused. "No, around it." He spoke again to Darrell, avoiding Pierman.

"There isn't any corn," Pierman said.

It peeved Darrell and confused the boy.

"Yes," the boy said finally. "Yes, there is."

"So you waited and shot Randy Grable?" Darrell said, avoiding Pierman's eyes.

"I wasn't planning to." Pierman realized the boy was finally talking to him. "I just wanted to scare him. I mean I wanted to scare Mr. Grable. I . . . I was going to send him a note to, you know, threaten him. About the books."

"Who'd you think you were shooting at?" Pierman asked.

The boy's eyes darted.

"The old guy."

"Couldn't you tell?"

"He was a long way off."

"A long way off," Pierman repeated and the boy nodded.

"You were just trying to scare him?" Pierman repeated.

"Yes." The boy's head bobbed up and down like a doll with a spring in its neck.

"And yet you managed to put two shots in Randy Grable. One in his head and one in his chest."

"Yeah," the boy said defensively. He waited on certainty again. "It was a mistake. Like I said."

Darrell had held back too long. "Where's the weapon?"

"I–." The boy's voice dropped away. "The paper said you guys have it."

"We've got some of it. Where's the rest?"

"I won't say." The boy was firm about it. "I don't want to get anybody else in trouble."

From behind his back, Darrell pulled out pair of handcuffs.

"You can take us to it or you can sit in jail," Darrell said and squeezed one cuff around the boy's thin wrist. "I reckon you'll do both."

The boy looked at Pierman, then his father, who also looked to Pierman for help, a tear running down one cheek.

"I'll put this simply to you, Matthew," Pierman said. "You're fucking with us."

Darrell and the father were indignant, Darrell, Pierman supposed, because he thought Pierman was going to let the boy up and the father because of Pierman's language. The boy looked away.

Pierman sighed. "I don't know whether you're trying to carry your self-proclaimed martyrdom to its logical conclusion, or whether you're just trying to screw with your old man's head, but I do know that what you're telling us is shit."

"Pierman," Darrell said, in warning.

"Mr. Pierman, deputy," he said, without looking at Darrell.

The boy's eyes were full. "What do you want?" he whined.

"Not what you want," Pierman said. "Deputy, finish taking his statement, and turn him over to his father."

"You can't–" Darrell began.

"Sure I can," Pierman said, cutting him off. "Prosecutorial discretion. Put the cuffs away." Darrell stared. "Now, deputy." He turned. "Mr. Barton, he's not to be out of your presence or your wife's until you hear from us."

No one moved. Darrell glowered. The elder Barton looked at Pierman suspiciously, certain of another surprise to come. Matthew cocked his head back and forth among them like a confused bird. Pierman opened his mouth to explain, then thought better of it.

"Get out of my office," he said quietly.

Darrell slipped a hand under the boy's arm and roughly pulled him upright. Still staring at Pierman, the father slowly rose. He carried no clear face; if his hostility was gone, so was his forbearance.

"Pray for your son," Pierman said uselessly.

"For him?" he said, "or you?"

Pierman turned to the window. He waited until they were gone before he used both hands to knead his face. He let Darrell open the door, he held it, and the boy walked through it. He could easily be wrong, way wrong. He had only the terror-stricken eyes of an abject, mercurial boy to say that he wasn't.

"Whom do I hate?" he asked aloud.

12

Calkins tried to call Pierman that night, but Pierman had pulled the wire from the jack. Calkins went to Pierman's apartment and pounded on the door, but Pierman had turned out the lights, the bottle of Scotch at his elbow long gone. Calkins tried calling me, but I told him he damned well knew better.

It was a surprise to no one then that, after seething for the better part of the night, Calkins entered Pierman's office the next morning, told Ginny to get out, and closed the door. He began by asking Pierman to classify what type of an "idiot" and "asshole" Pierman was. He put both his hands on Pierman's desk, leaned across it, and asked Pierman when he was going to grow up and start acting like a man. He told Pierman that Carter was the only real prosecutor the county had ever had and that his son wasn't even a cheap imitation. He told Pierman that Pierman was making his department look incompetent, that Pierman had betrayed him. "God damn you," he said.

He said that if Pierman wanted to be a fucking defense attorney and turn every criminal in the county loose, he ought to get the fuck out of the prosecutor's job and let someone who would do the job have it. Then, out of meanness, because he had been reluctant to say anything about it before to spare Pierman's feelings, he told Pierman that Purcell had rolled up the stroll and found nothing. The boy, Calkins said, running out of steam, was it, all they had left.

"You done?" asked Pierman, who sat back in his chair and held Calkins' angry eye without blinking throughout the tirade. "Tell me the last part again," he said evenly before Calkins could respond, "the part about Purcell."

"You mean about the queers."

"I mean, the part about fucking cops acting like the Gestapo, ruining people's lives, and, coincidentally, burning any bridges we might have had to Randy Grable's background. And did I hear right? Purcell didn't find out anything. Tell me the part about why that should be a surprise. That's the fucking part I'm talking about."

From down the hall, I could hear the ire, if not the words. It had drawn a crowd. In the middle of it, Ginny, the prosecutor's secretary, stood on legs at odd angles in the manner of discomfited young women, her arms crossed, tears on her cheeks. A couple of older women, clerks from other offices, looked angry as they tried to console her. The county treasurer looked uncertain and concerned. The planning commissioner looked amused.

They did not see me when I first entered the office. I closed the inner door loudly to get their attention, and they both turned, startled.

"They killed my dog," I said.

Neither man spoke at first. Finally, Pierman said, "I'm sorry, Judge. You said . . . ?"

"I'm here to report an incident," I said. "And a condition."

Both tried to concentrate on what I was saying, but they were slow, each still untangling himself from their argument.

"Last night," I said, "about midnight, after Sheriff Calkins here called me looking for you, I let my dog out. You recall Humphrey, Allen. He was a Great Dane. You played with him when he was a puppy. I liked to sit in the back yard with him while I tried to decide a difficult case. He was a good listener, particularly after my wife died."

I was telling them more than was necessary and more than either of them had a right to know, so I hurried on.

"A man who lives two blocks away heard Humphrey rummaging in something in the alley behind his house. This man said he called out a warning, but Humphrey, of course, was simple and stubborn and did not respond. So this man shot him. He fired four times and hit Humphrey once, which was more than enough. He used a large caliber handgun. It tore away a good portion of Humphrey's chest. This man said he purchased the gun recently to protect himself after the Grable incident because, in his words, 'no one is safe 'round here anymore.'" Said he was sorry and shrugged, 'just glad it wasn't a kid.'"

Neither man spoke for a time. Calkins, apparently for lack of anything better to say, said, "Well, Judge, did you report it?"

I opened my mouth and closed it. "I am reporting it," I said. With one fist clenched on my thigh, I pointed at Calkins. "To you," I said and pointed at Pierman, "And you."

Both men took interest in the spines of the case books on Pierman's shelves while I tried to regain some measure of composure.

"I am reporting to you," I said finally, "not that my dog was shot, but that there is a state of uncertainty and fear in this community that has never existed before in my lifetime. Death, murder in particular, in case you didn't already know it, undermines peoples' confidence in themselves and others. As a rule, we don't like that so we try and do something about it. And I'm telling you that people, not dogs, are going to be hurt if you two do not do something about it and quickly."

When I had gone, Pierman and Calkins looked at each other for a time.

"You got nothing from the people Purcell talked to in the capital?" Pierman asked. "No information worth pursuing in Randy Grable's background?"

"No. Nothing."

"The boy, Matthew," Pierman said. "He come off his statement? He still say he did it?"

"He still says that."

"You still checking his story?"

"We're still out there."

Pierman turned to the window. "You're clear," he said, "you understand, we're about to destroy a boy's life not because we have good evidence that this boy killed another human being but because someone—a person this boy probably doesn't know—killed a dog,"

Calkins held his breath, hearing the concession.

"Bring him in," Pierman said, his back still turned. When he still felt Calkins' presence, he said, "Staying to gloat?" Pierman heard the door close then.

At the end of the day, as Pierman unlocked his car, Calkins pulled up, blocking Pierman's car from behind.

"Hop in," Calkins said through the window. He leaned over and threw open the passenger door. "Come on. I'm blocking traffic here."

Pierman bit his lips and threw his briefcase in his car before he went to Calkins and leaned in the open door.

"I'm tired, I'm hungry, and if you've been laying in wait to argue with me some more, I'm not interested."

"I'm glad to hear you're hungry 'cause I'm taking you home to dinner."

Pierman looked over the roof of the squad car, deciding.

"So you gonna be rude to my wife?" Calkins said.

Pierman sighed and got in.

As they drove through Lindley, each was intensely aware of the other, but distrust and uncertainty kept them quiet. Finally, Calkins slowed and lifted a finger from the wheel. "Seen Lindley's stab at urban renewal?

The high school they had attended was a square, three-story, brown brick donut of classrooms surrounding a gymnasium. Like the Courthouse, it sat on a block of green lawn all to itself. Now, it looked like the leftovers of some giant child. The top floor had been eaten away, but the first two remained with jagged scallops along the top of the walls.

It was to have been converted into apartments for the elderly, Calkins explained. After the new high school was built, the one outside of town, the old building sat around for two or three years before the school board found a buyer. A developer finally comes along and pays their price. He's going to demolish the place and put up apartments. The only thing, Calkins says, is he didn't know as much as he let on and he didn't count on the federal money for the project running out.

"He's in bankruptcy and there she is, waiting for guys like you to sort her out in court," Calkins said. Before Pierman could say anything, Calkins began to hum a tune that Pierman finally recognized as the high school fight song.

""Cheer, cheer for old Lindley High," Calkins sang out in an offkey baritone. "The expert came to town and left you high and dry."

Laughing, Calkins looked over to see if his guest was entertained. Pierman smiled, understanding that Calkins had put down a marker.

The house was nestled in the middle ring of neighborhoods between the very old and the very new. The front was covered in tan brick; the rest as far as Pierman could see was wood siding painted yellow. To one side, a one-car garage was attached by an awning, and in the lawn next to it, under an adolescent oak, lay a huge tire. Multicolored plastic cups and a toy tractor were strewn about the sand in the center. All in all, it was about the same as the others in the neighborhood. The houses were all low, one-story affairs situated near the front of the quarter-acre lots so that they formed a rectangle with the back yards adjoined in one long open space. Calkins told Pierman he and his wife now considered this their vacation home; the place they came to get away from their jobs. Pierman had to tune out the song about "ticky-tacky" that played in his head.

"Find out anything more about young Barton today?" Pierman asked casually as they walked around to the back door.

Calkins stopped, his expression pained. "No business here, okay, Allen. It's our rule."

"Your house," Pierman said. "Your rules."

Calkins shrugged and looked away. "I get called at home a lot, Gloria gets upset once in a while. I don't talk about it here anymore'n I have to."

"You fellows just going to stand out there and sweat?"

The woman Pierman had seen at the jail held the door open for them. She was barefoot and dressed in a tube top and shorts. She reminded Pierman a little of a clothes pin–short, round, and solid– and brown, bobbed hair only added to the impression. She called Pierman by his first name, introduced herself, and extended her hand.

"I've seen you on the street," she said.

"You should've said something," Pierman said.

"She's shy," Calkins said, and herded them both inside.

Pierman noted that she squeezed her husband's arm as he passed but did not greet him with a kiss. In the kitchen, she halted in front of Calkins and waited while he removed first the gun and holster on his belt then a similar packet strapped to his ankle and locked both in a cupboard above the refrigerator. She saw Pierman's bemused expression but she did not step away from Calkins until the ritual was complete.

She led them into a family room appointed in the shades of deep orange, gold, and bronze of a Holiday Inn. She told Pierman to take off his tie. "Shoes, too, if you want," Gloria said, extending her foot, wiggling her toes, and giggling. She asked what she could get him and ran down a list that included milk, juice, pop, and iced tea.

"How about a beer?" Calkins said, and Pierman said yes to that before he saw her frown.

"Make it two," Calkins said without appearing to notice. He dropped into a recliner, pointed Pierman toward a couch, and pulled off his shoes.

"She doesn't like me drinking in front of Skeeter," Calkins said when they could hear glasses clinking in the kitchen.

"And where is Skeeter?" Pierman said.

"Right here."

Calkins clapped his hands toward a short hall on Pierman's left where a small face peeked around a door. The youngster raced down the hall, inexplicably banged into Pierman's knees, and dove into his father's arms. Calkins held the boy above his head and smiled into his face.

"Your mama calls you Scottie and your daddy calls you Skeet," Calkins chanted, rocking the boy in time while he laughed and squirmed.

Gloria put the drinks on a table and stood back to watch this ritual with approval. Calkins let the boy fall into his lap and turned him around to face Pierman.

"Oh, Scott," Gloria sighed and stalked off down the hall.

The boy's right eye danced uncontrollably in its socket. He wore cutoffs, and he was what Pierman's mother would've called brown as a berry, but when Pierman looked closer, he could see the darker bruises running down his right arm and leg.

Gloria came back with a black patch and a pair of glasses, which she strapped around the boy's flailing head. "Leave them on," she scolded. Then she remembered her company manners and introduced Pierman as Mr. Pierman. The boy turned shy and buried his face in his father's arm.

"My friends call me Allen," Pierman said. "Maybe you could call me that."

The boy gave him a sidelong glance. "Ayan," he said.

"How old are you, Scott?"

"'keet."

Gloria had taken a chair opposite the men. She rolled her eyes at her husband, who pretended not to notice.

"Okay," Pierman said, "so how old's Skeet?"

The boy put up his last three fingers, leaving the thumb and forefinger in a circle that he looked through.

"Close," his father said quickly. "You have to multiply that by two."

Calkins held up his own hands in front of the boy's face and counted off six, describing long arcs in the air with his index finger as he moved from fingertip to fingertip. The boy was more intent on the rhythm and the motion that what they demonstrated. Pierman caught resignation settle on his mother's face. He decided against asking the boy where he went to school.

The boy ate like a sparrow. He was right-handed, and in order to fork a piece of the meatloaf or scoop a spoonful of mashed potato, he lowered his head and cocked it to the left. As soon as he put the food in his mouth, he righted himself to chew. The swift, jerky motions were hypnotic. Pierman ordered himself to concentrate on the meal and the conversation.

They ate in the kitchen. After the initial consternation with her husband and her son, Gloria seemed genuinely pleased to feed Pierman. She talked animatedly throughout the meal under prompting from his polite questions.

She had gone to school in the next county, found an opening at a bank here, and met Joe when he came to cash a check one day. They'd had a small wedding, and she'd worked for a couple of years before Scott was born. She kept busy now with church and a homemakers club and, of course, she was the jail matron, but someday she'd like to have a job of her own. It was disgraceful what the county paid, especially when you stopped to think about the shit–her word– officers had to put up with.

"Allen works for the county, too," Calkins said. Until then, he had been content to occasionally correct the boy's manners and smile at appropriate points in his wife's stories.

Gloria told them to keep their forks and replaced the empty plates with mugs of coffee and slices of pie. The talk flagged. It occurred to Pierman they did not have company often. The boy asked to be excused, and Pierman complimented her on the meal.

"I don't imagine it was much after what you must get in Chicago," she said.

"I eat my own cooking in Chicago."

"A single man like you doesn't go out?" she teased, then blushed. "With all the restaurants–and girls–to choose from?"

Calkins had risen to refill their cups. "Let's hear about life in the city, Allen. Ever been mugged?"

"Joe!" Gloria scolded. "He wouldn't live in a neighborhood like that. Do you, Allen."

Pierman knew he was being pushed out on stage. They–she at any rate–expected the guest's age-old gift, a song for his supper, and they, after all, had told him their story. He obliged under her prodding.

His neighborhood was all right, but nothing fancy, just apartments filled mostly with young singles and childless couples. Yes, it was near the Lake, within walking distance anyway, but the El was closer and that was more important. His work was fine–but like everything else a lot of drudgery sometimes. Sure, he went out sometimes. He liked a storefront place in Evanston where you had to bring your own wine 'cause of the liquor laws left over from its days as the home of the Temperance movement. He didn't really go to clubs that much, just parties with friends now and then. Girlfriend? No, no one steady. He'd been engaged once, but she had a career, too, and it just didn't look like it was going to work once they sat down and thought about it.

Pierman realized he was making it sound worse than it was. He wasn't dissatisfied with his life. It just wasn't anything out of the ordinary, and instinct, or maybe the memory of his confrontation with

Calkins earlier in the day, made him careful about leaving the impression he thought he was any better off than they were.

It played to mixed reviews. Calkins leaned his chair back with his eyebrows raised and his lips pursed, nodding in the pauses at his wife. He looked like he had been vindicated, although whether of Pierman's attitudes or his wife's, it was hard to tell. With each of Pierman's answers, though, the gaiety and playfulness that punctuated Gloria's first questions receded until she sounded curt and forced, then stopped asking altogether.

"I've been to Chicago," she said, standing to take their plates. "The sixth grade went to the Museum of Science and Industry."

Calkins lowered his chair, eyeing her carefully. The dishes seemed to be rattling more loudly than they needed to, Pierman thought, and when she bumped an elbow in her haste to reach rubber gloves under the sink, he heard her swear under her breath. Her shoulder blades rotated fiercely as she deftly swiped the plates in a cloud of steam, but after a few minutes, they slowed.

"Scotty'd like that," she said, gazing out the window above the sink as suds slithered off her fingertips. "The museum, with the German sub. Do they still have that, Allen?"

"So far as I know."

"And the coal mine? And maybe a Cubs game. And the lights on that big fountain down the lake at night. My sister had a postcard."

Even small dreams die hard. They assume new shapes and billow again, crowding those who don't believe. Calkins hunched over his empty cup.

"We'll see," he said. "We'll just have to see."

Her humming drove them out. After a time, Pierman rose and said it was time to go. Calkins jumped up and said it was early yet, come out and see the shop. When he stopped to pull a bottle of bourbon and two glasses from the cupboard where he kept his guns, Gloria smiled benevolently on them both. Now they stood in the garage, squeezed between a workbench and a candy apple red 1968 Oldsmobile Cutlass that appeared to be fully restored.

"Not the 4-4-2," Pierman repeated, gazing at the car. "The next step down, but pretty damn hot."

Calkins had said it every time someone even glanced at the car. Pierman could not count the hours they had spent in it.

"So you never got rid of it," Pierman said.

Calkins sanded a piece of wood he picked up from the workbench. "It runs good. Why would I?"

Pierman brushed away some nails on the bench and set his glass down.

"When I was little, my mother could never come to terms with how often she had to tell me no," he said, leaning back against the bench and folding his arms. "When she said, 'we'll see,' it was just her way of saying no."

Calkins scowled. He opened a drawer in the workbench, took out a pack of cigarettes and a lighter, and lit a cigarette. He gave a Pierman an angry glance before turning his head and exhaling a cloud of smoke.

"You could stay at my place," Pierman said. "It's not big, but I've got a couch that folds out." Without asking, he took a cigarette from Calkins' pack and lighted it.

"You're a son of a bitch to figure out," Calkins said evenly. "One minute you're giving me polite hell for the way I treat my wife, the next you're asking me up."

"I don't much care to be put on display," Pierman said.

Calkins held up the piece and sighted it into the light from a window. It was the wing of a toy plane. The fuselage lay on the bench behind a vise.

"I didn't know you smoked," Pierman said.

"Not steady since Viet Nam," Calkins said, "Once in while, when I drink." He ground out the butt on his shoe, stripped it down to the filter, crushed that, and put it in his pocket. "I didn't know you'd quit," he said.

"Not since I became prosecutor," Pierman said and thought better of it, remembering Calkins' no business talk rule. "What's that, an old combat trick?"

"I prefer to think of it as a survival skill, then and now," Calkins said. "God help me if I left a butt around for Skeeter to find."

As if summoned, the boy appeared at the door, dressed in faded, thin pajamas.

"Let's pyay," he said looking back and forth between them, his eyes alight with possibility.

Calkins cupped the boy's head in his hand and pulled him to his leg. He told his son he was going to talk to Mr. Pierman, then led him onto the patio where he reached into a beat-up pan. He held his hand in the pan for several moments and brought up a dripping, loaded water pistol. "You can squirt ants or something," he told the boy. Then, embarrassed at the sympathetic grin that crossed Pierman's face, Calkins elaborately bowed toward the lawn chairs.

Pierman put the cigarettes and lighter in his pocket and brought the bottle. It was two thirds empty. He could not remember how full it was when they started. They sat quietly for a while, sipping and watching the boy, who had taken up a position on the step. With his head forever cocked, he leaned over the pistol, holding it ready with his elbows on his knees.

"It's good exercise for his eye," Calkins said.

"What happened?"

"Born with it. Muscles." The corners of Calkins' mouth turned down. It was another subject not be discussed at home.

The sun took its time setting in the flats, even for June. It had snagged on a long blade of cloud and bled Day-Glo pink and orange over the edge. Pierman wondered how, if he had noticed them at all, he had described colors like that before he saw them on posters in college.

The smoke from grills and murmured conversations drifted up to them. Gloria was engaged in one of them, standing on a patio with another woman two doors away. The garage provided them some cover on the right, but it was open on the left and in front of them. Pierman looked down the expanse of back yards, but more than a glance seemed like an intrusion.

"How do you know when to stop?" he asked, mostly for something to say. "I mean how do you know when you're mowing your neighbor's yard instead of your own?"

Calkins snorted as if he had been thinking the same thing.

"Wait till he mows first," he said. "Some years the grass's knee high before anybody makes the first move."

Calkins sat forward, dangling his empty glass between his knees.

"Kind of a shame, isn't it, the front being just for show. It's like everybody's circled the wagons." He banished the somber tone with a click of his cheeks. "But people can't stay cooped too long. They got to come out one side or the other eventually."

It made Pierman think about Elizabeth.

"Ayan."

The boy aimed the squirt gun at Pierman. Pierman began to raise his hands and make a playfully horrified face when Calkins sprang between them.

"No!" Calkins wrenched the gun from the boy's hand. The plastic cracked when it hit the garage. "Don't you ever, *ever* point a gun at people." Calkins' finger stabbed the air in front of the boy's face. "I told you." He grabbed the child's arm, jerked the child toward him and smacked him on the bottom. "I told you that."

"He didn't mean anything by it, Joe," Pierman said.

"Stay out of it," Calkins snapped back over his shoulder.

At first, the boy was stunned. Then his mouth opened wide and his cry lanced the peace of the neighborhood. Calkins stood over his son glaring, but he would not touch him again in any way. Gloria came back at a trot.

"What happened?" The sympathy in her voice could've been as much for the father as the son. "Scottie?" She cradled the boy, but he cried too hard to talk. "Joe?"

"He pointed the pistol at Allen."

An element of menace in Calkins' voice warned her not to ask for more. Confused, she looked to Pierman for explanation, but he'd been warned once, and all she got from him was a terse, confirming nod.

The boy's howl rose again in protest as she took him inside. Calkins stared at the ground, his eyes darting in fury, then followed them.

Pierman poured himself a finger of bourbon. He drummed his fingers on his lips and watched the sky recede. If you held your mind right, it was like a wave receding down the beach, leaving behind glistening stars. He tried hard not to hear the lowered, hostile voices behind him.

They reappeared after twenty minutes or so. From the doorway, her voice quivering, Gloria thanked Pierman for coming and hoped they'd see each other again.

Calkins watched her quickly turn back into the house before he sat down. The light above the kitchen sink shined through the window and glinted off his watch as he emptied the bottle into his glass.

"She'd turned off the phone," he said. He raised the glass to his lips, but only tapped the rim against his teeth. "Found it when I went inside. Bad timing. That's what the shouting was about."

Down the property lines, other windows glowed. Through an un-shaded patio door, Pierman watched blue figures jitter on a television screen. Out in the middle, fireflies winked loops of gold.

"We've all been under a lot of strain lately," Pierman said. "Gloria must know that. And the boy'll have forgotten about it by morning."

"Could've had a call. 'Bout Grable, 'bout any damned thing. She knew better," Calkins said, still explaining. "Where're the smokes?"

Pierman handed him the pack and the lighter from his pocket and watched him light one. "Take me home," he said. "You ought to be in there making up to her."

Calkins stared out into the neighborhood and pursed his lips. He emptied his glass in a one pull.

"Can't," he said. "I'm drunk and I can't drive and as officers of the court neither one of us can let me out on the road without violating our sacred oaths to uphold the laws of this state."

Calkins didn't act drunk. His words were not slurred and his hand, when he brought the cigarette to his lips, was sure, but the bourbon allowed him to renounce constraint. When he sucked the ember down to the filter, a resolute face emerged from the shadow. He would have to do it. The whole evening had just been dancing, a tango toward the inevitable.

Calkins flipped the butt away. Watching sparks arc into the grass, having seen Calkins' face, Pierman began to understand the dread of priests.

13

"I'll tell you a bedtime story," Calkins began. "Call it a souvenir, something I carried back from Viet Nam, like chopsticks for my uncle."

Drunk or not, Calkins found the recklessness that goes with it appealing. He sat with his back to the illuminated window and most of his face was lost in the shadow, but for an instant, Pierman saw his cheek furrow in what may have been a grin. Then it left.

"Anybody who made it back to the World has one," Calkins explained, making it sound entirely reasonable. "The story he won't tell anybody else.

"You keep it to yourself. But you tell it over and over in your head cause it's so rotten it's like somebody else did it."

He rocked his head from one side to the other, weighing it still.

"'Course, maybe to another guy it's nothing. Guy in my outfit from Nebraska got shook about spending the night in a Saigon cathouse. We're lighting up people damn near every day and he's worried about what somebody's going say about him fucking a whore."

He barked a laugh, the irony enough to gag him. After a silent moment, he started again.

"Or maybe it was something you did to stay alive. Or"–he absently flicked away a drop of sweat that tracked down from his temple–"or maybe, in a few cases, it was rough stuff. My-Lai stuff. Cutting off ears and shit. Worse." He turned mildly scornful. "The news boys played that shit up. What'd they know? They could leave when they wanted. I mean it was there, but not as bad as they'd have you think."

Calkins paused, listening to the echo of what he had said.

"Well, it was there," he said. "But it was all the same thing, stuff so strange and crazy you'd never thought it possible. I mean they tell you about it. Poison shit on pointed sticks. The kids, little children, with grenades. But they can't begin really to describe it." He turned his face away deeper into the shadows, and his voice, a hollow whisper, followed. "Strange," he said. "So strange."

Calkins' hand rose, palm up, still reasonable.

"'Course, you could tell yourself a hundred good reasons for doing it at the time. You'd get your ass shot off if you didn't, you'd go nuts, somebody told you to. Or the best one, the A-number one best one of all, because there was absolutely nothing and absolutely no one to stop you. Probably that's where it starts. When you find out that one part of you has to actually tell the other part not to do something, and maybe you find out that one part's not up to the job."

Again, the words sounded no better to him now that they had been spoken aloud, and he waved them away.

"Whatever it was, it got worse when you got home—back to where people knew you—or thought they did. Real quick, you started weeding out the people who didn't really want to hear it and I can tell you back then that was most of them."

Calkins blew out air.

"Who could fucking blame them? There were a few—the superpatriots or the ones you were real close to—they'd ask how it was, so you'd tell them little things, you know, just to kind of test the water. Maybe you'd tell them how you got your scar or how your balls'd draw up tight when the rounds were coming in. But pretty soon, you just ran out of people. It was stranger to them than it was to you, and it didn't take long for them to start tuning you out. Even the old guys, the vets. My Dad. God damn. My Dad."

The sweat ran off Calkins now, and the faint, sweet scent of the booze in it reached Pierman. As if he sensed it, too, Calkins pulled a handkerchief from his back pocket and wiped his face in one rough, circular sweep.

"If anybody actually believed you, they hated you," he said. "Just wrote you off altogether. But most wouldn't—couldn't?—believe and that just—what's the word?—reinforced the way you were already thinking about yourself. Sure, you knew these things happened and somebody had to've done them. But if everybody's acting like it couldn't've been you, why then it must not've been you. Sure as hell, it had to be somebody else who did that thing you never got far enough to tell anybody about, and you get to thinking that if you tell yourself that enough, it'll be true.

"Almost does the trick, too. Other things creep in—money, jobs, family—so you don't have to convince yourself so often. But it always comes back, sooner or later, always, and it still doesn't add up so you keep it to yourself and you turn it and you turn it, like a pointy, little puzzle piece, looking for a way, some goddamned way, to work it back in."

Dim-witted, addled moths buffeted the window, uneven, percussion for the falsetto whine of tires on the highway beyond. The subject though, the one on the surface at least, had turned the music on its head. Just as it had everything else, Pierman thought. Calkins' low resonance had been the melody, drawing the night down around them like a string on a hood. Now that it rested, the lines that backed it leaped forth, nearly deafening, haunted and incomplete.

Calkins sat rigid, almost in a crouch, with clenched fists and arms that could have been strapped to the chair. Hesitantly, Pierman leaned forward and touched him. "Joe?" His voice was thick, gentle, the voice one might use to wake a child or a lover. Calkins heard, but without the touch, Pierman could not have been sure. He felt the hard ridge of muscle below the elbow sink back toward the bone.

"We don't," Pierman said, not bothering to finish.

"We do." Calkins turned a rueful face out of the night, and Pierman saw the grief there tendered like a shy gift. "We do," Calkins repeated and turned away, giving himself back to the memory and the shadows.

$\approx$

He cleared his throat and said, "I went in Sixty-Nine, the year after we graduated. The Army told me I was a good 'un, a volunteer, a man who recognized his obligation to his country. That was hardly it; I was just facing facts. Anita—remember Anita down at the draft board?—she kept me out long as I was farming, but when that went under, that excuse was gone. It didn't make much difference. I was fucked up anyway, didn't know what I was going to do. I figured what the hell, I'll join up, make a little money for once, and think about it.

"I went from plowboy to doughboy in three months. In less than six, I arrived in the land of the creeping red rice paddy. The short-timers, the ones who were close to rotating out, tagged me with Alfalfa 'cause of the farm. By the time I left, they still called me Alf, but damned few were left who could remember why."

Calkins was quiet for a moment, then laughed.

"My unit was kind of like that 'Up with People' group that rolls through here every three or four years, only no women and a hell of lot more lethal. The lieutenant was from out East, a ROTC guy who stayed with it and got his chips called in when he graduated. At the other end of the scale was this kid from Missouri who acted like he'd never made it past the sixth grade. They tried to teach him about windage and elevation, but it didn't make sense to him. He always figured if he fired too high the first time, he'd just aim a little lower the next. He got lit up by a sniper who understood the principles of marksmanship better than he did. In between was some more white guys, a bunch of black guys, and a Chicano. There was even this grouchy little Italian from New York, just like in the fucking movies.

"And it was just like the recruiter said. 'Plenty of opportunity for advancement for the right individual.' Shit. The corporal re-upped to get off the line, and I got his stripe. Mortar worked as an effective deterrent to the advancement of our sergeant and I had three. I told myself it was because I was a little older than most of the others, a little more mature." He shrugged. "Age seemed to matter quite a bit then.

"Whatever it was, it was working out. I was even kind of proud. I mean it wasn't like I wanted anything to happen to anybody, but it had and I couldn't stop it, so I was proud of where I was. But you didn't show it. I just tucked it away and tried to keep us from getting killed. Most days I was scared, but I was handling it. Hell, I was even able to send a few bucks home to the old man."

The sweat had reappeared on Calkins' face. This time, he wiped it away with the palm of his hand then wiped his hand on his pants leg.

"One day," he said matter-of-factly, "we'd been laying out after a couple of weeks in the field, the C.O. shows up with a captain and an A.R.V.N."

"Arvin?" Pierman said.

"Army of the Republic of Viet Nam. South Vietnamese."

Calkins shook his head. The sweat from his face flew off onto the patio.

"Immediately, I didn't like it. They wore no metal–no insignia, no tags. The C.O. hands us over and leaves, quick. This captain—he said he was a captain, but who knows; he gave us a name, too, but I'm sure he lied—this guy, he tells us load up. They choppered us down the way and marched us to one of the villages. When we get there, this captain tells us to set a perimeter. Nobody comes, nobody goes. There weren't more'n a dozen hooches, but the clearing looked good-sized and we weren't that many so I started trotting off to do my share. But this captain calls me back and says me and the lieutenant are going with him. I asked him what was up, but he's a real hard ass behind his aviators. No questions, he says; he'll tell us what we need to know.

"So we stroll into the ville. Bigger than life. Just the four of us, like fucking gunfighters. There's nobody out, but I'm thinking all anybody's got to do is roll a grenade out the door and we're meat. This A.R.V.N. character marches up to one of the hooches and yells something in. Me and the lieutenant had our backs to him and all I can see are eyes, just eyes, peeping at us from the cracks in the doorways. The slope yells something again. I couldn't understand what he's saying, but it sounded like orders, real stern and barky.

"Finally, an old man comes out and bows. A.R.V.N. flips him around and pats him down while the captain checks out the hooch. They shoved the old man out in the middle of the compound and push him into a squat and start interrogating him, you know, loud enough so everybody can hear.

"I'm thinking these guys've got awful good intelligence or else they're plumb crazy for exposing themselves like that. The lieutenant was thinking the same thing 'cause he tells me not to get too far away from the hooch where we're standing, and if we have to open up, aim low. He wasn't telling me anything I didn't already know, but I guess he'd spotted the eyes, too. If something happened, we were both going to write those fuckers off and make excuses later.

"The old man, the chief, had a lot of dignity, but they were doing their best to break him of it. A.R.V.N.'s squatting down, yapping in his face, and he's got the old man's hands on top of his head. Every time the old man's elbows start to droop, A.R.V.N. gives him a little poke to get them up again. The captain's standing over them, kind of looking away, but listening close. The chief started answering the questions real polite. A.R.V.N.'d yap at him and he'd say something calm and reasonable. But A.R.V.N. kept badgering him. He kept yelling at him and poking at him and jabbering and not letting him finish. Finally, the old guy got pissed. He said something angry.

A.R.V.N. whips out his sidearm. He puts it in the old guy's ear and some woman, in one of the hooches, she screams."

Calkins sat bolt upright, his hands locked on the armrests of his chair.

"I don't know what kept me from opening up right then," he said, as the intensity of the memory faded, and he relaxed. "I suppose it must've been the scuffling we heard inside the hooch, and the crying, which was sort of muffled. It'd made the whole damn ville blink. The doors were closed, the eyes gone. It was quiet. All I could hear was my heart pounding in my pot.

"It'd made that pair out in the middle jumpy, too, the sons of bitches. They'd pushed the old man away and had their automatics trained on the hooch. Then the captain told A.R.V.N. to put them away. The slope drags the old guy back up on his feet and barks at him. He's like a goddamn terrier dog–all high-pitched, nippy–but the old man just looks at him and will not say a thing.

"A.R.V.N. and the captain look at each other kind of like they're trying to decide what to do next. Then, the captain nods and A.R.V.N. starts shouting, standing out there in the middle, turning 'round, like he's calling home the cows. Nothing happens, so the captain says to us—me and the lieutenant—flush 'em. It was just some more old people and the rest women and kids, but I was kind of rough 'cause I was spooked. One of the women was young, and her face and pajamas were all dirty and she was sniffling. I guessed she was the one who screamed—maybe she was the chief's daughter or something—and I gave her some extra shakes she didn't deserve. A little guy with his leg off, a brother or a husband, was with her, and A.R.V.N. climbed his case until he showed him some papers.

"When we had them all out and lined up, A.R.V.N. barks some more questions, but nobody says anything. They all kept their eyes on the ground. Then, A.R.V.N. changes his tune. It's like a lecture, maybe a pep rally, with the captain standing off to the side with his arms folded like the principal and the old man as the visual aid. A.R.V.N.'s waving his hands in the air and pointing back at the old man, who's still squatting with his hands on his head. Then, A.R.V.N. goes down the lines again, asking again. He stops at a little boy and tickles him under the chin, like he wants to show them he's not a son of a bitch, but the kid wants nothing to do with him. He kind of hides behind his mother and looks at me and the lieutenant with big eyes like we're supposed to do something. Jesus, what could I do?

"Then when A.R.V.N. gets to the end, where the guy with his leg off is, he offers him his sidearm and points to the old man. The captain acts kind of surprised by that. He sidles over to me and tells me to take the guy out if he takes the piece. But the woman's going crazy again, screaming and pounding on his chest, and the guy with his leg off just shakes his head.

"A.R.V.N. shrugs and looks at the captain for the go-ahead on the next step. I'm waiting for them to tell us to torch the place and trying to decide if I'm going to go along with it. But they don't. They drag the old fellow over to a tree and tie him with his back to it and his arms bent back around it. The captain pulls out a syringe and gives it to A.R.V.N. and he sticks the old guy. He says something short—couple of sentences maybe—to the people then he goes over and parks himself in the shade at the edge of the compound. The captain motions us over, too, and we're all supposed to sit down.

"I was damned glad to get off my feet, but I was still pretty edgy so I just took a knee 'cause I figure we may still have to get out of there quick. The lieutenant's down, too, but I notice he's got his weapon pointed at the crowd. The other two are just talking. They're chatting away in Vietnamese and taking sips from their canteens, waiting for the goddamn show to begin.

"It didn't take long. The old man's eyes got glassy and his head sagged like he was going to sleep. His legs'd buckle and he'd have to push himself up 'cause it hurt his arms when he sagged. But the old boy was a fighter. He'd slip down and he'd prop himself back up and he just kept doing it until finally he couldn't anymore, and he just hung there. He was so still I thought he was dead, and his people must've thought so, too, 'cause they've got their faces in the dirt whimpering. The captain kind of forgot himself in the middle of all this. He said, 'Looks like he's pacified.' He said it in English and looked over real quick to see if we heard. I pretended I didn't. Then he must've repeated it in Vietnamese 'cause A.R.V.N. laughed. The cocksucker laughed.

"But nobody's making any moves to leave. I mean, if the old guy's dead, they've made their point and I am ready, really ready, to get the hell out of there. Shit, it seemed like hours we sat there and nobody moving. And all the time, I can smell myself. The heat's coming off me and right up my nose and it was strong. There'd been a lot of times when I'd gone without washing, and after a while, you don't notice anymore. But when you start smelling yourself again, it's a bad sign. It's what animals, predators, smell, the fear.

"And then it started. The old man's hanging there and then he mumbles something, real quiet at first. Then he seized up. It was quick and hard, and his head bonked the tree. It must've been hollow cause it sounded like someone knuckling a ripe melon. That woke him, sort of. His eyes opened for a second and he said something and then he slumped and was quiet again for a while. Then it grabbed him again and his head hit. It lasted a little longer this time. He was shaking when it let go.

"The people were shocked at first; they acted like they'd seen a ghost. And the wailing started. The girl, the one I shook, she made a dive for the old man but the guy was too quick for her, even with his leg gone. He got her down and held there. A.R.V.N. raised his sidearm and threatened them, but they're all crying and not paying him any attention.

"A good one took the old guy about then. He thrashed 'round and hit his head four, five times. Jesus, it sounded like a woodpecker. Rapid. He's babbling something, maybe cussing A.R.V.N. 'cause that's who he's looking at when he gets off it. And then his eyes go glassy again and roll back into his head and he's pounding the tree again and again. He's jabbering and frothing and it's flying all over the place as he's hitting the tree.

"I'd seen people die, but Jesus, never like this. Never. The man's beating himself to death, and we're letting him do it. The women are holding their screaming kids for dear life. They're moaning and howling and rocking. I can't even hear his head thumping anymore, but I can see it and feel it every time he makes contact and I'm sure, dead fucking certain, that if it doesn't stop I am going to lose my mind. And just when I know I'm going right over the fucking edge, the old man screams. From way down deep, he screams. A-A-I-I-E-E. Right up the scale, every note, every fucking note, until his breath is gone."

Calkins panted, his breath gone, too.

"It was so quiet," he said finally, just shy of a whisper, in awe. "I mean the only sound is the kids whimpering 'cause the people've had the bejesus scared out of them. I don't know if the old man's dead or not. I'm sitting there with my head in my hands trying to hold it together, trying to sort it out and thinking God, it's over now.

"But the spasms still had him, see. He's still thumping but slower and it sounds kind of squishy, like somebody's pounding wet sand. I guess I couldn't believe it 'cause I looked up and there's that kid again, the one A.R.V.N. tried to get friendly with, staring at me. He wipes his nose with his hand but he won't take his eyes off me. And the others, they're looking at us, too. Lot of hate, and I'm feeling very exposed again.

"Next thing I know, I'm on my feet, aiming. I've told myself I just wanted to put the old guy out of his misery, but I don't think I really knew what I was going to do. I was all ready to squeeze it off when the captain tells me 'sit.'

"Like a dog, the way he said it, and I figure fuck him. 'Sergeant, look at me,' he says. I didn't want to. I didn't ever want to do anything that motherfucker said again. 'Look at me,' he says. 'Now!'

"I heard the click. And I knew what it was. And I looked. He's pointing his sidearm at my head. The son of a bitch was going to shoot me. 'Put it away,' he says, 'and sit down.' The people are watching this all very close, but it didn't make any difference. The old guy had stopped. He was just hanging. 'Sergeant!" the captain says. "Now!' Maybe he said it. Or I could've imagined it, but I did what he said. I just sat down."

$$\mathcal{D}$$

With the image of the chief before him, Calkins had flailed, too. Pierman thought he would tip the chair. Now, he was quiet, shrunken and drained. Pierman touched his arm again, sighing once deeply and looking away. All the other lights in the neighborhood were out now, and the night creatures had gathered above their heads in a frenzied attack on the glass.

"I'll be back," Pierman said.

He opened the door quietly, found the light switch above the sink, and turned it off. The drumming died away. But he could not wipe away all traces. The moon was in its third quarter, a vertical, cataracted eye that still reflected enough light to make the white handkerchief Calkins held to his face glow.

Pierman lighted a cigarette and nudged Calkins.

"Here," he said.

"So?"

"What do you want me to say?"

"Whatever you got on your mind."

"I'm still here."

Calkins could only nod.

"You did what you could, Joe."

"Wasn't much, was it. Can you stand the rest?"

"If you can."

Calkins thought that was the funniest thing he had ever heard. He laughed and laughed until he had to wipe his eyes with the handkerchief.

$$\mathcal{D}$$

"When it was over," he said after some time, "A.R.V.N. went to make sure the people got the point, whatever the hell it was. While he was doing that, the captain plopped himself down in front of us to make sure we did. I thought I was too numb, that I wouldn't hear him, but I did, every fucking word. We had just participated in a classified operation. The chief had been aiding the enemy. That was it, the whole explanation. Nothing about duty or patriotism or protecting our comrades in the field. Nothing to put a fine finish on it. This guy knew what we'd done. He was a pro.

"And the operative word was classified. We weren't to discuss it with anyone—our superiors, other guys in the outfit, nobody—and naturally, he had a whole fistful of incentives to encourage our coop- eration. He'd see to some passes if we needed them. Promotions'd be coming down soon, and if the rest of our records were good, we'd have no problems.

"But if we fucked him, there would be consequences, he said. Like court-martials for violating military secrets. I was too young and ignorant to realize it until later, but that was bullshit. Nobody in the Army'd want to push that shit out into the open.

"No, the real threat was the people in the ville. They knew what we looked like, he said, and we'd be dead if they told Charlie. He'd be leaving the area today, but we were staying. Double-cross him, and his A.R.V.N. friend had ways of making sure Charlie found out. I don't know if what he said was true. All I knew was I wanted to kill him right there and then. And he knew it. On the way out, he stayed behind me all the way.

"The other guys were itching to find out what happened—all the noise and crying and not a shot fired—but I didn't say anything. The lieutenant and I didn't even talk about it to each other. A pass came down a few days later. I knew where it came from and I hadn't asked for it, but I took it. I went to Saigon and trolled every dirty, filthy fucking place I could find. And all the time, I'm asking myself why me? Was there something in my record that made somebody think I was that vicious? Or was I just handy at the time?

Calkins snorted and shook his head.

"The only answer I got was what they'd done to the old man. An MP sat down next to me in one of those places. He's off-duty, wearing a loud, flowered shirt, but still doing the big, stupid MP bit. You know, warning boonie boys about the dangers of Saigon's seamier side. As if he knew shit. Well, he starts with the hookers and all the stuff they've got that'll rot your cock off down to the nub, but pretty soon he gets around to drugs. There's heroin, he says, comes down out of the mountains and they call it Ivory 'cause it's ninety-nine and so many hundredths percent pure. Saigon dealer'll give a guy a dose and he's hooked. Soon as he comes down, he goes into withdrawal and they've got themselves another customer. Stay away from that shit, he says. He was so fucking stupid I broke his nose.

"I'd overstayed my welcome by that time anyway. I got back a couple of days late, but nobody seemed to care. Hell, they were so damned glad to see me they had a promotion waiting. The lieutenant already had his and he was long gone. New outfit. Far away. I told them to stick it. I had two months to go, I said, and I was plenty happy right where I was.

"I wasn't, 'course. I was scared to death. I said I wasn't sure whether to believe the captain but that's now. Then I did. On the other hand, I wasn't going to let that animal buy me off like that either, and I guess it made me crazy. Most guys when they got close to their time got real cautious, and I didn't go out of my way to find trouble in the field. Hell, I spent most patrols looking over my shoulder, but I did a couple of hairy things when trouble came my way. Like when the sniper took out the kid from Missouri. I just stood up, in full view, and lit up the tree. Didn't aim, just emptied the magazine. One guy said I got him a time or two on the way down, too. Crazy shit like that. I wanted out of there so bad I didn't particularly care if it was dead or alive."

Pierman searched for anything that was hopeful. "But you got out," he said. "And alive."

"Alive," Calkins repeated, as if the word were new to him. He paused to think about it, then said, "You ever ask yourself if you should've gone?" Calkins searched Pierman's face and gave him a cockeyed smile when Pierman did not reply. "I know you have. I can see it in your face. Nothing to be ashamed of. Everyone who didn't go asks himself that. Even the ones who marched, at one point or another, they've asked. I mean, hell, we were the fucking sons of John Wayne, that famous Green Beret, so you got to wonder, don't you, if he wasn't right? 'Am I less a man 'cause I haven't been tested in battle?'

"My opinion?" Calkins said quickly, to cut off any response from Pierman. "Maybe. Maybe so. But the thing you got to remember is the price to find out is pretty damn steep. And after you pay it, you're always wondering what you gained and was it worth it." He laughed. "Seems like everybody's got some damned question, don't they."

"I came back here," Calkins said. "Had to. I had to get back to someplace where I knew what was right and what was wrong. It doesn't change around here. And I was lucky. People didn't especially want to hear any war stories, but nobody called me a baby killer or anything like a lot of other guys got. They might've hated the war for what it did, one way or the other, but nobody was blaming me for it. Hell, the Kiwanis asked me to speak to them, like I was a hero or something. But I mean it wasn't like somebody's trip to the Holy Land or winning their scholarship, was it, and I just didn't feel up to it.

"And that was all right with them. People just let me be and that's all I wanted, some time and some room to put it back together. I knew I could do it if I had that.

"It was pretty hard at first, but I got a job mixing feed at the Co-op and they kept me pretty busy. I didn't mind. It kept my mind off it. But I was drinking pretty hard then, at night, at home. Dad—I'd moved in with him--Dad didn't care for it, but I didn't want to go to the bars or the Legion or anyplace like that 'cause I was afraid I'd get liquored up and do something foolish. Besides, there weren't many people our age still around. They were like you, gone off somewhere to make their fortune."

"You could've called," Pierman said, but they both knew it wasn't so.

"And just what could you have done? Hell, man, you were still in school. How could you understand?"

Calkins stopped short, regretting the scorn some but not much. He shrugged.

"I wasn't fit to live with anyway. I mean, I was mad as hell at guys like you who got out of it. And if I'd found out you marched on top of that, you would've had a real problem on your hands."

"I didn't," Pierman said.

"Well, I guess it doesn't make a hell of a lot of difference now anyway," Calkins said and sat silently for a time.

"I almost called you once," he said. "But I figured it'd just open a whole new can of worms."

"What would?"

"I wanted you to thank your dad for me." Calkins shifted in his chair. "You've probably seen stories about guys who came back having nightmares and hitting the dirt whenever they heard a loud noise. I did, too. In the beginning. The first time was downtown under your father's office. Somebody hit the brakes to avoid an accident, and I'm on the sidewalk with my arms over my head. Busted my nose, I went down so hard. All these people are standing around looking at me, and I'm feeling pretty stupid, but your dad comes down and tells them to get the hell away. He gave me his handkerchief for my nose and asks me what's the matter. When I told him nothing, he just patted me and sent me on my way, like it happened every day. It was the most natural thing in the world as far as he was concerned, and there was nothing to be ashamed of."

Calkins hesitated. "I imagine he talked about it later." He made it sound more like a question and left an opening. "It's all right if he did, you know. Hell, everybody 'round here talks."

"I don't remember," Pierman said, lying. The old man had never said a thing about it, not in his son's presence, but it seemed so important to Calkins, who took his time digesting Pierman's answer.

"Well," Calkins said. "Well, maybe he didn't. And I guess I never got around to saying thanks." Calkins tapped the chair arm several times, then stood. "I should've said something 'cause he did me another favor, I think, later."

Again, Calkins paused, but Pierman still had no answer for him.

"I was handling it pretty well by then. In fact, I thought I was just about over it. The nightmares—they were always about that kid looking at me only I was the one in his place, sitting in a slope woman's lap rocking and hearing her howl in my ears—the nightmares were slowing down. I'd even stopped in at the Legion a couple of times and nothing'd happened.

"Anyway, it was at the fair. I'd been looking at the cattle and kind of thinking how we'd raised better. Some kids, maybe nine, ten years old, come rolling through the barn. They were playing grab ass and throwing cap balls. The noise and the commotion were spooking the animals. Me, too, for that matter. It made me feel kind of tight, quivery, you know, nervous; but I'm doing pretty good, I'm past the diving-for-cover stage. Then one of them brushed me—just sort of tapped me on the butt—and I grabbed him. Allen, Jesus, I nearly broke his arm. So help me, I almost broke his fucking arm.

The only thing that stopped me was the look on his face as I shook him. It was straight out of the nightmare, the look. I let him go and bolted."

Calkins stood, paced the patio once, and escaped back to his chair.

"For a while, I just drove around, shaking. Believe it or not, I felt worse about what I'd done to that boy than the old man on the tree. All I could think about was what I'd become. How it was never going to go away, and if it didn't what was I going to do? To me, to somebody else."

Out of the blue, Calkins laughed.

"So I turned myself in. I marched up to the jail at midnight, pounded on the door, and told Carl Teague, the sheriff then, here I am, this is what I did, lock me up. Carl, he was hardly the brightest bulb in the lamp, he scratches his head and puts me in the office. I heard him talking on the phone in his apartment there, but I couldn't make out what he said. A little later, somebody comes in and there's more talk.

"Whoever it was left and Carl comes back to read me the riot act. It was mostly half-hearted, about knowing better than doing what I did. He's going to keep me overnight to give me some time to think about it, but since I'd turned myself in and since I'm a vet, he's going to make me a trusty. I'm going to check the cells and keep things quiet. I'll help him serve breakfast in the morning and then he'll see what to do with me.

"The whole thing sounds far-fetched now, but I was so screwed up that night I just went along with it and then in the morning he turned me loose. He says it seems I've got too much time on my hands and he'll take care of some of it, if I'm willing. He'll make me a jailer on nights, weekends. He hasn't got much money to pay me, but if I think I need looking after, he'll do it in exchange for the work. Shit, any place else they'd've sent me to a shrink, but here they think a little work'll cure anything."

"And so, pretty soon you became a deputy," Pierman said.

"You don't have to sound smug. It's not like you did anything. It was your father."

"Joe, I don't know who it was."

"It sounds like him, though, doesn't it?"

"In some ways. What difference does it make?"

Pierman sensed they were almost back to where they started. The direct path, once they agreed to follow it, had led them back to the maze at the beginning. Calkins was still the guide, but now he sat silently, deciding whether to continue or end it here. And whether the one he led was still willing.

"I got pissed off after a while," Calkins said finally. "Here I was working two jobs and neither one paid for shit. I'd had my fill of long hours and rude inmates, and like it wasn't me who started all of it in the first place, by God, I was going to find out just what the hell was going on. I went roaring into Carl's office and unloaded on him. He just smiles. 'If you're as mad as you act," he said, 'you're making progress. Don't screw it up. There's some people think you show promise.'

"Promise! Get that? It's what people'd been stringing us along with all our lives. Remember Booth's class? Current events? Clip out a newspaper story, tell it to the class, and there's your A. Well, I never paid much attention until that summer we graduated. At commencement, they give us the bit about we've all got promise. If anybody's going to straighten out the world, it's got to be us, the pimply, horny little hopes of the world. Martin Luther King's dead, blacks are burning their cities, and Bobby Kennedy's going to wind up dying in a kitchen with a waiter holding his brains. Nixon's going to get us out of the war so I don't have to go, but first cops have to beat the shit out of hippies in Chicago."

Calkins checked himself and sighed.

"Sometimes all that stuff—the war, civil rights, free love, baby— it all seemed far away, out of reach, but when you talked to people they all seemed mad or sad and then you knew it was closer than you thought. I began to think there's not much use in promise, and I knew it after Viet Nam. It was a leash, holding me back when I wanted to run and dragging me on when I wanted to stop. It was just a word and somebody else's at that, but here's old Carl, telling me with a perfectly straight face that somebody believes in it, just like before, and I've got to believe it too or I'll screw up."

Calkins had run out of breath. Pierman heard him panting and realized it wasn't the same trip. Beyond the last stop, it was uncharted. Calkins had simply ducked his head and run. Now he'd hit a wall of pride and confusion, and it was Pierman's turn to lead.

"So you believed."

"Yeah!"

Calkins kicked away the chair. He prowled the patio a couple of times, then went to the edge to relieve himself. When he was done, he remained standing with his back to Pierman. He sucked in the humid night air and let it out slowly.

"Was there anything else?" Calkins said. "The good folks of Lindley were giving Alf, the homicidal feed-sacker, his second chance. He had to be grateful and that made him willing."

"It's nothing to be ashamed of."

Calkins wheeled. "Damn it. I'm not."

"Then don't give me bullshit about homicidal feed-sacker."

The bluntness of it set both back for a moment.

"It's just that I've swung back so hard," Calkins said. "There didn't seem to be anyplace to stop in between."

"And now you think you've got to carry the whole town? The county?"

Calkins slumped back into his chair.

"Sometimes," he admitted grudgingly. "But don't you see? That's how I started. Maybe I could live up to that promise if I just set my sights a little lower. I'll just take care of Lindley. Somebody else'll have to deal with the rest of the world. It should be easy. Everybody treats each other all right around here; I'll just be there to take out the odd ones."

"I think you're setting yourself up for a lot of disappointment, Joe."

"You would," Calkins said.

After they had glared at each other for a time, Pierman rose and walked to the edge of the patio. He was stiff from sitting so long. He put his hands under his belt and pushed against his lower back.

"And you came to the funeral to say thanks to the old man," he said, unable to keep the accusation out of it.

"I felt bad about you and your mom."

And now, after everything else, you've decided to be awful damn meek about it, Pierman thought. Again, Pierman sensed Calkins' struggle, the welling of instincts that told him to hold back and the summoning of will to wade out of them. And Pierman was tired of it, exhausted from throwing out the line and seeing it batted away, throwing again and missing.

"Joe, let's cut the crap. Why'd you invite me here tonight?"

Calkins looked at him and shrugged. "I didn't want any hard feelings after you changed your mind about bringing in the Barton kid. I wanted you to understand."

"Well, I got to tell you it hasn't worked. I'm clueless."

Calkins clasped his hands between his knees and leaned forward over them, his lips pursed. He looked up. "I said I'd swung back hard and couldn't find a place to stop in between. You would've. You always did. You do. You always see the other side and hold back a little."

Calkins rose and came to face Pierman.

"I've already got that disappointment you talked about. That kid in the field. Shot in broad daylight and burned to crisp. It was vicious and senseless, just like Viet Nam, only it wasn't strange people in a strange place. It was here. It made me scared again and mad and sad. And God *damn* you for making me say so."

For an instant, the light from the dead eye above them caught in Calkins' own, glittering and wild. Pierman's back stiffened. Then, Calkins blinked and turned.

"No jungles, Allen," he said, looking back over his shoulder. "Not here."

He put his hands in his pockets and bowed his head. He exhaled with force and pulled himself erect. "I'll get my keys."

Pierman stopped after a block and looked at his watch, twisting his wrist this way and that in the dark. It was after midnight and quiet above the sizzle of crickets. A barking dog somewhere off behind the houses reminded him of the volume of his steps on the pavement against the night.

He had declined the ride. He didn't know whether to be angry or sad, but he knew he wanted no more bush-league analysis. Calkins hadn't pressed. "I'll see you then," he said, and went inside. Pierman grabbed his jacket and cut east to the highway.

The bright lights along the highway made Pierman's eyes ache. In the distance, he could hear a semi entering Lindley, running the state road late to avoid the weigh stations on the interstate. The truck grumbled as it ran down the gears and the axles clanged over rough spots. Pierman came to a side street and turned down it quickly. He had not realized how raw his senses were.

The trouble with Calkins was the trouble with Lindley, Pierman thought. They presumed–on friendship, on history, on blood. People should have the courtesy to ask the mule to bear their burdens. He kicked high, scuffing his sole on the pavement, then laughed out loud at the public display.

Light from street lamps dripped through the trees into ragged yellow pools on the walk, and as though he waded through them,

Pierman felt refreshed.   He rarely walked in Chicago at this hour, he thought, and when he did, he stayed at the edge of the walk, away from buildings, where he could be sucked into an alley. Calkins was right about one thing at least. Lindley held out time and room to put things together.

Another light, above the street lamps, glowed in my house as he passed it. I did not understand either, Pierman thought when he heard a storm door stretch open ahead. Probably someone letting a cat out, Pierman guessed, but he veered into the street beyond the parked cars anyway and maintained his pace against the slow, bumbling seconds. Damn cops and judges for ghost stories, he thought. Finally, behind him now, the door sighed shut and a lock snapped, one last foreign sound.

Alone again, Pierman gave himself up to the impulse. He started to trot, an easy pace, not out of fear or away from anything. He moved like the moths, toward the pools, from one to the other, a little bit faster to reach the next. He felt blood stretch his veins and wind cool his chest. He could run to morning, if he did not reach home first.

14

Corn should be knee-high by the Fourth of July, they used to say as a rule of thumb. They still say it. It's traditional. It rhymes. But despair surely would mark its utterance now if the rule still applied.

Along the narrow, flat, back roads, the tough field hybrids, shocked by acrid chemicals, had already grown chest-high or more to form impenetrable walls on either side of Pierman's low-slung car. Propped up by the corn, the hazy white sky splayed, here and there, dropped like parachute silk to drape soft canopies of beans in adjoining fields, then jerked up again to rest on the tall stalks. Itched by dusty tassels and fuzzy leaves, the sky seesawed on the car, syncopated all the more by green monotony of the severely truncated landscape and the speed at which he drove.

Pierman parked across from the woods. The sun was not yet high, but the air was already thick with the moisture and dust it percolated off the crops. Sitting low, looking up and above the trees into the brilliance, Pierman was for a moment nauseous and dizzy and thought he could not breath. When it passed, he climbed out, removed his vest and tie, and threw them onto the seat with his jacket.

When he slammed the car door, a lookout crow issued a raw call to the flock to retreat back into the woods. A human counterpart wasn't far behind. A pickup truck slowed, and the driver hoisted himself up to look in as he rolled past Pierman's car. The brakes bawled behind Pierman as he searched for a place to climb the fence.

The driver said, "Lose something?"

Horseweeds and brambles had grown higher than the fence since the last time Pierman was here, and he saw no sign anyone else had been around since then.

"No," said Pierman, who continued to look for a place to put the first step.

"I know you?"

"If you've got to ask," Pierman said, turning now to look at the driver, "probably not."

A middle-aged man leaned out the truck window. He wore a red baseball cap advertising fertilizer, and his cheek bulged with a tobacco knob. The side of his face that was not drawn tight by the chaw was slatted and weathered. His expression implied he did not care for strangers with smart mouths.

"Illinois plates." The man jerked a thumb back over the truck bed toward Pierman's car and recited the number. "Any reason our sheriff shouldn't know that?"

"None that I can think of."

The man revved the truck in time with the working of his jaw.

"We had some trouble around here," he announced and spit. "Mind if I ask what you're doing?"

Pierman gave up and introduced himself.

"Hell," the man said, "that's different."

He turned off the truck and pushed back the cap. "They can go around," he said, although there was no traffic to do so. "How's it going?"

Pierman almost laughed. "You're taking me at my word?"

"Looked like lawyer clothes on that seat back there," the man said and spit again. "Paper said you were from Chicago and–"

"And you've got my plate if something happens."

The man's grin was lopsided and unapologetic.

"You live around here, mister?"

"Goss. Lou Goss."

The way he said it, Pierman understood the man expected him to know who he was, but it took a second.

"You reported the fire."

"I just happened to see the smoke," Goss said modestly. "Should've seen it sooner. Maybe it would've helped old Randy."

Old Randy. Already the kid was legend, Pierman thought, then remembered metal lumps that looked like lemon drops.

"I doubt it, Mr. Goss."

Goss frowned with only one corner of his mouth. "I had a problem getting through anyway. Line was buzzing, for some reason. But still, I feel bad. That's why I been kind of keeping an eye on things at this end since."

"I'll tell Paul. I'm sure he'll appreciate it."

"I reckon he knows."

The juice traveled a high trajectory this time. The man didn't need somebody telling him how to treat his neighbor.

"You planning to go in there, are you?" he asked.

Pierman said that was his plan.

"Something to do with evidence, I reckon," Goss said.

"Just trying to understand. Any reason why I shouldn't?"

When Goss realized he was being teased, he laughed.

"I wouldn't say you're dressed for it. Briars and such."

"So I see," Pierman said. "Any suggestions."

The man leaned back into the cab and tossed out a greasy bundle.

"Overalls," he said. "Those are my spares."

There was a faint odor of manure. Pierman said thanks while trying not to succumb to his inclination to hold them at arm's length.

"Need something to fortify you?" Goss asked.

Pierman expected him to produce a bottle or a Thermos, but Goss proffered a silver foil envelope of shredded tobacco. Pierman fished out the cigarettes he'd kept when he left Calkins' house.

"These'll do," he said.

"Shit," Goss said, "those'll kill you."

His engine roared when it caught. "No rush bringing them back," he shouted referring to the overalls as though Pierman would know exactly where to find him.

$$\mathcal{Q}$$

Pierman found an opening on the other side of the fence, kicked the weeds away on his side, and tossed the bundle over. He resisted the idea of using it until his pants snagged on the barbed wire at the top of the fence. The undergrowth thinned out twenty yards into the woods' shadow, and behind it, he made his way to the fence row that ran down the west side of the woods.

As he took off his clothes, both sunlight and shade touched his damp skin and made it quiver. The picture he had of himself standing not quite naked in briefs, over-the-calf socks, and wingtips made him laugh, but he could not deny the almost illicit thrill that went with it. He lingered for a moment, then forced himself to step into the rough, smothering fabric of the overalls.

The encounter with the farmer cheered him, too. The man had shown him a good deal of openness and generosity, sides of people, particularly these people, Pierman knew he too easily forgot. But that mood didn't last long either. Circumstances forced him to finally judge the man as a little too quick to trust and thus something of a fool. He took no pride in the conclusion.

Pierman hung his dress pants and white shirt on a fence post. He picked up a stick to sweep back the weeds and began walking along the fence row. Probably he was being conceited and not a little foolish himself. After all, just what did he expect to find? Actual evidence was unlikely. Weeks had passed. The vines and the quackgrass had grown so thick they had nearly thrown him once already. People with sharper eyes, better equipment, and a clearer idea of what they were doing had covered the woods before.

He stopped trying to recall the details of police reports and concentrated instead on picturing in his mind what he should be looking for. But he could not settle on what that would be. Spent shells, bits of cloth or paper, bent twigs? All crossed his mind and seemed ridiculous. Those might be the kinds of things that alone, in an hour, answered the questions of TV detectives, but he had defended enough cases to know that the value of physical evidence was directly proportional to the extent it could be used to leverage a confession from a defendant.

Pierman rejected that line of thinking and kept walking. He held onto only one thought, the one he'd left town with. Perhaps it was the defense attorney in him, but he would not be satisfied with the arrest of the Barton kid—or probably anyone else—until he had looked himself. He would have to take it from the beginning to understand. To that extent, he had told Goss the truth.

His racket—snapping brush, the swish of his stick, muttered obscenities—set off a chain reaction among the woods' creatures. Just ahead would be a tense silence. Then, in a burst, wings fluttered and crashed through the foliage; small claws scrabbled across the bark and dry scrap. With his head down, Pierman began to think of himself as a swimmer who hears water complain against the rending of strokes. And like the swimmer triumphant at the end, he found to his amazement, and perhaps relief, that nearly silent normality nevertheless flowed in behind him. Could a raw, overwrought boy cope with that? The question alone cleared Pierman's head.

Near a cement corner post, thick as a tree trunk, where the fence intersected with another on the woods' south side, the bottom strand of one of the rusty wire rectangles was broken and the one below it was bent. The broken tips were still clean and bright.

In his mind, Pierman felt the jolt as the wire snapped and the momentary panic as the climber's crotch sank toward the barbed wire atop the fence. Someone had crossed recently, he reasoned, ready to be pleased with himself until he remembered again that actually many had.

He considered crossing himself and walking the perimeter of the corn on the other side, but the wide, bent leaves looked like scimitars and he recalled the tractors passing so many times over the ground. If he was going to find anything, he decided again, it would be in the woods. With gnats swarming around his head, he moved over ten yards and started back through the woods. He would at least be methodical.

On the way back, Pierman again came to an old, gray tree laying across his path. Long dead, it had blown down out of the woods. The top had mashed the fence, and Pierman, mulling too many things on the first pass, had noticed it only long enough to step over the narrow end. Here, though, the trunk was thicker and he had to step up and onto it, but the bark was long gone and the slick soles of his dress shoes slipped on the bare wood. He planted the stick and caught himself, tottering between the stick and the trunk in a faceful of leaves from nearby branches.

Righting himself on the trunk, Pierman swore, then smiled when he reflexively looked around to see if someone was watching him. The tree was a bridge into the chamber of the woods, he could see, and his clumsiness had been hidden from the fence by a veil of low-hanging foliage. Only from the knees down might he show. At the other end, between two still healthy heirs, lay the stiff tentacles of the tree's uprooted base. A bit playfully, Pierman walked toward it. He kept his eyes on the roots for balance, but where the base sloped up, he slipped again. He pitched to the left into one of the younger trees. Reflexively, he reached for a bough above his head. A splinter gouged his palm. He grabbed his hand and sucked it, and when he looked up at the offending branch, he saw that it had been cut off near the base.

Pierman climbed back onto the dead tree and propped himself with his arm against the live one. The branch's stump was five or six inches long, maybe an inch in diameter, and angled upward slightly from the trunk. A rude thought occurred to him, but Pierman dismissed it along with the pain in his hand as his mind's instinctive attempt to distract. The end was only slightly discolored.

The branch had been pinched off, but not cleanly. Some sharp, twisted splinters pointed out from the upper right side and the bark there was peeled back to the trunk. Jumping down, Pierman searched the ground around the roots of the dead tree. He looked back up, then took the stick and poked up among the branches around the stump. A branch with dead leaves fell to his feet. A stiff, pointed strip of bark spiraled out from its end.

Pierman took a deep breath and silently ordered himself to calm down. Pierman stepped back onto the dead tree and leaned precariously on his toes closer to the stump. The live tree's bark hung in loose strips attached only at the top like narrow, ragged shingles. Hickory or maple? If he ever knew, he could not remember. Looking closely around the branch stump, he found one shingle that appeared to be looser that the others and wedged beneath it where it joined the tree, he saw a small piece of black plastic. He started to lift the bark strip to ease the plastic out, but stopped.

Pierman had to consider the chain of evidence, like the gun pieces found along the county highways. Only in this instance, the issue was compounded by the fact that making himself the first link in the chain also made him a potential witness at trial. Under the ethical rules of the profession, he could not try any case in which he could also be a witness. The fact that he stopped to think about it made Pierman realize that he wanted to try the case. But then it occurred to him that even seeing it made him the first link, and he decided, screw it, someone else could try it.

Gently, holding the plastic by as little of the edge as he could so as not to leave or smudge a print, he drew it out. It looked like electrician's tape, but thinner and without adhesive. It was also puckered around the edges, which made Pierman think it was probably torn from a larger piece. He took the cigarette pack from his pocket and slipped it under the cellophane.

Pierman looked around the branch stump for anything else. About a foot above the place where he found the plastic piece he found odd marks. On the tree's surface, at a place where a bark shingle had broken off, were two punctures, each in the shape of a triangle. They appeared to be no bigger than the width of his little finger, but Pierman resisted the urge to touch them out of concern that a forensics unit would most certainly need to examine them.

He looked carefully at the dead trunk for marks. When he found none, he gingerly stepped around the tree with the branch stump looking for other debris or footprints. Again, he saw nothing more. He raised the stick to rake through the leaves, but decided against that. Again, he did not want to disturb the scene any more than necessary before Calkins or Purcell sent in a batch of techs to do what they should have done the day the Grable kid was killed. Time to move on.

At the other end of the woods, he checked, and through the growth, he could just see his white shirt draped over the post. Satisfied, he moved over another ten yards and started through again, taking it slowly, tacking back and forth across a straight line, looking up now as well as down. He guessed he'd run out his string, but he wanted to be sure, within limits, of course.

In that frame of mind, Pierman stopped for one more look around the dead tree. Standing on the other side of the roots, looking out toward the fence, he saw that the suspect tree's twin also had a low bough overhanging the dead tree. Suspect tree. He told himself he was getting worse all the time. Still, he went around and walked the trunk again. The branch on the right was just as easy to reach, and if he was looking for a handhold, the right side felt more natural. Maybe whoever clipped the branch on the tree on the left side was left handed. But if whoever had been there wanted something to hang onto, why make it harder by cutting it off? Shit, he thought, he didn't know.

After a couple more hours, Pierman gave up. He had covered half the width of the woods and had nothing else to show for it other than burrs in his socks. He had found nothing that disproved the boy's story, but he had found nothing that proved it either. For the moment, that was enough.

He cleaned off his socks and unzipped the front of the overalls. He had long since sweated through the grease and they itched. Walking back to the fence, he decided to ask Goss to let him wash when he returned the clothes. The man probably had a tub, probably one of those with porcelain feet, rather than a shower, and it wouldn't do to ask him for a blow dryer, but really, a little soap and water was all Pierman needed before he headed back to town.

It wasn't. His clothes were gone. He thought at first he simply had gone to the wrong post, but a quick trip up and down the fence row showed him that wasn't so, and coming back to the first post, his head bowed and his hands on his hips, he noticed a quarter glinting up through the grass.

He cuffed the post. The reverberation sent up a flock of small birds down the line. Remembering suddenly the analysis of how Randy Grable had been shot, Pierman dropped and wheeled. Down low, he could not see through the growth, and with the birds gone, the only sound was a mosquito at his ear. Slowly, still on one knee and half afraid of what he might see, he pivoted, but he could see nothing through the corn on the other side of the fence.

He considered animals, but not long. Other than a dog maybe, only one animal in this woods was large enough and mischievous enough to steal his clothes. He was embarrassed, too. It would be like going back to town naked in a barrel. And, Christ, he would have to walk. His keys were in his pants. As quickly and quietly as he could, he made his way out to the road. The car was still there and still locked, his "lawyer" clothes baking on the passenger seat.

Pierman put his arms across the roof of the car and looked down the road. He thought of Calkins and wondered if Goss hadn't called him after all and if he hadn't taken the clothes as some sort of joke, perhaps to spite him for investigating on his own. He thought of Goss and wondered if he could have been wrong about the man's trusting nature. He came back to the possibility that he'd understood instinctively from the first, that his clothes had been taken not as a joke, but as a threat. For an instant, he was seized by the thought of running, but he didn't like the odds. He wasn't that fast, and the closest house was a half-mile away down an empty road. He would have to go back in and look.

Watching where he put his feet, Pierman climbed the fence again to go back into the woods and quickly found a bigger stick. He would start with the fence. If a coin had dropped out of his pants, perhaps his car keys had, too. He worked in widening rings away from the post. Nothing showed in the springy weeds. No wonder someone could get in and out of the woods undetected.

His handkerchief hung on a briar twenty-five or thirty yards out. Since it didn't snag until he grabbed it off, he assumed it had been placed. He looked around again, his senses up. He probed the bushes with the stick. He felt more than heard someone enter the space behind him. Rather than move forward, he leaned into a hard, backhand shot with the stick. The impact felt soft and Pierman knew he'd done no real damage. There was a grunt and squeal as the figure landed in a thicket. He spun and raised the stick.

"Don't!"

Kay struggled to roll away.

"Well," she demanded, when he just stood there glaring down at her. "Get me out of here."

Pierman yanked her up. Jeans and a T-shirt had kept her from getting too scratched, but blood trickled from a welt above her elbow. He offered her the handkerchief, which she snatched out of his hand.

"You could've broken my arm."

"Actually, I could've split your damn skull."

She daubed at the cut furiously. "Don't kid yourself."

He laughed and she threw the handkerchief back at him.

"Okay," he said. "You had your joke. It backfired–on both of us–but you shouldn't sneak up on people like that."

"I shouldn't? What about you? I'm here on my property and someone comes crashing through the trees. It's bad enough you've got me jittery with that talk about locked doors. You scared the hell out of me."

"I might say the same of you."

Her hair had been tied back in the heat, but the jolt had knocked it loose. She let it down and began to pick out nettles and bits of leaves. As Pierman watched, he realized the coveralls were open to the crotch. He turned and zipped.

"I'm sorry," he said back over his shoulder.

"What're you doing here?"

When he looked at her, she had a cool, still air. Something in it suggested that if he was not careful it could be made permanent.

"Come on," he said.

She refused his hand, but followed him into the shade. Sitting with their backs against separate trees, he told her about Matthew Barton. He saw no reason to go into things he could not explain, so he told her only that it was far from definite and that he had come to check some things first.

"Well, did you find anything?" Her tone was sarcastic.

He pulled out the cigarette pack and stretched the cellophane tight with his thumbs so she could see the plastic beneath it.

"Know what that is?"

She looked away from it as though it were a dead fly.

"Not much then," she said.

He did not understand her hostility.

"No," he said, "not much."

"It looks like the sheeting you put in a garden," she said. "Around strawberries maybe, in the spring. It holds in moisture."

"Thank you." Pierman looked around him and held his breath for a time. "Are these woods used for anything?"

"Nothing," she said. "At least they never used to be."

"No one comes back here then? Like to take timber out or prune it?"

"Prune it? You mean, thin it? We're farmers, not lumberjacks."

He wanted to shake her.

"So what in the hell are you doing back here then?"

"So why in the hell do I have to tell you?"

She did not blink.

"You're right," he said. "Give me back my clothes and I'm gone." He stood up. "I've already said I'm sorry, Kay. But it's still my job."

She picked up a twig and scraped at the moss on a root near her leg. Lowered to her task, her face was hidden under her long hair. When she finally got up, she turned without saying more and started for the far corner of the woods.

Pierman followed, bewildered. Except for direction, her course seemed random, straying with the thickest part of the undergrowth. The trees revolved them through a thousand ripe shades of green and gray toward a wispy white light they could never quite reach. Pierman had to steal it, catch it out of the corner of his eye. If he actually looked, it was gone.

"You were trespassing," Kay muttered.

It had not felt that way to Pierman, not until she arrived. Before that, he had had the sense that he was right where he was supposed to be. He chose not to argue with her.

In the corner, the trees broke for a brook that flowed under the two fences, a meandering third side to the triangle. He thought they would cross and duck under the fence to a car parked in the lane on the other side, but she turned and followed the grassy bank for a few yards. An old tree, standing apart from the rest, shaded the bank. She stopped there. His clothes lay at her feet on a large towel next to a white enameled pan full of blackberries.

"I was picking when I heard you," she said, her back to him.

Her shoulders rose and fell. Pierman admitted to himself he probably had scared the hell out of her. He grasped her shoulders and they went limp.

"Kay, I—"

She turned out of his hands and faced him, but he could not look at her. When he leaned over to pick up his clothes, she started like a fawn. She paused, then in one motion, crossed her arms over her waist and drew off her shirt.

He straightened, blinking. Her long hair fell back on breasts that were brown down to their darker centers. The shirt dropped from her hand at her side. His mouth opened, but she reached for his neck and pulled his face to hers before he could speak. In time, his hands came up to touch the smooth muscles of her back and they swayed.

They parted, and she first, then he, bent away. An instant later, when her arms encircled his neck again, she cupped him and, as always, he was astonished. His face dipped to the warm scent of her breasts as he followed her down.

Their rhythms arose from different needs. They fought, then merged, and together they rowed, under the piping of birds, into that bank of white light on currents of a landlocked sea.

ॐ

"I've been spending a lot of time back here lately," she said drowsily.

They lay on their backs, her head resting on Pierman's arm. A new breeze tightened their skin, gathering perspiration off them as if it needed the moisture for rain promised by the clouding sky.

"When I was little and wanted to run away, this is where I came," she said. "I'd bring a doll or a book and read and dream until I could go back."

"And you were doing that today?"

"Reliving my childhood? Maybe." She removed his hand from her breast but held it between both of hers. "And maybe not."

"Things that bad?"

"No. No, I guess not."

"Meaning?"

"I don't know." She squeezed his hand. "Maybe they're better."

He raised himself on one elbow. The berries had spilled. He gave her one and took one for himself.

"Just how premeditated was this?"

"I will admit only to being a little worried you wouldn't come back that time you went out to the road."

She suddenly turned away onto her side.

"But I didn't like being frightened," she said. "And I don't like your choice of words."

"Sorry."

After a while, she said, "Yeah. Well." She sat up and began to retrieve the berries.

"When he'll talk about it, like this morning, Daddy says the bitterness, the hate, are a waste. There's nothing we can do about it now and they just get in the way. We have to leave them to people like you, because it's your job."

"Does he believe it?"

"He's trying to talk himself into it."

"And you?"

"Not for a fucking second."

She rolled a berry between her thumb and forefinger.

"If you don't think about it too hard, it's almost easy to believe it never happened. The beans are up. It's turning green along the ditch again." She pointed with her free hand. "That's where the creek goes. They diverted it into that ditch years ago."

"But?" he said.

"But then people show up." She crushed the berry between her fingers and wiped them on the grass. "I already knew about the Barton kid. Your friend, the sheriff, was out this morning. First thing. He had to tell us, ask some questions."

Pierman sat up.

"Daddy cried when he left, and I think it was as much for that boy as it was for Randy. Can you believe it?" She sighed. "I hated your friend."

"For the way he made your father feel?"

"And the way he made me feel about Daddy. Or maybe just for reminding."

She hooked her hair behind her ear.

"Would you say that's awful?"

"I'd say it's understandable."

She willed a smile.

"Yes," she said, "I suppose you would."

She looked at him finally.

"The sheriff said you don't believe the boy. My father says you're timid. I told him he was wrong."

Pierman colored imagining the context of the conversation.

"Is that a way of saying you thought I might turn up here today?"

"Or hoped you wouldn't."

She let him pull her to him.

"It's your job that doesn't do much for me," she said. "I wonder if you don't risk having to understand too much."

"At this point, there's not much risk of that."

She remained still, as though she weren't certain. Back in the woods, a mourning dove called, forecasting rain. Suddenly, she nuzzled into his chest.

"I can't wait for this damned thing to be over."

"And what will you do then?" he asked, careful to put it in the singular.

"I don't know. Yet."

He lifted her face and held it in both hands before him for a moment before he kissed her.

"Ever bring anyone else back here?" he asked.

She smiled and pushed him down.

The rain began as he left the woods. It was steady and gentle, the kind farmers like.

Kay had walked back to the woods, but she didn't want Pierman to drive her home. It was near the middle of the afternoon, and they had been lucky her father—worse, Rodney, his moonstruck hired hand—hadn't come looking for her. There was no reason to push their luck with an unexpected appearance by Pierman and the questions that would raise. Indeed, even today, since your mother will not speak of it, only a few of us can say with any certainty who your father was.

Pierman took his time finding his way out. The cold drops soaked through the overalls and ran down his back and chest. It felt good and the clothes didn't matter. But the rain soon made him shiver, and as he willed himself not to hurry, he caught an echo from the depths of longing. The rain sounded like a wave that never reaches shore.

15

Large, dark eyes followed him. A sullen trooper stood in front of the tall oak doors at the top of the stairs on one side of the Courthouse. He rotated only his head to follow Pierman's car. Another trooper had taken up the same position on the next side. His gaze picked up Pierman's car and followed it when Pierman turned the corner. Both men wore aviators. They put Pierman in mind of the surveillance cameras in banks that swiveled as you passed. It was early the next day, and already his skin crawled.

Calkins had called twenty minutes ago, a little before six, as he was waking up. When Pierman answered after a half dozen rings, Calkins said, "Jesus, thank God." Before Pierman could ask what that was about, Calkin ordered Pierman to the Courthouse—"Now. No questions. Now."—and hung up. Pierman decided on the drive over that ignorance wasn't bliss; just refuge, a small, barren place to rest.

Fifteen, sixteen police cars–state, county, town–were parked at various spots around the building, several of them cockeyed, outside or across the yellow lines painted on the brick-paved streets. Pierman felt the hairs on the back of his neck rise. The problem with criminal defense work was that you came in after they'd cleaned up the mess; you always had to reconstruct. The problem for the prosecution, he was beginning to see, was that you came in at the beginning; you had to look at the mess.

Pierman parked on a side street off the square. A few of the geezers who took their exercise early stood on the sidewalk at one corner of the square so they could see two sides of the Courthouse. They turned to look expectantly at Pierman as he approached, but since he wore only a T-shirt, jeans, and a billboard cap to cover his mussed and unwashed hair, they dismissed him as someone curious but unconnected to the excitement.

As Pierman turned up the long, wide sidewalk leading to the Courthouse steps, the trooper at the door let his hand fall to his gun belt. Pierman decided to keep his hands out of his pockets, and it annoyed him. The trooper came down two steps and held his free hand up flat.

"Sorry. Building's closed."

"Why?"

"Please go back."

"I'm the prosecutor. Let me by."

One eyebrow arose from behind the trooper's sunglasses. Pierman imagined the man's eyes roaming his bedraggled appearance. Aggravated, Pierman stepped forward. He heard the pop when the man unsnapped the strap securing his weapon. Pierman stopped.

"Trooper," he said, "given the way I look, I'm willing to forget you did that, but it's time you took your hand away from that gun."

"Stay there."

The trooper backed up the steps and pulled open the door without taking his eyes off Pierman. He spoke to someone inside. In a few moments, Darrell appeared. Through the glass in the door, he looked at Pierman for much longer than Pierman thought necessary. Finally, he nodded. The trooper held the door open.

"Your fly's open," Pierman said as he passed. The trooper grabbed himself.

Four cops of various jurisdictions were huddled in the hallway. They stopped talking and watched as Darrell and Pierman walked toward the stairs.

"What's happened?" Pierman said.

"You don't know?" His voice cracked, and Pierman thought he was working hard to remain casual.

"No."

Darrell said nothing more.

"Why aren't we taking the elevator?" Pierman asked.

"You don't know." A statement this time.

"No."

"Won't work."

Darrell turned to Pierman at the first landing.

"Where were you yesterday?" Darrell was too young and inexperienced to keep the insinuating tone out of his voice.

"Why're you questioning me?"

For a time, they eyed each other, then Darrell turned back toward the stairs and Pierman followed. At the second landing, Pierman put his hand on Darrell's arm to turn him back and make him answer, but Darrell held up one threatening finger, biting his lips and looking away. Pierman backed off.

When Pierman's eyes cleared the last landing, he saw that the door to his office was open. Just inside the reception area on the floor lay a red blanket that looked like it had been thrown in a heap. From then on, Pierman took each step with increasing reluctance; each told him something more unpleasant and confusing. Sighing, he smelled a vague odor of human waste. A scuffed wingtip lay on its side a few feet outside the door. The shoe had a hole in the sole. A dark brown smear stretched from the shoe to a point somewhere beneath the blanket.

Calkins stood at the yellow ribbon that had been stretched across the opening into the stairwell. Darrell blocked Pierman from going further. He whispered in Calkins's ear, while Calkins looked at and through Pierman with the fixed gaze of an ice-blue anger. Calkins held the ribbon up to let Pierman stoop under.

"Take a deep breath. Look at this." Calkins said in a flat voice. "And watch where you step."

Calkins knelt and pulled back the blanket from the face of Willie, the janitor. It was waxy and tinged blue around the lips and ears. The tip of his tongue parted his lips in the corner of his mouth, but except for that, he looked as serene as he always did. His eyes were closed, and his hands were folded on his chest. It made Pierman think of the last time he had seen his father.

"He's . . . he looks like he's asleep," Pierman said instead.

"Don't be stupid," Calkins said. "He's laid out. Somebody took the time to put him back together." Calkins watched Pierman closely as his color changed. "Don't you do that, Allen. You've been through this before. Look again."

Calkins pointed to a maroon crescent across the bottom of the old man's Adam's apple. The blood had dried in jagged lines down his neck to the silver clasp of his bolo tie. A crusty, brown film dulled the clasp's gleam.

"Tell you anything?" Calkins said.

Pierman shook his head, swallowing hard.

"Strangled. His own fucking tie," Calkins said, his voice low and rasping, the cords seized. "Stood in front of Willie. Face to face." Calkins cleared his throat. "Took the end of the tie in one hand. Ran the buckle up into his throat with the other. Cinched him. Willie—" Calkins cleared his throat again—"watched."

Calkins tossed the blanket back across the old man's face. He stood. He looked into Pierman's door for a long moment, then at Pierman for an even longer time. "Go see about your office."

Clouds of silver dust sparkled in the window light as one of Purcell's technicians batted a brush full of fingerprint powder on a filing cabinet, carefully stepping around pieces of the telephone on the floor. Purcell stood propped on one arm leaning over Pierman's desk, studying one of the files.

"Buddy boy," Purcell said, glancing up at Pierman. "Nice outfit." He turned the folder around. "This yours, Al?"

Silver dabs, shimmering like watermarks, bordered the top page of the file. The name on the tab was Matthew Barton. Pierman reached out to pull the file closer, but Purcell caught his hand and turned it back and forth, looking at it closely before he let it go. It took Pierman a moment to drag his attention from Purcell back to the first page in the file. Across the top of it, someone had typed: "No. Wrong. You can do better."

𝒮

Pierman conducted his own interrogation. He righted an over-turned chair, stared down the horrified technician, and sat down. He smiled ingratiatingly at Purcell. Purcell, too, started to object, but curiosity got the better of him and he changed his mind. He told the technician to go bat powder somewhere else. "Perhaps the sheriff should step in," Pierman said.

He had been at his apartment since seven-thirty, eight, the night before, Pierman began, when Calkins came in. Purcell rested a hip on one corner of Pierman's desk and leaned back, his arms crossed. Calkins stood at the other corner, one thumb hooked in his gun belt, his face blank.

There had been no one with him, Pierman said, he had been alone. He had spent the evening reading some of his father's case files to see what he might be able to get if he sold the old man's civil practice. The files and his notes were still scattered on the floor of his living room, if they cared to look, although that really didn't prove a thing, of course, since he could have put them there anytime. He had gone to bed then. He was still alone. He'd been asleep when Calkins called. Pierman looked at Calkins, who nodded and looked away.

He'd had dinner with his mother before he went home. He gave the name of the restaurant; he assumed somebody there would confirm their presence.

He had spent the latter part of the afternoon getting ready for Warren Sley's trial. He had dictated the final witness and exhibit list and the jury instructions. At about five he'd handed the tape to

Ginny, the secretary, and told her it had to be done by this morning since trial would begin next Tuesday and D'Agostino was hounding him for the lists and the instructions.

He'd stopped to see Calkins at his office once in the afternoon before that and tried to reach him again by telephone later. No, he didn't know times. He assumed the dispatcher could provide that information since the man had told Pierman each time that Calkins was out and he could leave a message, which he did. Purcell looked at Calkins, who nodded. Pierman said he didn't see that anything earlier than that was relevant.

No, Pierman said, leaning forward, ticking off points on his fingers, he didn't know what Willie was doing in his office, but the man was the janitor, wasn't he, and had the run of the building. No, he said, touching the index finger of his right hand to the ring finger of his left, he didn't have a thing against Willie, nor did he know anyone who did. He'd known Willie all his life, and he was harmless. No, he said, holding up both hands and turning them, there were no signs of blood or bruising from an act of violence on him, but they were welcome to look closer if they wanted. No, he hadn't typed the message. Why would he? He may have considerable doubts about the boy's guilt, but just typing words on a page wouldn't change the boy's circumstances. Yes, the type looked like it came off the office typewriter, but tests obviously were necessary to confirm that. No, he didn't know who would've typed the message. No, he didn't know what to make of it.

Sure, Pierman said, picking up the pace a little, letting in a little edge, he could certainly understand if they and every other fucking cop he had encountered that morning looked at him with suspicion. He wasn't dumb. Nothing had ever really happened here 'til he came to town and now they'd had two murders in a month, one in his own office.

Joe didn't need to interrupt, Pierman said, raising a hand to cut Calkins off. He understood, Pierman said, and actually, as an officer of the court and a concerned citizen, he would like to continue to cooperate. But speaking as a defense attorney, the fact of the murders and the timing of his return to town really didn't add up to probable cause, and, really, if they needed anything further, as prosecutor, he'd have to say that they'd better fucking Mirandize him.

Pierman hooked his thumbs in the loops of his jeans, leaned back, and crossed his legs. He moistened his finger and concentrated on wiping a spot from his sneaker. "Now," he said, "where do you guys want to go from here?"

Purcell and Calkins looked at each other. The room's weather broke.

"God, you're a touchy son of a bitch," Purcell said. He hoisted himself off the desk and turned toward the window. "When's the last the time you saw your secretary?"

"I believe I told you that before," Pierman said. "Your question makes me think I'm not back on the team." He rose as if to leave.

Calkins stepped forward and put his hand on Pierman's arm. Purcell had turned from the window, watching. "Tell him," Purcell said.

"Ginny's missing," Calkins said. "Her parents called the town boys last night when she didn't come home. She was supposed to be working late here, according to her mother."

"And she's supposed to be involved in this how?"

Calkins shrugged. "You tell us," Purcell said.

Pierman moved Calkins aside. He went to the reception area. The pages of the jury instructions he intended to propose were stacked neatly in the center of her desk. The top page was half finished; the last word typed on the page was gibberish. Pierman took a pencil from a cup on the desk and used the eraser to press a corner of the eject button of the transcriber. A cassette was still in the machine.

"Anybody look for her last night?" Pierman asked Calkins, who had followed him.

"She's an adult, Allen," Calkins said. "She gets to come and go as she pleases. Nobody thought anything about it until I called this morning to see if they noticed anything around here last night."

"The answer's no then. Anybody looking for her now?"

"Of course."

Pierman felt a little sick, but his mind still functioned. He stared at Willie's body. He looked at the last word on the jury instructions. He thought about the elevator not working.

"How 'd you find this?" he asked.

"Deputy Dawg," Purcell said from the doorway.

"Darrell was coming into town to do paperwork before the end of his shift," Calkins said. "Saw a light in your window. He went in to investigate."

Pierman went to the outside door. He raised his hand, snapped his fingers at Darrell, who had remained at the stairwell to act as gate-keeper, and waved him over.

"You call for backup when you came in here?" Pierman demanded.

Pierman's summons and tone annoyed Darrell. He looked away, starting to resist, but Calkins, standing behind Pierman, a half smile on his face, snapped his fingers on his leg and raised his eyebrows.

"The town don't have anybody on after midnight," Darrell said. His eyes slid over to Purcell. "And I was told anybody else'd be just too far away."

"So you came into a large, dark building alone."

"Well, yeah."

"Which is either brave or foolish or maybe both. And you found what we see here."

"Yeah."

"You search the building?"

"I called it in immediately."

"You search the building?"

"What for?"

"Ginny."

Darrell swallowed. "I maintained the integrity of the crime scene until other units arrived," he said.

"And courage has its limits. Write it up just that way, Darrell," Pierman said. He turned to Purcell. "Your guys look?"

"We didn't know she'd been here until just a little bit ago. No purse, no blood, nothing."

"But the instructions she was working on aren't done, the last sentence isn't complete, and the last word on the page is nonsense."

"We're supposed to proofread her work?"

Ignoring Purcell, Pierman turned to Calkins. "Why's the elevator off?"

Calkins said he didn't know; they had not got that far yet.

"The switch is up here somewhere," Pierman said to Calkins. "Where?"

Calkins led them all around a partition at one end of the floor to a plywood door in one corner of a storage area. A purse hung on the knob.

"Open it," Pierman said.

"Wait," Purcell said. "We'll dust it."

"Fuck that," Calkins said.

He pulled a black flashlight with the length and heft of a tire iron from Darrell's belt and drew his revolver. He stepped to one side. When Darrell turned the knob from the other side the door, he nudged it open an inch.

The flashlight beam found her feet first. As it traveled up Ginny's body, Pierman saw that her ankles and hands were bound with the beige cords from his phone. Her hose had been jammed in her mouth but the gag was unnecessary. A bruise like a strawberry birthmark swelled the left side of her face from her forehead to her cheek.

Calkins stepped inside, knelt, and felt her throat. "Still with us. Call an ambulance."

Behind them, Cross, the coroner, had slipped in, unnoticed as usual.

"It's here," he said, in his solemn, reasonable way.

"How'd you know?" Calkins said.

"You mean if I didn't do it?" Pierman said.

"Cheap shot."

"You think so?"

They were alone in Pierman's disheveled, gray-speckled office. Calkins had taken the chair Pierman had earlier. Pierman stood at the window.

Ginny had gone on one stretcher, Willie another, but their destination, a hospital in the next county, was the same, so together they rode in Cross's hearse.

The distance had always frightened his mother, Pierman recalled as he watched the wagon pull away from the square. Carter would note the appearance of another acquaintance on the obituary page, and she would say, "I'll go here or I'll go there, but not in between. I want someone who's certified to say when they can stop working on me." Carter had "gone" in his sleep at home. It had been one of her comforts in those first days, but that seemed a decade ago.

Darrell had been dispatched to tell Ginny's folks, and Purcell was off somewhere in the building. Pierman didn't know or care where. There had been another argument. Purcell had wanted the whole building closed for the day so that he and his men could go over it. Calkins said that would only create more fear, and Lindley, by God, had had enough of that. Pierman told them both to shut up. They could close off the fourth floor, and Purcell could get what he wanted elsewhere before the building opened at 8:30. It was just after seven, one more day to which Pierman could see no end.

Below, the small knot of onlookers had grown to a sizeable crowd that lined the sidewalk on the two sides of the square that Pierman could see. They stood with their arms folded or their hands thrust in their back pockets. They spoke to one another and nodded gravely. From where Pierman stood, they acted as though they understood perfectly.

"Just like old times." Pierman said. "A body. A crowd. Everybody pissing on each other's shoes."

Without turning, he said, "I'll assume it was Purcell's idea. About me."

A newcomer arrived. Two members of the crowd pointed up at Pierman as they filled him in. Pierman considered waving but decided it could be construed as flippant.

"For Christ's sake, Allen," Calkins said. "It was talk. People were looking for you yesterday. It was speculation."

The newcomer was bold. He broke from the crowd and approached the door, probably to put a question to the trooper.

"And Ginny?" Pierman said. "She played into it how exactly?"

"There was no 'exactly.' There's talk around the building that she was sweet on you."

"Willie catches us in some compromising situation, and we dispose of him. And then maybe I dispose of her or had her waiting somewhere? We were playing it that way?"

"Something like that."

"She and I are single and we're both of age. I don't see a motive in that, although it is entirely logical, since there hadn't been a murder for years until I got back to town."

"Yeah, I believe you mentioned that. Before you told us to fuck ourselves."

The newcomer briefly returned to the group, then headed around the building, perhaps to see what was going on at another door.

"I wonder why it's so hard for us to believe that maybe it's one of us. I mean, it wouldn't surprise me if you and Purcell treated a stranger, an outsider, to that kind of thinking, but you were ready to believe that shit, Joe."

"Allen, you're damn near a stranger, and I'd believe damn near anything to get this straightened out." Pierman heard the stiff leather of Calkins' gun belt creak as he shifted his feet. "Maybe that's not true. And I don't believe it now."

"Apology accepted." Pierman turned away from the window. "I didn't know about Ginny. I guessed. But my guess was better educated than yours."

He explained that he knew Willie came back to close down the building at night and how he knew it. He chose not to say that part of his hunch was based on a deep-seated suspicion of the cops' effectiveness.

"Somebody took the time to lay Willie out, you said. That was either a cruel joke or whoever killed him did it reluctantly. I gave him the benefit of the doubt."

"'Course," Calkins said, looking away, "you would."

"Suppose whoever was here just to break into my office," Pierman said. "Forget why for now. He doesn't expect to find Ginny, but he doesn't necessarily want to harm her when he does. Maybe he does only what he has to to avoid recognition."

"Braining her is only what he has to?"

"He killed Willie."

They batted it around. The fact that Willie came back at around 6 p.m. each day told them approximately when Ginny was attacked and Willie murdered. Since they had found no evidence of a break-in, the killer either had a key, knew someone who would let him in, or hid in the building after it closed. They figured the assailant approached Ginny from behind, while she was turned away from the only door into the prosecutor's office typing the jury instructions, and struck her before she could see him. If that were so, the fact that the left side of her face was injured made it likely that the assailant was left handed or at least had used his left hand. They theorized that Willie either found the killer rifling Pierman's office or he found Ginny when he went to turn off the elevator, then found the killer in the office. Either way, they were reasonably certain that Willie could have identified the man; otherwise, why kill him?

"Must've rattled the guy," Calkins said. "He forgot to turn out the lights."

"Or not, "Pierman said.

Calkins looked up perplexed.

"He took the time to lay out Willie. He dragged him over to Ginny's desk. He hung her purse from a door knob. He left a light on. One light. My light."

"He wanted her to be found."

"But none too quickly."

"Better chances," Calkins said. "It wouldn't get dark until around eight or so. Nobody'd really notice until it got dark, and even then, they'd just think you were working late."

"If they bothered to look up at all."

Calkins thought the remark odd and waited for an explanation. Pierman offered none.

"So, I'll ask the question out loud," he said. "Whom do we know who kills standup, face to face, does it in daylight, and in a way that not only covers his tracks but helps police find his victims?"

Calkins looked at Pierman as though he was prepared to be resentful, but in the end, he nodded agreement.

"You want to know how I spent my day yesterday?" Pierman said. Leaving out his encounter with Kay, he told Calkins about walking the woods and finding the tree and the marks on it. As he did, he pulled the cigarette pack from his pocket and teased off the cellophane wrapper so that the piece of plastic sheeting remained in it. He held it out to Calkins.

"So, what do you wrap in plastic and hang from a stub in a tree?"

To his credit, Calkins had already asked himself the question and had an answer ready. "A rifle you're going to use later."

"So let's ask the previous question a different way: Is there anybody in Holoce County who knows enough, is cold enough, arrogant enough, to do all this?"

Calkins' eyes skittered aside. He had obviously asked himself that question, too, and for a moment, Pierman thought he would offer up a name. When Calkins did not, Pierman shrugged.

"I'll tell you who is not capable of that, who could not possibly have done Willie anyway because he was sitting in your jail, and that's Matthew Barton. It's time to turn him loose."

Calkins put his hands in his pockets and stared at the floor. Pierman gave him time to work it through. Pierman knew he could simply call the jail and order the release, but he was like Calkins at that point, sick of turmoil.

"I mean," Pierman said, trying to make a joke of it, "even the killer's told us we're wrong on Barton."

Calkins finally shrugged. "I don't reckon he was telling us anything anyway."

Pierman heard something in the way he said it. "Us. Who's us?"

"D'Agostino called yesterday," Calkins said. He had a hard time looking at Pierman. He spoke to the bookshelf over Pierman's shoulder. "He called while you were out."

D'Agostino had proposed that Calkins put Wesley Sley in the same cell as Matthew Barton. If Barton had anything of value to say, Sley would pass it on to Calkins in exchange for slack on the burglary charge.

Pierman did not know where to begin. "The sheriff's department cuts plea agreements now?" he sputtered.

"You were out."

"Fuck yes, I was out. I was doing what you guys should've been doing two goddamned months ago."

"It's Sley's third felony count," Calkins continued as though he had not heard Pierman. "He's a petty thief looking at a habitual offender charge. Convict on this one, he's gone for twenty-five years, more. He was motivated."

"And you put an adult and a juvenile together in the same cell." Pierman said. He leaned across his desk, talking past Calkins. "Put aside the fact that there are statutes against that. While I'm trying to figure out how much damage that does to the case against each of them, I'll be sure to let the county attorney know you meant well when the boy's folks sue you for offering him up in satisfaction of Mr. Sley's appetites."

"Meaning?"

"Even you, Joe, are not that naive."

As soon as he said it, Pierman thought the differences in their beliefs about who each had been and who each had become could not have been made clearer if he'd popped them with a flash. For a moment without measure in time, they considered each other in sorrow, waiting for the queasy slosh of loss and remorse to subside.

"Why is this guy looking out for that boy?" Calkins said.

"Why did he not kill Ginny?"

"The library charge remains?"

"Make the call. Get him out."

"Sure," Calkins said, rising. "Call it the benefit of doubt."

The sun shined directly into Pierman's window. He felt its warmth on the back of his head, but for a long time after Calkins left, he sat staring into the shadow that extended like a long corridor from his chair. The morning's images appeared like portraits along it: Calkins walking out and down the stairs so stooped he appeared headless. Darrell's contemptuous stare. Purcell, arrogance personified, perched on his desk. The sequence changed each time he made the trip, but the images at the end were always the same, a half-finished piece of paper, an overturned shoe.

In his head, he made lists of what he should feel, then reduced them. Grief, if not anguish; alarm, if not terror; indignation, if not outrage; culpability, if not guilt. It was easy, almost automatic. He did it again and they were gone. Abruptly, he swiveled the chair into the light and was grateful when his eyes ached back into the middle of his skull.

He turned back into the room, and as the red circles cleared from his eyes, he saw again what a mess the place was. He looked at his watch; it was almost nine. He should call his mother, tell her what happened, try to keep her calm. But then he had no phone. He could go home. That would probably be better, but then what if he was needed here? He looked at his watch again. Purcell might be back soon and it wouldn't look good if he slipped out. It did occur to him that there were other phones in the building he could use, but he told himself he did not feel up to answering the questions of his fellow officeholders, and he did not dwell long on that thought.

He started by putting away files. There was nothing else to do, and nobody else to do it for him. Purcell's tech had taken the Barton file and a couple under it, but there were others strewn around the desk and on the floor. Was Purcell done? Pierman worked carefully around the gray splotches. Two files were flagged for arraignments. He checked his desk calendar; they were, of course, set for that morning. He grasped the calendar in both hands and slapped it onto desk once, twice before he got himself back under control.

A half hour later, the office looked cleaner than it had when he moved in. He had attacked the cleaning, letting the tremors work themselves out through his limbs, but all the tissues in his office and Ginny's area were now gone, and his handkerchief was filthy. He was ready to throw it away when he remembered there was still one more mess and still no one to take care of it. The closest restroom was in the jury room on the third floor. The instantly averted eyes of the prim welfare director reminded him the guards were now gone. He ducked quickly into the jury room, where I found him.

The hot water was making the building's old pipes clank when I put my head tentatively in the door from the courtroom. Pierman had found a bucket, a sponge, and some cleaner; he was filling the bucket.

"Botsford heard someone rattling 'round in here," I said. "She is understandably a little jumpy this morning. She asked me to investigate."

"Welcome to the club," he said, without looking up. "Tell Bots' it was the ghost of janitors past."

I sucked in some breath. "Not a good morning," I said carefully. "Damned right."

He jerked the bucket from the sink. Some of the steaming water sloshed onto his jeans. It must've burned his thighs, but he did not flinch.

"What're you doing?" I asked.

"Cleaning up. Getting things back to normal. You'd want that, wouldn't you?"

"Yes," I said. "Yes, that's good." I put a thumbnail between my front teeth and leaned back against the long table that took up most of the room. "You'll need the rest of the day to sort things out, I imagine. I'll grant a continuance on the two you've got slated for this morning."

"Thank you."

"Botsford can call defense counsel. You'll have enough to do, I suspect, especially without a secretary for a while."

"For that reason, you may as well continue the Sley trial on Tuesday. I can't be ready now."

"I see," I said skeptically. "You know, of course, D'Agostino will be in here demanding that his client be released on bail."

"Then release him. No objection."

Pierman put the bucket on the floor and faced me.

"Found my replacement yet?"

"No."

"You have less than a week."

"Is that a threat?"

"Promise kept. Contract performed. Call it what you want."

I started a little stroll around the long table.

"Your mother called me this morning just as I was leaving." Pierman's head snapped around. "She didn't want to bother you. In fact, she didn't seem to know how to get ahold of you. Nevertheless, she seemed intent on knowing what was going on. At the time, I didn't know anything was going on. I ran into the sheriff as he was coming out. He told me." I put my hands in my back pockets and rocked. "I've called your mother back. I think she's calmer now."

Pierman bent over the table.

"And now you're going to ask me how I can run out on my poor mother at a time like this."

"No, actually, I'm not." I wedged a thumbnail between my teeth again for a moment. "Actually, she said she wished you were back in Chicago."

"Meaning?"

"Well, I suppose, like most mothers, she does not care to see her child in distress."

"You're walking me into the weeds. We both know about that. Dad and you used to say that's where we lawyers lay the traps." Pierman straightened. "I've gone far enough. Say it."

The room was purposely spartan. Its walls were painted an off-white and bare, and it was furnished only with the table and a dozen hard, straight-backed chairs. Having to decide tough questions of liberty and money makes juries skittish creatures, even the stolid, diligent types impaneled here. It was therefore my opinion that efficient decisions were made when distractions and amenities were denied.

The one exception to the decor was a wood carving of the state seal, which hung on one barren wall. As large and round as a garbage can lid, it depicted a bison bounding away from a settler chopping down a tree. It had been given to one of my predecessors by a local craftsman, and even as a young lawyer advising obstreperous clients in that room, I had recognized that the artist's spirit far exceeded his skill.

Jurors obviously appreciated it far more than I did. During deliberations, many had felt the need to touch it. Perhaps they stood as I stood then, brooding, trying to decide if there was anything left to say. Particularly on the bison's head and the settler's wide-brimmed hat, they had darkened the wood with their oils and worn it smooth. A touch for luck, perhaps for hope.

"You know what I think," I said, reaching out to the settler's hat. "How many times must we ask you to dance?"

♫

Even by the time Pierman got back to the fourth floor, the water was warm enough to release the stench from the brown streak that ran from the hallway into his office door. Nate McQueen found him sitting back on his heels, swallowing back a retch.

"I'm surprised you weren't here sooner," Pierman said hoarsely, not bothering to rise.

"You accusing me of something?" McQueen's eyes were alight with amusement and he smiled, but through the fright mask it was hard to tell.

"No more than wiretapping."

"What is that smell?"

"Willie."

"Man, always you were a cold bastard."

"Your business here is?

"Thought you might need this." McQueen took a beige phone from a box he carried under his arm. "See? Even remembered your color."

Pierman stood, waved him into the office, and followed him through the reception area. McQueen walked slowly; his head turning to take it all in.

"How did you know I needed a phone?"

McQueen turned. The smile remained in place, but the light in his eyes shrank to pinpoints like old television sets when they were turned off.

"Your buddy Calkins called me. Told me what happened. I put you at the top of my list. As always."

Pierman waved him forward again, wanting him in and out of the office as quickly as possible. McQueen turned completely around examining Pierman's office.

"This is way cleaner than the last time I was in here. What happened?"

"You don't know?" Pierman heard Darrell's words come out of his mouth and wondered if he was any better than Purcell, putting the spotlight on a guy merely because he disliked him. McQueen's smile drifted.

"I know you don't think much of me, Mr. Prosecutor, but I hate what happened to those people."

"Willie and I were what you could call business acquaintances," McQueen said when Pierman was silent too long. "I'm considered by my colleagues to be the expert on the courthouse phone system."

He knelt by the jack box.

"Yes," he said, looking around the office slowly. "I'm the one who installed it so I'm the one they send to fix it. Always had to see Willie to get the key to the switch room."

He looked around slowly once more before taking a screwdriver from his belt and applying it to one of the screws.

"Why don't you just plug the line into the jack?" Pierman asked impatiently.

"How do I know the line wasn't yanked and the jack damaged?"

Pierman did not know whether the killer had yanked the line from the jack or not, but it made him wonder.

"You always check that?"

McQueen smiled back over shoulder. "Always."

Pierman decided that he was no better than Purcell.

"You here yesterday?" he asked and was surprised when McQueen said he was.

"Treasurer's office," he said. "About two. You want a technical explanation for what was wrong?"

"You have to get Willie's key to the switch room?"

"Yup."

"You give it back to him?"

"Yup."

"Where is the switch room?"

McQueen pivoted on his haunch, leaned back against the bookcase, and considered Pierman.

"This floor, end of the hall," he said. "Next to the elevator box."

He smiled, inviting another question. Pierman obliged.

"What time did you leave?"

McQueen frowned, as though disappointed with the quality of the question. "Don't know. I had two more jobs after that. Company's got the records." He turned back to the jack. "You can check them."

Pierman noted that he fished the innards out of the box with his left hand, but when he reattached the faceplate, he turned the screwdriver with his right. When McQueen tried to slip the screwdriver back into one of the loops on his toolbelt, he missed and it fell to the floor. Pierman reached down to hand it back to him, but McQueen pulled on a cord between the belt and the screwdriver and snatched it away. He grinned at Pierman, who saw then that all the tools on the belt were attached to it by cord.

"Go up light and tie 'em tight." McQueen said.

"What does that mean?"

"It's what the old guys say about how to carry your tools when you go up a pole. They just never say it till you've dropped your tools a couple times to learn the lesson."

"Never met the girl, your secretary," McQueen said, switching subjects before Pierman could think of anything to say. "Nice chick, was she?"

Pierman froze at the leer. "She's not dead."

"Never said she was, man. Never said she was."

McQueen connected the line between the jack and phone base, picked it up the handset to listen for the dial tone, and smacked his hands in approval.

"I reckon you'll have to turn that Barton kid loose now," he said, looking up, shifting subjects again.

"What makes you say that?"

"There can't be more'n one guy roaming round this county killing people, can there?" That boy was in jail when this happened."

Pierman was relieved that it was as obvious to someone else as it was to him.

"But then, you've still got those damn books," McQueen was saying. "If you ask me"—he stopped, looked at Pierman, daring him—"by God, even if you don't, I think you ought to let that kid off." McQueen's face was reddening, and he flexed his hands at his side. "It's the same old shit 'round here. Always afraid, can't ever tell kids the truth. It ain't all goody-goody out there, and we don't like to leave a lot of room for different. So I want to know, what're you going to do about it, man. What?"

McQueen stared, his chest heaving.

Pierman remembered the books in Mrs. McQueen's bedroom, but there was no accounting for this.

"I'm discussing no cases with you, Nate."

McQueen's eyes went blank for a moment, then it passed. "Yeah, sure," he said, straightening up. "So," he said, full of good humor again, "how're you and Kay getting along?"

"If you're done, get out."

McQueen smiled and threw Pierman a two-finger salute.

"I'll let you know, I hear anything."

❧

Pierman trembled, more with fury, he thought at first, than with fear. The man seemed bent on creating some kind of contest between them. It was as though he planned their encounters like a cunning practical joke designed to prick every exposed nerve Pierman had, and for the life of him, Pierman could not see why. Whatever differences Pierman had had with McQueen long ago were, at most, insignificant now.

The outburst raised the other issue, though. It moved the question of McQueen's persistent antagonism to the edge of rational explanation and maybe that was what made him shake now. He asked himself, not for the first time, what had made Kay drop McQueen and why she did it when she did. He remembered Calkins' hand dropping to his gun in Billie's bedroom and his reference to McQueen as a wild man. He wondered what they knew, instinctively or otherwise, but could not bring themselves to say. He considered again the question of which hand McQueen favored and decided again he couldn't really say. And once more, in light of those questions, he asked the old question, the one he'd asked himself all morning whenever his eyes fell on the old man's diplomas, the one he'd asked himself once a day since he'd come home. Then, more than before, he doubted he could ever say.

The door was locked that evening. He had to pound and finally call her name before Elizabeth peeked through the curtain. She did not speak or cry; she simply clung. He recalled more faces and more words, added to the old ones. His grip tightened. She resisted at first. It was as if he was tilting her off the edge of the world.

16

The transcript of the recorded statement Pierman took from the Barton boy that Saturday, the next day, was part of the evidence Detective Purcell's team gathered later. He did not want to share it with me at the time. Indeed, he was so brash as to admit that he might want to look into *my* role in what he described as "this whole fucking mess."

I could investigate my role myself, without Detective Purcell's assistance. I knew the prosecutor. I had seen to his appointment. It was not a problem to obtain the statement.

Pierman was good at his job. The statement's tone is calm, matter of fact; its language nearly clinical in its precision. In no way does it convey its cost, either to Matthew Barton or to Pierman.

Pierman found Matthew Barton early that morning sitting on a step in the shadows of the stairs leading to Carter's office. Pierman had planned to spend the morning closing files. The boy's arms were folded across his knees and his forehead rested on his forearms. He lifted his head only slightly at the sound of Pierman's footsteps on the stairs.

The boy cleared his throat by way of giving notice that he was there, then said hoarsely, "Can I talk to you?"

"What'd you do, Matthew? Celebrate your release by spending the night outside my door?"

The boy lifted his head higher, looking at Pierman for the first time. His shirt was short sleeved, button down, and wrinkled. He wore it over jeans and black sneakers. His eyes were red and sunken and his skin, where it wasn't broken out, was gray.

Of note, the bridge of his nose was swollen, and his lower lip was pulled to one side. A scab that ran from his lip was a fraction too long and too wide to be part of the acne on his chin. Below the boy's shirt collar in the middle of a net of wrinkles, there was a maroon stain, as though someone had grabbed a fistful of the boy's shirt and wiped his chin with it.

"The Courthouse is locked," the boy said. "I didn't know where else to find you." He turned his head to rake his nose across his sleeve and winced.

"If it's about the books, you ought to get an attorney," Pierman said.

"It's not."

Running his eyes over the boy once more, Pierman sighed and agreed, "Probably not."

When he'd sat the boy on the couch in the waiting area and offered him a pop, Pierman tipped his chin at the boy's face and asked, "Get that in jail?"

The boy shook his head slowly, as if the answer were uncertain and required long thought. He did not care to meet Pierman's gaze. "I'm not supposed to be here," he said and glanced toward the door.

Pierman stood away from the boy so that he could see him, leaning back against the secretary's desk.

"Beware the damned?"

The boy nodded.

"Your old man must look worse than you then if you're here."

The boy grinned, but it made him wince again.

"You need a doctor?"

The boy shook his head.

"You want some ice?"

Again, he shook his head.

"Want to charge him?"

The boy looked up, incredulous. "No."

Pierman folded his arms and studied his shoes, willing his tone to even. "What can I do for you, Matthew?"

"I wanted to say thanks."

"You're not off the hook. There's still the books."

The boy wearily closed his eyes; it was, in his mind, just another example of how stupid adults were.

"You . . . did you really think I did it, killed that guy?"

"No, but you knew that."

The boy nodded gravely, considering. He said, "Maybe there's something else you should know."

The way he was screwing up his courage by such deliberate turns made Pierman put aside his impulse to suspect anything the boy might say.

"Matthew?"

"Sley? The queer the cops put in with me? He knows who killed Grable."

Pierman blinked a couple of times before he said, "Does he."

"Yeah," the boy said a little too quickly for Pierman's tastes.

Pierman drew a chair from his conference room, placed it in front of the boy, and sat. "Well, Matthew," he said when the boy offered nothing more, "who?"

The boy rubbed his hand on his jeans and rocked slightly. "He didn't say a name."

Shaking him would have made Pierman feel better. Instead, he smiled to show the boy they would take things at his pace. "All right then, Matthew. What did he say?"

The boy met Pierman's gaze and studied him for one last long moment before he looked away. A glance now and then to see how it was going was all Pierman got from him after that until he was through.

"He goosed me," the boy began. "When we were in line for some of the shit they call meals over there. I told him, I said don't try that fag stuff on me, and he thought that was kind of funny, I guess, 'cause he was bigger and older than me."

Now that he had started, words fell out of him.

"He said I was pretty spunky for a kid, and he thought that was funny, too, I guess 'cause of the word. He said I was pretty ballsy 'specially in view of the fact I was facing a murder charge. We were going to be roomies, he said, and I said well, don't fuck with me or I'd do to him what I'd done to Grable. He kind of laughed at me again and said if I was going to tell somebody that in there I ought to learn not to whine when I said it. Then, he kind of held up his hands and said it was okay with him 'cause he'd play it however I wanted 'cause I was his ticket out of there. And I said I didn't know what he was talking about and then he told me exactly what he was supposed to do, about how he was supposed to get me to talk to him about it and he would tell the cops what I said."

"God, he was stupid," the boy said, shaking his head in disbelief. "He actually told me what he was going to do. Is that, like, legal? Putting him in with me to get me to talk?"

"It happens," Pierman said since answering directly and honestly seemed obstructive to him at the time.

"Well," the boy said, "I told him, I said I didn't have anything he wanted since I'd already confessed. He said I was an idiot, that another guy other than him might beat the shit out of me for saying that 'cause it meant I was worthless and anyway I should never, ever give away the cookies when I'm holding the jar."

The boy squirmed a little in his chair and looked around.

"And then he thinks about it some and says it doesn't matter. He's got merchandise—his word, he was proud he knew it—he's got merchandise, he says, that'll interest the sheriff. And you. My story, he says, just would've been easier to sell."

Pierman interrupted. "What did he mean by that, Matthew, that he had merchandise?"

The boy shrugged.

"He said he'd thought about it and he'd figured it out. He said his own lawyer hadn't believed him, but fuck him, he was going to fire him and peddle the story himself. Then, they turned us both loose all of sudden and the last thing he said to me as we were walking out was he was always a lucky guy. He'd just hang onto the cookies until he needed them. It was my first lesson in crime, he said. I ought to remember it."

"How do you know that whatever Sley knows is about the murder?"

"He said his cookies were Grable flavor. God, he's stupid."

Pierman stood at the window, looking down. The pickups and boxy cars were starting to fill the square. People still came to town on Saturdays to live their lives. Pierman could tell those who had heard about the most recent events. They stopped, looked up, and scanned the Courthouse as they got out of their trucks or cars. One or two pointed out his office to children or a spouse. Pierman doubted they did that before yesterday.

Maybe Sley was not as stupid as the boy thought. Plea bargains are, as the name implies, transactions; goods and services exchanged between criminals and courts. Sley seemed to think that whatever goods he had to offer were not enough to get him where he wanted to go, which was anywhere but jail. He needed to improve his bargaining position. Whatever the Barton boy had to say might've done that, but he didn't need it. Letting Matthew into his cell improved his bargaining position so much that not only did he get out of jail he likely got out of the charges. And he kept the cookies, whatever their flavor, perhaps to use another time. No wonder he freely told the boy about his plan.

Running through the logic of it again, Pierman doubted that Sley was that strategic. D'Agostino was. Sley was more the tactical type. He'd stolen D'Agostino's plan and fired him. Regardless, the strategy and tactics were sound. Except to the extent they relied on Calkins' desperation, Pierman respected them. They just needed to be put to better use.

"Matthew," Pierman said finally, "You just bought your way out of the book problem."

The boy turned to Pierman, appalled. "I don't want out."

"If your information produces results . . . ." Pierman considered the matter some more. "Even if doesn't, I will tell the Court you voluntarily came forward with information in an effort to help authorities resolve the murder." He began to phrase it as if he were in court, rehearsing it to see how it sounded. "That would be evidence of remorse and your desire to comply with the rules of society. The charges should accordingly be dropped." Pierman shrugged out of the persona. "You're out."

"I just told you," the boy said, his voice becoming shrill, "I'm not looking for a way out."

"I know." From the window, Pierman looked back and down at him. "Mostly, you came here to show up your old man, Sley, and me."

"No," the boy began, but Pierman cut him off.

"Same thing with the books. That was showing up your old man, his church, your school, maybe, given adolescent self-absorption, Lindley as a whole."

"That's not true," the boy said, his voice cracking.

"Like the rest of us, though," Pierman said, "you're inconsistent. You're a big proponent of freedom of speech and, I presume from that, tolerance, but you call Mr. Sley a 'fag'. I can live with inconsistency. I'm quite willing to accept good results from bad reasons.

Which is to say I don't much care why you're here, if it's going to help us out with the Grable case."

Pierman shrugged.

"I suppose it's an occupational strain on martyrs and revolutionaries, keeping motives pure—sorting them out, not letting the personal pollute the ideal or letting the ideal put too pretty a face on the personal—so the ends won't be tainted by the means. I 'spect only zealots or psychopaths always get it right, but then that's what sets them apart, isn't it? They just don't—can't?—care."

The boy had tears on his face. "Why're you saying this?"

"I think your punishment—what's going to get to you more than jail or restitution—ought to be to deny you what you want, notoriety, martyrdom. And it's time you grew up."

Pierman listened to the last part echo in his head.

"Pull yourself together," he said. "I'm going to get a tape."

❁

Loud, startling, and slightly disheveled, Calkins landed like Sunday's paper on Pierman's doorstep that night. At eleven, eleven-thirty, he pounded Pierman's door.

"Police," he barked and pounded again. "Open up."

He smirked, gratified at Pierman's flushed expression of confusion and annoyance when he yanked open the door.

"You sleeping?" He looked Pierman up and down, making a point of taking in Pierman's T-shirt, running shorts, and bare feet. "Get some clothes on. We're stepping out."

Pierman blocked the door, his hand still on the knob, refusing to be moved.

"You find him?" he asked. He had called Calkins and ordered him to bring in Sley as soon as the Barton boy had left.

"I got a lead," Calkins said. "Let's go see if it's any good."

Calkins had on a khaki-colored T-shirt, jeans, running shoes, and a foam-and-mesh, yellow, billed cap that spelled out in green letters the name of a Little League team sponsor. His shirttail was half out, the cap was cockeyed, and he smelled of beer. Pierman saw no badge, gun, or anything else that would identify Calkins as a police officer.

"You on duty or off?" he asked.

Calkins propped himself on the doorframe, crossed his left leg across his right, and pulled up his pants leg. He wore a small revolver in an ankle holder. "On," he said, without weaving or stumbling in that awkward position. "Always on."

Pierman tried one more time. "We on business or just howling at the moon?"

"Both," Calkins said brightly. "Call it undercover work."

The fact that Calkins was driving the restored Cutlass Pierman had seen in his garage and not his patrol car did nothing to allay Pierman's concerns, but they did not go far. Calkins parked alongside a small brick building a couple of blocks from the Courthouse. With his window down, Pierman caught odors of fried food, cigarette smoke, and sweat.

"Ever been to Skelly's?" Calkins asked, still cheerful.

"Joe, I want to know what you have in mind."

"A little beer. A little conversation."

Calkins reached under the seat and produced a wire coat hanger.

"A little abortion?" Pierman said acidly.

"You always know the right thing to say," Calkins said. "Stay here. Be back in a second."

Pierman watched Calkins trot down the alley behind the building. He quickly straightened up and stared ahead at the sound of footsteps. In the outside mirror, Pierman could see a young couple barely out of their teens weave in tandem toward the car. The woman was on full display with a tight, scooped halter, short-short cutoffs, and platform shoes. The man had his hand in the back pocket of her jeans. He talked loudly and crudely about the points of the woman's anatomy he found appealing. She giggled. A braced paralysis spread across Pierman's arms and chest. They passed without noticing him, and he hissed out the breath he had held. In many ways, he recognized, he was his mother's son.

"Okay." Calkins appeared at the window. Pierman jumped. "Let's go."

Calkins caught the wooden screen door before it slammed. He pointed Pierman to the right toward a table in the corner nearest the door, then eased Pierman aside so he could take the corner chair. It gave him a clear view of both the door and the bar. Calkins pulled a rumpled pack of cigarettes from the front pocket of his jeans, put it in the center of the table, and nodded an invitation to Pierman. Pierman yielded to desire, lighting one with the book of matches Calkins had tucked under the cellophane. A box fan suspended on chains above them noisily caught the smoke and sent it packing toward the far corner of the room.

The place held light and color dear, caching them in pockets around the edges. Facing them along the wall on their right, a man reflectively sipped beer while he waited for a pinball machine to chime his scores. His furrowed face was orange with light that seeped up from the machine through the bottom of his mug. Enough light spilled over on a table behind the player for Pierman to make out the couple he had seen outside. Their heads were close and their hands were locked between them on the table so that the man's upraised thumb teased the woman's nipple. She smiled dreamily and swayed in time to the chipped voice of a woman singing country on the jukebox behind them.

Across the room, a neon beer sign threw down a corrosive purple cast on amber bottles behind the bar. Two young men with long, greasy hair stood at the rail, working their way through a stack of tipboards. Sparse, patchy beards appeared in the flash of the flame tongue that licked up from the ashtray between them each time one tossed in a used card and lit it. The erratic pulsing light of an inaudible Saturday Night Live sketch played across the back of a man with his head down on his arms at the end of the bar. Behind him in shadow was another figure, a large figure, seated at a table near a set of double doors, but the green exit sign that lived above the doors was not bright enough for Pierman to tell more than that.

Calkins had scanned the room, then watched Pierman do the same.

"You act like you never been in a dive before," he said, snorting at Pierman's slightly offended expression. "Hell, this is Lindley's one and only."

"And Sley's supposed to be here?" Pierman demanded.

But Calkins was intent on the figure at the back, who turned out to be a woman. She approached ponderously, tacking toward them like a gelatinous bowling pin. The flat black beehive that cupped her round face was immobile, but extra flesh swung from side to side with each step as though she carried a bag around her waist under her apron.

"Skelly!" Calkins welcomed her as though he owned the place. "It's about time. We're thirsty."

"In my place, likes as you are obliged to address me as Miss Skelly."

"Miss Skelly," Calkins corrected himself wryly and looked down at his hands, which he had folded on the table. With only the weak light from the street to illuminate her face, Pierman could not make out her eyes, which were sunk deep in black slits between her brow and swollen cheeks.

"Thought we had an understanding," she said, drawing the towel she held in one hand through her other hand as she glared down at Calkins.

"That we did and do," he said. He had to tip his chair back on its hind legs to take her all in. When he loosely crossed his legs, he put one hand on the ankle with the holster he had shown Pierman earlier. "If we didn't, I'd be in uniform and there'd be a marked car outside."

She thrust herself up on tiptoe to see over the curtain into the street. The jaundiced street light turned her pudgy lips black and threw spackled makeup into relief. When she tipped her head back, a growth with the texture of cauliflower bloomed from among the folds of her neck.

"Been a long time since you been in to see me on pleasure, Joey-boy," she said coyly, landing on her heels and smiling down at Calkins.

"Just pull us a couple of beers," Calkins said, suddenly put off by the game.

She waddled off in a huff and Calkins brought his chair down on all fours. "Our hostess," he confided.

"Jesus, she's something straight out of a Fellini movie."

Calkins looked away. "I guess I wouldn't know."

Pierman watched her fill the mugs. She said something to the two unwashed men at the bar. One sneaked a look over his shoulder. They picked up the tipboards and put them in their pocket.

"Every once in a while," Calkins said, smiling back at the guys at the bar, "somebody starts yammering to close her down. Mostly it's hens in church circles or some store owner who's had his window busted on a rowdy night." He tucked in his chin and frowned. "We listen but we never do it. Even trash's got to go someplace. Skelly keeps it in one place so's we can keep an eye it."

"And the agreement?"

Calkins nodded, almost sad. "We don't come in or raid, long as she keeps them quiet. And she does pretty well." He suddenly grinned and slid his eyes over to Pierman. "As you might imagine."

When Skelly returned with the beers, she gave Pierman her full leering attention. "Who's your friend?" she asked Calkins without looking his way.

Pierman started to introduce himself, but Calkins cut him off.

"Just that. A friend."

"Joey, honey, I ain't seen *him* before," she said, sidling up to Pierman. Her belly caressed his arm. "State? Maybe excise?"

"Why do you say that, Miss Skelly?" Pierman said, amused.

"Oh my, and he's polite," she said, pinching Pierman's cheek. "Must be state," she said pointedly to Calkins.

"Well, honey," she said, turning back to Pierman and caressing his cheek with the back of her forefinger, "I can't think of any other reason your friend, the sheriff, and you, a stranger, would be in here 'less it's about that Grable boy's murder, and I'd bet your friend, the sheriff"–she tilted her high, black head in Calkins' direction–"like so many other areas of his sorry-ass life, just isn't up to handling that himself."

Pierman took her hand from his face, kissed the back of it, and put it back on her hip. He cocked his head toward the guy at that end of the bar.

"That Billy McQueen drooling on your woodwork?"

"Sure, sugar," she said, looking at the back of her hand and smiling, "He keeps that end mighty clean."

Pierman smiled back at her.

"He a regular?"

"This here's a bar. He's a drunk."

She turned her hand back and forth in front of her face as though admiring a ring.

"When was the last time you saw him before that Grable boy was killed?"

She dropped her hand and stared at Pierman.

"Son of a bitch," she said. "I think it was a night, no, two, before that boy was killed."

Pierman turned very serious. "And you think that because?"

"Because it was a memorable night. Billy actually had money for his tab for once. He came in, drank heavy, even by his standards, and paid cash. Son of a bitch."

"Where'd he get the money?" Pierman said.

"Damned if I know." She held out her wet tray to Calkins. "Speaking of paying."

Calkins looked annoyed, put out with Pierman and her. "Billy gets to run a tab," he said, "and I don't?"

The woman shook the tray under his nose.

"Ain't nothing in this life free, 'specially not cop beer."

Calkins dropped a couple of singles on the tray. Pierman added a five on top.

"For the conversation," he said.

"Shit," she said, shaking beer off the five and tucking it up under her apron, "in that case, I'll tell you something else memorable. Billy's boy rolled in here 'bout midnight and took him home. I don't remember the last time I'd seen the boy and surely not with his dad. Well-known fact, his boy hates him."

$$\text{\textit{2}}$$

When she had gone, Calkins said, "Maybe you want to go wash your lips."

Pierman ignored the remark, thinking about what she had said.

"Let's do a reality check," he said. "Did Nate tell us he intended to meet his old man here, but didn't? That he couldn't find him?"

Calkins pursed his lips. "That's what he said."

Pierman and Calkins looked at each other, but Pierman was not seeing him. Instead, he reviewed what else he had seen and heard when they'd last seen Bill McQueen and searched his house.

"What's LURP?" Pierman asked finally.

"What?"

"LURP. L-U-R-P. I'm asking you what it is."

When Pierman used the word the first time, Calkins' eyes locked on him then ambled off.

"What makes you think I'd know anything about it?"

"Because it has something to do with military service, probably Viet Nam."

Without warning, Calkins turned surly.

"Neither of which you'd know a thing about."

"Not a thing," Pierman agreed simply.

For a while, Calkins sat quietly, eyes fixed on shadows in the middle of the tavern, and sipped his beer in short, quick takes that he seemed to suck through his teeth.

"L-R-R-P," he said finally. He put the beer down and looked at Pierman. "Long Range Reconnaissance Patrol."

"Which is what, please?"

"A small unit, five, maybe six, who went behind enemy lines, if you could call them lines, to reconnoiter." He picked up his beer and sipped again.

"And?"

"And. Shit, and." He swallowed the last third of the mug and wiped his mouth. "And sometimes they did other things. Ambushes. Sometimes, they were advanced as sniper teams."

"They have a radio man?"

"Sure, that's how you got in or out, but they didn't spend a lot of time on the radio, not if they liked living. Those guys were more about being quiet, moving, staying out of sight."

Calkins took one of his cigarettes, lighted it, and blew a large cloud of smoke out of the side of his mouth. He did not blink or take his eyes off Pierman; he appreciated Pierman enough to know where he was going.

"Safe to say, then," Pierman said, "these would be men who knew how to move quietly without being tracked and would, on occasion, kill at long range."

"Yes, they would be such men," Calkins said.

"Did you know McQueen had something to do with that?

"That's how he spent his time in Viet Nam. That's how he got that scar. He and his patrol got caught out. Had to fight their way out by hand.

"All this time you've known that?"

Calkins shrugged. "Small town. I've known."

"And every time I've asked you who around here was capable of killing in the way we've seen you've said you didn't know."

"Don't know."

"How can you say that?"

Calkins shrugged again, but he kept his eyes on Pierman's. "Don't know."

Pierman stared at him, then grappled for a couple of dollars in the pocket of his jeans and tossed them on the table.

As he turned to walk, Calkins said, "Allen. Aren't you a little curious about what I've got in mind?"

When Pierman stopped and turned back to him, Calkins sighed, leaned back his chair, and looked away.

"Aren't you just a little afraid," he said, "of what I might do?"

$\mathfrak{D}$

"Sure you are," Calkins said amiably when Pierman took his seat again. "Sometimes, I am, too."

He waved two fingers at Skelly at the back of the room. While they waited for her to waddle her way to the bar then to their table, Calkins stared at his hands, which he had folded across his stomach.

"I mean, hell," he said, "you got to wonder. Guy goes off to war, kills some people, it's always going to be a question."

Pierman did not respond, his agreement implicit. When Skelly brought the beer, Pierman slid the money he had thrown on the table toward her and waved her away without taking his eyes off Calkins.

"You have no way to understand, so I'll explain it," Calkins said when she left. "You still won't understand, but this is how it works," he said, finally looking up at Pierman, his expression kindly and sad.

"I will never again feel things like I did then. Happy, sad, pissed off, funny, any feeling I had. Nothing that strong, nothing that changed so quick, never again." He drank half his beer in two swallows. "I will never be as intimate with anyone—not my wife, not anyone else—as I was with those men then. And I'm not talking about sex." He waved the notion away. "I'm talking about knowing what's in somebody else's head and heart at any time without being told. You're the guy who's good with words, you can put the fucking poetry to it, but I don't reckon you can." Pierman started to open his mouth, but Calkins said, "And don't try now."

245

Calkins took the last cigarette from the pack, lighted it, and blew out a cloud.

"The intensity of it was too scary, least for some. Those guys won't talk about it, ever, to anyone. Other guys liked it so much they keep trying to get it back. They read every fucking book ever written about that goddamn place, join the Legion, tell the war stories. But that'll never work either, cause what they don't talk about much is the price you pay getting there."

He smiled, considering the irony.

"You know, blood. The currency of war. Your blood, your buddy's blood, enemy blood. We all had it and we were all fighting to keep it or take it. I never used to know what preachers meant when they said you had to be 'washed in the blood' to be saved, to be one with God, but after that I did. I learned it there, and this part *is* like sex, 'cause it's all 'bout bodily fluid. Swapping fluid makes you feel. Swapping fluid makes you intimate."

He stubbed out the cigarette and leaned back his chair.

"You can explain what makes you do the things you have to do any way you want," he said reasonably. "Training, duty, your survival, your buddies' survival. Paint it however you want, it's still about blood. And the question is: when it's over and it's time to move on, now that you know you can do it, that you *are* capable of taking blood, to keep yours, to keep men you love from losing theirs, would you— could you?—do it again?"

He snickered.

"What's the old joke? 'Why does a dog lick his balls? Because he can?'"

He brought the chair down, put his arms through the chain of wet mug rings on the table, and leaned toward Pierman.

"At some point, every one of us who was there'll ask himself that question. Most of us try to avoid it long as we can. That's what jobs and family are for. They distract. But in the end, each of us'll ask, and only each of us can answer.

"The question you asked is pretty much the same question, and the honest answer—the only one I'm going to give you—is, if the circumstances're right, I'm the only one *I* know who's capable of it in Holoce County. I can't—and won't—speak for McQueen."

♋

The pinball machine was mercifully quiet, the player gone after what seemed like twenty, thirty dollars in coins. The couple left shortly after him. The man had trouble getting the woman out; he had to put his arm around her and cup her breast for extra leverage. It looked like it hurt, but she only giggled and nibbled his ear. At the bar, Skelly washed glasses while the two men at the bar drooped closer to the rail.

Pierman could think of nothing to say when Calkins finished. He nodded once, and Calkins eased his eyes away. They sat like that for some time, neither able to look at the other, before Pierman went to the bar, ordered two more beers and another pack of cigarettes from the now sullen Skelly, and brought them back to the table.

Pierman was tilting his head one way and another to read the obscenities carved in the table when the screen door slammed behind him. Calkins pulled his hat lower over his brow and softly said, "Showtime."

He told Pierman to stay put and steadied the back of his chair with one hand as he stood so that it would not squeak. Sley had his arms around the shoulders of the pair at the bar, ordering them another round. Calkins placed himself between the door and bar.

"Wes-ley," Calkins said in falsetto, reminding Pierman of someone calling a dog home to dinner.

Sley turned, blinked, and bolted for the double doors at the back. When he hit the crash bars, the doors burst open to admit a half foot of night and stopped. Sley's momentum carried him forward. He dropped to the floor holding his head as the doors sighed shut.

Only Calkins knew what to do at first. He barged through Sley's friends, who had stepped away from the bar and stared, and jerked the thrashing man to his feet.

"This man's hurt, Miss Skelly. I'll do you favor and get him some attention."

"Bastard!" Skelly shouted. "Motherfucker!"

She came up from behind the bar with a sawed-off baseball bat and pounded it on the bar as she advanced on Calkins.

"Come in here, beat up my customers. You fucked me."

Calkins pushed Sley's head back to the ground with one hand, kneeled, and began reaching for the gun on his ankle. Pierman caught Skelly's arm on the way up as she came out from behind the bar, and after a struggle, twisted the bat out of her hand.

"You want to press charges, see me in the morning," he said in a low voice. He held her arm close against her, trying to keep his body between Skelly and Calkins. He tipped his chin to the men at the bar. "We'll talk about unauthorized gambling while we're at it."

"Who the fuck're you?" Skelly spit and yanked herself out of his grasp.

"The prosecutor. Now shut up."

Calkins had dragged Sley backward by the collar until he could open the double doors with his rump. With one hand, he reached through the crack and unwound the coat hanger he'd twisted through the handles outside.

"Joe. Let's go," Pierman said. He backed away from Skelly, waving the bat he still held behind him to guide himself out, but Calkins was long gone. Pierman nearly fell backward in his haste to follow.

Calkins had Sley draped on his belly across the hood of the Cutlass, patting him down. He heard Pierman approach.

"Thanks, Allen," he said calmly, not looking around, "but you should've kept your mouth shut. She didn't need to know who you were."

Pierman's fingers wound and rewound around the bat as he checked up and down the street and tried to slow his heart rate. The club clattered on the pavement when it landed twenty yards away. He stepped in close to Calkins.

"It's bad enough you doing something like this," he said, "but to get me involved? Are you nuts?"

"I wouldn't worry," Calkins said, backing Pierman away with his forearm. "Nobody's going to believe Skelly. But if you need to, you can tell them the truth. I led you into it. You wouldn't've stood for it if you'd known, and I dumped you before you saw anything I could really be charged for."

Calkins let Sley down, but held him pinned and moaning against the car with a hand on his back.

"That would be the truth, wouldn't it, Allen? You didn't expect a thing? 'Are you on duty or off?' 'Are we on business or just howling at the moon?'"

"He's going to kill me, man," Sley suddenly yowled.

Calkins spun him around. "Shut up." Calkins spiked Sley on the bridge of the nose with the bill of his cap. Sley squealed and grabbed his nose.

"Are you going to kill him?" Pierman asked, putting a hand on Calkins arm. "Is that why you had to drink before you came to see me tonight? Are we back to blood?"

"I'm going to talk to him, Allen," Calkins said. He removed Pierman's hand gently, but the effort to restrain himself, to be reasonable, seemed to take a lot out of him, and he sighed. "I'm going to find out what we need to know."

"How far do you intend to go to do that?" Pierman said. "What you've—we've—done already could be explained."

Calkins took a set of cuffs from his back pocket.

"Wesley, my boy," he said, "would you like to get in the car?"

Sley looked from one silent face to the other before nodding.

"Say it," Calkins ordered.

"Yes."

"See?" Calkins muttered as much to himself as to Pierman. "Voluntary. No coercion. No kidnaping."

He turned Sley gently, put the cuffs on, and, with one hand on Sley's head, folded him into the front seat. He closed the door, tugged his keys from his jeans, and started around the car. Pierman started to step off the curb to follow, but Calkins laid his fingertips on Pierman's chest, holding him gently at arm's length.

"I've never done anything like this before, Allen." He let his hand fall. "If that helps any."

Pierman came no further. His whiskers felt sharp in his palm, and when he rubbed his face, their rasp filled his head for what seemed like a long time.

"Neither have I," he said finally.

"Stay close to your office. I 'spect somebody'll be up to see you."

As Calkins got in the car, he said, "Wesley, how 'bout a little bedtime story?"

The whimpers grew louder, longer, nearly frenzied. The car radio came on loud, an oldies station, the music of their generation. Pierman stepped back onto the curb.

17

Pierman waited until noon the next day before he could stand it no longer and called.

Why yes, Gloria said, she surely did answer the sheriff's phone on Sundays 'cause the county was too damned cheap to pay for a dispatcher on a generally slow day. And no, Gloria said, Joe was not there. She didn't know where he was. That wasn't really unusual, Gloria said, since the sheriff, without enough help, was gone at all hours doing things he never told her about.

"But since you asked, Allen," Gloria said, "why don't you know where my husband is? He told me he was going to see you last night after he'd drunk a bellyful of beer."

He told her truthfully they had followed up a lead in the Grable matter and that he hadn't seen Joe since midnight. Saying more at that point seemed unnecessary and unwise. His father used to say, putting a rock on a fire sometimes put it out.

Cross buried Willie at one that day. He did it for free. Since Willie had no money, Cross put enough embalming fluid in him to keep him until Sunday, when he figured people would most likely attend a funeral for a man with no family and few friends, donated a cardboard casket, and ordered an opening in the corner of the old cemetery reserved for paupers. Cross cut to the chase, however. He scheduled only graveside rites, skipping a service at the funeral home. He was a compassionate enough man, but free was free.

When he arrived, Pierman found there were more than he'd expected. To his surprise, Pierman spotted Purcell, watching from an unmarked car parked down the lane. Pierman made a point of waving as he got out of his car. Two elderly women in dark, veiled hats and flower-print dresses came from the tiny church Willie attended. They took seats on the first of two rows of chairs that been set up facing the casket, as though they were family. Jenks, the local newspaper reporter Pierman had done everything in his power to avoid since Randy Grable was murdered, wandered in just before the service began and sat on the end of the back row. He had thrown on a houndstooth jacket over an open, stained shirt and striped, seersucker pants to gather pathos for Monday's edition.

The pasty, young preacher obviously was an ascetic. Like a coat hanger, he carried more than wore a brittle, black Sears suit that was size or two too big, and it was easy to imagine that his lank, brown hair had been chopped by someone standing over a newspaper laid on his kitchen floor. Pierman wondered whether his lifestyle choices were a function of his theology or the church board who called and paid him.

A crestfallen look came over the preacher's horsey face when he stepped before the casket and sized up the house, but he quickly tucked it away and did his duty. He brought a hand to his wispy goatee, fixed his eyes on the old ladies, and directed them in a bleating voice not to grieve. Brother Willis Dunbar might now be living a better life than he had ever known on this earth. He was a good and simple man who had worked hard for his community. But it all depended. We were all sinners, and until we, each of us—his eyes fell on Jenks then Pierman—gave ourselves up to the Lord we could not entertain even the faintest hope of knowing life everlasting.

The preacher harangued them for several more minutes, but Pierman had stopped listening. The man had picked the wrong time to ride down hard on the living and hedge his bets on the dead. Pierman may not have believed a word the preacher said, but he bowed his head with the others and, for a moment, for Willie's sake, let himself hope.

The old ladies tottered forward to compliment the young man when he was done. As Pierman watched him smile down on them with hoarded benevolence, Jenks sidled up.

"What'd you think?" he asked.

"Of the sermon? I really had no idea whom he was talking to."

"Yes, I was thinking I should've brought a tape recorder. I certainly don't know what his rush was. The guest of honor wasn't in any hurry."

"Might have something to do with how much he's getting paid."

"That's cynical."

"So's your funeral suit. Order it from Barnum and Bailey?"

Jenks had been a small-town reporter too long to allow his dignity to interfere with his work.

"Good one. I'll have to remember it," he said, riffling through his pad until he found a clean page and poised his pen over it. "I don't suppose you've changed your mind about talking about the current conflict."

"No."

"Not after it's moved into the very *heart* of your office?"

"For that reason most of all."

"That could look quite suspicious."

"Of whom?"

Jenks shifted his skinny spider's frame uncomfortably, then raised his hand with an exasperated flourish.

"Well, you, of course."

Pierman smiled at him. "Then you know something I don't."

For a moment, they were quiet while each decided that calling the other a liar would not end well.

"Well, then," Jenks said, "maybe you'd be good enough to tell our readers why you came today."

Pierman brought his hand to his forehead as if to shade his eyes, then quickly put it in his pocket.

"Why does anybody come to these things?" he said and watched Jenks write it down. His gaze made Jenks uncomfortable.

"We weren't off the record, you know."

"I didn't say we were."

"That's not going to look so good in print either. I must tell you that."

"Then I'll have to trust you not to print it."

Jenks looked at what he'd written. He tore off the sheet, crumpled it, and placed it in Pierman's hand, curling Pierman's fingers around it.

"So much of good writing is tone," Jenks said. "I don't think I care to jeopardize that with flippancy in this piece."

๛

Pierman did not wave this time. He went straight to Purcell's car.

"I'm surprised to see you," Pierman said, putting his hands on the side of the car, leaning down toward the open window, invading Purcell's space.

"I'm surprised to be here," Purcell said. He leaned away from Pierman reflexively, but in a car, he could only go so far. "Your sheriff was supposed to cover this. Nobody can find him. Where is he?"

"Not my day to watch him."

"Well, I was going to call you anyway. Got the forensics back on that stuff in the woods. About what we expected. A piece of plastic sheeting and a piece of a tree. Maybe if you told me how you came across it and what you think it is."

"I don't think I want to see it in the newspaper, thank you."

Purcell leaned away again, this time to appraise Pierman. "Do I know what you're talking about?"

"Sure you do. The local press knows about that little flyer you took at me up in my office the day we found Willie and Ginny. I've always thought it a good idea for cops to be seen and not heard."

Purcell rapped the steering wheel with the heel of his hand. "Calkins must've been running his mouth."

"No, it was you. Jenks hung his striped ass out this very window before he wandered into the service, didn't he."

Purcell's jaw bulged as he started the car.

"One of these days, your hunches aren't going to pan out. You're going to be knee-deep in shit without anybody to pull you out. You just cinched it for me. I'm done with you."

The pea gravel ticked off the bumper: to Pierman's ear, a highly satisfying sound.

"Don't like using them much," said the old man with the engineer's cap. Cross had introduced him as the cemetery caretaker. The finger he raised was as thick, knuckled, and hooked as the backhoe he jabbed the air toward. "Damn tires tear up the sod. Makes mowing tough."

The vault man was stout, middle-aged, and dressed in moss-colored work clothes. He nodded impatiently. It was Sunday. He'd heard it all before.

"Wouldn't've thought of using it for your Pop," the caretaker said, directing his lecture to Pierman. "Only use that thing in this corner. Plenty of room."

The man's phlegmy voice was too loud by half in the cool shade. Talking too long to the deaf, Pierman thought, but as they gathered on either side of the chrome frame that held the casket poised over the grave, Pierman saw the crimson webs float over the slats of his yellowed cheeks and picked up the fruity odor of cheap wine.

"Watch your step," the vault man said, as he moved Pierman aside so that he could get to the crank on the frame.

"Yah," the caretaker bellowed like he was driving mules. "Stones here don't stay fast."

He peeled off the cap and waved it around him toward the rows of small, cement rectangles nearby. They were pushed in level with the ground. Names and dates had been scratched on the tops when the cement was wet.

"Can't afford a base for them," the caretaker said. "Winters push them up."

As the vault man cranked the casket into the hole, the caretaker pulled a long, paisley bandana from his hip pocket and wiped away the sweat and the saliva that foamed in tiny bubbles at the corners of his mouth.

"Don't have to make them, you know. The stones. County won't pay for them, not here in this corner." The caretaker blew his nose with a honk and bored out each nostril before he put the bandana away. "But I always have a little goo left over when I set the fancy stones. Did a batch this morning, matter of fact."

Since no one cared enough to remark on it, the caretaker continued as though he was obliged to fill the air.

"Your big can works best, like what they get cling peaches in over at the school cafeteria. That's where I get mine. Saw them down the middle." The caretaker shook his head and laughed. "Trouble is, by the time I get around to it, I have a hell of time remembering the dates."

He stepped forward to seesaw the lowering straps out from under the casket while the vault man went to get his wagon.

"I don't imagine you'll have any trouble remembering the date on this one," Pierman said, hoping to prod him into doing something not to forget.

"Can's a mighty handy thing to have in this line of work," the caretaker said, chuckling.

Cross touched Pierman's arm. "Thank you," he whispered. "I'm leaving. You don't have to stay."

Pierman nodded his understanding, then shook his head.

"Had a feller once," the caretaker was saying. "He'd gone off to New York City and made a pile. Gave most of it to some college 'cause he was a bachelor feller and didn't have family. You a bachelor?"

Pierman smiled and nodded.

"Well, when this feller died, see, he wanted to be buried with his folks over in J." The hooked forefinger came up and dabbed the air in the direction of another section. "But they cremated him, see. And since his people was all gone and nobody thought to buy him an urn, they put his ashes in a can and shipped him here. Maxwell House coffee can. Good to the last drop. Ain't that something?"

The caretaker cackled.

"I kep' it on a shelf nearly a year thinking maybe somebody'd do something about it, but they never did, so I buried him that way. Yah. More'n a million, and him in a can." The caretaker wiped away the foam from his mouth with the back of his hand. "We're kinda democratic 'round here. Treat them all the same once they're in."

He moved three rolls of sod to give the vault man a clear path to the hole. When the wagon was centered, the vault man ran the rattling chain through the pulley attached to the top of the wagon frame and lowered the cement box. Like Willie with his watch, Pierman thought, hand over hand. The caretaker stood beside Pierman now, watching the vault man down in the hole covering the box with two square lids.

"Won't keep the worms out," the old man said. "Not like your better models. But the ground'll cave once it settles if you don't have them. Makes for a bumpy ride on a mower."

The vault man hoisted himself out of the grave, tied up the chain, and sucked a click out of his cheek. "Gotta go," he said.

"Yah," the caretaker said and waved.

He and Pierman stood for a time.

"You wanting to say some words?" the caretaker asked.

"I'm no preacher."

As the man nodded, Pierman nudged a stray clod into the hole with his toe. He took his wallet from his back pocket. He had two twenties, which he held out to the caretaker.

"How much longer do you suppose it would take to use a shovel on this one?"

The caretaker leisurely removed his cap, scratched his bristly gray hair with it still in his hand, and ladled it back on.

"Not that much longer, I reckon. On this one."

"Want some help?"

The caretaker took in Pierman's suit, tie, and dress shoes. A ragged snicker started up his chest, but when he saw Pierman's expression, he stifled it.

"Nah," he said. "Don't like that goddamned machine anyway."

Pierman turned to leave.

"I won't forget the date on this one," the caretaker called.

Behind him, Pierman heard the first shovelfuls hit the vault. The clods sounded deep and throaty, adagio bursts on an unsnared drum.

The silence on the other end when Pierman picked up the phone that night made him a little queasy, but it didn't last long, certainly not long enough for him to attribute it to any particular one of the many fears that ran through his head as he dozed in a chair in his living room.

"You haven't called," Kay sighed at last.

"I've had my hands full," he said, suddenly furious at her for the way he knew she would make him feel.

"I saw you in the cemetery today. They laid my brother's stone last week."

It was Pierman's turn to pause.

"I saw you, too," he said.

"I know."

He had thought he recognized the pickup truck parked across the cemetery as he walked away from the caretaker. He went closer, stopped behind one of the maples, and peered around it. She stood over a sparkling new marble stone. Her head was bent, and a white tail hung from the fist at her mouth.

"It's crooked," she said faintly.

"What? I'm sorry?"

"The stone. They set it crooked."

"The caretaker has wine for breakfast."

He had been drawn almost before he realized it. He could have gone to her, and without a word, she would have let him hold her while she shuddered against his chest. But he stayed, and the bark where he had placed his hand bit his fingertips. The shudders would pass and then where would they be? And wasn't she the one who understood that long before he did?

The sound of falling dirt was gone. The old man's steady, rhythmic grunts were all he could hear, and for once, it was sound that counted. He listened, then gradually he backed away. Still, when he turned, he hoped she wouldn't see.

"So how have you been?" she said.

Silences had become a meddlesome third party to the conversation.

"Kay," he said back across the void.

"Just forget it," she snapped. "And thanks for nothing. You let that Barton, that kid, go."

"Kay."

"Nate was right. You are such a chickenshit."

He barely heard the dial tone over the echoes in his skull.

18

Without preamble Darrell said, "Where is he?"

Pierman knew whom he meant. He said, "I don't know."

Darrell went straight to Pierman's apartment early Monday morning when the graveyard shift ended. He got Pierman out of bed. Pierman was tired of talking to cops on his doorstep in his underwear.

"There's talk you and him went to Skelly's Saturday night," Darrell said.

"Yes."

"They say he drug Sley out of there. They say you wrestled Skelly for a club while he was doing it."

Pierman was always careful not to ask a client directly about things he did not want to know. He thought Darrell was doing the same thing now.

"Do they," Pierman said. He concentrated on looking Darrell in the eye.

"His wife tells me he's took a vacation." Under stress, Darrell forgot his professional aspirations and reverted to our patois. "She don't seem worried, but she don't act like she knows where he is."

Pierman concentrated on keeping surprise off his face.

"Don't seem like a good time to take a vacation. With this Grable matter."

"No," said Pierman, more distractedly than he intended.

"So where is he?"

"I don't know."

Darrell required time to formulate his response.

"Well," he said, turning and tossing a hand in the air. "I'd sure as hell like to know why not."

⚲

Gloria answered the door to the apartment in the jail. No surprise, Pierman noted. This morning, she favored an accusatory look.

"You wait there."

She left him on the other side of the door while she stepped back into the shadows of the apartment. From inside, Pierman could hear the low, indistinct grumble of the building's other occupants. By this time, Calkins probably had tuned it out, but Pierman doubted Gloria ever did.

She returned with a package, a small box wrapped in grocery bag paper and sealed with strapping tape.

"The livestock's hungry," she said. "I'm busy."

"You're always feeding them, Gloria. What's going on?"

She studied his face.

"He said give you that. Said you might need it. Said tell you, do what he said. I figured you knew what's going on."

"I don't."

It was not an answer she expected. She blinked away a stricken look. She turned her face back into the shadows of her home, her eyes roaming across toys scattered on the floor.

"Welcome to the fucking club," she said, her eyes returning to Pierman. She was nearly amused at his reaction to her language.

"You'll be pleased to know," she said, "he puts more faith in you than me. He said you'd figure it out."

⚲

Calkins had said he was to wait in his office, somebody'd be along to see him. As Pierman walked from the jail to the courthouse, he looked around the square, hoping to see Sley or Calkins waiting for him. All he saw were the loafers, who were already gathering on the bench. They waved, but Pierman was already checking the other side of the square.

When he got to his office in the courthouse, he called Edith at his father's office, but she had no messages for him. Really, she said, why should there be?

He tried to think of whom else he could call, but he realized that he did not know who Calkins' friends were now or much of anything about his personal life. He decided against calling Gloria to find out.

He pulled the tape recorder from the filing cabinet and placed it carefully on the corner of his desk. He found a new cassette in the bottom drawer of Ginny's desk and jammed it into the recorder. At his desk, he swiveled around to punch in the air conditioner. The cool air blew up the back of his chair onto his neck and settled around the gap between his cuffs and the tops of his thin socks. He took a deep breath, but still had to print Sley's name and the date on the cassette to make it legible. He pulled a new legal pad from the filing cabinet, sharpened two pencils, and placed them at his left hand within easy reach. He looked at his watch. It was 8:17 a.m.

Pierman got up and went to the coat tree, where he searched his jacket for cigarettes. He'd left them at home, but he had plenty of change. He put on the jacket and started for the door, but stopped. *Stay close to your office.*

As he hung his jacket back on the coat tree, he saw Calkins' package, which he had tossed onto the filing cabinet in his rush to get to the office and organize. He turned it over and around before holding it before him on his fingertips like a waiter carrying drinks on a tray. It seemed heavy for its size.

He passed up the notion of shaking it but considered closing the door. No, he decided, after an inordinate amount of time. He didn't want to give Sley the slightest excuse not to come in.

He broke two pencils trying to pry up and tear the strapping tape before he rifled Ginny's desk a second time and found a pair of scissors. When he had the paper off, he looked at it front and back. On one side was the name, address, and logo of the grocery store where the Calkins family evidently shopped. On the plain side, there was only Pierman's name, written in Calkins' illegible hand and looking little different than it had when they were in fifth grade. From the markings on the cardboard box under the paper, Pierman concluded that Skeeter had sometime in the recent past received a new pair of shoes. The box, too, was sealed. Pierman broke a third pencil before finding the scissors under the wrapping paper. The ankle holster Calkins had worn Saturday night was nestled in a bed of newspaper. It was full.

Pierman heard footsteps in the hall and looked up, poised. They passed. Pierman set the box down on his desk like it contained a vital organ. He sat back, then swiveled his chair around and punched off the air conditioner. He was shivering.

♒

One side of Pierman's stomach gnawed at the other. It was past noon, but hunger had little to do with it. He had checked the recorder at least twice, the last time singing "Jeremiah was a bullfrog, was a good friend of mine," and quickly erasing it. Twice he had tried to read, to sort through rules and cases on evidence and authorized uses of force. Twice, too, he had lifted the phone—once for Calkins, once for Kay—and replaced it without dialing. He trusted Calkins. He hated him. He could love Kay. He might hate her. Mostly, he tried to keep at bay the thought that something had gone wrong, that Sley had turned out to be tougher than Calkins thought or, worse, that Calkins got caught up in what he was doing.

He had heard footsteps all morning, some real, some imagined, and each time, he had fought their wheedling. That's why he was startled that Sley should just appear, not out of nowhere necessarily, but like a cutout in a fun house, suddenly pushed upright in the doorway to his office.

Sley waited for a signal to enter. His clothes were not torn, nor were they any dirtier than they had been two nights ago. There were no marks on him, other than the discolored knot on his forehead and an abrasion at the top of his nose that connected his eyebrows.

Both knew what was going to happen, although each seemed reluctant to start. Without speaking, Pierman beckoned Sley to a chair. Sley dragged his feet getting there. He looked blanker, more pliable, even if not yet entirely cooperative. He had nothing to say, no threats, no dares, until Pierman turned on the tape recorder and read him his rights.

"The fucker was going to shoot me up. He gave me some shit 'bout what he'd done in Viet Nam and–"

"Calkins said *he'd* done it."

"Yeah. And he said he was going to do it again. To *me.*"

Pierman decided to let the tape run.

"Did he hit you?"

"No."

"Did he touch you in any way?"

"You saw what he did."

"I saw you run into a door as you were fleeing a police officer. I believe there was a roomful of people who also saw that. I saw you subsequently resist that officer's order to get in his car," Pierman said for the benefit of the tape. "Did he show you a needle?"

"No."

"Or a pill?"

"No, but—"

"And he did not give you a drug of any type?"

"Well, no."

"But you believed he would."

"Fuck, yes. He drags my ass out into the country. No people, no lights. He's smiling some goofy smile. What was I supposed to think?"

"Just that, I imagine," Pierman said. Under the diffidence, he rejoiced.

🙎

"First of all," Sley said, "I ain't queer."

Pierman had no idea why Sley chose to start with that. He had allowed Sley's outrage at the way he had been treated to peter out, then stared at him until Sley could stand the silence no longer.

"Big hair, tight clothes, shall we say, 'a precise manner,'" Pierman said, shrugging, goading. "Who'm I to say?"

"Now see, that's the point," Sley said. "There's a difference 'tween stylish and queer." He had pronounced it "diff'ernce." "If I was queer, the last thing I'd do is advertise it, 'specially in this town. You'd do nothing but create problems for yourself. You couldn't get a job, people'll think you'll rape their children, you'd probably get the shit beat out of you on a fairly regular basis."

"Employment is a high priority with you?"

"You're not listening to me. That's what made it so strange. I mean, that McQueen guy made a pass at me."

Sley now had Pierman's attention.

"Which McQueen? Father or son?"

"Son." Sley stopped to consider the issue. "I 'spect booze's boiled all the sap out of the old man's wood," he said absently.

"When?"

"I don't know. Before that Grable kid was killed, I know that. Maybe two months."

"And?"

"We were in Turk's."

"Not Skelly's?"

"Not that night. Skelly's too low rent for him."

Sley waived the interruption away.

"McQueen's sitting by himself in the back by the can, kind of watching the room, not talking to anybody, like he does when he comes in. He acts like he's lonely, but he's such a weird fuck nobody with any sense'll go near him. Know what I mean?"

"I appreciate the lesson in group dynamics."

The remark peeved Sley. He thought he might just clam up, but Pierman pressed the lever he knew he had.

"Would you like to speak to the sheriff again?"

"He was kind of out of it," Sley said finally.

"Nate McQueen?"

"Yes, McQueen, goddamnit."

"I didn't think he drank. 'Cause of his father."

"Yeah, he says he don't, but I've seen him take a drink now and then, and there's been a couple of times I thought maybe he wasn't opposed to other forms of controlled substances."

"Meaning?"

"He looked wound up, not relaxed like he would be with booze."

"He seems to be wound up, agitated, all the time."

"These times it was more than usual."

Pierman wondered at the plural but set it aside for later.

"Scary," he said.

"No shit."

Sley slouched in the chair, crossed his legs wide, and folded his arms loosely across his stomach, getting comfortable with the telling.

"I don't think I'd seen him out of it before, but he was this time. When I walked by him to go to can, he said something about liking the way my jeans fit. You might imagine that a stylish guy like me had heard that before, so I asked him, I said flat out, 'You making a pass?' And he kinda pulled back in his chair and shook his head, like he was surprised it'd come out of his mouth.

"He said, like he was talking to himself, he said that he'd made a mistake, he'd fucked up. He'd broken his rule. He said goddamn he was tired of the rule. Then, he kind of remembers I'm standing there and he looks at me with those funky fucking eyes of his and he said forget it. Said if I told anybody what he'd said he'd have to kill me. Said he knew how to do it so's nobody'd know. And all the time he's saying it, he's got that crazy grit-teeth smile on. Like he's biting a fart. Then he ran a finger down that scar of his. Needless to say, I moved on."

"That it?" Pierman said, acting unimpressed.

"Fuck, no, that ain't it. What's it is I saw that Grable kid go up to him maybe a month later in the same damn bar, say something to him, and put a hand on McQueen. A queer hand. Ran it across his shoulders like you would with a woman.

"McQueen jerked away like he'd been scorched, said something hostile back, and bolted. I reckon McQueen wasn't nearly as drunk or out of it or whatever as he was the night he came after me. Otherwise, he'd have gone after that fine young ass, I imagine. Don't you?"

Sley looked proud of himself. Pierman kept his expression flat.

"That's it?"

"Yeah," Sley said, deflated. "That's it."

"What do you want for this?"

Sley turned a shade paler.

"Your crazy fucking friend said I wasn't supposed to ask."

Pierman walked Sley through it twice more, boring in on times, dates, precise words, and anyone else who was present in the bar on either occasion. Sley mewled over Pierman's orders to stay in town but out of sight. He didn't really want to risk his skin by hanging around. Pierman lifted the handset on his phone and offered to let Sley discuss it with Calkins at the jail. The bluff did what it was supposed to do: It settled Sley down and told Pierman Sley didn't know where Calkins was.

When Sley left, Pierman slouched back into his chair. Sley's story was far from enough to make an arrest, let alone obtain a conviction. Both would require much more leg work. With Calkins gone who knew where or for how long, Pierman could think of only one way to evaluate whether it was worthwhile to push things in that direction.

The question of whether employing that method was in his interests or the county's occurred to him, but he refused to dwell on it.

Her father answered.

"She's not much interested in talking to you these days."

"I know," Pierman said. "Would you put her on anyway, please?"

"I kind of got my orders on this thing."

"Is she there?" Pierman knew he would not lie.

"Yes."

"Then let me talk to her, please."

Until now, Pierman had not stopped to think what a relief it had been to deal with the family through Kay. The father was tough, but the scar was just forming and Pierman hated the idea of picking at it. He stabbed instead.

"It's business, Paul."

Seconds passed before the receiver bumped something hard. A minute or two passed before she picked it up.

"I hate you for what you just did," she said.

"When you and Nate McQueen were engaged, did you take him back in your woods? Did you ever show him your spot?"

For once, he caught her off guard, but she would be no less honest than her father. "He saw as much as you." Quickly recovered, she could be more so. "In every way."

Pierman's consolation was that in the silence he found he could not hate her.

"For the next few days, Kay, please," Pierman said, "stay away from him."

He did not know whether she heard him. In time, Paul Grable came back on the line.

"I'm hanging it up now," he said.

As he tried to decide whether to call Darrell or Purcell, Pierman's eyes fell on the shoe box he had put on the filing cabinet before Sley arrived. He heard again footsteps in the hall and looked toward them, poised. When they passed, he went out into the reception area and closed and locked the door. When he returned to his office, he closed that door and brought the box to his desk.

Other than the gun, there was only wadded newspaper in the box. In one wad he spread on his desk to make sure he had not missed a note from Calkins, there was an oily spot over a personal item in a column of them, the paper's best read section. It read: "Mr. and Mrs. Philip Timmins, Tammy, Tom and Kevin ate catfish Friday night at the home of Philip's mother, Mrs. Mona Everett." Pierman wondered: Why was Mrs. Everett's name different from her son's? Was Kevin an "accident" or had Phil just found another woman with less regard for alliteration? Would he again know a time when he would not question every damn thing?

He picked up Calkins' present and held it flat in his hand. The pistol nearly spilled out into his lap when he unsnapped the strap around the hammer. His thumbnail broke on the cylinder, and he had to settle for turning the gun to cautious angles at arm's length. Four silvery cones peeked out into the window light from the smooth, blue-black holes. He assumed one more and thought it curious. Didn't revolvers hold six or was that just folk wisdom from westerns and cop shows? It was a small gun.

Against the tips of his last three fingers, the grip's ridges felt sharp, rougher than they looked. He pushed the lever above his thumb and the cylinder sprang open. Brass clattered onto the desk. Pierman threaded the small cones back in with an annoyed grunt. He laid his forefinger along the barrel, then jerked it back. The gun was so stubby, his finger nearly drooped over the muzzle. He hooked his finger lightly over the trigger guard—it felt more natural there anyway—and planted his elbows on the desk to sight it. The quivering gradually stopped. Across the room, the top button of his jacket was eclipsed.

Pierman got up and went to the other side of the room. He pointed the gun as he seen on TV—legs wide and bent, arms stiff, right hand cupped in the left. Instantly, the edge of his chair dissolved. In the window one floor down and across the street, the realtor's secretary came into focus. He thought she must be out of range. He knew he could not be sure. She wore a shiny barrette. It dissolved into a gold corona. It glowed around the black knob at the end of the barrel.

He tried again. He was faster. Once more, faster still. The fourth time, he held it. Then he stepped forward. His arms were still rigid, but they lowered with each step toward the window until he could see down into street. How much would you have to lead a car? A pedestrian?

Many of his colleagues in Chicago carried guns, but he had never felt sufficiently threatened to think about it for long. His only experience with guns was when he was eleven. For Christmas, as he had asked, the old man had given him a BB gun but withheld the BBs until after dinner when he could show the boy how to use it. All morning, Pierman had held rifle, fondled it actually. All morning, he had dreamed of plinking the tree ornaments, blowing the fragile, ripe balls, one by one into a billion glistening flakes. Looking once more at the secretary's barrette, Pierman had to put the pistol down until the mood passed.

Even empty, the holster was stiff enough to hold its shape. Which was best? Right or left? Inside the ankle or out? He could not remember how Calkins wore it. Pierman was right-handed; he decided inside-left. He walked around the desk twice. He wished he had a mirror and laughed; he was not trying on shoes. He snapped the gun in.

It never occurred to him that he might have it wrong or that he might have to get used to it. The weight put him off balance. He barked the knob of his other ankle during a third circuit of the desk. His sock fell down. To use the gun, Pierman realized, he would have to stop, stoop, lift his cuff, unsnap the strap, draw, and aim. And then, with a piddling thing like this, where? Head or chest? And after all that time, would it matter?

Pierman tried it just to see and went back to his chair. He put the whole rig back in the box, replaced the lid, and laid the box in the drawer where the tape recorder had been.

⚘

I imagine him doing this with a tight, sedulous smile. I imagine a similar expression, a bit more wistful or rueful perhaps, meandering around his bleached eyes later when he might've been able to talk about it.

Calkins had taught him well. On that day, Pierman would say, he was no different from other men at one point, maybe more, in their lives. On that day, for a time, he was taken in tow, seized by a kind of rapture, something that lurks beyond the basic human impulse toward finite perfection.

Until, of course, he stopped to consider. There was the clumsiness, the inconvenience, the mess—always with people, he would say, the mess. Kind of like sex the first time, he would say. He would note aloud that the comparison was hardly original nor was it intended to be as negative as it sounded. And he would think to himself that my generation, with all of its supposedly ignorant virgins, probably wouldn't understand it. But the truth of it was that right or wrong never entered the mind when the time came. Only the hassle, he would say, again putting it in generational terms, and how immeasurable is that?

What he would not say about that day is what we both would have understood, if for different reasons. McQueen appalled him, more than ever.

19

We have his dictated notes for evidence of what he did over the next few days. Judging by the wind and road noise, he dictated them into a handheld while driving from one place to another. The recordings are professional, beginning with his identification of himself and the date, continuing with detailed and thorough summaries of the people he talked to and what he found out, and ending with his affirmation, subject to the penalties for perjury, that the statements were true and correct. He does not mention the name of anyone he intended the notes for, although it is reasonable to assume he knew that they would eventually wind up in the hands of his successor or Calkins or Darrell. I would like to think he intended me to be among his audience, but what he felt I can only imagine.

ॐ

The implements—a plow, a planter, a harrow, a hay baler, a corn picker, a rake, a mower, an elevator—were neatly arrayed under a line of trees along the back of the barn lot, tongues forward for easy connection. An old tractor stood among them, but until Goss called, Pierman did not see him.

"Wouldn't have took you for an early riser," Goss said, poking his head up from behind one of the tall rear tractor tires. The tractor was hitched to a rake, and Goss held a grease gun. He wore smudged khaki work clothes and a billboard cap.

"You chewing yet this morning?" Pierman asked.

Wary, Goss shook his head.

"Then, it must be early. Here." Pierman handed over the recently washed overalls and a fresh bag of Red Man. "Thanks. Sorry I didn't get them back to you sooner."

"Not a problem." Goss looked at the bundle suspiciously before tossing it up on the tractor seat and plugging the nozzle of the grease gun onto a fitting.

"Haying today?" Pierman asked.

"Sun's out," Goss said, settling it. He pumped the handle on the grease gun until the sickly green jelly oozed out around the connection. "Maybe you, too, though I 'spect it's a different sort."

"Pardon?"

"I 'spect you're making hay. We don't hardly know each other well enough for chitchat. Excuse me."

He moved Pierman aside to get to the other end of the rake.

"Mr. Goss."

"Lou'll do." He gave Pierman a wry smile.

"Lou. The day of the fire, you said the phone wasn't working right. You said the line was buzzing."

"I said that."

"Were they working on them that day?"

"Yeah." But he stopped to search his memory. "Yeah, they were," he said with certainty.

"How do you know?"

"Well, now, I saw the truck," Goss said as though Pierman had been impertinent again.

"Where?"

"Down there." Goss directed the grease gun across a corn field toward the road.

"Near the woods?"

"They had one of those little tents up on the line," Goss said.

Pierman thought about that for a moment. "Was it raining?" he said.

"Nah," Goss said in a way that implied Pierman had said something stupid.

"Had it been raining?"

Goss saw that Pierman was serious. He shook his head.

"Kind of hot that day, as I remember," Pierman said.

Goss looked around the ground at his feet. His adam's apple bobbed twice.

"Makes you wonder what they'd need a tent for," he said.

"Yes, sir. It does."

Goss pushed his cap back and wiped his brow with the back of his hand.

"I didn't see anybody. You reckon maybe I wasn't supposed to?"

"Thanks, Lou."

Goss didn't want to shake hands. He said it was the grease.

"You don't suppose somebody would've come in and stole that truck?" he asked as Pierman turned to go. Pierman looked at him for a moment, without answering.

"I'll keep this to myself," Goss said.

"I know," said Pierman. "I appreciate it."

At the phone company, general managers came and went, but Hanna Gerber remained. If you wanted something done, you called her, not them. Miz Gerber, as even her elders instinctively addressed her, did not ask permission of or beg forgiveness from those around her, as her superiors did.

She had started as a data entry clerk the Monday after she and Pierman graduated from high school. When Pierman called her not long after he returned from Goss's farm, she was the office manager.

Miz Gerber was a tall, big-boned woman, and every day from the age of about three on, at the behest of her rigid faith, she put on an ankle-length, straight skirt and a shapeless blouse and nestled a small, white, net cap atop her upswept, lacquered hair. If she had worn anything else when Pierman pulled up to the gate into the maintenance area, he would not have recognized her.

She did not give him a chance to get out of the car. Before he could open the door, she crossed the gap between the car and the gate, leaned down into his open window, and said: "Explain to me again why I didn't tell you no on this deal."

"Because when you were a girl, you thought I had a certain roguish charm," Pierman said, grinning. "And this evening I promised you ice cream and a ride in my little red sports car."

They both knew she had been sweet on him in school, but he had never treated her with anything more than respect. Unlike others in their class, he had never made fun of her size, appearance, or religion, but like other boys and men down to the present day, he had been wary of her tart manner. Pierman accordingly was surprised to see that she had colored.

"That pretty much makes me a fool beyond compare then, doesn't it," she said.

The gate was part of a head-high, chain-link fence that knitted a paved lot to the back of the office building. Miz Gerber pulled a bristling ball of keys from the pocket of her denim skirt and opened the gate's padlock. She pushed the gate wide and pointed him around the corner of the building toward a row of three service vans parked nose out against the building's back wall.

"Who drives which vehicle?" Pierman said when he got out.

"We've got three repairmen. They can drive any one of them."

"I'll bet they don't. I'll bet each guy favors one van over the others."

"Who're you interested in?"

He smiled his flirting smile. "All of them."

He took a pair of leather driving gloves from his trunk. She remembered enough about him to be amused but only for a second.

"You obviously think somebody here did something. You call me and ask me to let you look in our trucks and see our work orders—after we're closed—and not to tell anybody about doing it. You put my job on the line, and maybe you're putting me in harm's way. I think I get to ask some questions."

"You get to ask. I don't know I can answer."

She put the keys back in her pocket and folded her arms.

"If I tell you that you are cooperating in a homicide investigation and that these measures are necessary to avoid either alerting or embarrassing a person considered to be a suspect, would that satisfy you?" Pierman said.

She considered him. He gave her the smile for the third time.

"Oh, well, sure, that's different." She still had not smiled.

She took the keys from her pocket again and walked to the first van. "This one's McQueen's," she said and waited for Pierman to react. When he did not, she shrugged and unlocked it. She identified the repairman who used each of the other two vans as she unlocked them.

Pierman stood at the rear of the middle one looking at the equipment, tools, and parts stored in it for some time. He stepped gingerly into the rear of the van so that none of his clothes touched or snagged any of the shelving and opened tool and parts drawers in the shelving, careful to touch only the edges with his gloved hands. At McQueen's van and the third van, he did the same things, giving each the same amount of time as he had the first van. That was merely to keep Miz Gerber from guessing whom he was interested in. He only needed a fraction of the time he took to see what he expected to see.

In McQueen's van, as in the other two, was a drawer full of screwdrivers, including two big ones with rubber-insulated handles that could be used to hit a secretary without breaking the skin. In McQueen's van, as in the other two, was a roll of black plastic sheeting.

Miz Gerber said the repairmen cut pieces from it as necessary to temporarily protect cable splices from moisture. Or, Pierman thought, wrap a sniper's rifle to protect it from the elements. In McQueen's van, as in the other two, was a pair of long-handled pruning shears. Sometimes, Miz Gerber said, they had to pinch back tree branches to get to overhead lines. Or, Pierman thought, make a hook to hang a sniper's rifle in a tree. In McQueen's van, as in the other two, was a pair of stirrups that the repairmen strapped to their calves to climb poles and trees. On the inside of each stirrup was a spike. It was shaped like a pyramid. It would leave a triangular puncture mark in a pole or a tree. Neither Miz Gerber or Pierman discussed what those were used for.

"Can we take these out of service for the next day or so?" Pierman asked, when he climbed out of the last van and closed the rear doors.

"Sure," Miz Gerber said, "with a court order. It's not like we don't have things to do with them." She shrugged. "Course, you want to take just one out of service, I could probably arrange that."

Pierman weighed the advantages of getting Purcell and his lab techs in to go over the van against the disadvantages of tipping his hand to McQueen. A lot of time had passed. The most the techs would find would be Ginny's hair or skin on a screwdriver and that would not tie McQueen to Grable, only to Ginny. He had looked for but not seen hair, tissue, or blood on any of the tools in McQueen's van.

"Let's look at the work orders," he said.

In her narrow, concrete block office, she handed him a sheaf of about 50 pink pages. She had told him on the telephone that the repairmen did not go out without a work order and that work orders were only issued through the office. From that, he assumed McQueen could not have tampered with the records of his work activities. Pierman asked Miz Gerber to produce the work orders for each repairman for the week of Randy Grable's murder.

It took him about ten minutes to thumb through the papers. Twice, he consulted the large map of the company's territory behind Miz Gerber's desk. Not one work order showed a job near Lou Goss's or Paul Grable's farms. The closest job was, as McQueen had said, several miles away and he had been assigned to it. The "time on" the job was noted. The "time off" was blank. The form indicated that the person who called in the fault had not left a name.

"This all of them?" Pierman asked, holding up the sheaf.

"How long we known each other?"

"I'll need to take these with me."

"I've already made copies for our file."

Miz Gerber had stood against the door, playing with a loose strand of hair at her neck and looking away, trying to give Pierman privacy. She moistened her fingers, pulled the strand through them, and tucked it back up behind her ear.

Without looking back toward Pierman, she said quietly, "You have any thoughts about what I ought to do when Nate finds out you've been here and I helped you. You think maybe he'll decide he ought to kill me, too?"

"What makes you think it's McQueen?"

She shrugged and smiled. "I know my boys. 'Specially the ones with a demon here and there."

"What're his demons?"

"Nothing that made me think he killed Paul Grable's boy, if you're asking that." She touched her cap. "It's just I know a sinner when I see one."

Pierman pursed his lips. "Maybe he didn't. Let's work on keeping this between us, and I don't think you'll have a problem."

She looked at him with sadness. Lying was a sin. She nodded once.

"I'm not getting any younger and I never was pretty," she said. "I think I'll drive your little car 'bout ninety, and if we survive, you buy me a sundae."

"Hey," the young, pear-shaped man shouted. "Fuck off."

He charged from the shadows behind the library, his right arm raised. Pierman had been walking along the stroll, peering into the darkness around the loading docks and doorways, trying to find the black man Kay and he had encountered there before. Pierman stepped to one side to avoid the ill-aimed swing and stiff-armed the man so that he toppled backward. Pierman held out his hand to help the man up, but he batted it away.

"Fuck off."

Pierman shrugged and knelt beside the man on the ground. "I need to find the black guy."

"Fuck off." The pear-shaped man looked away. He rubbed his chest where Pierman had made contact. Over his shoulder, Pierman saw the face of the older, bald man he had met before emerge out of the shadows.

"Where is he, the black guy?" Pierman asked patiently.

"Let's see. Black queen gets arrested in mass roust and thrown in jail with white straights. Why, I guess he got the shit stomped out of him. I guess he lost his job. I guess he lost his family. He *was* married, you know. And I guess he don't come around here no more."

"Ah," Pierman said. "I heard about that."

"Sure you did, asshole. Since you're the one who sicced those cops on us. Why else do they show up the day after you and the slut were here? Asshole motherfucker, you lied to us. You didn't tell us you were law."

Pierman look around. He counted the shadows, six men gathering to see what was going on, but they kept their distance. He reached around behind him to his pocket, and the pear-shaped man crab-walked away backward out of reach.

"Easy," Pierman said. "Whether you believe it or not, I didn't send the cops. That was someone else." He held out his hand. "Ever seen this guy here?"

Earlier in the day, he had gone to the jail, searched Calkins' records, and found a mugshot taken of McQueen from some years before when he'd been run in for a fight. "Nope," Gloria had said, glowering at him from the doorway as he riffled through the files. "No news here. You?"

The man glanced toward the photograph. His eyes lingered a moment too long before he looked away again.

"When did you see him last?" Pierman asked.

"Fuck off," he said, rolling to one side and pushing himself to his feet. "You come here again, I know some people like leather and gags. They'll play Mardi Gras and stuff beads up your ass. Maybe I'll call them. Maybe I'll call them right now."

He trotted off, tugging at a tear in the seat of his short shorts.

Pierman held out the photograph, turning in a circle for the others to see. "Anybody ever see this guy here?"

The others turned away from him as he tried to meet their eyes. When he got to the place where the older man peeked out, his face dissolved back into the dark.

Pierman decided not to see whether the pear-shaped man would make good on his promise. It had been a long shot anyway.

He kept an eye over his shoulder for a block or so, but he did not see anything or hear the footsteps behind him until he was nearly back to his car. When he spun around, the older man jumped back and held up his hands.

The man giggled and passed his hand over his mustache.

"Is that guy killing us?" he asked.

"He may have killed two men, one of whom was homosexual," Pierman said.

"My, you're very careful not to give offense." He giggled again. Something to do with nerves, Pierman thought. "May I see that picture again?"

Pierman stepped toward him and gingerly handed him the photograph. The man used reading glasses dragged from his baggy Bermuda shorts to examine it.

"Phillip, isn't it?" Pierman said.

The terror peeked out before he clamped it back behind the first serious, grown-up expression Pierman had seen.

"Questions and a good memory for names," he said, looking at the photograph again. "Qualities held in low regard around here."

He extended the photo to Pierman but would not release it until he had Pierman's attention and said, "Allen."

"I don't know his name," the man said when he saw that he had made his point. He cocked his chin at the photo. "But I've seen him. Here. He's kind of dishy, but he always looked risky. Like he was pissed off. Like maybe he didn't like having to be gay. Like maybe he liked rough stuff. Might have been the scary grin."

"Did you ever see him with the young guy I showed you before?"

The man shook his head.

"But you do remember seeing this guy, and he was trolling."

"An unfortunate choice of words."

"What would you prefer?"

"Yes, I have seen him here." The man shrugged. "And he was participating."

"How often? When was the last time?"

The man shrugged again. "I don't know. Maybe every month or six weeks or so. Only cops and whores keep book. The last time? Maybe a couple, three months ago."

"Not since then?"

The man turned and looked back across the plaza toward the library. He scanned the street along which they stood.

"Many of us who come here have secrets that we will go to extreme lengths to protect. My friend, the angry little number whose shorts you tore tonight, has a mother whose heart he could not bear to break. No doubt she knows, but he barely escaped the last roust.

"I believe him when he says he's gone to call the rough friends. If I stand here under the street lights much longer, some cop will think I'm propositioning you. Best we both left now."

Pierman watched him walk back toward the library. When he was nearly there, the man stopped, craned his neck, and lowered his shoulders, sighing off a scratchy skin.

ॐ

And then he came to me, first thing, on the morning of the next day.

No coat, a wrinkled shirt, and tie at half mast. His eyes sat back deep and red behind the glasses. I could remember feeling the way he looked when I'd been up all night prepping for a trial. I usually threw up at least once before it began. I wondered about him.

He appeared in the door and said he needed to see me alone, here, in chambers, and, yes, it was more important than the bail hearing that was set in a half hour.

He closed the door and put a handheld on my desk. He took one of the leather chairs across from me, drew a deep breath, and splayed his hands in front of him on my desk. He had, he said, reason to believe Nate McQueen killed Randy Grable and Willie. He wanted, he said, to tell me what those reasons were.

Without notes or a file in front of him, he told me about McQueen's background, both as a soldier and a gay man. He explained what he had found in the woods and how it tied into McQueen's occupation. He nailed the lies about McQueen being with his father and about someone with a telephone van being in a place they were not supposed to be on the morning Randy Grable was killed. He punched the play button on the recorder, and with the tape cued past the point where he and Sley had talked about Calkins, as I found out later, he let me listen to Sley talk about McQueen making a pass at him in a bar and Randy Grable making a pass at McQueen.

And a half hour later, he looked me in the eye and said, barely above a whisper, "I want warrants. I need one to search McQueen's apartment, his personal vehicle, and his work van. I also want an arrest warrant. Make it second degree. A grand jury can bump it to first later."

282

I had seen lawyers make weaker arguments with straighter faces. Indeed, long ago, I had made it a rule of thumb that the more certain the lawyer's spiel, the more proof he would have to provide before I would believe him. So I did not answer Pierman at first, for it would have been discouraging.

Instead, when I could stand my own silence no longer, I said, "And you think McQueen killed Grable because he was afraid a younger man would expose him as a homosexual?"

"Yes," Pierman said, an edge of impatience in it as though I was being obtuse.

"And that he would've then killed Willie to avoid being found out?"

"He had access to the building in his job, and we think Willie found him rummaging through my files to see where we were in the Grable investigation."

"We being?"

"Joe Calkins and myself."

I made a greater show of looking around the room than was probably necessary.

"Your shadow, the sheriff, is not with you today."

"No."

"I would've thought he would be."

"It's a big job. He's probably working on other things this morning."

"I heard he was on vacation," I said. "Seemed strange to me."

"He's not told me that."

I took my time peeling the cellophane off a cigar and lighting it. I knew his father. I knew him. He would not lie; he would be artful.

"Perhaps not," I said.

I reviewed the notes I had taken again. Absently, I said: "You read about these Viet Nam veterans cracking up, killing people, themselves. I don't remember it happening with my generation after our war. It's amazing how often it happens."

Pierman was silent so long I looked up.

"No, Judge," he said, when he had my attention, "what's amazing is, given the shit your generation dropped them into, what's amazing is how well adjusted most of them are. What's amazing is it doesn't happen more often."

Perhaps he was thinking of Calkins. I could think of nothing to say. Beyond the matter at hand, we had just run out of other things to talk about.

"Sorry, Allen," I said. "You don't have nearly enough. It's all circumstantial. I see nothing that ties McQueen directly to either victim. You can't put him at the scene of either murder and you have nothing that puts him in proximity to either victim at or near the times of their deaths. I can't do it."

He had the fallback ready. "Give me the warrants," he said. "Let me bring him to question him, then a grand jury can make the call on the final charges and whether they stick."

"What prosecutor do you know who can't make a grand jury give him anything he wants?"

Pierman stared, then closed his eyes and bowed his head for almost as long. When he looked up, I started. He wore his father's reptile gaze.

"Give me just the search warrant, then."

"No, Allen. You and Calkins have to get more."

"You owe me one, Judge. In fact, you owe me two."

"Two?"

"Yes, two. Come on. Let me play the hunch."

I can see now, as I could not then, that he whipsawed me deliberately.

"A hunch," I said. "You're not allowed hunches. You've got to have evidence."

"You know what I have. I can't get more without a warrant. Give me the warrant. You owe me."

"I don't owe you."

"Sure, you do. Twice.

"You keep saying that. What do you mean, twice?"

"You really want to discuss it?"

"Tell me or get out."

He smiled his father's cold smile, crossed his legs wide, and wrapped his hands around his bent knee.

"Two. Easy," he said. "One, for agreeing to be prosecutor. But you knew that. Two, for screwing my mother before the old man died."

It was the last thing I expected him to say. It rendered me numb and stupid. I opened my mouth to rebut him, but nothing came out. "I didn't," I said finally.

"You didn't."

"No."

He leaned forward, reached across my desk, and picked up the phone. "Let's call her," he said.

"No!" I grabbed the handset from him and replaced it on the hook.

"Your mother never broke her vows to your father."

It was all I could think to say. He nodded his head once, as though he expected as much.

"Your partner and your friend invited you into his house after your wife died, and what did you do? You tried to seduce his wife. How's that going, by the way?"

"You didn't really know," I said and he shrugged. He shrugged.

"I always wondered why, after a time, she couldn't bring herself to look at either Dad or you when you were at our table." He put the tip of his tongue to his top lip, raised his eyebrows, and smiled. "I played a hunch. I'm good at it. Give me the warrant."

The skeins of anger and shame that swirled in my gut became so tangled and knotted I cannot say, even now, from whom or to whom they ran. I only wanted him out of my chambers. I took the form from a drawer in my desk.

"Fill in what you want," I said. "Do it right."

And, God help me, I signed it and backhanded it across the desk.

20

By the time Pierman found Darrell, it was midafternoon. Pierman considered calling Purcell to serve the warrant but decided that Darrell, being by far the easier of the two to manipulate, was his man. For his part, when Darrell looked at the name on the warrant, he marched into Calkins' office, took down one of the riot guns, and checked the load. "Ready," he said, snapping the gun shut.

"Jesus, Darrell," Pierman said, "what do you think we're doing here?"

"Hunting somebody that's a damned sight better shot than me."

Darrell eased to a stop in the alley behind a large, older home painted battleship gray.

"I didn't realize he lived this close," Pierman said.

Most of what had been the back yard was now a lot for cars with rusted wheel wells and dingy, ragged vinyl roofs. They distracted Darrell.

"To what," he said finally.

"To me," Pierman said. "My folks' house. It's only a couple, three blocks."

"He not here," Darrell said. "Car's gone." In a small town, we know what each other drives.

"I imagine he's at work," Pierman said.

He was too nonchalant, and they had gotten to know each other. Darrell turned away from the yard and looked at him.

"You know he's at work."

"I called Hanna, yeah."

"Maybe she give him an extra assignment?"

Pierman decided Darrell was smarter than he had given him credit for, and for that reason, he said nothing.

"Who exactly you serving that warrant on then?"

"I'm hoping for a landlord."

Darrell continued to look at Pierman.

"I got a feeling my boss has put himself in a box," he said. "I got a feeling you're going in after him. So I guess my question at this point is: You putting me on the slide with you?"

Pierman leaned forward to look at the house through the windshield. He did not dare eye contact. Darrell's ambition, a quality upon which in this instance Pierman relied, sounded fragile.

"Deputy," he said and sighed. "If you don't want to do this . . . ." He let the sentence hang.

Darrell released his breath in a hiss that ended in "Shit." He held out his hand. "Let's have them."

Pierman automatically reached for the papers inside his coat, but when his fingers touched them, he stopped. They suddenly seemed too precious and volatile to entrust to anyone else, particularly Darrell.

"Why don't you get this thing out of sight?" Pierman suggested and left the car.

❦

The landlord lived behind one of three blue doors on the first floor. Judging from the row of six, rusting, black mailboxes outside the front door and the landlord's appearance, Pierman decided he probably had carved up the family home to finance his retirement. An old, unshaven man, bent as a dog's hind leg, he trailed a greasy smell, like reheated beef, behind him as they trudged up the central staircase to McQueen's apartment on the second floor.

"Meal was late," the old fellow said. They huddled outside McQueen's door while he dithered with a key ring.

"What?" Darrell snapped.

"Meal. They brought it late, the wheels. Not been feeling good. They won't come tomorrow."

Pierman wondered if he was bargaining: bring me lunch and I'll open the door.

"The holiday," the man said, only to commiserate.

"Just open it," Darrell said. He was jumpy and in no mood to be charitable.

McQueen's apartment was a scene from Pierman's college days, a place he had more than a decade before. Tall windows threw shadows in rooms of patched, plaster walls the color of mushrooms. Rust tongues licked webs in cracked, porcelain fixtures. Maroon paisleys on a cloth stretched across the ceiling strained light from overhead to the color of weak tea. Block-and-board shelves held a stereo, albums, and candles. The only thing missing, Pierman thought, was a print of Van Gogh's goddamn "Starry Night" taped to the wall above the faded, mangy-armed, tomato-red couch.

Pierman stood transfixed in the doorway of McQueen's living room. Having looked over the apartment to see how much of a job lay ahead and to make sure McQueen was not, in fact, home, Darrell came up behind Pierman and looked over his shoulder.

"Bet we find dope."

"Because the moon is in the seventh house?"

Darrell looked at Pierman as though he had spoken in tongues.

The search produced results as banal as Pierman's first impression. Nothing came from the kitchen or the living room. Shadow threads drooped and clung like webs when Darrell flipped on the overhead light in the bedroom; Pierman's head brushed the trough of a fishnet tacked to the ceiling. In a corner—we love our corners, Pierman thought—a mattress laid on the floor, its gray sheets corded at the foot. On the window sill above the mattress, Pierman noted a soiled but empty ashtray and a high-intensity light, and around the mattress, paperbacks in stacks, some almost to the sill.

Pierman recognized the room's odor about the time Darrell pulled the sandwich bag from under the mattress and shook it at him. Papers and a few brown flakes were all that was left, but the discovery set Darrell off on a new frenzy.

While Darrell rummaged through a clothes closet under the eaves, Pierman's eye fell on a sepia photograph in a tarnished filigree frame that sat on a chipped, fiberboard dresser. A woman in a wide-brimmed hat and flowered dress knelt beside a white-haired toddler in front of an old car. The woman's face was shadowed and stony; the child smiled and waved with a blurred hand. Several seconds passed before Pierman saw that the woman probably was too old to be the child's mother.

"Come here," Darrell said, his voice muffled.

A moist, hot, violet glow spilled out of a door at the back of the closet. In an attic area under the eaves, aluminum foil lined the walls, throwing nourishment from a grow light back on a half-dozen, waist-high plants.

"Look at this shit," Darrell said. "I told you."

Pierman was not surprised. Even the guy's dope was old fashioned, but with his disposition, he probably had to round off the edges.

"Would you say you're incensed?" Pierman asked.

"You bet your ass I am."

"Incensed and marijuana frequently go hand in hand," Pierman said.

Darryl was as oblivious to the joke as Pierman suspected he would be.

"Sheriff said you knew dope."

"Did he. Let's go."

"Where?"

"Like Red Riding Hood. To grandmother's house. To see what we find there."

Darrell looked at the plants, his face red in the heat, and started to protest.

"We've found nothing," Pierman said.

They were nearly out the door when the telephone rang. Neither one of them moved at first.

"Just pick it up," Pierman said finally.

Bewilderment stretched Darrell's round face oval as he listened then thrust the handset at Pierman.

"Your mother," he said.

Pierman took a moment to throttle back questions and answers that careened through his head.

"Mother," he said, "how did you get this number?"

"Allen, come home. Come home now." Her voice snagged and stretched. "Somebody's here."

When she said it, he knew. He told her to stay calm. He told her to leave it to him. He spoke slowly and distinctly, as much for him as for her.

"Allen—" Her voice started up the scale.

"Listen!" He lowered his voice. "Just listen. No panic. All right?" He heard her panting. "All right."

"Yes," she whispered.

"Good. Put him on."

The line went dead, then Pierman heard something hard clatter against the receiver. It was impossible to think around the picture of McQueen juggling metal and flesh.

"That's what I call great situation management."

"McQueen." Pierman waved Darrell back.

"Funny thing. Back I come from getting a little bite of supper, and I'm feeling real good about myself 'cause I'm bringing a little something back for my poor old landlord. He's worried he's not getting fed tomorrow, you know. And what do I find parked outside my house? A fucking cop car."

Pierman silently cursed Darrell for not doing what he told him to do.

"So I asked myself what is a sheriff's deputy doing at my house? Hasn't he talked to my lifelong friends, the prosecutor and his flunky, the sheriff? Doesn't he know that I left word? No intrusions. I could think of only one thing to do, naturally. I decided to drop by and ask if you'd passed that word to the troops. Only one thing. You weren't here. Just Ma."

"I've got a warrant, Nate."

"Nate now, is it?"

"I've got warrants," Pierman said, touching the papers in his pocket again for assurance. "And statements."

"Liar."

"Why should I lie?"

But they both knew the answer, and for a while, neither spoke.

"Nate, you ought to turn yourself in."

"Say." McQueen drew it out, smothering the suggestion completely. "Find the greenhouse yet."

"Yes, but it doesn't make any difference."

"Then you didn't look behind the foil." He gave it a moment to sink in. "Go ahead. Take a peek. No hurry here."

Pierman couldn't bring himself to put the phone down. He gave Darrell hasty instructions and slumped against a wall while he waited. Darrell came back with a box of rifle shells and a green canvas holster on a web belt. Some of the shells were gone, and the holster was empty.

"Dug a hole in the lathe," Darrell said, thrusting the articles forward like an offering.

"Found them," Pierman said into the phone. "So what?"

"So what!"

McQueen's voice became distant and muffled. In the background, Pierman heard his mother moan.

"McQueen!" he shouted. "Leave her alone!"

"Then let's not get upset," McQueen ordered. He chuckled. "Now, guess which one I've got."

Pierman clenched his teeth. "Has to be the pistol. Army issue from the holster, probably a souvenir from Viet Nam."

"Very good. But it doesn't have to be the pistol?"

"Sure it does. You scattered the rifle around telephone poles all over the county." Pierman lost the struggle to keep his voice even. "You sure as hell didn't leave it hanging in that fucking tree."

He waited for an angry reply, or worse, another sound from his mother, but all he heard was air.

"Well," McQueen said after a time.

"So what are we going to do about it?"

Darrell had slipped away. Pierman caught him at the door.

"Where're you going?" Pierman snapped, his hand covering the mouthpiece.

"He could kill her," Darrell said, looking sheepish, then defiant.

"He will kill her if you and whatever cavalry you were going to call go charging over there. Stay here. McQueen!"

After a moment, "Yo."

"You've made your point. You've got my mother and a gun. I can hold off the cops for a while but not forever. You want a head start, take it. Go."

"How much of a start?"

"How much you need?"

But McQueen had already abandoned the idea.

"You'd still come, wouldn't you. I know you. You'd never threaten, you'd never brag, you'd just fucking do it. You're so fucking stubborn. And with radios and computers and telephones. You'd still find me. I know those things. I'm the one keeps them up."

Pierman heard something uncharacteristic, a trace of hopelessness perhaps, in the man's voice.

Yes," he said, to encourage McQueen in that direction. "Yes, you are."

"But I'm just a tool," McQueen said. "The tool with the tools. I know more about these things than anybody around here. Communications."

He repeated the word, several times, changing the inflection, toying with it, until another idea, another more delightful plaything entered his head and he laughed.

"Fucking Lindley. There's not even a TV station to call, no cameras to read a statement of my accomplishments for, before I waste this old bitch."

Elizabeth howled. "Shut up!" McQueen shouted, and Pierman heard the slap of flesh on flesh. "She doesn't listen," McQueen said calmly.

"So shoot her," Pierman said softly.

It wasn't calculated, not at first; he had been sorting through ways out and it slipped.

After a time, McQueen said, "I don't think I heard you."

The fact that it had made McQueen pause encouraged Pierman.

"Didn't you? You're the one called me a cold bastard."

McQueen was stubbornly silent. Pierman had to listen hard for his breathing to be sure he was still there. Then he heard McQueen juggle the receiver and speak faintly. Elizabeth screamed.

"Your ma doesn't think much of your idea," McQueen said.

Pierman rested his forehead against the wall and squeezed his eyes shut.

"Think what'll come next," he said softly. "You're right. Sooner or later, we'll come. There'll be a lot of us. A ring of cops—country cops—not very sophisticated, just very edgy 'cause they've never been involved in something like this before."

He looked at Darrell to make sure he was still there and to judge his reaction. Darrell gave him the finger.

"Think," Pierman said. "The first shot, it's not hard to imagine what'll come next. They'll light up the house. You've seen it on TV, in the movies, in slow motion. The splinters and the glass'll shred you if the bullets don't. Hell, Nate, you were in Viet Nam, firefights. You tell me what it'd be like."

Pierman waited. In the background, he could hear his mother sobbing, then gagging.

"One more thing," he said, just louder than a whisper. "Who's going to be left standing when it's over. Me, for damn sure, I promise you. I'm not doing anything stupid." He paused, winding up to throw it out hard. "And certainly your old grandma. We'll have to bring her down to try and talk you out, but I'll tell you something, McQueen. Far as I'm concerned, it'd be just for show. Right now, I'd want her to watch." Pierman gave it a moment. "And if you want press, I'll arrange it. The old lady'd probably like one last clipping to finish out that scrapbook she keeps on her dresser."

Pierman held his breath. A moment before, it sounded like truth. Now it echoed as bluffs and lies, dangerous, stupid lies.

"What's he saying?" Darrell asked.

"Nothing. Shut up. McQueen!"

"I'm here."

"What's it going to be?"

"You."

"Me?"

"Yeah, the two of us. We'll talk."

"I told you. I'm not crazy."

"But you think I am. I'm not. Come see."

He sounded sober, subdued.

"You want me out?" he asked, when Pierman did not respond.

"Yes."

"Then we talk. I leave here. You leave there. We meet. No one else."

"You bringing the gun?"

"You coming alone?"

"Neither one of us has any reason to believe the other," Pierman said, nearly in despair.

"Sure we do. We have every reason. We're friends. We'll meet at the birthplace of friendship. The old school." McQueen chuckled. "Who'd have thought we'd ever be of the old school?"

In Pierman's mind, he ran down the tunnels, but none seemed any brighter than the others.

"I don't leave here until the deputy has checked on my mother. He calls me back here, I leave."

Something in the way Pierman agreed, the certainty of it perhaps, made McQueen pause. Something had happened while he was enjoying his little joke.

"I'll wait a half hour," he said, trying to match Pierman's authoritative tone. When that drew no reaction, he added helpfully, as one might when offering a cup of coffee, "I could come over there and kill you."

"I thought neither one of us was crazy."

Pierman put the receiver down.

To his credit, Darrell hated the idea and said so immediately. Pierman didn't understand. He was upset. If he was thinking straight, he'd know things weren't done this way. McQueen could take off. That would be bad enough, but someone could get killed.

Skeptics will point to Darrell's failure to put names to his final argument as evidence that he included himself among the possibilities. With Pierman so naively frank about his plans, what was to stop McQueen from ambushing Darrell when he came to Elizabeth's door. Given the urgency of the moment, though, that grants Darrell too much understanding of McQueen and Pierman too little.

Pierman sat on the couch with his eyes closed and his chin atop his folded hands, like a child ready to accept the price of mischief he knows he will commit again.

"Give me your keys," he demanded when Darrell finished.

"No way."

Darrell jammed his hands in his pockets, more to protect their contents than to underscore his feelings. But Pierman had no intention of wrestling him. In Darrell's tone, Pierman had already heard him admit to too many possibilities.

"He wants me at the old high school," Pierman said, putting it simply and logically. The school was ten, maybe twelve blocks away. His mother's house was two. It would take time for Darrell to get to his mother, see if she was all right, and call Pierman. "I've got less than half an hour. I could run, but I won't make it."

Darrell unhooked the full ring from its place next to his gun on his belt but stopped and held it against his chest.

"What makes you think you're some kind of hero? Or you just plain suicidal?"

Darrell opened the fist over Pierman's lap. The heavy, jangling ring hit him at the joint. The pain was exquisite.

❧

Pierman waited until he heard the outside door click shut. As he dialed, he glanced at his watch, then remembered he had not checked it when the deal was struck. He estimated ten minutes. That would be enough time to cover a couple of miles into the country, and he swore.

When she picked up the phone, he said, "You all right?"

"I'm glad you called."

"*Are* you all right?"

The phone had rung several times, and he had no way to interpret the relief he had heard.

"Yes," she said finally.

"Answer yes or no. Is there anyone there with you?"

"Yes."

"Your father?"

"Yes."

"Anyone else?"

"No, Allen. Damn you. Haven't you scared us enough already?"

He heard her take a deep breath and release it slowly.

"Is this over?" she asked, having put anger aside. "Are you okay?"

He heard the beckoning, but he was well practiced now. The answer he looked for had been nestled in her anger. On everything else, he clamped a lid.

"I want you to go," he instructed, careful to keep his voice low and even. "Do it now. I'm not trying to frighten you, but you have to leave. Now."

"Allen?"

"Now. Go to a motel or a neighbor's. Check with the sheriff's office in the morning. They'll know."

Words like gnats whined out of the receiver, but he could stay on the line no longer. No telling what Darrell might do if he could not get through. Or so Pierman told himself.

*

The question that aggravates those who still talk about it is the one Darrell raised: Why would Pierman agree to such an arrangement? Answering it requires more questions: Had it become that personal between McQueen and him? Was it a matter of besting his father? Me? Was it expediency to protect Elizabeth? If so, why did he keep his word? Was he protecting Calkins? Did he not trust the police? Did he fear so much for Kay? Did he expect to become a hero? Did he truly see no other way?

I have, of course, asked myself the same question, as I know you have and will, more times than we will count. And I will tell you in all honesty I do not know the answer. I have come to believe that it was an irrational choice born of all those impulses and maybe more. Which is to say, it was born of love, even if we cannot say clearly for whom or what.

21

A burst of static announced another stream of jumbled codes. To Pierman's untrained ear, they were impossible to decipher, but the dispatcher's drone persuaded him that Darrell had not yet sounded an alarm. He turned off the radio and hunkered down; no sense in drawing attention to a stranger driving the deputy's car.

To keep his mind occupied, he let figures under street lights tell him stories. Two boys, their overlong, damp, T-shirts plastered to their chests, dragged baseball bats over breaks in the sidewalk and snickered at the sound, like bullfrogs. A dog straining at its leash ahead of a middle-aged couple strolling hand in hand was merely an excuse. An oblong beach ball jammed in the open back door of a Caravan corked a week of sunburns and beer to be had at the lake.

In the dark intervals, though, Pierman's memory told him another story, over and over. "She's all right. Maybe a little hysterical." But Darrell had had to shout to make himself heard. "I'm going to call a doctor."

Pierman parked short of the school and checked the mirror before exposing himself under the light of an opened door. One car passed, another turned. Pierman dismissed them. Headlights spoke to the presence and direction of others. He had only his own to be concerned with now.

Lindley thought well of education at the turn of the century. A precious block had been devoted to the old high school, a lot large enough to cut a broad patch of sky away from the old treetops that obscured expansive views anywhere else near the town's core.

The mood of the half-eaten ruin below was not nearly so clear or serene. The jagged top was outlined in silver, clawing at rays from still hidden security lights in the alleys along the back and side. The shavings fell back inside, diagonally, across what was left of the upper windows. It presented a dark, sullen face. Shamed, it averted gray eyes, but its hair stood on end.

Before slinking away bankrupt, the developer had chained the front doors and stretched snow fence of chicken wire and lath around the rubble at the base of the building, but those measures, Pierman saw, were merely nods to some lawyer's admonitions about liability. All the window glass was gone, salvaged before the money ran out. He bent the chicken wire to step over it and picked a low, black rectangle he remembered as leading into the band room.

The floor was deeper than he thought. He sprawled, grit settling on his face. He scrambled. Nothing followed: No movement, no sound.

In fact, for all the silence and the landscape, Pierman could've rolled down the lip of a lunar crater. The interior walls that had swallowed and channeled the brute, feral energy of the place were reduced to chest-high mounds of debris here and there. The shadows that covered them were deep, and they bowed as if to cradle the pewter bowl of light out in the center of what once was the gymnasium's basketball court.

Pierman considered calling, but if McQueen were there, he couldn't have missed the clumsy entrance. And if he had something in mind, he would've come prepared.

Pierman, too, was prepared, he thought, but not to be caught stupidly, red-eyed and frozen like a jack-lighted deer. Instead, he moved in the shadows. Stooping, placing his feet carefully, he waved his arms in low arcs before him, like a blind man who's dropped his dog's leash or an infant just getting his legs.

"Bang, bang. Dead meat."

Pierman dove. Something sharp, a stray nail perhaps, ripped his thigh when he landed. The voice came from the darkness on the other side of the gray cup.

"Ollie, ollie, oxen free."

As Pierman crawled forward, McQueen stepped into the light. It caught the whites of his eyes and the scar on his neck as he tipped back his head.

"Ladies and gentlemen. Will you rise and join me in honoring our country?"

McQueen marched in place, his fists held out chest-high, one on top of the other, as though carrying a flag, before the whites winked out.

"Remember, Allen? Before each game?" He held his arms out to each side, then dropped them. "Okay, preliminaries over. Let's toss it up."

He addressed the shadows, turning, uncertain exactly where Pierman was. What mattered to Pierman was that his hands had been empty.

It was at this point, we believe, Pierman nestled the handheld recorder into a pile of bricks, where it was found later. There are sounds of scraping and Pierman's hobbling steps forward, away from the machine.

"You're hurt," McQueen said.

A black stain in the shape of a bowling pin appeared around the rip in Pierman's slacks.

"Does it matter?" he asked.

"Come on. I don't want you bleeding out. Fix it."

"What are your plans?" Pierman asked.

He bent to wrap a handkerchief around the leg and thus did not see McQueen's hand slip behind his back.

"I was thinking maybe hostage."

Pierman had imagined that it would be the muzzle that would fill his vision, but he was, in the end, an optimist, picturing the worst in daylight. In reality, what seized his attention was the pencil-thin gleam that ran the length of the black tube resting on McQueen's fist.

"You're a trusting bastard," McQueen said, filling the long silence Pierman left him. He stepped forward and jammed his free hand under Pierman's arms, then ran it around Pierman's waistband and up and down each leg.

The course was laid. "No," Pierman said as though tired.

When McQueen stepped back, Pierman willed himself to follow the path of the gleam up McQueen's arm to his face and the eyes hidden deep in the shadow of his brow.

"No, not entirely," he said louder.

McQueen stepped back again, ears pricked.

"Calkins?"

"You wore him out, made him do things he didn't like. He's gone."

"Who?"

"The deputy. Anybody else he can round up. You've got time, though. My mother is hysterical. The deputy'll have to find a doctor first. You'll get some warning, too. They're not smart or cunning. Not like you. They'll come roaring up with sirens and bullhorns. Mind if I walk? The leg hurts."

The gun stayed level, following Pierman around the edge of the light, but McQueen didn't try to stop him.

"So what are you expecting, Pierman?"

"Expect? You stalk and assassinate a boy, then do your damnedest to avoid it the next time? I can't *expect* anything from you; you've shown me that. What I *want* is you put the gun down and walk out with me." He shrugged. "But I don't expect it."

"So you were stupid to come here. Let's go."

"No."

"Yes. Let's go."

Pierman felt the blood trickle down his shin and thought his heart must be pumping faster. Why didn't he feel it?

"No is no, Nate. I'm not going anywhere."

"Then I'll make you."

"And I'll resist."

"You tried that once—long time ago." McQueen tipped the muzzle of the gun back and traced the silvery line on his neck with the sight. He teeth shined in the light. "And the last time I was in a serious fight, I came out on top."

"Then you understand I might fight a little harder and the outcome will be less certain. Under the circumstances."

"Damn you!"

The words ricocheted around the shell like bingo balls before McQueen spoke again.

"Don't talk down to me. You are not arguing some case." The gun came up an inch. "Or maybe you are. Tell me—in lawyer talk if you can't do it any other way–tell me why I shouldn't plug you, just for the pure satisfaction of it, and be on my way. Go on. What would a guy in your business call it? Show cause."

Pierman shrugged. "You don't want to. You're supposed to be my friend. You said you didn't want to hurt me. You didn't want to hurt others. Examples: Willie, Ginny." But then Pierman chuckled and shrugged again. "Sorry. I forgot. I'm not playing that game either."

McQueen stroked his beard. He had let the gun fall to his thigh, but Pierman made no advance. He was entirely deferential.

"I'm going to sit down. The leg's getting shaky." He moved to a long pile covered in shimmering plastic sheeting and sat. He peeled back a corner of the plastic.

"I suppose this is appropriate," he said. "You know what these are? Planks from the old bleachers."

"You're not leaving me many choices."

McQueen shook the gun like an accusing finger, his voice rising. Pierman prayed for a little more time.

"You want to hear the Golden Rule, the one you live by in a small town. You know it already, although you may not've put it in so many words. It's an equation. Be as good as you can be without being better than anyone else."

McQueen pointed the gun steadily. "Shut . . . up."

"No." But Pierman looked away. "I can't see more than two choices: You give up or you shoot me. Since I doubt you'll surrender, I'll just have my say."

Pierman could feel McQueen's eyes on him, watching him from far back in the man's head, twin animals each in its lair. He hugged his injured leg to his chest for a moment, letting the tearing muscle fog, then clear his mind. He put it down slowly, replacing it with both hands like a heavy urn. Almost there.

"It's a lie, that equation. We both know it. No way to solve it. I couldn't stand it. I left. Not you. No, you came back from what I understand was a truly shitty war and burrowed right in, wallowed in it, I should say. Took complete advantage of it, which makes you kind of a loser."

McQueen's head snapped around down the line of his arm. Pierman ignored him.

"What's going on with that apartment? You making up for time you lost in Viet Nam? You trying to relive a childhood you never had, as a hippie, as some radical college student? Shit, even your dope's old fashioned." Pierman crossed his arms and shook his head. "Given your volatile nature, I had you pegged as a PCP man myself. Pig drugs would be plentiful around here."

McQueen jacked the slide on the breech of the automatic.

"I'm sure it's loaded." Pierman waved a hand, annoyed at the interruption.

"Not that it makes much difference," he said, turning back to his previous thought. "Under the Golden Rule, nobody's going to tell you you're a loser too often. Everybody knows everybody else too well for that, and even losers have their place. You can pretty much think what you like about yourself and you don't even have to do that too often. Just when you're bored or maybe when that rare thing comes up that calls your way of life into question. Yeah, maybe then, and it starts to eat at you again."

"I should just hurt you," McQueen said. "Blow your balls off or something. I don't have to listen to this."

Pierman stopped to consider. "True," he said finally and frowned. "You don't have to listen to this. Randy Grable already reminded you. You're a gay man in a small, backward town."

"Damn you."

"Damn me? Damn you. That boy could expose you, he'd seen you trolling behind the library. There's some news'd split open your comfortable little cocoon. Not only would folks around here know you were some half-loopy loser, they'd know you were gay to boot. What really bothered you? That finally you'd have to admit that to yourself or your grandma'd find out?"

"You're wrong."

"What? You telling me you thought you were shooting Paul Grable?" Pierman raised his hand, thumb and forefinger at right angle, and jabbed it at McQueen. "There! To pay him back for firing your old man?" He jabbed again. "There! 'Cause his daughter was the first to see what you are? There! To defend Lindley against book banners?" Pierman's brow furrowed. "Two shots or three, by the way?"

"You're wrong." McQueen's voice took a dangerous turn up the scale.

"Well, it's got to be one or the other. You either intended to shoot the boy or you intended to shoot the old man. I don't really think you're so noble that you'd try the old man. I mean, for Christ sake, you used *your* old man as a beard while you planted your rifle."

Pierman looked at McQueen. "And look what it cost you. Willie. Ginny. She didn't die, by the way. You probably knew that, but she says the headaches and blurred vision aren't going away."

"I didn't mean to . . ."

Pierman finished it for him. "Got out of hand, didn't it."

McQueen had retreated a step and lowered his head. "That was your fault."

"My fault? I forgot. I was another variable in your twisted equation. I was missed opportunity. If you could put this over on me, finally, what—after twenty years?—well, that might make it worthwhile. Hell, that would just frost the cake. Only look at you. Missed opportunity all over again. I give you one last chance to pull it off and you're just standing there."

But McQueen wasn't. He was crouched, aiming with both hands.

"You've changed my mind."

"Too bad." Pierman straightened himself, staring. "Well?"

But McQueen still hesitated, and in the moment, Pierman knew he'd played it too long.

"You want me to do it," McQueen said in wonder.

He drew his clasped hands back to his chest and bowed his head to them, following the thought.

"You've got statements and warrants, but no case. You need a confession. If I go with you, you'll have it. If I kill you, everything else won't matter. Somebody knows we're here. I'm the only who could've done it."

He threw his head back, eyes aglitter.

"You've done it again. You're going to fuck me over by doing nothing."

It started as a snicker or a whimper from deep down. It gained momentum as it rose. He threw back his head and laughed until two glistening trails creeped toward his temples.

"You can still run." Pierman stood, shouting to make himself heard over his own terror and the lunatic howl. "You've got time."

The man's head fell forward. For a time, he was silent. Then he pivoted to profile. His arm came up, and with it, his face and the hard, gritted smile.

"Say you're sorry."

"What?"

"You called me a son of a bitch once. Say you're sorry."

They had come no further, Pierman thought, and he, too, might have laughed but for the anger, a last surge of rage at McQueen and his own infernal impotence. It seized him around the arms and chest and left only his voice free.

"No."

"Come on. Two little words."

"No," Pierman said just above a whisper.

"Your fault then."

McQueen swiveled the gun and slowly brought the barrel back toward his face. "No choices." He opened his mouth, the smile swallowed by a third black hole, empty, ready, receptive.

Pierman lunged, but the injured leg gave way. He scrabbled in the rubble until metal pressed against his ear stilled him. On his hands and knees, against the pressure of the muzzle, he turned his head and looked up.

"Mean it?" McQueen said. "Or you just hate to see *your* opportunity slip away?"

McQueen shrugged.

"Whatever. It'll do."

Time stretched, place wheeled, and Pierman wondered how he could be both witness and victim. Three shadows in the face above him dissolved away into night. There were two cracks and blinding, hot spatter, and Pierman understood. McQueen lay dead on his back before him.

"Darrell?"

Pierman pushed himself up and turned toward the place where he thought the shots came from. Amid the sulphur was another smell that made him gag. He wiped his face on his sleeve, and it was better.

"Joe!"

At the edge of the light, Calkins stood, like a diver, knees bent, hands joined above his head.

"You followed me?"

But Calkins did not answer. The only sound was the body twitching a tattoo on the floor behind Pierman. Calkins listened, stone-faced and rapt, to what I must believe was an echo from his jungle.

$$\mathcal{Q}$$

I hear: "Joe. He's dead."

I imagine: Pierman saw the glint and the flash, a comet he had already launched to meet. He hugged the burning tail and rode the dizzying spiral. Wind whistled the question in his ears; he may have screamed it aloud. Then all stopped. No matter. Caught between earth and sun, he landed in a heap on the moon.

RESTITUTION

Your grandmother was in no shape to do it, so your mother and I buried your father in the plot your grandfather purchased in the new cemetery across town. At the time, whether you believe it or not, I gave no thought to putting distance between Carter and Allen.

McQueen we put in the paupers' corner of the old cemetery, as far from Willie as we could get him, but still. Some weeks later, the old woman who raised him came forward with a concrete stone molded out of a ham can and etched with a nail. The caretaker set it free of charge, but he says it's damn near more trouble than it's worth. It heaves up in the spring and nicks the blades of his mower.

Calkins had to resign, of course, but the grand jury cleared him, called it an accident, as I knew it would. I had the brash D'Agostino appointed prosecutor, and his ambitions made him more malleable than Pierman, by far. The tender of permanent appointment required that he recognize that the citizens of Holoce County could stomach no more turmoil and that he present the case to the grand jury accordingly. Calkins' use of Allen as both pointer and bait made him negligent beyond understanding but not criminally culpable. D'Agostino made the case.

Calkins left Holoce County when the divorce became final. I know nothing more about him.

Much of your mother's story since then you know, of course. Answers to questions you have about her now you'll have to demand from her or, at the very least, someone other than me.

And I should leave it at that. Despite what laymen think, law and morality are rarely the same, and I think now I know only law. But I'll not let it go yet, not if you want me to be honest. Not if you want me to be complete.

Word spread quickly. Night owls, Jenks among them, followed the sirens' commotion, found the red lights playing carousel beams across the face of the school, and started working the phones. We celebrated the Fourth anyway.

We hold a parade each year. It's nothing out of the ordinary, certainly not enough to attract people from surrounding counties. They hold their own, and the themes, the unspoken ones that inspire the official clichés, are pretty much the same: We're good people, and we thrive because of it.

So we preach to the converted and everyone looks forward to it. For a month beforehand, the paper runs any number of well-read stories about who the grand marshal will be, the number of units, who's sponsoring them, who registered then backed out. It caused quite a stir one year when the high school band director, a young fellow fresh out of school but already looking for the next, brief stop on his career path, refused to march without compensation. The band had expenses and priorities, he said, like competitions in August. The school board, Paul Grable among them, said the young man's priorities—*values* was the word they used—were misplaced. The band marched that year, and the director was gone by fall. I didn't think about it at the time. It was the way things were.

On the day after Allen died, there was no such controversy. Most said it was dandy, one of the best parades in years.

The route goes by my house. I watched from the porch, and I'd have to say the women enjoyed it most. It's not often they're given their do unashamedly. The den mothers beamed across the ranks of the young scouts, and the shy, blushing fair queen contestants waived and tittered from the backs of the convertibles. The exception might have been Amanda's Mini-Majorettes. They high-stepped in ragged lines to music blaring from a box bouncing on Amanda's wide hip. But for all their eye shadow and carefully stiff, gathered hair, they seemed not to have much fun. Their sequined suits bagged where they should've stretched. Their faces locked in grimaces when they tossed their batons then dissolved more into relief than pride when they caught them. I suppose it made their mothers happy, though, and they'll learn soon enough.

The men tended to disguise their pleasure behind duty, something they better understood and appreciated. They fretted over the overheated engines of the idling convertibles, and the color guard looked grim behind the flags slanted against the arcs of their bellies. Still, the firemen tried to outdo each other with siren solos, and others, in fezzes and earrings, tootled from toy vans.

What little appetite I had for it I soon lost. I went back inside long before it was over, but the rest isn't hard to imagine. The parade ended at the fairgrounds on the edge of town. The Eastern Star served barbeque-blackened chicken and slaw. The congressman recalled the spirit of radicals and dissenters—he called them patriots—the preacher thanked God we inherited it, and the people listened but anxiously for night drew down onto the fields beyond. It differed little from the one before, hard and clear as a sapphire's heart, but below it, at the horizon, was a gentle line of light, mellow as a slice of cheese. Not until that was gone, the people knew, could dreams begin again.

The rockets shattered on the dark. A million sparkling flakes fell on the hearts of those reclined on blankets below. Their beats quickened, but it is to be excused. It cannot be helped. We allow it only once a year, and the embers soon fade.

We are sentenced by time. We are sentenced to time.

Before you go too far, that you should know as well.

ACKNOWLEDGMENTS

I am grateful to my friends, Ellen and Bruce England, for their careful and thoughtful reading of the manuscript. They made this a much better book. Flaws that remain accordingly are mine. Thanks, too, and love to Jane, who let me do just about everything in this life I ever wanted to do but never let me go.

ABOUT THE AUTHOR

John Gastineau brings his experience with life in the country and his expertise in law to his new thriller, *The Judge's Brief.*

Gastineau was raised on a farm in central Indiana. He worked as a newspaper reporter, photographer, and editor before going back to school to earn his law degree. Gastineau practiced as a litigator and general civil practitioner for twenty-four years.

Gastineau lives with his wife in Indiana and spends time with their family in Arizona and Australia.

CPSIA information can be obtained
at www.ICGtesting.com
Printed in the USA
FSOW02n1109041017
39510FS